Jeeves, Jeeves, Jeeves

Three Novels
By P. G.
Wodehouse

 AN EQUINOX BOOK/PUBLISHED BY AVON BOOKS

JEEVES, JEEVES, JEEVES was originally published in three separate volumes as: *How Right You are, Jeeves, Stiff Upper Lip, Jeeves,* and *Jeeves and the Tie That Binds.*

A condensed version of *Stiff Upper Lip, Jeeves* was serialized in *Playboy* Magazine.

AVON BOOKS
A division of
The Hearst Corporation
959 Eighth Avenue
New York, New York 10019

How Right You Are, Jeeves © 1960 by P. G. Wodehouse; *Stiff Upper Lip, Jeeves* © 1962 by P. G. Wodehouse; *Jeeves and the Tie That Binds* © 1971 by P. G. Wodehouse.

Published by arrangement with Simon & Schuster, Inc.

ISBN: 0-380-00627-8

First Equinox Printing, March, 1976

EQUINOX TRADEMARK REG. U.S. PAT. OFF. AND IN OTHER COUNTRIES, MARCA REGISTRADA, HECHO EN U.S.A.

Printed in the U.S.A.

Contents

How Right You Are, Jeeves

• 1 •

JEEVES PLACED the sizzling eggs and b. on the breakfast
table, and Reginald (Kipper) Herring and I, licking the
lips, squared our elbows and got down to it. A lifelong
buddy of mine, this Herring, linked to me by what are
called imperishable memories. Years ago, when striplings,
he and I had done a stretch together at Malvern House,
Bramley-on-Sea, the preparatory school conducted by that
prince of stinkers, Aubrey Upjohn, M.A., and had frequently stood side by side in the Upjohn study awaiting the
receipt of six of the juiciest from a cane of the type that biteth like a serpent and stingeth like an adder, as the fellow
said. So we were, you might say, rather like a couple of old
sweats who had fought shoulder to shoulder on Crispin's
Day, if I've got the name right.

The *plat du jour* having gone down the hatch, accompanied by some fluid ounces of strengthening coffee, I was
about to reach for the marmalade, when I heard the telephone tootling out in the hall and rose to attend to it.

"Bertram Wooster's residence," I said, having connected with the instrument. "Wooster in person at this end. Oh, hullo," I added, for the voice that boomed over the wire was that of Mrs. Thomas Portarlington Travers of Brinkley Court, Market Snodsbury, near Droitwich—or, putting it another way, my good and deserving Aunt Dahlia. "A very hearty pip-pip to you, old ancestor," I said, well pleased, for she is a woman with whom it is always a privilege to chew the fat.

"And a rousing toodle-oo to you, you young blot on the landscape," she replied cordially. "I'm surprised to find you up as early as this. Or have you just got in from a night on the tiles?"

I hastened to rebut this slur.

"Certainly not. Nothing of that description whatsoever. I've been upping with the lark this last week, to keep Kipper Herring company. He's staying with me till he can get into his new flat. You remember old Kipper? I brought him down to Brinkley one summer. Chap with a cauliflower ear."

"I know who you mean. Looks like Jack Dempsey."

"That's right. Far more, indeed, than Jack Dempsey does. He's on the staff of the *Thursday Review*, a periodical of which you may or may not be a reader, and has to clock in at the office at daybreak. No doubt, when I apprise him of your call, he will send you his love, for I know he holds you in high esteem. The perfect hostess, he often describes you as. Well, it's nice to hear your voice again, old flesh and blood. How's everything down Market Snodsbury way?"

"Oh, we're jogging along. But I'm not speaking from Brinkley. I'm in London."

"Till when?"

"Driving back this afternoon."

"I'll give you lunch."

"Sorry, can't manage it. I'm putting on the nosebag with Sir Roderick Glossop."

This surprised me. The eminent brain specialist to whom she alluded was a man I would not have cared to lunch with myself, our relations having been on the stiff side since the night at Lady Wickman's place in Hertfordshire when, acting on the advice of my hostess's daughter Roberta, I had punctured his hot-water bottle with a darning needle in the small hours of the morning. Quite unintentionally, of course. I had planned to puncture the h.-w.b. of his nephew, Tuppy Glossop, with whom I had a feud on, and unknown to me they had changed rooms. Just one of those unfortunate misunderstandings.

"What on earth are you doing that for?"

"Why shouldn't I? He's paying."

I saw her point—a penny saved is a penny earned and all that sort of thing—but I continued to be surprised. It amazed me that Aunt Dahlia, presumably a free agent, should have selected this very formidable loony-doctor to chew the midday chop with. However, one of the first lessons life teaches us is that aunts will be aunts, so I merely shrugged a couple of shoulders.

"Well, it's up to you, of course, but it seems a rash act. Did you come to London just to revel with Glossop?"

"No, I'm here to collect my new butler and take him home with me."

"New butler? What's become of Seppings?"

"He's gone."

I clicked the tongue. I was very fond of the major-domo in question, having enjoyed many a port in his pantry, and this news saddened me.

"No, really?" I said. "Too bad. I thought he looked a little frail when I last saw him. Well, that's how it goes. All flesh is grass, I often say."

"To Bognor Regis, for his holiday."

I unclicked the tongue.

"Oh, I see. That puts a different complexion on the matter. Odd how all these pillars of the home seem to be dashing away on toots these days. It's like what Jeeves was telling me about the great race movements of the middle ages. Jeeves starts his holiday this morning. He's off to Herne Bay for the shrimping, and I'm feeling like that bird in the poem who lost his pet gazelle or whatever the animal was. I don't know what I'm going to do without him."

"I'll tell you what you're going to do. Have you a clean shirt?"

"Several."

"And a toothbrush?"

"Two, both of the finest quality."

"Then pack them. You're coming to Brinkley tomorrow."

The gloom which always envelops Bertram Wooster like a fog when Jeeves is about to take his annual vacation lightened perceptibly. There are few things I find more agreeable than a sojourn at Aunt Dahlia's rural lair. Picturesque scenery, gravel soil, main drainage, company's own water and, above all, the superb French cheffing of her French chef, Anatole, God's gift to the gastric juices. A full hand, as you might put it.

"What an admirable suggestion," I said. "You solve all my problems and bring the bluebird out of a hat. Rely on me. You will observe me bowling up in the Wooster sports model tomorrow afternoon with my hair in a braid and a song on my lips. My presence will, I feel sure, stimulate Anatole to new heights of endeavor. Got anybody else staying at the old snake pit?"

"Five inmates in all."

"Five?" I resumed my tongue-clicking. "Golly! Uncle Tom must be frothing at the mouth a bit," I said, for I knew the old buster's distaste for guests in the home. Even a single weekender is sometimes enough to make him drain the bitter cup.

"Tom's not there. He's gone to Harrogate with Cream."

"You mean lumbago."

"I don't mean lumbago. I mean Cream. Homer Cream.

4

Big American tycoon, who is visiting these shores. He suffers from ulcers, and his medicine man has ordered him to take the waters at Harrogate. Tom has gone with him to hold his hand and listen to him of an evening, while he tells him how filthy the stuff tastes."

"Antagonistic."

"What?"

"I mean altruistic. You are probably not familiar with the word, but it's one I've heard Jeeves use. It's what you say of a fellow who gives selfless service, not counting the cost."

"Selfless service, my foot. Tom's in the middle of a very important business deal with Cream. If it goes through, he'll make a packet, free of income tax. So he's playing up to him like a Hollywood yes man."

I gave an intelligent nod, though this of course was wasted on her because she couldn't see me. I could readily understand my uncle-by-marriage's mental processes. T. Portarlington Travers is a man who has accumulated the pieces of eight in sackfuls, but he is always more than willing to shove a bit extra away behind the brick in the fireplace, feeling—and rightly—that every little bit added to what you've got makes just a little bit more. And if there's one thing that's right up his street, it is not paying income tax. He grudges every penny the Government nicks him for.

"That is why, when kissing me goodbye, he urged me with tears in his eyes to lush Mrs. Cream and her son Willie up and treat them like royalty. So they're at Brinkley, dug into the woodwork."

"Willie, did you say?"

"Short for Wilbert."

I mused. Willie Cream. The name was familiar, somehow. I seemed to have heard it or seen it in the papers somewhere. But it eluded me.

"Adela Cream writes mystery stories. Are you a fan of

hers? No? Well, start boning up on them directly you arrive, because every little helps. I've bought a complete set. They're very good."

"I shall be delighted to run an eye over her material," I said, for I am what they call an a-something of novels of suspense. Aficionado, would that be it? "I can always do with another corpse or two. We have established, then, that among the inmates are this Mrs. Cream and her son Wilbert. Who are the other three?"

"Well, there's Lady Wickham's daughter Roberta."

I started violently, as if some unseen hand had goosed me.

"What? Bobbie Wickham? Oh, my gosh!"

"Why the agitation? Do you know her?"

"You bet I know her."

"I begin to see. Is she one of the gaggle of girls you've been engaged to?"

"Not actually, no. We were never engaged. But that was merely because she wouldn't meet me halfway."

"Turned you down, did she?"

"Yes, thank goodness."

"Why thank goodness? She's a one-girl beauty chorus."

"She doesn't try the eyes, I agree."

"A pippin, if ever there was one."

"Very true, but is being a pippin everything? What price the soul?"

"Isn't her soul like mother makes?"

"Far from it. Much below par. What I could tell you . . . but no, let it go. Painful subj."

I had been about to mention fifty-seven or so of the reasons why the prudent operator, if he valued his peace of mind, deemed it best to stay well away from the redheaded menace under advisement, but realized that at a moment when I was wanting to get back to the marmalade it would occupy too much time. It will be enough to say that I had long since come out of the ether and was fully cognizant of the fact that in declining to fall in with my suggestion

6

that we should start rounding up clergymen and bridesmaids, the beazel had rendered me a signal service, and I'll tell you why.

Aunt Dahlia, describing this young blister as a one-girl beauty chorus, had called her shots perfectly correctly. Her outer crust was indeed of a nature to cause those beholding it to rock back on their heels with a startled whistle. But while equipped with eyes like twin stars, hair ruddier than the cherry, oomph, *espièglerie* and all the fixings, this B. Wickham had also the disposition and general outlook on life of a ticking bomb. In her society you always had the uneasy feeling that something was likely to go off at any moment with a pop. You never knew what she was going to do next or into what murky depths of soup she would carelessly plunge you.

"Miss Wickham, sir," Jeeves had once said to me warningly at the time when the fever was at its height, "lacks seriousness. She is volatile and frivolous. I would always hesitate to recommend as a life partner a young lady with quite such a vivid shade of red hair."

His judgment was sound. I have already mentioned how with her subtle wiles this girl had induced me to sneak into Sir Roderick Glossop's sleeping apartment and apply the darning needle to his hot-water bottle—and that was comparatively mild going for her. In a word, Roberta, daughter of Lady Wickham of Skeldings Hall, Herts, and the late Sir Cuthbert, was pure dynamite, and better kept at a distance by all those who aimed at leading the peaceful life. The prospect of being immured with her in the same house, with all the facilities a country house affords an enterprising girl for landing her nearest and dearest in the mulligatawny, made me singularly dubious about the shape of things to come.

I was tottering under this blow when the old relative administered another, and it was a haymaker.

"And there's Aubrey Upjohn and his stepdaughter,

Phyllis Mills," she said. "That's the lot. What's the matter with you? Got asthma?"

I took her to be alluding to the sharp gasp which had escaped my lips, and I must confess that it had come out not unlike the last words of a dying duck. But I felt perfectly justified in gasping. A weaker man would have howled like a banshee. There floated into my mind something Kipper Herring had once said to me. "You know, Bertie," he had said, in philosophical mood, "we have much to be thankful for in this life of ours, you and I. However rough the going, there is one sustaining thought to which we can hold. The storm clouds may lower and the horizon grow dark, we may get a nail in our shoe and be caught in the rain without an umbrella, we may come down to breakfast and find that someone else has taken the brown egg, but at least we have the consolation of knowing that we shall never see Aubrey Gawd-help-us Upjohn again. Always remember this in times of despondency," he said, and I always had. And now, here the bounder was, bobbing up right in my midst. Enough to make the stoutest-hearted go into his dying-duck routine.

"Aubrey Upjohn?" I quavered. "You mean *my* Aubrey Upjohn?"

"That's the one. Soon after you made your escape from his chain gang he married Jane Mills, a friend of mine with a colossal amount of money. She died, leaving a daughter. I'm the daughter's godmother. Upjohn's retired now and going in for politics. The hot tip is that the boys in the back room are going to run him as the Conservative candidate in the Market Snodsbury division at the next by-election. What a thrill it'll be for you, meeting him again. Or does the prospect scare you?"

"Certainly not. We Woosters are intrepid. But what on earth did you invite him to Brinkley for?"

"I didn't. I only wanted Phyllis, but he came along, too."

"You should have bunged him out."

8

"I hadn't the heart to."

"Weak, very weak."

"Besides, I needed him in my business. He's going to present the prizes at Market Snodsbury Grammar School. We've been caught short, as usual, and somebody has got to make a speech on ideals and the great world outside to those blasted boys, so he fits in nicely. I believe he's a very fine speaker. His only trouble is that he's stymied unless he has his speech with him and can read it. Calls it referring to his notes. Phyllis told me that. She types the stuff for him."

"A thoroughly low trick," I said severely. "Even I, who have never soared above the 'Yeoman's Wedding Song' at a village concert, wouldn't have the crust to face my public unless I'd taken the trouble to memorize the words, though, actually, with the 'Yeoman's Wedding Song' it is possible to get by quite comfortably if you keep on singing 'Ding dong, ding dong, ding dong, I hurry along.' In short—"

I would have spoken further, but at this point, after urging me to put a sock in it, and giving me a kindly word of warning not to step on any banana skins, she rang off.

· 2 ·

I CAME away from the telephone on what practically amounted to leaden feet. Here, I was feeling, was a nice bit of box fruit. Bobbie Wickham, with her tendency to stir things up and with each new day to discover some new way of staggering civilization, would by herself have been bad enough. Add Aubrey Upjohn, and the mixture became too rich. I don't know if Kipper, when I rejoined him, noticed that my brow was sicklied o'er with the pale cast of thought, as I have heard Jeeves put it. Probably not, for he was tucking into toast and marmalade at the moment, but it was. As had happened so often in the past, I was conscious of an impending doom. Exactly what form this would take I was of course unable to say—it might be one thing or it might be another—but a voice seemed to whisper to me that somehow, at some not distant date, Bertram was slated to get it in the gizzard.

"That was Aunt Dahlia, Kipper," I said.

"Bless her jolly old heart," he responded. "One of the very best, and you can quote me as saying so. I shall never forget those happy days at Brinkley, and shall be glad at any time that suits her to cadge another invitation. Is she up in London?"

"Till this afternoon."

"We fill her to the brim with rich foods, of course?"

"No, she's got a lunch date. She's browsing with Sir Roderick Glossop, the loony-doctor. You don't know him, do you?"

"Only from hearing you speak of him. A tough egg, I gather."

"One of the toughest."

"He was the chap, wasn't he, who found the twenty-four cats in your bedroom?"

"Twenty-three," I corrected. I like to get things right. "They were not my cats. They had been deposited there by my cousins Claude and Eustace. But I found them difficult to explain. He's a rather bad listener. I hope I shan't find him at Brinkley, too."

"Are you going to Brinkley?"

"Tomorrow afternoon."

"You'll enjoy that."

"Well, shall I? The point is a very moot one."

"You're crazy. Think of Anatole. Those dinners of his! Is the name of the peri who stood disconsolate at the gate of Eden familiar to you?"

"I've heard Jeeves mention her."

"Well, that's how I feel when I remember Anatole's dinners. When I reflect that every night he's dishing them up and I'm not there, I come within a very little of breaking down. What gives you the idea that you won't enjoy yourself? Brinkley Court's an earthly Paradise."

"In many respects, yes, but life there at the moment has its drawbacks. There's far too much of that where-every-prospect-pleases-and-only-man-is-vile stuff buzzing around

11

for my taste. Who do you think is staying at the old doss-house? Aubrey Upjohn."

It was plain that I had shaken him. His eyes widened, and an astonished piece of toast fell from his grasp.

"Old Upjohn? You're kidding."

"No, he's there. Himself, not a picture. And it seems only yesterday that you were buoying me up by telling me I'd never have to see him again. The storm clouds may lower, you said, if you recollect . . ."

"But how does he come to be at Brinkley?"

"Precisely what I asked the aged relative, and she had an explanation that seems to cover the facts. Apparently, after we took our eye off him he married a friend of hers, one Jane Mills, and acquired a stepdaughter, Phyllis Mills, whose godmother Aunt Dahlia is. The ancestor invited the Mills girl to Brinkley, and Upjohn came along for the ride."

"I see. I don't wonder you're trembling like a leaf."

"Not like a leaf, exactly, but . . . yes, I think you might describe me as trembling. One remembers that fishy eye of his."

"And the wide, bare upper lip. It won't be pleasant having to gaze at that across the dinner table. Still, you'll like Phyllis."

"Do you know her?"

"We met out in Switzerland last Christmas. Slap her on the back, will you, and give her my regards. Nice girl, though goofy. She never told me she was related to Upjohn."

"She would naturally keep a thing like that dark."

"Yes, one sees that. Just as one would have tried to keep it dark if one had been mixed up in any way with Palmer the poisoner. What ghastly garbage that was he used to fling at us when we were serving our sentence at Malvern House. Remember the sausages on Sunday? And the boiled mutton with caper sauce?"

"And the margarine. Recalling this last, it's going to be a strain having to sit and watch him getting outside pounds of the best country butter. Oh, Jeeves," I said, as he shimmered in to clear the table, "you never went to a preparatory school on the south coast of England, did you?"

"No, sir, I was privately educated."

"Ah, then you wouldn't understand. Mr. Herring and I were discussing our former prep-school beak, Aubrey Upjohn, M.A. By the way, Kipper, Aunt Dahlia was telling me something about him which I never knew before and which ought to expose him to the odium of all thinking men. You remember those powerful end-of-term addresses he used to make to us? Well, he couldn't have made them if he hadn't had the stuff in his grasp, all typed out, so that he could read it. Without his notes, as he calls them, he's a spent force. Revolting, that, Jeeves, don't you think?"

"Many orators are, I believe, similarly handicapped, sir."

"Too tolerant, Jeeves, far too tolerant. You must guard against this lax outlook. However, the reason I mention Upjohn to you is that he has come back into my life, or will be so coming in about two ticks. He's staying at Brinkley, and I shall be going there tomorrow. That was Aunt Dahlia on the phone just now, and she demands my presence. Will you pack a few necessaries in a suitcase or so?"

"Very good, sir."

"When are you leaving on your Herne Bay jaunt?"

"I was thinking of taking a train this morning, sir, but if you would prefer that I remained till tomorrow—"

"No, no, perfectly all right. Start as soon as you like. What's the joke?" I asked, as the door closed behind him, for I observed that Kipper was chuckling softly. Not an easy thing to do, of course, when your mouth's full of toast and marmalade, but he was doing it.

"I was thinking of Upjohn," he said.

I was amazed. It seemed incredible to me that anyone who had done time at Malvern House, Bramley-on-Sea, could chuckle, softly or otherwise, when letting the mind dwell on that outstanding menace. It was like laughing lightly while contemplating one of those horrors from outer

13

space which are so much with us at the moment on the motion-picture screen.

"I envy you, Bertie," he went on, continuing to chuckle. "You have a wonderful treat in store. You are going to be present at the breakfast table when Upjohn opens his copy of this week's *Thursday Review* and starts to skim through the pages devoted to comments on current literature. I should explain that among the books that recently arrived at the office was a slim volume from his pen dealing with the Preparatory School and giving it an enthusiastic build-up. The formative years which we spent there, he said, were the happiest of our life."

"Gadzooks!"

"He little knew that his brain child would be given to one of the old lags of Malvern House to review. I'll tell you something, Bertie, that every young man ought to know. Never be a stinker, because if you are, though you may flourish for a time like a green bay tree, sooner or later retribution will overtake you. I need scarcely tell you that I ripped the stuffing out of the beastly little brochure. The thought of those sausages on Sunday filled me with the righteous fury of a Juvenal."

"Of a who?"

"Nobody you know. Before your time. I seemed inspired. Normally, I suppose, a book like that would get a line and a half in the Other Recent Publications column, but I gave it six hundred words of impassioned prose. How extraordinarily fortunate you are to be in a position to watch his face as he reads them."

"How do you know he'll read them?"

"He's a subscriber. There was a letter from him on the correspondence page a week or two ago, in which he specifically stated that he had been one for years."

"Did you sign the thing?"

"No. Ye Ed is not keen on underlings advertising their names."

14

"And it was really hot stuff?"

"Red hot. So eye him closely at the breakfast table. Mark his reaction. I confidently expect the blush of shame and remorse to mantle his cheek."

"The only catch is that I don't come down to breakfast when I'm at Brinkley. Still, I suppose I could make a special effort."

"Do so. You will find it well worth while," said Kipper, and shortly afterward popped off to resume the earning of the weekly envelope.

He had been gone about twenty minutes when Jeeves came in, bowler hat in hand, to say goodbye. A solemn moment, taxing our self-control to the utmost. However, we both kept the upper lip stiff, and after we had kidded back and forth for a while, he started to withdraw. He had reached the door when it suddenly occurred to me that he might have inside information about this Wilbert Cream of whom Aunt Dahlia had spoken. I have generally found that he knows everything about everyone.

"Oh, Jeeves," I said. "Half a jiffy."

"Sir?"

"Something I want to ask you. It seems that among my fellow guests at Brinkley will be a Mrs. Homer Cream, wife of an American big butter-and-egg man, and her son Wilbert, commonly known as Willie, and the name Willie Cream seemed somehow to touch a cord. Rightly or wrongly I associate it with trips we have taken to New York, but in what connection I haven't the vaguest. Does it ring a bell with you?"

"Why, yes, sir. References to the gentleman are frequent in the tabloid newspapers of New York, notably in the column conducted by Mr. Walter Winchell. He is generally alluded to under the sobriquet of Broadway Willie."

"Of course! It all comes back to me. He's what they call a playboy."

"Precisely, sir. Notorious for his escapades."

"Yes, I've got him placed now. He's the fellow who likes to let off stink bombs in night clubs, which rather falls under the head of carrying coals to Newcastle, and seldom cashes a check at his bank without producing a gat and saying, 'This is a stick-up.'"

"And . . . No, sir, I regret that it has for the moment escaped my memory."

"What has?"

"Some other little something, sir, that I was told regarding Mr. Cream. Should I recall it, I will communicate with you."

"Yes, do. One wants the complete picture. Oh, gosh!"

"Sir?"

"Nothing, Jeeves. A thought has just floated into my mind. All right, push off, or you'll miss your train. Good luck to your shrimping net."

And I'll tell you what the thought was that had floated. I have already indicated my qualms at the prospect of being cooped up in the same house with Bobbie Wickham and Aubrey Upjohn—for who could tell what the harvest might be? If in addition to these two heavies I was also to be cheek by jowl with a New York playboy apparently afflicted with bats in the belfry, it began to look as if this visit would prove too much for Bertram's frail strength, and for an instant I toyed with the idea of sending a telegram of regret and oiling out.

Then I remembered Anatole's cooking and was strong again. Nobody who has once tasted them would wantonly deprive himself of that wizard's smoked offerings. Whatever spiritual agonies I might be about to undergo at Brinkley Court, Market Snodsbury, near Droitwich, residence there would at least put me several *Suprêmes de foie gras au champagne* and *Mignonettes de poulet petit duc* ahead of the game. Nevertheless, it would be paltering with the truth to say that I was at my ease as I thought of what lay before me in darkest Worcestershire, and the hand that lit the after-breakfast gasper shook quite a bit.

At this moment of nervous tension the telephone suddenly gave tongue again, causing me to skip like the high hills, as if the Last Trump had sounded. I went to the instrument all of a twitter.

Some species of butler appeared to be at the other end.

"Mr. Wooster?"

"On the spot."

"Good morning, sir. Her ladyship wishes to speak to you. Lady Wickham, sir. Here is Mr. Wooster, M'lady."

And Bobbie's mother came on the air.

I should have mentioned, by the way, that during the above exchange of ideas with the butler I had been aware of a distant sound of sobbing, like background music, and it now became apparent that it was from the larynx of the relict of the late Sir Cuthbert that it was proceeding. There was a short intermission before she got the vocal cords working, and while I was waiting for her to start the dialogue I found myself wrestling with two problems that presented themselves: the first, What on earth is this woman ringing me up for?; the second, Having got the number, why does she sob?

It was Problem A that puzzled me particularly, for ever since that hot-water-bottle episode my relations with this parent of Bobbie's had been on the strained side. It was, indeed, an open secret that my standing with her was practically that of a rat of the underworld. I had had this from Bobbie, whose impersonation of her mother discussing me with sympathetic cronies had been exceptionally vivid, and I must confess that I wasn't altogether surprised. I mean to say, no hostess extending her hospitality to a friend of her daughter's likes to have the young visitor going about the place puncturing people's hot-water bottles and leaving at three in the morning without stopping to say goodbye. Yes,

17

I could see her side of the thing all right, and I found it extraordinary that she should be seeking me out on the telephone in this fashion. Feeling as she did so allergic to Bertram, I wouldn't have thought she'd have phoned me with a ten-foot pole.

However, there, beyond question, she was.

"Mr. Wooster?"

"Oh, hullo, Lady Wickham."

"Are you there?"

I put her straight on this point, and she took time out to sob again. She then spoke in a hoarse, throaty voice, like Tallulah Bankhead after swallowing a fish bone the wrong way.

"Is this awful news true?"

"Eh?"

"Oh dear, oh dear, oh dear!"

"I don't quite follow."

"In this morning's *Times*."

I'm pretty shrewd, and it seemed to me, reading between the lines, that there must have been something in the issue of the *Times* published that morning that for some reason had upset her, though why she should have chosen me to tell her troubles to was a mystery not easy to fathom. I was about to institute inquiries in the hope of spearing a solution, when in addition to sobbing she started laughing in a hyenaesque manner, making it clear to my trained ear that she was having hysterics. And before I could speak there was a dull thud suggestive of some solid body falling to earth, I knew not where, and when the dialogue was resumed, I found that the butler had put himself on as an understudy.

"Mr. Wooster?"

"Still here."

"I regret to say that her ladyship has fainted."

"It was she I heard going *bump*?"

"Precisely, sir. Thank you very much, sir. Goodbye."

He replaced the receiver and presumably went about his domestic duties, these no doubt including the loosening of the stricken woman's corsets and burning feathers under her nose, leaving me to chew on the situation without further bulletins from the front.

It seemed to me that the thing to do here was to get hold of a *Times* and see what it had to offer in the way of enlightenment. It's a paper I don't often look at, preferring for breakfast reading the *Mirror* and the *Mail,* but Jeeves takes it in and I have occasionally borrowed his copy with a view of having a shot at the crossword puzzle. It struck me as a possibility that he might have left today's issue in the kitchen, and so it proved. I came back with it, lowered myself into a chair, lit another cigarette and proceeded to cast an eye on its contents.

At a cursory glance, what might be called swoon material appeared to be totally absent from its columns. The Duchess of something had been opening a bazaar at Wimbledon in aid of a deserving charity, there was an article on salmon fishing on the Wye, and a cabinet minister had made a speech about conditions in the cotton industry, but I could see nothing in these items to induce a loss of consciousness. Nor did it seem probable that a woman would have passed out cold on reading that Herbert Robinson (26) of Grove Road, Ponder's End, had been jugged for stealing a pair of green-and-yellow checked trousers. I turned to the cricket news. Had some friend of hers failed to score in one of yesterday's county matches owing to a doubtful l-b-w decision?

It was just after I had run the eye down the Births and Marriages that I happened to look at the Engagements, and a moment later I was shooting out of my chair as if a spike had come through its cushioned seat and penetrated the fleshy parts.

"Jeeves!" I yelled, and then remembered that he had long since gone with the wind. A bitter thought, for if ever

there was an occasion when his advice and counsel were
of the essence, this occ. was that occ. The best I could do,
tackling it solo, was to utter a hollow g. and bury the face
in the hands. And though I seem to hear my public tut-tut-
ting in disapproval of such neurotic behavior, I think the
verdict of history will be that the paragraph on which my
gaze had rested was more than enough to excuse a spot of
face-burying.

It ran as follows:

FORTHCOMING MARRIAGES
The engagement is announced between
Bertram Wilberforce Wooster of Berkeley
Mansions, W.1, and Roberta, daughter of
Lady Wickham of Skeldings Hall, Herts.,
and the late Sir Cuthbert Wickham.

· 3 ·

WELL, AS I was saying, I had several times when under the influence of her oomph taken up with Roberta Wickham the idea of such a merger, but—and here is the point I would stress—I could have sworn that on each occasion she had declined to co-operate, and that in a manner which left no room for doubt regarding her views. I mean to say, when a girl, offered a good man's heart, laughs like a bursting paper bag and tells him not to be a silly ass, the good man is entitled, I think, to assume that the whole thing is off. In the light of this announcement in the *Times* I could only suppose that on one of these occasions, unnoticed by me possibly because my attention had wandered, she must have drooped her eyes and come through with a murmured "Right ho." Though when this could have happened, I hadn't the foggiest.

It was, accordingly, as you will readily imagine, a Bertram Wooster with dark circles under his eyes and a brain threatening to come apart at the seams who braked sports model on the following afternoon at the front door of Brinkley Court—a Bertram who, in a word, was asking himself what the dickens all this was about. Nonplused more or less sums it up. It seemed to me that my first move must be to get hold of my fiancée and see if she had anything to contribute in the way of clarifying the situation.

As is generally the case at country houses on a fine day, there seemed to be nobody around. In due season the gang would assemble for tea on the lawn, but at the moment I could spot no friendly native to tell me where I might find Bobbie. I proceeded, therefore, to roam hither and thither about the grounds and messuages in the hope of locating her, wishing that I had a couple of bloodhounds to aid me in my task, for the Travers demesne is a spacious one and there was a considerable amount of sunshine above, though none, I need scarcely mention, in my heart.

And I was tooling along a mossy path with the brow a bit wet with honest sweat, when there came to my ears the unmistakable sound of somebody reading poetry to someone, and the next moment I found myself confronting a mixed twosome who had dropped anchor beneath a shady tree in what is known as a leafy glade.

They had scarcely swum into my ken when the welkin started ringing like billy-o. This was due to the barking of a small dachshund, who now advanced on me with the apparent intention of seeing the color of my insides. Milder counsels, however, prevailed, and on arriving at journey's end he merely rose like a rocket and licked me on the chin, seeming to convey the impression that in Bertram Wooster he had found just what the doctor ordered. I have noticed before in dogs this tendency to form a beautiful friendship immediately on getting within sniffing distance of me. Something to do, no doubt, with the characteristic Wooster smell, which for some reason seems to speak to their deeps. I tickled him behind the right ear and scratched the base of his spine for a moment or two; then, these civilities concluded, I switched my attention to the poetry group.

It was the male half of the sketch who had been doing the reading, a willowy bird of about the tonnage and general aspect of David Niven, with ginger hair and a small mustache. As he was unquestionably not Aubrey Upjohn, I assumed that this must be Willie Cream, and it surprised me a bit to find him dishing out verse. One would have expected a New York playboy, widely publicized as one of the lads, to confine himself to prose, and dirty prose at that. But no doubt these playboys have their softer moments.

His companion was a well-stacked young featherweight, who could be none other than the Phyllis Mills of whom Kipper had spoken. Nice but goofy, Kipper had said, and a glance told me that he was right. One learns, as one goes through life, to spot goofiness in the other sex with an unerring eye, and this exhibit had a sort of mild, Soul's Awakening kind of expression which made it abundantly clear that, while not a supergoof like some of the female goofs I'd met, she was quite goofy enough to be going on with. Her whole aspect was that of a girl who at the drop of a hat would start talking baby talk.

This she now proceeded to do, asking me if I didn't think that Poppet, the dachshund, was a sweet little doggie. I assented rather austerely, for I prefer the shorter form more generally used, and she said she supposed I was Mrs. Travers' nephew, Bertie Wooster, which, as we know, was substantially the case.

"I heard you were expected today. I'm Phyllis Mills," she said, and I said I had divined as much and that Kipper had told me to slap her on the back and give her his best, and she said, "Oh, Reggie Herring? He's a sweetie-pie, isn't he?" and I agreed that Kipper was one of the sweetie-pies and not the worst of them, and she said, "Yes, he's a lambkin."

23

This duologue had, of course, left Wilbert Cream a bit out of it, just painted on the backdrop as you might say, and for some moments, knitting his brow, plucking at his mustache, shuffling the feet and allowing the limbs to twitch, he had been giving abundant evidence that in his opinion three was a crowd and that what the leafy glade needed to make it all that a leafy glade should be was a complete absence of Woosters. Taking advantage of a lull in the conversation, he said, "Are you looking for someone?"

I replied that I was looking for Bobbie Wickham.

"I'd go on looking, if I were you. Bound to find her somewhere."

"Bobbie?" said Phyllis Mills. "She's down at the lake, fishing."

"Then what you do," said Wilbert Cream, brightening, "is follow this path, bend right, sharp left, bend right again and there you are. You can't miss. Start at once, is my advice."

I must say I felt that, related as I was by ties of blood, in a manner of speaking, to this leafy glade, it was a bit thick being practically bounced from it by a mere visitor, but Aunt Dahlia had made it clear that the Cream family must not be thwarted or put upon in any way, so I did as he suggested, picking up the feet without anything in the nature of back chat. As I receded, I could hear in my rear the poetry breaking out again.

The lake at Brinkley calls itself a lake, but when all the returns are in it's really more a sort of young pond. Big enough to mess about on in a punt, though, and for the use of those wishing to punt, a boathouse has been provided with a small pier or landing stage attached to it. On this, rod in hand, Bobbie was seated, and it was for me the work of an instant to race up and breathe down the back of her neck.

"Hey!" I said.

"Hey to you with knobs on," she replied. "Oh, hullo, Bertie. You here?"

"You never spoke a truer word. If you can spare me a moment of your valuable time, young Roberta—"

"Half a second, I think I've got a bite. No, false alarm. What were you saying?"

"I was saying—"

"Oh, by the way, I heard from Mother this morning."

"I heard from her yesterday morning."

"I was kind of expecting you would. You saw that thing in the *Times*?"

"With the naked eye."

"Puzzled you for a moment, perhaps?"

"For several moments."

"Well, I'll tell you all about that. The idea came to me in a flash."

"You mean it was you who shoved that communiqué in the journal?"

"Of course."

"Why?" I said, getting right down to it in my direct way. I thought I had her there, but no.

"I was paving the way for Reggie."

I passed a hand over my fevered brow.

"Something seems to have gone wrong with my usually keen hearing," I said. "It sounds just as if you were saying 'I was paving the way for Reggie.' "

"I was. I was making his path straight. Softening up Mother on his behalf."

I passed another hand over my f.b.

"Now you seem to be saying 'Softening up Mother on his behalf.' "

"That's what I am saying. It's perfectly simple. I'll put it in words of one syllable for you. I love Reggie. Reggie loves me."

"Reggie," of course, is two syllables, but I let it go.

25

"Reggie who?"

"Reggie Herring."

I was amazed.

"You mean old Kipper?"

"I wish you wouldn't call him Kipper."

"I always have. Dash it," I said with some warmth, "if a fellow shows up at a prep school on the south coast of England with a name like Herring, what else do you expect his playmates to call him? But how do you mean you love him and he loves you? You've never met him."

"Of course I've met him. We were in the same hotel in Switzerland last Christmas. I taught him to ski," she said, a dreamy look coming into her twin-star-likes. "I shall never forget the day I helped him unscramble himself after he had taken a toss on the beginners' slope. He had both legs wrapped round his neck. I think that is when love dawned. My heart melted as I sorted him out."

"You didn't laugh?"

"Of course I didn't laugh. I was all sympathy and understanding."

For the first time the thing began to seem plausible to me. Bobbie is a fun-loving girl, and the memory of her reaction when in the garden at Skeldings I had once stepped on the teeth of a rake and had the handle jump up and hit me on the tip of the nose was still laid away among my souvenirs. She had been convulsed with mirth. If, then, she had refrained from guffawing when confronted with the spectacle of Reginald Herring with both legs wrapped round his neck, her emotions must have been very deeply involved.

"Well, all right," I said. "I accept your statement that you and Kipper are that way. But why, that being so, did you blazon it forth to the world, if blazoning forth is the expression I want, that you were engaged to me?"

"I told you. It was to soften Mother up."

26

"Which sounded to me like delirium straight from the sick bed."

"You don't get the subtle strategy?"

"Not by several parasangs."

"Well, you know how you stand with Mother."

"Our relations are a bit distant."

"She shudders at the mention of your name. So I thought if she thought I was going to marry you and then found I wasn't, she'd be so thankful for the merciful escape I'd had that she'd be ready to accept anyone as a son-in-law, even someone like Reggie, who, though a wonder man, hasn't got his name in Debrett and isn't any too hot financially. Mother's idea of a mate for me has always been a well-to-do millionaire or a duke with a large private income. Now do you follow?"

"Oh, yes, I follow all right. You've been doing what Jeeves does, studying the psychology of the individual. But do you think it'll work?"

"Bound to. Let's take a parallel case. Suppose your Aunt Dahlia read in the paper one morning that you were going to be shot at sunrise."

"I couldn't be. I'm never up so early."

"But suppose she did? She'd be pretty worked up about it, wouldn't she?"

"Extremely, one imagines, for she loves me dearly. I'm not saying her manner toward me doesn't verge at times on the brusque. In childhood days she would occasionally clump me on the side of the head, and since I have grown to riper years she has more than once begged me to tie a brick around my neck and go and drown myself in the pond in the kitchen garden. Nevertheless, she loves her Bertram, and if she heard I was to be shot at sunrise, she would, as you say, be as sore as a gumboil. But why? What's that got to do with it?"

"Well, suppose she then found out it was all a mistake

27

and it wasn't you but somebody else who was to face the firing squad. That would make her happy, wouldn't it?"

"One can picture her dancing all over the place on the tips of her toes."

"Exactly. She'd be so all over you that nothing you did would be wrong in her eyes. Whatever you wanted to do would be all right with her. Go to it, she would say. And that's how Mother will feel when she learns that I'm not marrying you after all. She'll be so relieved."

I agreed that the relief would, of course, be stupendous.

"But you'll be giving her the inside facts in a day or two?" I said, for I was anxious to have assurance on this point. A man with an engagement notice in the *Times* hanging over him cannot but feel uneasy.

"Well, call it a week or two. No sense in rushing things."

"You want me to sink in?"

"That's the idea."

"And meanwhile what's the drill? Do I kiss you a good deal from time to time?"

"No, you don't."

"Right ho. I just want to know where I stand."

"An occasional passionate glance will be ample."

"It shall be attended to. Well, I'm delighted about you and Kipper or, as you would prefer to say, Reggie. There's nobody I'd rather see you center-aisle-ing with."

"It's very sporting of you to take it like this."

"Don't give it a thought."

"I'm awfully fond of you, Bertie."

"Me, too, of you."

"But I can't marry everybody, can I?"

"I wouldn't even try. Well, now that we've got all that straight, I suppose I'd better be going and saying 'Come aboard' to Aunt Dahlia."

"What's the time?"

"Close on five."

28

"I must run like a hare. I'm supposed to be presiding at the tea table."

"You? Why you?"

"Your aunt's not here. She found a telegram when she got back yesterday saying that her son Bonzo was sick of a fever at his school, and raced off to be with him. She asked me to deputy-hostess for her till her return, but I shan't be able to for the next few days. I've got to dash back to Mother. Ever since she saw that thing in the *Times*, she's been wiring me every hour on the hour to come home for a round-table conference. What's a guffin?"

"I don't know. Why?"

"That's what she calls you in her latest 'gram. Quote. 'Cannot understand how you can be contemplating marrying that guffin.' Close quote. I suppose it's more or less the same as a gaby, which was how you figured in one of her earlier communications."

"That sounds promising."

"Yes, I think the thing's in the bag. After you, Reggie will come to her like rare and refreshing fruit. She'll lay down the red carpet for him."

And with a brief "Whoopee!" she shot off in the direction of the house at forty or so m.p.h. I followed more slowly, for she had given me much food for thought, and I was musing.

Strange, I was thinking, this strong pro-Kipper sentiment in the Wickham bosom. I mean, consider the facts. What with that *espièglerie* of hers, which was tops, she had been pretty extensively wooed in one quarter and another for years, and no business had resulted, so that it was generally assumed that only something extra special in the way of suitors would meet her specifications and that whoever eventually got his nose under the wire would be a king among men and pretty warm stuff. And she had gone and signed up with Kipper Herring.

Mind you, I'm not saying a word against old Kipper. The salt of the earth. But nobody could have called him a knockout in the way of looks. Having gone in a lot for boxing from his earliest years, he had the cauliflower ear of which I had spoken to Aunt Dahlia and in addition to this a nose which some hidden hand had knocked slightly out of the straight. He would, in short, have been an unsafe entrant to have backed in a beauty contest, even if the only other competitors had been Boris Karloff, King Kong and Oofy Prosser of the Drones.

But then, of course, one had to remind oneself that looks aren't everything. A cauliflower ear can hide a heart of gold, as in Kipper's case it did, his being about as gold as they come. His brain, too, might have helped to do the trick. You can't hold down an editorial post on an important London weekly paper without being fairly well fixed with the little gray cells, and girls admire that sort of thing. And one had to remember that most of the bimbos to whom Roberta Wickham had been giving the bird through the years had been of the huntin', shootin' and fishin' type, fellows who had more or less shot their bolt after saying "Eh, what?" and slapping their leg with a hunting crop. Kipper must have come as a nice change.

Still, the whole thing provided, as I say, food for thought, and I was in what is called a reverie as I made my way to the house, a reverie so profound that no turf accountant would have given any but the shortest odds against my sooner or later bumping into something. And this, to cut a long story s., I did. It might have been a tree, a bush or a rustic seat. In actual fact, it turned out to be Aubrey Upjohn. I came on him round a corner and rammed him squarely before I could put the brakes on. I clutched him round the neck and he clutched me about the middle, and for some moments we tottered to and fro, linked in a close embrace. Then, the mists clearing from my eyes, I saw who it was that I had been treading the measure with.

Seeing him steadily and seeing him whole, as I have heard Jeeves put it, I was immediately struck by the change that had taken place in his appearance since those get-togethers in his study at Malvern House, Bramley-on-Sea, when with a sinking heart I had watched him reach for the whangee and start limbering up the shoulder muscles with a few trial swings. At that period of our acquaintance he had been an upstanding old gentleman about eight feet six in height, with burning eyes, foam-flecked lips and flame coming out of both nostrils. He had now shrunk to a modest five foot seven or thereabouts, and I could have felled him with a single blow.

Not that I did, of course. But I regarded him without a trace of the old trepidation. It seemed incredible that I could ever have considered this human shrimp a danger to pedestrians and traffic.

I think this was partly due to the fact that at some point in the fifteen years since our last meeting he had grown a mustache. In the Malvern House epoch, what had always struck a chill into the plastic mind had been his wide, bare upper lip, a most unpleasant spectacle to behold, especially when it twitched. I wouldn't say the mustache softened his face, but being of the walrus or soup-strainer type it hid some of it, which was all to the good. The upshot was that instead of quailing, as I had expected to do when we met, I was suave and debonair, possibly a little too much so.

"Oh, hullo, Upjohn!" I said. "Yoo-hoo."

"Who you?" he responded, making it sound like a reverse echo.

"Wooster is the name."

"Oh, Wooster?" he said, as if he had been hoping it would be something else, and one could understand his feelings, of course. No doubt he, like me, had been buoying himself up for years with the thought that we should never meet again and that, whatever brickbats life might have in

31

store for him, he had at least got Bertram out of his system. A nasty jar it must have been for the poor bloke having me suddenly pop up from a trap like this.

"Long time since we met," I said.

"Yes," he agreed in a hollow voice, and it was so plain that he was wishing it had been longer that conversation flagged, and there wasn't much in the way of feasts of reason and flows of soul as we covered the hundred yards to the lawn where the tea table awaited us. I think I may have said "Nice day, what?" and he may have grunted, but nothing more.

Only Bobbie was present when we arrived at the trough. Wilbert and Phyllis were presumably still in the leafy glade, and Mrs. Cream, Bobbie said, worked in her room every afternoon on her new spine-freezer and seldom knocked off for a cuppa. We seated ourselves, and had just started sipping when the butler came out of the house bearing a bowl of fruit and hove to beside the table with it.

Well, when I say "butler," I use the term loosely. He was dressed like a butler and he behaved like a butler, but in the deepest and truest sense of the word he was not a butler.

Reading from left to right, he was Sir Roderick Glossop.

· 4 ·

At the Drones Club and other places I am accustomed to frequent you will often hear comment on Bertram Wooster's self-control or sangfroid, as it's sometimes called, and it is generally agreed that this is considerable. In the eyes of many people, I suppose, I seem one of those men of chilled steel you read about, and I'm not saying I'm not. But it is possible to find a chink in my armor, and this can be done by suddenly springing eminent loony-doctors on me in the guise of butlers.

It was out of the q. that I could have been mistaken in supposing that it was Sir Roderick Glossop who, having delivered the fruit, was now ambling back to the house. There could not be two men with that vast bald head and those bushy eyebrows, and it would be deceiving the customers to say that I remained unshaken. The effect the apparition had on me was to make me start violently, and we all know what happens when you start violently while holding a full cup of tea. The contents of mine flew through the air and came to rest on the trousers of Aubrey Upjohn, M.A., moistening them to no little extent. Indeed, it would scarcely be distorting the facts to say that he was now not so much wearing trousers as wearing tea.

I could see the unfortunate man felt his position deeply, and I was surprised that he contented himself with a mere "Ouch!" But I suppose these solid citizens have to learn to curb the tongue. Creates a bad impression, I mean, if they start blinding and stiffing as those more happily placed would do.

But words are not always needed. In the look he now shot at me I seemed to read a hundred unspoken expletives. It was the sort of look the bucko mate of a tramp steamer would have given an able-bodied seaman who for one reason or another had incurred his displeasure.

"I see you have not changed since you were with me at Malvern House," he said in an extremely nasty voice, dabbing at the trousers with a handkerchief. "Bungling Wooster we used to call him," he went on, addressing his remarks to Bobbie and evidently trying to enlist her sympathy. "He could not perform the simplest action such as holding a cup without spreading ruin and disaster on all sides. It was an axiom at Malvern House that if there was a chair in any room in which he happened to be, Wooster would trip over it. The child," said Aubrey Upjohn, "is father of the man."

"Frightfully sorry," I said.

"Too late to be sorry now. A new pair of trousers ruined. It is doubtful that anything can remove the stain of tea from white flannel. Still, one must hope for the best."

Whether I was right or wrong at this point in patting him on the shoulder and saying "That's the spirit!" I find it difficult to decide. Wrong, probably, for it did not seem to soothe. He gave me another of those looks and strode off, smelling strongly of tea.

"Shall I tell you something, Bertie?" said Bobbie, follow-ing him with a thoughtful eye. "That walking tour Upjohn was going to invite you to take with him is off. You will get no Christmas present from him this year, and don't expect him to come and tuck you up in bed tonight."

I upset the milk jug with an imperious wave of the hand.

"Never mind about Upjohn and Christmas presents and walking tours. What is Pop Glossop doing here as the butler?"

"Ah! I thought you might be going to ask that. I was meaning to tell you sometime."

"Tell me now."

"Well, it was his idea."

I eyed her sternly. Bertram Wooster has no objection to listening to drivel, but it must not be pure babble from the padded cell, as this appeared to be.

"His idea?"

"Yes."

"Are you asking me to believe that Sir Roderick Glossop got up one morning, gazed at himself in the mirror, thought he was looking a little pale and said to himself, 'I need a change. I think I'll try being a butler for a while'?"

"No, not that, but . . . I don't know where to begin."

"Begin at the beginning. Come on now, young B. Wick-ham, smack into it," I said, and took a piece of cake in a marked manner.

The austerity of my tone seemed to touch a nerve and kindle the fire that always slept in this vermilion-headed menace to the common weal, for she frowned a displeased frown and told me for heaven's sake to stop goggling like a dead halibut.

"I have every right to goggle like a dead halibut," I said coldly, "and I shall continue to do so as long as I see fit. I am under a considerable nervous s. As always seems to happen when you are mixed up in the doings, life has be-come one damn thing after another, and I think I am justified in demanding an explanation. I await your statement."

"Well, let me marshal my thoughts."

She did so, and after a brief intermission during which I finished my piece of cake, proceeded. "I'd better begin by telling you about Upjohn, because it all started through him. You see, he's egging Phyllis on to marry Wilbert Cream."

"When you say egging—"

"I mean egging. And when a man like that eggs, something has to give, especially when the girl's a pill like Phyllis, who always does what Daddy tells her."

"No will of her own?"

"Not a smidgeon. To give you an instance, a couple of days ago he took her to Birmingham to see the repertory company's performance of Chekhov's *Sea Gull*, because he thought it would be educational. I'd like to catch anyone trying to make me see Chekhov's *Sea Gull*, but Phyllis just bowed her head and said, 'Yes, Daddy.' Didn't even attempt to put up a fight. That'll show you how much of a will of her own she's got."

It did indeed. Her story impressed me profoundly. I know Chekhov's *Sea Gull*. My Aunt Agatha had once made me take her son Thos to a performance of it at the Old Vic, and what with the strain of trying to follow the cockeyed goings on of characters called Zarietchnaya and Medvienko and having to be constantly on the alert to prevent Thos making a sneak for the great open spaces, my suffering had been intense. I needed no further evidence to tell me that Phyllis Mills was a girl whose motto would always be: "Daddy knows best." Wilbert had only got to propose and she would sign on the dotted line because Upjohn wished it.

"Your aunt's worried sick about it."

"She doesn't approve?"

"Of course she doesn't approve. Going over to New York so much, you must have heard of Willie Cream."

36

"Why, yes, news of his escapades has reached me. He's a playboy."

"Your aunt thinks he's a screwball."

"Many playboys are, I believe. Well, that being so, one can understand why she doesn't want those wedding bells to ring out. But," I said, putting my finger on the *res* in my unerring way, "that doesn't explain where Pop Glossop comes in."

"Yes, it does. She got him here to observe Wilbert."

I found myself fogged.

"Cock an eye at him, you mean? Drink him in, as it were? What good's that going to do?"

She snorted impatiently.

"Observe in the technical sense. You know how these brain specialists work. They watch the subject closely. They engage him in conversation. They apply subtle tests. And sooner or later . . ."

"I begin to see. Sooner or later he lets fall an incautious word to the effect that he thinks he's a poached egg, and then they've got him where they want him."

"Well, he does something which tips them off. Your aunt was moaning to me about the situation, and I suddenly had this inspiration of bringing Glossop here. You know how I get sudden inspirations."

"I do. That hot-water-bottle episode."

"Yes, that was one of them."

"Ha!"

"What did you say?"

"Just 'Ha!' "

"Why 'Ha!'?"

"Because when I think of that night of terror, I feel like saying 'Ha!' "

She seemed to see the justice of this. Pausing merely to eat a cucumber sandwich, she continued.

"So I said to your aunt, 'I'll tell you what to do,' I said. 'Get Glossop here,' I said, 'and have him observe Wilbert

Cream. Then you'll be in a position to go to Upjohn and pull the rug from under him.' "

Again I was not abreast. There had been, as far as I could recollect, no mention of any rug.

"How do you mean?"

"Well, isn't it obvious? 'Rope in old Glossop,' I said, 'and let him observe. Then you'll be in a position,' I said, 'to go to Upjohn and tell him that Sir Roderick Glossop, the greatest alienist in England, is convinced that Wilbert Cream is round the bend and to ask him if he proposes to marry his stepdaughter to a man who at any moment may be marched off and added to the membership list of Colney Hatch.' Even Upjohn would shrink from doing a thing like that. Or don't you think so?"

I weighed this.

"Yes," I said, "I should imagine you were right. Quite possibly Upjohn has human feelings, though I never noticed them when I was in *statu pupillari*, I believe the expression is. One sees now why Glossop is at Brinkley Court. What one doesn't see is why one finds him buttling."

"I told you that was his idea. He thought he was such a celebrated figure that it would arouse Mrs. Cream's suspicions if he came here under his own name."

"I see what you mean. She would catch him observing Wilbert and wonder why—"

"—and eventually put two and two together—"

"—and start Hey-what's-the-big-idea-ing."

"Exactly. No mother likes to find that her hostess has got a brain specialist down to observe the son who is the apple of her eye. It hurts her feelings."

"Whereas, if she catches the butler observing him, she merely says to herself, 'Ah, an observant butler.' Very sensible. With this deal Uncle Tom's got on with Homer Cream, it would be fatal to risk giving her the pip in any way. She would kick to Homer, and Homer would draw himself up and say, 'After what has occurred, Travers, I

38

would prefer to break off the negotiations,' and Uncle Tom would lose a packet. What is this deal they've got on, by the way? Did Aunt Dahlia tell you?"

"Yes, but it didn't penetrate. It's something to do with some land your uncle owns somewhere, and Mr. Cream is thinking of buying it and putting up hotels and things. It doesn't matter, anyway. The fundamental thing, the thing to glue the eye on, is that the Cream contingent have to be kept sweetened at any cost. So not a word to a soul."

"Quite. Bertram Wooster is not a babbler. No spiller of the beans he. But why are you so certain that Wilbert Cream is loopy? He doesn't look loopy to me."

"Have you met him?"

"Just for a moment. He was in a leafy glade, reading poetry to the Mills girl."

She took this big.

"Reading poetry? To *Phyllis*?"

"That's right. I thought it odd that a chap like him should be doing such a thing. Limericks, yes. If he had been reciting limericks to her, I could have understood it. But this was stuff from one of those books they bind in limp purple leather and sell at Christmas. I wouldn't care to swear to it, but it sounded to me extremely like Omar Khayyám."

She continued to take it big.

"Break it up, Bertie, break it up! There's not a moment to be lost. You must go and break it up immediately."

"Who, me? Why me?"

"That's what you're here for. Didn't your aunt tell you? She wants you to follow Wilbert Cream and Phyllis about everywhere and see that he doesn't get a chance of proposing."

"You mean that I'm to be a sort of private eye or shamus, tailing them up? I don't like it," I said dubiously.

"You don't have to like it," said Bobbie. "You just do it."

· 5 ·

WAX IN THE HANDS of the other sex, as the expression is,
I went and broke it up as directed, but not blithely. It is
never pleasant for a man of sensibility to find himself
regarded as a buttinski and a trailing arbutus, and it was
thus, I could see at a g., that Wilbert Cream was penciling
me in. At the moment of my arrival he had suspended the
poetry reading and had taken Phyllis' hand in his, evidently
saying or about to say something of an intimate and tender
nature. Hearing my "What ho," he turned, hurriedly released the fin and directed at me a look very similar to the
one I had recently received from Aubrey Upjohn. He
muttered something under his breath about someone,
whose name I did not catch, apparently having been paid
to haunt the place.

"Oh, it's you again," he said.

Well, it was, of course. No argument about that.

"Kind of at a loose end?" he said. "Why don't you settle down somewhere with a good book?"

I explained that I had just popped in to tell them that tea was now being served on the main lawn, and Phyllis squeaked a bit, as if agitated.

"Oh, dear!" she said. "I must run. Daddy doesn't like me to be late for tea. He says it's not respectful to my elders."

I could see trembling on Wilbert Cream's lips a suggestion as to where Daddy could stick himself and his views on respect to elders, but with a powerful effort he held it back.

"I shall take Poppet for a walk," he said, chirruping to the dachshund, who was sniffing at my legs, filling his lungs with the delicious Wooster bouquet.

"No tea?" I said.

"No."

"There are muffins."

"Tchah!" he ejaculated, if that's the word, and strode off, followed by the low-slung dog, and it was borne in upon me that here was another source from which I could expect no present at Yuletide. His whole demeanor made it plain that I had not added to my little circle of friends. Though going like a breeze with dachshunds, I had failed signally to click with Wilbert Cream.

When Phyllis and I reached the lawn, only Bobbie was at the tea table, and this surprised us both.

"Where's Daddy?" Phyllis asked.

"He suddenly decided to go to London," said Bobbie.

"To London?"

"That's what he said."

"Why?"

"He didn't tell me."

"I must go and see him," said Phyllis, and buzzed off.

Bobbie seemed to be musing.

"Do you know what I think, Bertie?"

"What?"

"Well, when Upjohn came out just now, he was all of a doodah, and he had this week's *Thursday's Review* in his hand. Came by the afternoon post, I suppose. I think he had been reading Reggie's comment on his book."

This seemed plausible. I number several authors among my acquaintance—the name of Boko Fittleworth is one that springs to the mind—and they invariably become all of a doodah when they read a stinker in the press about their latest effort.

"Oh, you know about that thing Kipper wrote?"

"Yes, he showed it to me one day when we were having lunch together."

"Very mordant, I gathered from what he told me. But I don't see why that should make Upjohn bound up to London."

"I suppose he wants to ask the editor who wrote the thing, so that he can horsewhip him on the steps of his club. But of course they won't tell him, and it wasn't signed, so . . . Oh, hullo, Mrs. Cream."

The woman she was addressing was tall and thin with a hawklike face that reminded me of Sherlock Holmes. She had an ink spot on her nose, the result of working on her novel of suspense. It is virtually impossible to write a novel of suspense without getting a certain amount of ink on the beezer. Ask Agatha Christie or anyone.

"I finished my chapter a moment ago, so I thought I would stop for a cup of tea," said this litterateuse. "No good overdoing it."

"No. Quit when you're ahead of the game, that's the idea. This is Mrs. Travers' nephew, Bertie Wooster," said Bobbie with what I considered a far too apologetic note in her voice. If Roberta Wickham has one fault more pronounced than another, it is that she is inclined to introduce me to people as if I were something she would much have

42

preferred to hush up. "Bertie loves your books," she added, quite unnecessarily, and the Cream started like a Boy Scout at the sound of a bugle.

"Oh, do you?"

"Never happier than when curled up with one of them," I said, trusting that she wouldn't ask me which of them I liked best.

"When I told him you were here, he was overcome."

"Well, that certainly is great. Always glad to meet the fans. Which of my books do you like best?"

And I had got as far as "Er" and was wondering, though not with much hope, if "All of them" would meet the case, when Pop Glossop joined us with a telegram for Bobbie on a salver. From her mother, I presumed, calling me some name which she had forgotten to insert in previous communications. Or, of course, possibly expressing once more her conviction that I was a guffin, which, I thought, having had time to ponder over it, would be something in the nature of a bohunkus or a hammerhead.

"Oh, thank you, Swordfish," said Bobbie, taking the telegram.

It was fortunate that I was not holding a teacup as she spoke, for hearing Sir Roderick thus addressed I gave another of my sudden starts and, had I had such a cup in my hand, must have strewn its contents hither and thither like a sower going forth sowing. As it was, I merely sent a cucumber sandwich flying through the air.

"Oh, sorry," I said, for it had missed the Cream by a hair's breadth.

I could have relied on Bobbie to shove her oar in. The girl had no notion of passing a thing off.

"Excuse it, please," she said. "I ought to have warned you. Bertie is training for the Jerk The Cucumber Sandwich event at next year's Olympic Games. He has to be practicing all the time."

On Ma Cream's brow there was a thoughtful wrinkle, as though she felt unable to accept this explanation of what had occurred. But her next words showed that it was not on my activities that her mind was dwelling but on the recent Swordfish. Having followed him with a keen glance as he faded from view, she said, "This butler of Mrs. Travers'. Do you know where she got him, Miss Wickham?"

"At the usual pet shop, I think."

"Had he references?"

"Oh, yes. He was with Sir Roderick Glossop, the brain specialist, for years. I remember Mrs. Travers saying Sir Roderick gave him a supercolossal reference. She was greatly impressed."

Ma Cream sniffed. "References can be forged."

"Good gracious! Why do you say that?"

"Because I am not at all easy in my mind about this man. He has a criminal face."

"Well, you might say that about Bertie."

"I feel that Mrs. Travers should be warned. In my *Blackness at Night* the butler turned out to be one of a gang of crooks, planted in the house to make it easy for them to break in. The inside stand, it's called. I strongly suspect that this is why this Swordfish is here, though of course it is quite possible that he is working on his own. One thing I am sure of, and that is that he is not a genuine butler."

"What makes you think that?" I asked, handkerchiefing my upper slopes, which had become considerably bedewed. I didn't like this line of talk at all. Let the Cream get firmly in her nut the idea that Sir Roderick Glossop was not the butler, the whole butler and nothing but the butler, and disaster, as I saw it, loomed. She would probe and investigate, and before you could say "What ho" would be in full possession of the facts. In which event, *bim* would go Uncle Tom's chance of scooping in a bit of easy money. And ever since I've known him, failure to get his hooks on any stray cash that's floating around has always put him out

44

of touch with the bluebird. It isn't that he's mercenary; it's just that he loves the stuff."

Her manner suggested that she was glad I had asked her that.

"I'll tell you what makes me think it. He betrays his amateurishness in a hundred ways. This very morning I found him having a long conversation with Wilbert. A real butler would never do that. He would feel it was a liberty."

I contested this statement.

"Now there," I said, "I take issue with you, if taking issue means what I think it means. Many of my happiest hours have been passed chatting with butlers, and it has nearly always happened that it was they who made the first advances. They seek me out and tell me about their rheumatism. Swordfish looks all right to me."

"You are not a student of criminology, as I am. I have the trained eye, and my judgment is never wrong. That man is here for no good."

I could see that all this was making Bobbie chafe, but her better self prevailed and she checked the heated retort. She is very fond of T. Portarlington Travers, who, she tells me, is the living image of a wirehaired terrier now residing with the morning stars but at one time very dear to her, and she remembered that for his sake the Cream had to be deferred to and handled with gloves. When she spoke, it was with the mildness of a cushat dove addressing another cushat dove from whom it was hoping to borrow money.

"But don't you think, Mrs. Cream, that it may be just your imagination? You have such a wonderful imagination. Bertie was saying only the other day that he didn't know how you did it. Wrote all those frightfully imaginative books, I mean. Weren't you, Bertie?"

"My very words."

"And if you have an imagination, you can't help imagining. Can you, Bertie?"

"Dashed difficult."

Her honeyed words were wasted. The Cream continued to dig her toes in like Balaam's ass, of whom you have doubtless heard.

"I'm not imagining that that butler is up to something fishy," she said tartly. "And I should have thought it was pretty obvious what that something was. You seem to have forgotten that Mr. Travers has one of the finest collections of old silver in England."

This was correct. Owing possibly to some flaw in his mental make-up, Uncle Tom has been collecting old silver since I was so high, and I suppose the contents of the room on the ground floor where he parks the stuff are worth a princely sum. I knew all about that collection of his, not only because I had had to listen to him for hours on the subject of sconces, foliation, ribbon wreaths in high relief and gadroon borders, but because I had what you might call a personal interest in it, once having stolen an eighteenth-century cow-creamer for him. (Long story. No time to go into it now. You will find it elsewhere in the archives.)

"Mrs. Travers was showing it to Willie the other day, and he was thrilled. Willie collects old silver himself."

With each hour that passed I was finding it more and more difficult to get a toehold on the character of W. Cream. An in-and-out performer, if ever there was one. First, all that poetry, I mean, and now this. I had always supposed that playboys didn't give a hoot for anything except blondes and cold bottles. It just showed once again that half the world doesn't know how the other three quarters lives.

"He says there are any number of things in Mr. Travers' collection that he would give his back teeth for. There was an eighteenth-century cow-creamer he particularly coveted. So keep your eye on that butler. I'm certainly going to keep mine. Well," said the Cream, rising, "I must be getting back to my work. I always like to rough out a new chapter before finishing for the day."

She legged it, and for a moment silence reigned. Then Bobbie said, "Phew!" and I agreed that "Phew!" was the *mot juste*.

"We'd better get Glossop out of here quick," I said.

"How can we? It's up to your aunt to do that, and she's away."

"Then I'm jolly well going to get out myself. There's too much impending doom buzzing around these parts for my taste. Brinkley Court, once a peaceful country house, has become like something sinister out of Edgar Allan Poe, and it makes my feet cold. I'm leaving."

"You can't till your aunt gets back. There has to be some sort of host or hostess here, and I simply must go home tomorrow and see Mother. You'll have to clench your teeth and stick it."

"And the severe mental strain to which I am being subjected doesn't matter, I suppose?"

"Not a bit. Does you good. Keeps your pores open."

I should probably have said something pretty cutting in reply to this, if I could have thought of anything, but as I couldn't I didn't.

"What's Aunt Dahlia's address?" I said.

"Royal Hotel, Eastbourne. Why?"

"Because," I said, taking another cucumber sandwich, "I'm going to wire her to ring me up tomorrow without fail, so that I can apprise her of what's going on in this joint."

• 6 •

I FORGET how the subject arose, but I remember Jeeves once saying that sleep knits up the raveled sleeve of care. Balm of hurt minds, he described it as. The idea being, I took it, that if things are getting sticky, they tend to seem less glutinous after you've had your eight hours.

Applesauce, in my opinion. It seldom pans out that way with me, and it didn't now. I had retired to rest taking a dim view of the current situation at Brinkley Court and opening my eyes to a new day, as the expression is, I found myself taking an even dimmer. Who knew, I asked myself as I pushed the breakfast egg away practically untasted, what Ma Cream might not at any moment uncover? And who could say how soon, if I continued to be always at his side, Wilbert Cream would get it up his nose and start attacking me with tooth and claw? Already his manner was that of a man whom the society of Bertram Wooster had fed to the tonsils, and one more sight of the latter at his elbow might quite easily make him decide to take prompt steps through the proper channels.

Musing along these lines, I had little appetite for lunch, though Anatole had extended himself to the utmost. I winced every time the Cream shot a sharp, suspicious look at Pop Glossop as he messed about at the sideboard, and the long, loving looks her son Wilbert kept directing at Phyllis Mills chilled me to the marrow. At the conclusion of the meal he would, I presumed, invite the girl to accompany him again to that leafy glade, and it was idle to suppose that there would not be pique on his part, or even chagrin, when I came along, too.

Fortunately, as we rose from the table, Phyllis said she was going to her room to finish typing Daddy's speech, and my mind was eased for the nonce. Even a New York playboy, accustomed from his earliest years to pursue blondes like a bloodhound, would hardly follow her there and press his suit.

Seeming himself to recognize that there was nothing constructive to be done in that direction for the moment, he said in a brooding voice that he would take Poppet for a walk. This, apparently, was his invariable method of healing the stings of disappointment, and an excellent thing of course from the point of view of a dog who liked getting around and seeing the sights. They headed for the horizon and passed out of view, the hound gamboling, he not gamboling but swishing his stick a good deal in an overwrought sort of manner; and I, feeling that this was a thing that ought to be done, selected one of Ma Cream's books from Aunt Dahlia's shelves and took it out to read in a deck chair on the lawn. And I should no doubt have enjoyed it enormously, for the Cream unquestionably wielded a gifted pen, had not the warmth of the day caused me to drop off into a gentle sleep in the middle of Chapter Two.

Waking from this some little time later and running an eye over myself to see if the raveled sleeve of care had been knitted up—which it hadn't—I was told that I was wanted on the telephone. I hastened to the instrument, and Aunt Dahlia's voice came thundering over the wire.

"Bertie?"

"Bertram it is."

"Why the devil have you been such a time? I've been hanging on to this damned receiver a long hour by Shrewsbury clock."

"Sorry. I came on winged feet, but I was out on the lawn when you broke loose."

"Sleeping off your lunch, I suppose?"

"My eyes may have closed for a moment."

"Always eating, that's you."

"It is customary, I believe, to take a little nourishment at about this hour," I said rather stiffly. "How's Bonzo?"

"Getting along."

"What was it?"

"German measles, but he's out of danger. Well, what's all the excitement about? Why did you want me to phone you? Just so that you could hear Auntie's voice?"

"I am always glad to hear Auntie's voice, but I had a deeper and graver reason. I thought you ought to know about all these lurking perils in the home."

"What lurking perils?"

"Ma Cream for one. She's hotting up. She entertains suspicions."

"What of?"

"Pop Glossop. She doesn't like his face."

"Well, hers is nothing to write home about."

"She thinks he isn't a real butler."

From the fact that my eardrum nearly split in half I deduced that she had laughed a jovial laugh.

"Let her think."

"You aren't perturbed?"

"Not a bit. She can't do anything about it. Anyway, Glossop ought to be leaving in about a week. He told me he

50

didn't think it would take longer than that to make up his mind about Wilbert. Adela Cream doesn't worry me."

"Well, if you say so, but I should have thought she was a menace."

"She doesn't seem so to me. Anything else on your mind?"

"Yes, this Wilbert Cream–Phyllis Mills thing."

"Ah, now you're talking. That's important. Did young Bobbie Wickham tell you that you'd got to stick to Wilbert closer than—"

"A brother?"

"I was going to say porous plaster, but have it your own way. She explained the position of affairs?"

"She did, and it's precisely that that I want to thresh out with you."

"Do what out?"

"Thresh."

"All right, start threshing."

Having given the situation the best of the Wooster brain for some considerable time, I had the *res* all clear in my mind. I proceeded to decant it.

"As we go through this life, my dear old ancestor," I said, "we should always strive to see the other fellow's side of a thing, the other fellow in the case under advisement being Wilbert Cream. Has it occurred to you to put yourself in Wilbert Cream's place and ask yourself how he's going to feel, being followed around all the time? It isn't as if he was Mary."

"What did you say?"

"I said it wasn't as if he was Mary. Mary, as I remember, enjoyed the experience of being tailed up."

"Bertie, you're tight."

"Nothing of the kind."

"Say 'British constitution.' "

I did so.

"And now 'She sells sea shells by the sea shore.' "

51

I reeled it off in a bell-like voice.

"Well, you seem all right," she said grudgingly. "How do you mean he isn't Mary? Mary who?"

"I don't think she had a surname, had she? I was alluding to the child who had a little lamb with fleece as white as snow, and everywhere that Mary went the lamb was sure to go. Now I'm not saying that I have fleece as white as snow, but I *am* going everywhere that Wilbert Cream goes, and one speculates with some interest as to what the upshot will be. He resents my constant presence."

"Has he said so?"

"Not yet. But he gives me nasty looks."

"That's all right. He can't intimidate me."

I saw that she was missing the gist.

"Yes, but don't you see the peril that looms?"

"I thought you said it lurked."

"*And* looms. What I'm driving at is that if I persist in this porous plastering, a time must inevitably come when, feeling that actions speak louder than words, he will haul off and bop me one. In which event, I shall have no alternative but to haul off and bop *him* one. The Woosters have their pride. And when I bop them, they stay bopped till nightfall."

She bayed like a foghorn, showing that she was deeply stirred.

"You'll do nothing of the sort, unless you want to have an aunt's curse delivered on your doorstep by special messenger. Don't you dare to start mixing it with that man, or I'll tattoo my initials on your chest with a meat ax. Turn the other cheek, you poor fish. If my nephew socked her son, Adela Cream would never forgive me. She would go running to her husband—"

"—and Uncle Tom's deal would be dished. That's the very point I'm trying to make. If Wilbert Cream is bust one, it must be by somebody having no connection with the

Travers family. You must at once engage a substitute for Bertram."

"Are you suggesting that I hire a private detective?"

" 'Eye' is the more usual term. No, not that, but you must invite Kipper Herring down here. Kipper is the man you want. He will spring to the task of dogging Wilbert's footsteps, and if Wilbert bops him and he bops Wilbert, it won't matter, he being outside talent. Not that I anticipate that Wilbert will dream of doing so, for Kipper's mere appearance commands respect. The muscles of his brawny arms are strong as iron bands, and he has a cauliflower ear."

There was a silence of some moments, and it was not difficult to divine that she was passing my words under review, this way and that dividing the swift mind, as I have heard Jeeves put it. When she spoke, it was in quite an awed voice.

"Do you know, Bertie, there are times—rare, yes, but they do happen—when your intelligence is almost human. You've hit it. I never thought of young Herring. Do you think he could come?"

"He was saying to me only the day before yesterday that his dearest wish was to cadge an invitation. Anatole's cooking is green in his memory."

"Then send him a wire. You can telephone it to the post office. Sign it with my name."

"Right ho."

"Tell him to drop everything and come running."

She rang off, and I was about to draft the communication, when, as so often happens to one on relaxing from a great strain, I became conscious of an imperious desire for a little something quick. Oh, for a beaker full of the warm south, as Jeeves would have said. I pressed the bell, accordingly, and sank into a chair, and presently the door opened and a circular object with a bald head and bushy eyebrows manifested itself, giving me quite a start. I had quite forgotten that ringing bells at Brinkley Court under prevailing conditions must inevitably produce Sir Roderick Glossop.

It's always a bit difficult to open the conversation with a blend of brain specialist and butler, especially if your relations with him in the past have not been too chummy, and I found myself rather at a loss to know how to set the ball rolling. I yearned for that drink as the hart desireth the water-brook, but if you ask a butler to bring you a whisky and soda and he happens to be a brain specialist, too, he's quite apt to draw himself up and wither you with a glance. All depends on which side of him is uppermost at the moment. It was a relief when I saw that he was smiling a kindly smile and evidently welcoming this opportunity of having a quiet chat with Bertram. So long as we kept off the subject of hot-water bottles, it looked as if all would be well.

"Good afternoon, Mr. Wooster. I had been hoping for a word with you in private. But perhaps Miss Wickham has already explained the circumstances? She has? Then that clears the air, and there is no danger of your incautiously revealing my identity. She impressed it upon you that Mrs. Cream must have no inkling of why I am here?"

"Oh, rather. Secrecy and silence, what? If she knew you were observing her son with a view to finding out if he was foggy between the ears, there would be umbrage on her part, or even dudgeon."

"Exactly."

"And how's it coming along?"

"I beg your pardon?"

"The observing. Have you spotted any dippiness in the subject?"

"If by that expression you mean have I formed any definite views on Wilbert Cream's sanity, the answer is no. It is most unusual for me to be able to make up my mind after even a single talk with the person I am observing, but in young Cream's case I remain uncertain. On the one hand, we have his record."

"The stink bombs?"

"Exactly."

"And the check-cashing with leveled gat?"

"Precisely. And a number of other things which one would say pointed to a mental unbalance. Unquestionably Wilbert Cream is eccentric."

"But you feel the time has not yet come to measure him for the straight waistcoat?"

"I would certainly wish to observe further."

"Jeeves told me there was something about Wilbert Cream that someone had told him when we were in New York. That might be significant."

"Quite possibly. What was it?"

"He couldn't remember."

"Too bad. Well, to return to what I was saying, the young man's record appears to indicate some deep-seated neurosis, if not actual schizophrenia, but against this must be set the fact that he gives no sign of this in his conversation. I was having quite a long talk with him yesterday morning, and found him most intelligent. He is interested in old silver, and spoke with a great deal of enthusiasm of an eighteenth-century cow-creamer in your uncle's collection."

"He didn't say he *was* an eighteenth-century cow-creamer?"

"Certainly not."

"Probably just wearing the mask."

"I beg your pardon?"

"I mean crouching for the spring, as it were. Lulling you into security. Bound to break out sooner or later in some direction or other. Very cunning, these fellows with deep-seated neuroses."

He shook his head reprovingly.

"We must not judge hastily, Mr. Wooster. We must keep an open mind. Nothing is ever gained by not pausing to weigh the evidence. You may remember that at one time

I reached a hasty judgment regarding your sanity. Those twenty-three cats in your bedroom."

I flushed hotly. The incident had taken place several years previously, and it would have been in better taste, I considered, to have let the dead past bury its dead.

"That was explained fully."

"Exactly. I was shown to be in error. And that is why I say I must not form an opinion prematurely in the case of Wilbert Cream. I must wait for further evidence."

"And weigh it?"

"And, as you say, weigh it. But you rang, Mr. Wooster. Is there anything I can do for you?"

"Well, as a matter of fact, I wanted a whisky and soda, but I hate to trouble you."

"My dear Mr. Wooster, you forget that I am, if only temporarily, a butler and, I hope, a conscientious one. I will bring it immediately."

I was wondering, as he melted away, if I ought to tell him that Mrs. Cream, too, was doing a bit of evidence weighing, and about him, but decided on the whole better not. No sense in disturbing his peace of mind. It seemed to me that having to answer to the name of Swordfish was enough for him to have to cope with for the time being. Given too much to think about, he would fret and get pale.

When he returned, he brought with him not only the beaker full of the warm south, on which I flung myself gratefully, but a letter which he said had just come for me by the afternoon post. Having slaked the thirst, I glanced at the envelope and saw that it was from Jeeves. I opened it without much of a thrill, expecting that he would merely be informing me that he had reached his destination safely and expressing a hope that this would find me in the pink as it left him at present. In short, the usual guff.

It wasn't the usual guff by a mile and a quarter. One glance at its contents and I was gosh-ing sharply, causing Pop Glossop to regard me with a concerned eye.

"No bad news, I trust, Mr. Wooster?"

"It depends what you call bad news. It's front-page stuff, all right. This is from Jeeves, my man, now shrimping at Herne Bay, and it casts a blinding light on the private life of Wilbert Cream."

"Indeed? This is most interesting."

"I must begin by saying that when Jeeves was leaving for his annual vacation, the subject of W. Cream came up in the home, Aunt Dahlia having told me he was one of the inmates here, and we discussed him at some length. I said this, if you see what I mean, and Jeeves said that, if you follow me. Well, just before Jeeves pushed off, he let fall that significant remark I mentioned just now, the one about having heard something about Wilbert and having forgotten it. If it came back to him, he said, he would communicate with me. And he has, by Jove! Do you know what he says in this missive? Give you three guesses."

"Surely this is hardly the time for guessing games?"

"Perhaps you're right, though they're great fun, don't you think? Well, he says that Wilbert Cream is a . . . what's the word?" I referred to the letter. "A kleptomaniac." I said. "Which means, if the term is not familiar to you, a chap who flits hither and thither pinching everything he can lay his hands on."

"Good gracious!"

"You might even go so far as 'Lor' lummel'"

"I never suspected this."

"I told you he was wearing the mask. I suppose they took him abroad to get him away from it all."

"No doubt."

"Overlooking the fact that there are just as many things to pinch in England as in America. Does any thought occur to you?"

"It most certainly does. I am thinking of your uncle's collection of old silver."

"Me, too."

"It presents a grave temptation to the unhappy young man."

"I don't know that I'd call him unhappy. He probably thoroughly enjoys lifting the stuff."

"We must go to the collection room immediately. There may be something missing."

"Everything except the floor and ceiling, I expect. He would have had difficulty in getting away with those."

To reach the collection room was not the work of an instant with us, for Pop Glossop was built for stability rather than speed, but we fetched up there in due course and my first emotion on giving it the once-over was one of relief, all the junk appearing to be in *statu quo*. It was only after Pop Glossop had said "Woof!" and was starting to dry off the brow, for the going had been fast, that I spotted the hiatus.

The cow-creamer was not among those present.

• 7 •

THIS COW-CREAMER, in case you're interested, was a silver jug or pitcher or whatever you call it, shaped, of all silly things, like a cow with an arching tail and a juvenile-delinquent expression on its face, a cow that looked as if it were planning, next time it was milked, to haul off and let the milkmaid have it in the lower ribs. Its back opened on a hinge and the tip of the tail touched the spine, thus giving the householder something to catch hold of when pouring. Why anyone should want such a revolting object had always been a mystery to me, it ranking high up on the list of things I would have been reluctant to be found dead in a ditch with, but apparently they liked that sort of jug in the eighteenth century, and, coming down to more modern times, Uncle Tom was all for it and so, according to the evidence of the witness Glossop, was Wilbert. No accounting for tastes is the way one has to look at these things, one man's caviar being another man's major general, as the old saw says.

However, be that as it may and whether you liked the bally thing or didn't, the point was that it had vanished, leaving not a wrack behind, and I was about to apprise Pop Glossop of this and canvass his views, when we were joined by Bobbie Wickham. She had doffed the shirt and Bermuda shorts which she had been wearing and was now dressed for her journey home.

"Hullo, souls," she said. "How goes it? You look a bit hot and bothered, Bertie. What's up?"

I made no attempt to break the n. gently.

"I'll tell you what's up. You know that cow-creamer of Uncle Tom's?"

"No, I don't. What is it?"

"Sort of cream-jug kind of thing, ghastly but very valuable. One would not be far out in describing it as Uncle Tom's ewe lamb. He loves it dearly."

"Bless his heart."

"It's all right blessing his heart, but the damn thing's gone."

The still summer air was disturbed by a sound like beer coming out of a bottle. It was Pop Glossop gurgling. His eyes were round, his nose wiggled, and one could readily discern that this news item had come to him not as rare and refreshing fruit but more like a buffet on the base of the skull with a sockful of wet sand.

"Gone?"

"Gone."

"Are you sure?"

I said that sure was just what I wasn't anything but.

"It is not possible that you may have overlooked it?"

"You can't overlook a thing like that."

He re-gurgled.

"But this is terrible."

"Might be considerably better, I agree."

60

"Your uncle will be most upset."

"He'll have kittens."

"Kittens?"

"That's right."

"Why kittens?"

"Why not?"

From the look on Bobbie's face, as she stood listening to our crosstalk act, I could see that the inner gist was passing over her head. Cryptic, she seemed to be registering it as.

"I don't get this," she said. "How do you mean it's gone?"

"It's been pinched."

"Things don't get pinched in country houses."

"They do if there's a Wilbert Cream on the premises. He's a klep-whatever-it-is," I said, and thrust Jeeve's letter on her. She perused it with an interested eye and having mastered contents said, "Cor chase my Aunt Fanny up a gum tree," adding that you never knew what was going to happen next these days. There was, however, she said, a bright side.

"You'll be able now to give it as your considered opinion that the man is as loony as a coot, Sir Roderick."

A pause ensued during which Pop Glossop appeared to be weighing this, possibly thinking back to coots he had met in the course of his professional career and trying to estimate their dippiness as compared with that of W. Cream.

"Unquestionably his metabolism is unduly susceptible to stresses resulting from the interaction of external excitations," he said, and Bobbie patted him on the shoulder in a maternal sort of way, a thing I wouldn't have cared to do myself, though our relations were, as I have indicated, more cordial than they had been at one time, and told him he had said a mouthful.

"That's how I like to hear you talk. You must tell Mrs. Travers that when she gets back. It'll put her in a strong position to cope with Upjohn in this matter of Wilbert and

61

Phyllis. With this under her belt, she'll be able to forbid the banns in no uncertain manner. 'What price his metabolism?' she'll say, and Upjohn won't know which way to look. So everything's fine."

"Everything," I pointed out, "except that Uncle Tom is short one ewe lamb."

She chewed the lower lip.

"Yes, that's true. You have a point there. What steps do we take about that?"

She looked at me, and I said I didn't know, and then she looked at Pop Glossop, and he said he didn't know.

"The situation is an extremely delicate one. You concur, Mr. Wooster?"

"Like billy-o."

"Placed as he is, your uncle can hardly go to the young man and demand restitution. Mrs. Travers impressed it upon me with all the emphasis at her disposal that the greatest care must be exercised to prevent Mr. and Mrs. Cream taking—"

"Umbrage?"

"I was about to say offense."

"Just as good, probably. Not much in it either way."

"And they would certainly take offense, were their son to be accused of theft."

"It would stir them up like an egg whisk. I mean, however well they know that Wilbert is a pincher, they don't want to have it rubbed in."

"Exactly."

"It's one of the things the man of tact does not mention in their presence."

"Precisely. So, really, I cannot see what is to be done. I am so baffled."

"So am I."

"I'm not," said Bobbie.

I quivered like a startled what-d'you-call it. She had

spoken with a cheery ring in her voice that told an experienced ear like mine that she was about to start something. In a matter of seconds by Shrewsbury Clock, as Aunt Dahlia would have said, I could see that she was going to come out with one of those schemes or plans of hers that not only stagger humanity and turn the moon to blood but lead to some unfortunate male—who on the present occasion would, I strongly suspected, be me—getting immersed in what Shakespeare calls a sea of troubles, if it was Shakespeare. I had heard that ring in her voice before, to name but one time, at the moment when she was pressing the darning needle into my hand and telling me where I would find Sir Roderick Glossop's hot-water bottle. Many people are of the opinion that Roberta, daughter of Lady Wickham of Skeldings Hall, Herts, and the late Sir Cuthbert, ought not to be allowed at large. I string along with that school of thought.

Pop Glossop, having only a sketchy acquaintance with this female of the species and so not knowing that from childhood up her motto had been "Anything goes," was all animation and tell-me-more.

"You have thought of some course of action that it will be feasible for us to pursue, Miss Wickham?"

"Certainly. It sticks out like a sore thumb. Do you know which Wilbert's room is?"

He said he did.

"And do you agree that if you snitch things when you're staying at a country house, the only place you can park them in is your room?"

He said that this was no doubt so.

"Very well, then."

He looked at her with what I have heard Jeeves call a wild surmise.

"Can you be . . . Is it possible that you are suggesting . . . ?"

63

"That somebody nips into Wilbert's room and hunts around? That's right. And it's obvious who the people's choice is. You're elected, Bertie."

Well, I wasn't surprised. As I say, I had seen it coming. I don't know why it is, but whenever there's dirty work to be undertaken at the crossroads, the cry that goes round my little circle is always "Let Wooster do it." It never fails. But though I hadn't much hope that any words of mine would accomplish anything in the way of averting the doom, I put in a rebuttal.

"Why me?"

"It's young man's work."

Though with a growing feeling that I was fighting in the last ditch, I continued rebutting.

"I don't see that," I said. "I should have thought a mature, experienced man of the world would have been far more likely to bring home the bacon than a novice like myself, who as a child was never any good at hunt-the-slipper. Stands to reason."

"Now don't be difficult, Bertie. You'll enjoy it," said Bobbie, though where she got that idea I was at a loss to understand. "Try to imagine you're someone in the Secret Service on the track of the naval treaty which was stolen by a mysterious veiled woman diffusing a strange exotic scent. You'll have the time of your life. What did you say?"

"I said 'Ha!' Suppose someone pops in?"

"Don't be silly. Mrs. Cream is working on her book. Phyllis is in her room, typing Upjohn's speech. Wilbert's gone for a walk. Upjohn isn't here. The only character who could pop in would be the Brinkley Court ghost. If it does, give it a cold look and walk through it. That'll teach it not to come butting in where it isn't wanted, ha, ha."

"Ha, ha," trilled Pop Glossop.

I thought their mirth ill-timed and in dubious taste, and I let them see it by my manner as I strode off. For of course I did stride off. These clashings of will with the opposite sex always end with Bertram Wooster bowing to the inev. But I was not in jocund mood, and when Bobbie, speeding me on my way, called me her brave little man and said she had known all along I had it in me, I ignored the remark with a coldness which must have made itself felt.

It was a lovely afternoon, replete with blue sky, beaming sun, buzzing insects and what not, an afternoon that seemed to call to one to be out in the open with God's air playing on one's face and something cool in a glass at one's side, and here was I, just to oblige Bobbie Wickham, tooling along a corridor indoors on my way to search a comparative stranger's bedroom, this involving crawling on floors and routing under beds and probably getting covered with dust and fluff. The thought was a bitter one, and I don't suppose I have ever come closer to saying "Faugh!" It amazed me that I could have allowed myself to be let in for a binge of this description simply because a woman wished it. Too bally chivalrous for our own good, we Woosters, and always have been.

As I reached Wilbert's door and paused outside, doing a bit of screwing the courage to the sticking point, as I have heard Jeeves call it, I found the proceedings reminding me of something, and I suddenly remembered what. I was feeling just as I had felt in the old Malvern House epoch when I used to sneak down to Aubrey Upjohn's study at dead of night in quest of the biscuits he kept there in a tin on his desk; and there came back to me the memory of the occasion when, not letting a twig snap beneath my feet, I had entered his sanctum in pajamas and a dressing gown, to find him seated in his chair, tucking into the biscuits himself. A moment fraught with embarrassment. The What-does-this-mean-Wooster-ing that ensued and the aftermath next morning—six of the best on the old spot— had always remained graven on the tablets of my mind, if that's the expression I want.

Except for the tapping of a typewriter in a room along

the corridor, showing that Ma Cream was hard at her self-appointed task of curdling the blood of the reading public, all was still. I stood outside the door for a space, letting "I dare not" wait upon "I would," as Jeeves tells me cats do in adages, then turned the handle softly, pushed—also softly—and, carrying on into the interior, found myself confronted by a girl in housemaid's costume who put a hand to her throat like somebody in a play and leaped several inches in the direction of the ceiling.

"Coo!" she said, having returned to terra firma and taken aboard a spot of breath. "You gave me a start, sir!"

"Frightfully sorry, my dear old housemaid," I responded cordially. "As a matter of fact, you gave *me* a start, making two starts in all. I'm looking for Mr. Cream."

"I'm looking for a mouse."

This opened up an interesting line of thought.

"You feel there are mice in these parts?"

"I saw one this morning, when I was doing the room. So I brought Augustus," she said, and indicated a large black cat who until then had escaped my notice. I recognized him as an old crony with whom I had often breakfasted, I wading into the scrambled eggs, he into the saucer of milk.

"Augustus will teach him," she said.

Now, right from the start, as may readily be imagined, I had been wondering how this housemaid was to be removed, for of course her continued presence would render my enterprise null and void. You can't search rooms with the domestic staff standing on the sidelines, but on the other hand it was impossible for anyone with any claim to being a *preux chevalier* to take her by the slack of her garment and heave her out. For a while the thing had seemed an impasse, but this statement of hers that Augustus would teach the mouse gave me an idea.

"I doubt it," I said. "You're new here, aren't you?"

She conceded this, saying that she had taken office only in the previous month.

66

"I thought as much, or you would be aware that Augustus is a broken reed to lean on in the matter of catching mice. My own acquaintance with him is a long standing one, and I have come to know his psychology from soup to nuts. He hasn't caught a mouse since he was a slip of a kitten. Except when eating, he does nothing but sleep. Lethargic is the word that springs to the lips. If you cast an eye on him, you will see that he's asleep now."

"Cool So he is."

"It's a sort of disease. There's a scientific name for it. Trau-something. Traumatic symplegia, that's it. This cat has traumatic symplegia. In other words, putting it in simple language adapted to the lay mind, where other cats are content to get their eight hours, Augustus wants his twenty-four. If you will be ruled by me, you will abandon the whole project and take him back to the kitchen. You're simply wasting your time here."

My eloquence was not without its effect. She said "Cool" again, picked up the cat, who drowsily muttered something which I couldn't follow, and went out, leaving me to carry on.

•8•

THE FIRST thing I noticed when at leisure to survey my surroundings was that the woman up top, carrying out her policy of leaving no stone unturned in the way of charming the Cream family, had done Wilbert well where sleeping accommodation was concerned. What he had drawn when clocking in at Brinkley Court was the room known as the Blue Room, a signal honor to be accorded to a bachelor guest, amounting to being given star billing, for at Brinkley, as at most country houses, any old nook or cranny is considered good enough for the celibate contingent. My own apartment, to take a case in point, was a sort of hermit's cell in which one would have been hard put to it to swing a cat, even a smaller one than Augustus—not of course that one often wants to do much cat-swinging. What I'm driving at is that when I blow in on Aunt Dahlia, you don't catch her saying "Welcome to Meadowsweet Hall, my dear boy. I've put you in the Blue Room, where I am sure you will be comfortable." I once suggested to her that I be put there, and all she said was *"You?"* and the conversation turned to other topics.

The furnishing of this Blue Room was solid and Victorian, it having been the G.H.Q. of my Uncle Tom's late father, who liked things substantial. There was a four-poster bed, a chunky dressing table, a massive writing table, divers chairs, pictures on the walls of fellows in cocked hats bending over females in muslin and ringlets, and over at the far side a cupboard or armoire in which you could have hidden a dozen corpses. In short, there was so much space and so many things to shove things behind that most people, called on to find a silver cow-creamer there, would have said, "Oh, what's the use?" and thrown in the towel.

But where I had the bulge on the ordinary searcher was that I am a man of wide reading. Starting in early boyhood, long before they were called novels of suspense, I've read more mystery stories than you could shake a stick at, and they have taught me something—*viz.,* that anybody with anything to hide invariably puts it on top of the cupboard or, if you prefer, the armoire. This is what happened in *Murder at Mistleigh Manor, Three Dead on Tuesday, Excuse My Gat, Guess Who* and a dozen more standard works, and I saw no reason to suppose that Wilbert Cream would have deviated from routine. My first move, accordingly, was to take a chair and prop it against the armoire, and I had climbed on this and was preparing to subject the top to a close scrutiny when Bobbie Wickham, entering on noiseless feet and speaking from about eighteen inches behind me, said, "How are you getting on?"

Really, one sometimes despairs of the modern girl. You'd have thought that this Wickham would have learned at her mother's knee that the last thing a fellow in a highly nervous condition wants, when he's searching someone's room, is a disembodied voice in his immediate rear asking him how he's getting on. The upshot, I need scarcely say, was that I came down like a sack of coals. The pulse was rapid, the blood pressure high, and for a while the Blue Room pirouetted about me like an adagio dancer.

When reason returned to its throne, I found that Bobbie, no doubt feeling after that resounding crash that she was better elsewhere, had left me and that I was closely entangled in the chair, my position being in some respects similar to that of Kipper Herring when he got both legs wrapped round his neck in Switzerland. It seemed improbable that I would ever get loose without the aid of powerful machinery.

However, by pulling this way and pushing that, I made progress, and I'd just contrived to de-chair myself and was about to rise, when another voice spoke.

"For Pete's sake!" it said, and, looking up, I found that it was not, as I had for a moment supposed, from the lips of the Brinkley Court ghost that the words had proceeded, but from those of Mrs. Homer Cream. She was looking at me, as Sir Roderick Glossop had recently looked at Bobbie, with a wild surmise, her whole air that of a woman who is not abreast. This time, I noticed, she had an ink spot on her chin.

"Mr. Wooster!" she yipped.

Well, there's nothing much you can say in reply to "Mr. Wooster!" except "Oh, hullo," so I said it.

"You are doubtless surprised," I was continuing, when she hogged the conversation again, asking me (a) What I was doing in her son's room and (b) What in the name of goodness I thought I was up to.

"For the love of Mike," she added, driving her point home.

It is frequently said of Bertram Wooster that he is a man who can think on his feet, and if the necessity arises he can also use his loaf when on all fours. On the present occasion I was fortunate in having had that get-together with the housemaid and the cat Augustus, for it gave me what they call in France a *point d'appui*. Removing a portion of chair which had got entangled in my back hair, I said with a candor that became me well, "I was looking for a mouse."

If she had replied, "Ah, yes indeed. I understand now. A mouse, to be sure. Quite," everything would have been nice and smooth, but she didn't.

"A mouse?" she said. "What do you mean?"

Well, of course, if she didn't know what a mouse was, there was evidently a good deal of tedious spadework before us, and one would scarcely have known where to start. It was a relief when her next words showed that that "What do you mean?" had not been a query but more in the nature of a sort of heart cry.

"What makes you think there is a mouse in this room?"

"The evidence points that way."

"Have you seen it?"

"Actually, no. It's been lying what the French call *perdu*."

"What made you come and look for it?"

"Oh, I thought I would."

"And why were you standing on a chair?"

"Sort of just trying to get a bird's-eye view, as it were."

"Do you often go looking for mice in other people's rooms?"

"I wouldn't say often. Just when the spirit moves me, don't you know?"

"I see. Well . . ."

When people say "Well" to you like that, it usually means that they think you are outstaying your welcome and that the time has come to call it a day. She felt, I could see, that Woosters were not required in her son's sleeping apartment, and realizing that there might be something in this, I rose, dusted the knees of the trousers, and after a courteous word to the effect that I hoped the spine-freezer on which she was engaged was coming out well left the presence. Happening to glance back as I reached the door,

71

I saw her looking after me, that wild surmise still functioning on all twelve cylinders. It was plain that she considered my behavior odd, and I'm not saying it wasn't. The behavior of those who allow their actions to be guided by Roberta Wickham is nearly always odd.

The thing I wanted most at this juncture was to have a heart-to-heart talk with that young *femme fatale*, and after roaming hither and thither for a while I found her in my chair on the lawn, reading the Ma Cream book in which I had been engrossed when these doings had started.

She greeted me with a bright smile, and said, "Back already? Did you find it?"

With a strong effort I mastered my emotion and replied curtly but civilly that the answer was in the negative.

"No," I said, "I did not find it."

"You can't have looked properly."

Again I was compelled to pause and remind myself that an English gentleman does not slosh a sitting redhead, no matter what the provocation.

"I hadn't time to look properly. I was impeded in my movements by half-witted females sneaking up behind me and asking how I was getting on."

"Well, I wanted to know." A giggle escaped her. "You did come down a wallop, didn't you? How art thou fallen from heaven, oh Lucifer, son of the morning, I said to myself. You're so terribly neurotic, Bertie. You must try to be less jumpy. What you need is a good nerve tonic. I'm sure Sir Roderick would shake you up one, if you asked him. And meanwhile?"

"How do you mean, 'And meanwhile'?"

"What are your plans now?"

"I propose to hoik you out of that chair and seat myself in it and take that book, the early chapters of which I found most gripping, and start catching up with my reading and try to forget."

"You mean you aren't going to have another bash?"

"I am not. Bertram is through. You may give this to the press, if you wish."

"But the cow-creamer. How about your Uncle Tom's grief and agony when he learns of his bereavement?"

"Let Uncle Tom eat cake."

"Bertie! Your manner is strange."

"Your manner would be strange if you'd been sitting on the floor of Wilbert Cream's sleeping apartment with a chair round your neck, and Ma Cream had come in."

"Golly! Did she?"

"In person."

"What did you say?"

"I said I was looking for a mouse."

"Couldn't you think of anything better than that?"

"No."

"And how did it all come out in the end?"

"I melted away, leaving her plainly convinced that I was off my rocker. And so, young Bobbie, when you speak of having another bash, I merely laugh bitterly," I said, doing so. "Catch me going into that sinister room again! Not for a million pounds sterling, cash down in small notes."

She made what I believe, though I wouldn't swear to it, is called a *moue*. Putting the lips together and shoving them out, if you know what I mean. The impression I got was that she was disappointed in Bertram, having expected better things, and this was borne out by her next words.

"Is this the daredevil spirit of the Woosters?"

"As of even date, yes."

"Are you man or mouse?"

"Kindly do not mention that word 'mouse' in my presence."

"I do think you might try again. Don't spoil the ship for a hap'orth of tar. I'll help you this time."

"Ha!"

"Haven't I heard that word before somewhere?"

"You may confidently expect to hear it again."

"No, but listen, Bertie. Nothing can possibly go wrong if we work together. Mrs. Cream won't show up this time. Lightning never strikes twice in the same place."

"Who made that rule?"

"And if she does . . . Here's what I thought we'd do. You go in and start searching, and I'll stand outside the door."

"You feel that will be a lot of help?"

"Of course it will. If I see her coming, I'll sing."

"Always glad to hear you singing, of course, but in what way will that ease the strain?"

"Oh, Bertie, you really are an abysmal chump. Don't you get it? When you hear me burst into song, you'll know there's peril afoot and you'll have plenty of time to nip out of the window."

"And break my bally neck?"

"How can you break your neck? There's a balcony outside the Blue Room. I've seen Wilbert Cream standing on it, doing his daily dozen. He breathes deeply and ties himself into a lovers' knot and—"

"Never mind Wilbert Cream's excesses."

"I only put that in to make it more interesting. The point is that there is a balcony and once on it you're home. There's a water pipe at the end of it. You just slide down that and go on your way, singing a gypsy song. You aren't going to tell me that you have any objection to sliding down water pipes. Jeeves says you're always doing it."

I mused. It is true that I have slid down quite a number of water pipes in my time. Circumstances have often so moulded themselves as to make such an action imperative. It was by that route that I had left Skeldings Hall at three in the morning after the hot-water-bottle incident. So, while it would be too much, perhaps, to say that I am never happier than when sliding down water pipes, the prospect of doing so caused me little or no concern. I began to see that there was something in this plan she was mooting, if mooting is the word I want.

What tipped the scale was the thought of Uncle Tom. His love for the cow-creamer might be misguided, but you couldn't get away from the fact that he was deeply attached to the beastly thing, and one didn't like the idea of him coming back from Harrogate and saying to himself, "And now for a refreshing look at the old cow-creamer," and finding it was not in residence. It would blot the sunshine from his life, and affectionate nephews hate like the dickens to blot the sunshine from the lives of uncles. It was true that I had said, "Let Uncle Tom eat cake," but I hadn't really meant it. I could not forget that when I was at Malvern House, Bramley-on-Sea, this relative by marriage had often sent me postal orders sometimes for as much as ten bob. He, in short, had done the square thing by me, and it was up to me to do the s.t. by him.

And so it came about that some five minutes later I stood once more outside the Blue Room with Bobbie beside me, not actually at the moment singing in the wilderness but prepared so to sing if Ma Cream, modeling her stategy on that of the Assyrian, came down like a wolf on the fold. The nervous system was a bit below par, of course, but not nearly so much so as it might have been. Knowing that Bobbie would be on sentry-go made all the difference. Any gangster will tell you that the strain and anxiety of busting a safe are greatly diminished if you've a lookout man ready at any moment to say "Cheese it, the cops!"

Just to make sure that Wilbert hadn't returned from his hike, I knocked on the door. Nothing stirred. The coast seemed c. I mentioned this to Bobbie, and she agreed that it was as c. as a whistle.

"Now a quick run-through, to see that you have got it straight. If I sing, what do you do?"

"Nip out of the window."

"And...?"

"Slide down the water pipe."

"And...?"

"Leg it over the horizon."

"Right. In you go, and get cracking," she said, and I went in.

The dear old room was just as I'd left it, nothing changed, and my first move, of course, was to procure another chair and give the top of the armoire the once-over. It was a setback to find that the cow-creamer wasn't there. I suppose these kleptomaniacs know a thing or two and don't hide the loot in the obvious place. There was nothing to be done but start the exhaustive search elsewhere, and I proceeded to do so, keeping an ear cocked for any snatch of song. None coming, it was with something of the old debonair Wooster spirit that I looked under this and peered behind that, and I had just crawled beneath the dressing table in pursuance of my researches, when one of those disembodied voices which were so frequent in the Blue Room spoke, causing me to give my head a nasty bump.

"For goodness sake!" it said, and I came out like a pickled onion on the end of a fork, to find that Ma Cream was once more a pleasant visitor. She was standing there, looking down at me with a what-the-hell expression on her finely chiseled face, and I didn't blame her. Gives a woman a start, naturally, to come into her son's bedroom and observe an alien trouser seat sticking out from under the dressing table.

We went into our routine.

"Mr. Wooster!"

"Oh, hullo."

"It's you *again?*"

"Why, yes," I said, for this of course was perfectly correct, and an odd sound proceeded from her, not exactly a hiccup and yet not quite not a hiccup.

"Are you still looking for that mouse?"

"That's right. I thought I saw it run under there, and I was about to deal with it regardless of its age or sex."

"What makes you think there is a mouse here?"

"Oh, one gets these ideas."

"Do you often hunt for mice?"

"Fairly frequently."

An idea seemed to strike her.

"You don't think you're a cat?"

"No, I'm pretty straight on that."

"But you pursue mice?"

"Yes."

"Well, this is very interesting. I must consult my psychiatrist when I get back to New York. I'm sure he will tell me that this mouse-fixation is a symbol of something. Your head feels funny, doesn't it?"

"It does rather," I said, for the bump I had given it had been a juicy one, and the temples were throbbing.

"I thought as much. A sort of burning sensation, I imagine. Now you do just as I tell you. Go to your room and lie down. Relax. Try to get a little sleep. Perhaps a cup of strong tea would help. And . . . I'm trying to think of the name of that alienist I've heard people over here speak so highly of. Miss Wickham mentioned him yesterday. Bossom? Blossom? Glossop, that's it, Sir Roderick Glossop. I think you ought to consult him. A friend of mine is at his clinic now, and she says he's wonderful. Cures the most stubborn cases. Meanwhile, rest is the thing. Go and have a good rest."

At an early point in these exchanges I had started to sidle to the door, and I now sidled through it, rather like a diffident crab on some sandy beach trying to avoid the attentions of a child with a spade. But I didn't go to my room and relax, I went in search of Bobbie, breathing fire. I wanted to take up with her the matter of that absence of the burst of melody. I mean, considering that a mere couple of bars of some popular song hit would have saved me from an experience that had turned the bones to water and whitened the hair from the neck up, I felt entitled to demand an explanation of why those bars had not emerged.

I found her outside the front door at the wheel of her car.

"Oh, hullo, Bertie," she said, and a fish on ice couldn't have spoken more calmly. "Have you got it?"

I ground a tooth or two and waved the arms in a passionate gesture.

"No," I said, ignoring her query as to why I had chosen this moment to do my Swedish exercises. "I haven't. But Ma Cream got me."

Her eyes widened. She squeaked a bit.

"Don't tell me she caught you bending again?"

"Bending is right. I was halfway under the dressing table. You and your singing," I said, and I'm not sure I didn't add the word "forsooth!"

Her eyes widened a bit farther, and she squeaked another squeak.

"Oh, Bertie, I'm sorry about that."

"Me, too."

"You see, I was called away to the telephone. Mother rang up. She wanted to tell me you were a nincompoop."

"One wonders where she picks up such expressions."

"From her literary friends, I suppose. She knows a lot of literary people."

"Great help to the vocabulary."

"Yes. She was delighted when I told her I was coming home. She wants to have a long talk."

"About me, no doubt?"

"Yes, I expect your name will crop up. But I mustn't stay here chatting with you, Bertie. If I don't get started, I shan't hit the old nest till daybreak. It's a pity you made such a mess of things. Poor Mr. Travers, he'll be broken-hearted. Still, into each life some rain must fall," she said, and drove off, spraying gravel in all directions.

If Jeeves had been there, I would have turned to him and said, "Women, Jeeves!" and he would have said, "Yes, sir" or possibly, "Precisely, sir," and this would have healed the bruised spirit to a certain extent, but as he wasn't I

78

merely laughed a bitter laugh and made for the lawn. A go at Ma Cream's goose-flesher might, I thought, do something to soothe the vibrating ganglions.

And it did. I hadn't been reading long when drowsiness stole over me, the tired eyelids closed, and in another couple of ticks I was off to dreamland, slumbering as soundly as if I had been the cat Augustus. I awoke to find that some two hours had passed, and it was while stretching the limbs that I remembered I hadn't sent that wire to Kipper Herring, inviting him to come and join the gang. I went to Aunt Dahlia's boudoir and repaired this omission, telephoning the communication to someone at the post office who would have been well advised to consult a good aurist. This done, I headed for the open spaces again, and was approaching the lawn with a view to getting on with my reading when, hearing engine noises in the background and turned to cast an eye in their direction, blow me tight if I didn't behold Kipper alighting from his car at the front door.

• 9 •

THE DISTANCE from London to Brinkley Court being a hundred miles or so, and not much more than two minutes having elapsed since I had sent off that telegram, the fact that Kipper was now outside the Brinkley front door struck me as quick service. It lowered the record of the chap in the motoring sketch which Catsmeat Potter-Pirbright sometimes does at the Drones Club smoking concert where the fellow tells the other fellow he's going to drive to Glasgow and the other fellow says, "How far is that?" and the fellow says, "Three hundred miles" and the other fellow says, "How long will it take you to get there?" and the fellow says, "Oh, about half an hour, about half an hour." The "What-ho" with which I greeted the back of his head as I approached was tinged, accordingly, with a certain bewilderment.

At the sound of the old familiar voice he spun around with something of the agility of a cat on hot bricks, and I saw that his dial, usually cheerful, was contorted with anguish, as if he had swallowed a bad oyster. Guessing now what was biting him, I smiled one of my subtle smiles. I would soon, I told myself, be bringing the roses back to his cheeks.

He gulped a bit, then spoke in a hollow voice, like a spirit at a séance.

"Hullo, Bertie."

"Hullo."

"So there you are."

"Yes, here I am."

"I was hoping I might run into you."

"And now the dream's come true."

"You see, you told me you were staying here."

"Yes."

"How's everything?"

"Pretty fruity."

"Your aunt well?"

"Fine."

"You all right?"

"More or less."

"Capital. Long time since I was at Brinkley."

"Yes."

"It looks about the same."

"Yes."

"Nothing much changed, I mean."

"No."

"Well, that's how it goes."

He paused and did another splash of gulping, and I could see that we were about to come to the nub, all that had gone before having been merely what they call *pourparlers*. I mean the sort of banana oil that passes between statesmen at conferences conducted in an atmosphere of the utmost cordiality before they tear their whiskers off and get down to cases.

I was right. His face working as if the first bad oyster had been followed by a second with even more spin on the ball, he said, "I saw that thing in the *Times*, Bertie."

I dissembled. I ought, I suppose, to have started bringing those roses back right away, but I felt it would be amusing to kid the poor fish along for a while, so I wore the mask.

"Ah, yes. In the *Times*. That thing. Quite. You saw it, did you?"

"At the club, after lunch. I couldn't believe my eyes."

Well, I hadn't been able to believe mine, either, but I didn't mention this. I was thinking how like Bobbie it was, when planning this scheme of hers, not to have let him in on the ground floor. Slipped her mind, I suppose, or she may have kept it under her hat for some strange reason of her own. She had always been a girl who moved in a mysterious way her wonders to perform.

"And I'll tell you why I couldn't. You'll scarcely credit this, but only a couple of days ago she was engaged to *me*."

"You don't say?"

"Yes, I jolly well do."

"Engaged to you, eh?"

"Up to the hilt. And all the while she must have been contemplating this ghastly bit of treachery."

"A bit thick."

"If you can tell me anything that's thicker, I shall be glad to hear it. It just shows you what women are like. A frightful sex, Bertie. There ought to be a law. I hope to live to see the day when women are no longer allowed."

"That would rather put a stopper on keeping the human race going, wouldn't it?"

"Well, who wants to keep the human race going?"

"I see what you mean. Yes, something in that, of course."

He kicked petulantly at a passing beetle, frowned awhile and resumed.

"It's the cold, callous heartlessness of the thing that shocks me. Not a hint that she was proposing to return me

82

to store. As short a while ago as last week, when we had a bite of lunch together, she was sketching out plans for the honeymoon with the greatest animation. And now this! Without a word of warning. You'd have thought that a girl who was smashing a fellow's life into hash would have dropped him a line, if only a postcard. Apparently that never occurred to her. She just let me get the news from the morning paper. I was stunned."

"I bet you were. Did everything go black?"

"Pretty black. I took the rest of the day thinking it over, and this morning wangled leave from the office and got the car out and came down here to tell you . . . " He paused, seeming overcome with emotion.

"Yes?"

"To tell you that, whatever we do, we mustn't let this thing break our old friendship."

"Of course not. Damn silly idea."

"It's such a very old friendship."

"I don't know when I've met an older."

"We were boys together."

"In Eton jackets and pimples."

"Exactly. And more like brothers than anything. I would share my last bar of almond rock with you, and you would cut me in fifty-fifty on your last bag of acid drops. When you had mumps, I caught them from you, and when I had measles, you caught them from me. Each helping each. So we must carry on regardless, just as if this had not happened."

"Quite."

"The same old lunches."

"Oh, rather."

"And golf on Saturdays and the occasional game of squash. And when you are married and settled down, I shall frequently look in on you for a cocktail."

"Yes, do."

"I will. Though I shall have to exercise an iron self-restraint to keep me from beaning that pie-faced little horn-swoggler, Mrs. Bertram Wooster, nee Wickham, with the shaker."

"Ought you to call her a pie-faced little hornswoggler?"

"Why, can you think of something worse?" he said, with the air of one always open to suggestions. "Do you know Thomas Otway?"

"I don't believe so. Pal of yours?"

"Seventeenth-century dramatist. Wrote *The Orphan*. In which play these words occur: 'What mighty ills have not been done by Woman? Who was't betrayed the Capitol? A woman. Who lost Marc Anthony the world? A woman. Who was the cause of a long ten years' war and laid at last old Troy in ashes? Woman. Deceitful, damnable, destructive Woman.' Otway knew what he was talking about. He had the right slant. He couldn't have put it better if he had known Roberta Wickham personally."

I smiled another subtle smile. I was finding all this extremely diverting.

"I don't know if it's my imagination, Kipper," I said, "but something gives me the impression that at moment of going to press you aren't too sold on Bobbie."

He shrugged a shoulder.

"Oh, I wouldn't say that. Apart from wishing I could throttle the young twister with my bare hands and jump on the remains with hobnailed boots. I don't feel much about her one way or the other. She prefers you to me, and there's nothing more to be said. The great thing is that everything is all right between you and me."

"You came all the way here just to make sure of that?" I said, moved.

"Well, there may possibly also have been an idea at the back of my mind that I might get invited to dig in at one of those dinners of Anatole's before going on to book a room at the Bull and Bush in Market Snodsbury. How is Anatole's cooking these days?"

"Superber than ever."

"Continues to melt in the mouth, does it? It's two years since I bit into his products, but the taste still lingers. What an artist!"

"Ah!" I said, and would have bared my head, only I hadn't a hat on.

"Would it run to a dinner invitation, do you think?"

"My dear chap, of course. The needy are never turned from our door."

"Splendid. And after the meal I shall propose to Phyllis Mills."

"What?"

"Yes, I know what you're thinking. She is closely related to Aubrey Upjohn, you are saying to yourself. But surely, Bertie, she can't help that."

"More to be pitied than censured, you think?"

"Exactly. We mustn't be narrow-minded. She is a sweet, gentle girl, unlike certain scarlet-headed Delilahs who shall be nameless, and I am very fond of her."

"I thought you scarcely knew her."

"Oh, yes, we saw quite a bit of each other in Switzerland. We're great buddies."

It seemed to me that the moment had come to bring the good news from Aix to Ghent, as the expression is.

"I don't know that I would propose to Phyllis Mills, Kipper. Bobbie might not like it."

"But that's the whole idea, to show her she isn't the only onion in the stew, and that if she doesn't want me, there are others who feel differently. What are you grinning about?"

As a matter of fact, I was smiling subtly, but I let it go.

"Kipper," I said, "I have an amazing story to relate."

I don't know if you happen to take Old Doctor Gordon's Bile Magnesia, which when the liver is disordered gives instant relief, acting like magic and imparting an inward glow? I don't myself, my personal liver being always more or less in mid-season form, but I've seen the advertise-

85

ments. They show the sufferer before and after taking, in the first case with drawn face and hollow eyes and the general look of one shortly about to hand in his dinner pail, in the second all beans and buck and what the French call *bien être*. Well, what I'm driving at is that my amazing story had exactly the same effect on Kipper as the daily dose for adults. He moved, he stirred, he seemed to feel the rush of life along his keel, and while I don't suppose he actually put on several pounds in weight as the tale proceeded, one got the distinct illusion that he was swelling like one of those rubber ducks which you fill with air before inserting them in the bathtub.

"Well, I'll be blowed!" he said, when I had placed the facts before him. "Well, I'll be a son of a what-not!"

"I thought you would be."

"Bless her ingenious little heart! Not many girls would have got the gray matter working like that."

"Very few."

"What a helpmeet! Talk about service and co-operation. Have you any idea how the thing is working out?"

"Rather smoothly, I think. On reading the announcement in the *Times*, Wickham senior had hysterics and swooned in her tracks."

"She doesn't like you?"

"That was the impression I got. It has been confirmed by subsequent telegrams to Bobbie in which she refers to me as a guffin and a gaby. She also considers me a nincompoop."

"Well, that's fine. It looks as though, after you, I shall come to her like . . . It's on the tip of my tongue."

"Rare and refreshing fruit?"

"Exactly. If you care to have a bet on it, five bob will get you ten that this scenario will end with a fade-out of Lady Wickham folding me in her arms and kissing me on the brow and saying she knows I will make her little girl happy. Gosh, Bertie, when I think that she—Bobbie, I mean, not

Lady Wickham—will soon be mine and that shortly after yonder sun has set I shall be tucking into one of Anatole's dinners, I could dance a saraband. By the way, talking of dinner, do you suppose it would also run to a bed? The Bull and Bush is well spoken of in the Automobile Guide, but I'm always a bit wary of these country pubs. I'd much rather be at Brinkley Court, of which I have such happy memories. Could you swing it with your aunt?"

"She isn't here. She left to minister to her son Bonzo, who is down with German measles at his school. But she rang up this afternoon and instructed me to wire you to come and make a prolonged stay."

"You're pulling my leg."

"No, this is official."

"But what made her think of me?"

"There's something she wants you to do for her."

"She can have anything she asks, even unto half my kingdom. What does she . . . " He paused, and a look of alarm came into his face. "Don't tell me she wants me to present the prizes at Market Snodsbury Grammar School, like Gussie?"

He was alluding to a mutual friend of ours of the name of Gussie Fink-Nottle, who, hounded by the aged relative into undertaking this task in the previous summer, had got pickled to the gills and made an outstanding exhibition of himself, setting up a mark at which all future orators would shoot in vain.

"No, no, nothing like that. The prizes this year will be distributed by Aubrey Upjohn."

"That's a relief. How is he, by the way? You've met him, of course?"

"Oh, yes, we got together. I spilled some tea on him."

"You couldn't have done better."

"He's grown a mustache."

"That eases my mind. I wasn't looking forward to seeing that bare upper lip of his. Remember how it used to make us quail when he twitched it at us? I wonder how he'll re-act when confronted with not only one former pupil but two, and those two the very brace that have probably haunted him in his dreams for the last fifteen years. Might as well unleash me on him now."

"He isn't here."

"You said he was."

"Yes, he was and he will be, but he isn't. He's gone up to London."

"Isn't anybody here?"

"Certainly. There's Phyllis Mills—"

"Nice girl."

"—and Mrs. Homer Cream of New York City, N.Y., and her son Wilbert. And that brings me to the something Aunt Dahlia wants you to do for her."

I was pleased, as I put him hep on the Wilbert-Phyllis situation and revealed the part he was expected to play in it, to note that he showed no signs of being about to issue the Presidential veto. He followed the setup intelligently, and when I had finished said that of course he would be only too willing to oblige. It wasn't much, he said, to ask of a fellow who esteemed Aunt Dahlia as highly as he did and who ever since she had lushed him up so lavishly two summers ago had been wishing there was something he could do in the way of buying back.

"Rely on me, Bertie," he said. "We can't have Phyllis tying herself up with a man who on the evidence would appear to be as nutty as a fruit cake. I will be about this Cream's bed and about his board, spying out all his ways. Every time he lures the poor girl into a leafy glade, I will be there, nestling behind some wild flower all ready to pop out and gum the game at the least indication that he is planning to get mushy. And now, if you would show me to my room, I will have a bath and a brush-up so as to be all sweet and fresh for the evening meal. Does Anatole still do those Timbales de ris de veau Toulousiane?"

"And the Sylphides à la crême d'écrevisses."

"There is none like him, none," said Kipper, moistening the lips with the tip of the tongue and looking like a wolf that has just spotted its Russian peasant. "He stands alone."

· 10 ·

As I HADN'T the remotest which rooms were available and
which weren't, getting Kipper dug in necessitated ringing
for Pop Glossop. I pressed the button and he appeared, giving me, as he entered, the sort of conspiratorial glance the
acting secretary of a secret society would have given a friend
on the membership roll.

"Oh, Swordfish," I said, having given him a conspiratorial
glance in return, for one always likes to do the civil thing,
"this is Mr. Herring, who has come to join our little group."

He bowed from the waist—not that he had much waist.

"Good evening, sir."

"He will be staying some time. Where do we park him?"

"The Red Room suggests itself, sir."

"You get the Red Room, Kipper."

"Right ho."

"I had it last year. 'Tis not as deep as a well nor as wide
as a church door, but 'tis enough, 'twill serve," I said, recall-

ing a gag of Jeeves's. "Will you escort Mr. Herring thither, Swordfish?"

"Very good, sir."

"And when you have got him installed, perhaps I could have a word with you in your pantry," I said, giving him a conspiratorial glance.

"Certainly, sir," he responded, giving me a conspiratorial glance.

It was one of those big evenings for conspiratorial glances.

I hadn't been waiting in the pantry long when he navigated over the threshold, and my first act was to congratulate him on the excellence of his technique. I had been much impressed by all that "Very good, sir," "Certainly, sir," bowing-from-the-waist stuff. I said that Jeeves himself couldn't have read his lines better, and he simpered modestly and said that one picked up these little tricks of the trade from one's own butler.

"Oh, by the way," I said, "where did you get the Swordfish?"

He smiled indulgently.

"That was Miss Wickham's suggestion."

"I thought as much."

"She informed me that she had always dreamed of one day meeting a butler called Swordfish. A charming young lady. Full of fun."

"It may be fun for her," I said with one of my bitter laughs, "but it isn't so diverting for the unfortunate toads beneath the harrow whom she plunges so ruthlessly into the soup. Let me tell you what occurred after I left you this afternoon."

"Yes, I am all eagerness to hear."

"Then pin your ears back and drink it in."

If I do say so, I told my story well, omitting no detail however slight. It had him Bless-my-soul-ing throughout, and when I had finished he *t'ck-t'ck-t'ck-ed* and said it must have been most unpleasant for me, and I said that "unpleasant" covered the facts like the skin on a sausage.

"But I think that in your place I should have thought of an explanation of your presence calculated to carry more immediate conviction than that you were searching for a mouse."

"Such as?"

"It is hard to say on the spur of the moment."

"Well, it was on the spur of the m. that I had to say it," I rejoined with some heat. "You don't get time to polish your dialogue and iron out the bugs in the plot when a woman who looks like Sherlock Holmes catches you in her son's room with your rear elevation sticking out from under the dressing table."

"True. Quite true. But I wonder . . . "

"Wonder what?"

"I do not wish to hurt your feelings."

"Go ahead. My feelings have been hurt so much already that a little bit extra won't make any difference."

"I may speak frankly?"

"Do."

"Well, then, I am wondering if it was altogether wise to entrust this very delicate operation to a young fellow like yourself. I am coming round to the view you put forward when we were discussing the matter with Miss Wickham. You said, if you recall, that the enterprise should have been placed in the hands of a mature, experienced man of the world, and not in those of one of less ripe years who as a child had never been expert at hunt-the-slipper. I am, you will agree, mature, and in my earlier days I won no little praise for my skill at hunt-the-slipper. I remember one of the hostesses whose Christmas parties I attended comparing me to a juvenile bloodhound. An extravagant encomium, of course, but that is what she said."

I looked at him with a wild surmise. It seemed to me that there was but one meaning to be attached to his words.

"You aren't thinking of having a pop at it yourself?"

"That is precisely my intention, Mr. Wooster."

"Lord love a duck!"

"The expression is new to me, but I gather from it that you consider my conduct eccentric."

"Oh, I wouldn't say that, but do you realize what you are letting yourself in for? You won't enjoy meeting Ma Cream. She has an eye like . . . What are those things that have eyes? Basilisks, that's the name I was groping for. She has an eye like a basilisk. Have you considered the possibility of having that eye go through you like a dose of salts?"

"Yes, I can envisage the peril. But the fact is, Mr. Wooster, I regard what has happened as a challenge. My blood is up."

"Mine froze."

"And you may possibly not believe me, but I find the prospect of searching Mr. Cream's room quite enjoyable."

"Enjoyable?"

"Yes. In a curious way it restores my youth. It brings back to me my preparatory-school days, when I would often steal down at night to the headmaster's study to eat his biscuits."

I started. I looked at him with a kindling eye. Deep had called to deep, and the cockles of the heart were warmed.

"Biscuits?"

"He kept them in a tin on his desk."

"You really used to do that at your prep school?"

"Many years ago."

"So did I," I said, coming within an ace of saying, "My brother!"

He raised his bushy eyebrows, and you could see that his heart's cockles were warmed, too.

"Indeed? Fancy that. I had supposed the idea original with myself, but no doubt all over England today the rising generation is doing the same thing. So you too have lived in Arcady? What kind of biscuits were yours? Mine were mixed."

"The ones with pink and white sugar on?"

93

"In many instances, though some were plain."

"Mine were ginger nuts."

"Those are very good, too, of course, but I prefer the mixed."

"So do I. But you had to take what you could get in those days. Were you ever copped?"

"I am glad to say, never."

"I was once. I can feel the place in frosty weather still."

"Too bad. But these things will happen. Embarking on the present venture, I have the sustaining thought that if the worst occurs and I am apprehended, I can scarcely be given six of the best bending over a chair, as we used to call it. Yes, you may leave this little matter entirely to me, Mr. Wooster."

"I wish you'd call me Bertie."

"Certainly, certainly."

"And might I call you Roderick?"

"I shall be delighted."

"Or Roddy? Roderick's rather a mouthful."

"Whichever you prefer."

"And you are really going to hunt the slipper?"

"I am resolved to do so. I have the greatest respect and affection for your uncle and appreciate how deeply wounded he would be, were this prized object to be permanently missing from his collection. I would never forgive myself if in the endeavor to recover his property, I were to leave any—"

"Stone unturned?"

"I was about to say 'avenue unexplored.' I shall strain every—"

"Sinew?"

"I was thinking of the word 'nerve'."

"Just as *juste*. You'll have to bide your time, of course."

"Quite."

"And await your opportunity."

"Exactly."

"Opportunity knocks but once."

"So I understand."

"I'll give you one tip. The thing isn't on top of the cupboard or armoire."

"Ah, that is helpful."

"Unless of course he's put it there since. Well, anyway, best of luck, Roddy."

"Thank you, Bertie."

If I had been taking Old Doctor Gordon's Bile Magnesia regularly, I couldn't have felt more of an inward glow as I left him and headed for the lawn to get the Ma Cream book and return it to its place on the shelves of Aunt Dahlia's boudoir. I was lost in admiration of Roddy's manly spirit. He was well stricken in years, fifty if a day, and it thrilled me to think that there was so much life in the old dog still. It just showed . . . well, I don't know what, but something. I found myself musing on the boy, Glossop, wondering what he had been like in his biscuit-snitching days. But except that I knew he wouldn't have been bald then, I couldn't picture him. It's often this way when one contemplates one's seniors. I remember how amazed I was to learn that my Uncle Percy, a tough old egg with apparently not a spark of humanity in him, had once held the metropolitan record for being chucked out of Covent Garden balls.

I got the book, and ascertaining after reaching Aunt Dahlia's lair that there remained some twenty minutes before it would be necessary to start getting ready for the evening meal, I took a seat and resumed my reading. I had had to leave off at a point where Ma Cream had just begun to spit on her hands and start filling the customers with pity and terror. But I hadn't put more than a couple of clues and a mere sprinkling of human gore under my belt when the door flew open, and Kipper appeared. And as the eye rested on him, he too filled me with pity and terror, for his map was flushed and his manner distraught. He looked like Jack

Dempsey at the conclusion of his first conference with Gene Tunney, the occasion, if you remember, when he forgot to duck.

He lost no time in bursting into speech.

"Bertie! I've been hunting for you all over the place!"

"I was having a chat with Swordfish in his pantry. Something wrong?"

"Something wrong!"

"Don't you like the Red Room?"

"The Red Room!"

I gathered from his manner that he had not come to beef about his sleeping accommodations.

"Then what is your little trouble?"

"My little trouble!"

I felt that this sort of thing must be stopped at its source. It was only ten minutes to dressing-for-dinner time, and we could go on along these lines for hours.

"Listen, old crumpet," I said patiently. "Make up your mind whether you are my old friend Reginald Herring or an echo in the Swiss mountains. If you're simply going to repeat every word I say—"

At this moment Pop Glossop entered with the cocktails, and we cheesed the give-and-take. Kipper drained his glass to the lees and seemed to become calmer. When the door closed behind Roddy, and he was at liberty to speak, he did so quite coherently. Taking another beaker, he said, "Bertie, the most frightful thing has happened."

I don't mind saying that the heart did a bit of sinking. In an earlier conversation with Bobbie Wickham, it will be recalled that I had compared Brinkley Court to one of those joints the late Edgar Allan Poe used to write about. If you are acquainted with his works, you will remember that in them it was always tough going for those who stayed in country houses, the visitor being likely at any moment to encounter a walking corpse in a winding sheet with blood all over it. Prevailing conditions at Brinkley were perhaps not

96

quite as testing as that, but the atmosphere had undeniably become sinister, and here was Kipper more than hinting that he had a story to relate which would deepen the general feeling that things were hotting up.

"What's the matter?" I said.

"I'll tell you what's the matter," he said.

"Yes, do," I said, and he did.

"Bertie," he said, taking a third one. "I think you will understand that when I read that announcement in the *Times* I was utterly bowled over?"

"Oh, quite. Perfectly natural."

"My head swam and—"

"Yes, you told me. Everything went black."

"I wish it had stayed black," he said bitterly, "but it didn't. After awhile the mists cleared, and I sat there seething with fury. And after I had seethed for a bit I rose from my chair, took pen in hand and wrote Bobbie a stinker."

"Oh, gosh!"

"I put my whole soul into it."

"Oh, golly."

"I accused her in set terms of giving me the heave-ho in order that she could mercenarily marry a richer man. I called her a carrot-topped Jezebel whom I was thankful to have got out of my hair. I—oh, I can't remember what else I said but, as I say, it was a stinker."

"But you never mentioned a word about this when I met you."

"In the ecstasy of learning that that *Times* thing was just a ruse and that she loved me still, it passed completely from my mind. When it suddenly came back to me just now, it was like getting hit in the eye with a wet fish. I reeled."

"Squealed?"

"Reeled. I felt absolutely boneless. But I had enough strength to stagger to the telephone. I rang up Skeldings Hall and was informed that she had just arrived."

"She must have driven like an inebriated racing motorist."

"No doubt she did. Girls will be girls. Anyway, she was there. She told me with a merry lilt in her voice that she had found a letter from me on the hall table and could hardly wait to open it. In a shaking voice I told her not to."

"So you were in time."

"In time, my foot. Bertie, you're a man of the world. You've known a good many members of the other sex in your day. What does a girl do when she is told not to open a letter?"

I got his drift.

"Opens it?"

"Exactly. I heard the envelope rip, and the next moment . . . No, I'd rather not think of it."

"She took umbrage?"

"Yes, and she also nearly took my head off. I don't know if you have ever been in a typhoon on the Indian Ocean."

"No, I've never visited those parts."

"Nor have I, but, from what people tell me, what ensued must have been very like being in one. She spoke for perhaps five minutes—"

"By Shrewsbury Clock."

"What?"

"Nothing. What did she say?"

"I can't repeat it all, and wouldn't if I could."

"And what did you say?"

"I couldn't get a word in edgewise."

"One can't sometimes."

"Women talk so damn quick."

"How well I know it! And what was the final score?"

"She said she was thankful that I was glad to have got her out of my hair, because she was immensely relieved to have got me out of hers, and that I had made her very happy because now she was free to marry you, which had always been her dearest wish."

In this hair-raiser of Ma Cream's which I had been perusing there was a chap of the name of Scarface McColl, a gangster of sorts, who, climbing into the old car one morning and twiddling the starting key, went up in fragments owing to a business competitor's having inserted a bomb in his engine, and I had speculated for a moment, while reading, as to how he must have felt. I knew now. Just as he had done, I rose. I sprang to the door, and Kipper raised an eyebrow.

"Am I boring you?" he said rather stiffly.

"No, no. But I must go and get my car."

"You going for a ride?"

"Yes."

"But it's nearly dinner time."

"I don't want any dinner."

"Where are you going?"

"Herne Bay."

"Why Herne Bay?"

"Because Jeeves is there, and this thing must be placed in his hands without a moment's delay."

"What can Jeeves do?"

"That," I said, "I cannot say, but he will do something. If he has been eating plenty of fish, as no doubt he would at a seashore resort, his brain will be at the top of its form, and when Jeeves's brain is at the top of its form, all you have to do is press a button and stand out of the way while he takes charge."

· 11 ·

It's CONSIDERABLY more than a step from Brinkley Court to
Herne Bay, the one being in the middle of Worcestershire
and the other on the coast of Kent, and even under the best
of conditions you don't expect to do the trip in a flash. On
the present occasion, held up by the Arab steed's getting
taken with a fit of the vapors and having to be towed to a
garage for medical treatment, I didn't fetch up at journey's
end till well past midnight. And when I rolled round to
Jeeves's address on the morrow, I was informed that he had
gone out early and they didn't know when he would be back.
Leaving word for him to ring me at the Drones, I returned
to the metropolis and was having the predinner keg of nails
in the smoking room when his call came through.

"Mr. Wooster? Good evening, sir. This is Jeeves."

"And not a moment too soon," I said, speaking with the
emotion of a lost lamb which after long separation from the
parent sheep finally manages to spot it across the meadow.
"Where have you been all this time?"

"I had an appointment to lunch with a friend at Folkestone, sir, and while there was persuaded to extend my visit in order to judge a seaside bathing-belles contest."

"No, really? You do live, don't you?"

"Yes, sir."

"How did it go off?"

"Quite satisfactorily, sir, thank you."

"Who won?"

"A Miss Marlene Higgins of Brixton, sir, with Miss Lana Brown of Tulse Hill and Miss Marilyn Bunting of Penge honorably mentioned. All most attractive young ladies."

"Shapely?"

"Extremely so."

"Well, let me tell you, Jeeves, and you can paste this in your hat, shapeliness isn't everything in this world. In fact, it sometimes seems to me that the more curved and lissome the members of the opposite sex, the more likely they are to set hell's foundations quivering. I'm sorely beset, Jeeves. Do you recall telling me once about someone who told somebody he could tell him something which would make him think a bit? Knitted socks and porcupines entered into it, I remember."

"I think you may be referring to the ghost of the father of Hamlet, Prince of Denmark, sir. Addressing his son, he said, 'I could a tale unfold whose lightest word would harrow up thy soul, freeze thy young blood, make thy two eyes, like stars, start from their spheres, thy knotted and combined locks to part and each particular hair to stand on end like quills upon the fretful porpentine."

"That's right. Locks, of course, not socks. Odd that he should have said porpentine when he meant porcupine. Slip of the tongue, no doubt, as so often happens with ghosts. Well, he had nothing on me, Jeeves. It's a tale of that precise nature that I am about to unfold. Are you listening?"

"Yes, sir."

"Then hold on to your hat and don't miss a word."

When I had finished unfolding, he said, "I can readily appreciate your concern, sir. The situation, as you say, is one fraught with anxiety—" which is pitching it strong for Jeeves, he as a rule coming through with a mere "Most disturbing, sir."

"I will come to Brinkley Court immediately, sir."

"Will you really? I hate to interrupt your holiday."

"Not at all, sir."

"You can resume it later."

"Certainly, sir, if that is convenient to you."

"But now . . ."

"Precisely, sir. Now, if I may borrow a familiar phrase—"

"—is the time for all good men to come to the aid of the party?"

"The very words I was about to employ, sir. I will call at the apartment at as early an hour tomorrow as is possible."

"And we'll drive down together. Right," I said, and went off to my simple but wholesome dinner.

It was with—well, not quite an uplifted heart—call it a heart lifted about halfway, that I started out for Brinkley on the following afternoon. The thought that Jeeves was at my side, his fish-fed brain at my disposal, caused a spot of silver lining to gleam through the storm clouds, but only a spot, for I was asking myself if even Jeeves might not fail to find a solution of the problem that had raised its ugly head. Admittedly expert though he was at joining sundered hearts, he had rarely been up against a rift within the lute so complete as that within the lute of Roberta Wickham and Reginald Herring, and as I remember hearing him say once, 'tis not in mortals to command success. And at the thought of what would ensue, were he to fall down on the assignment, I quivered like something in aspic. I could not forget that Bobbie, while handing Kipper his hat, had expressed in set terms her intention of lugging me to the altar rails and signaling to the clergyman to do his stuff. So, as I drove along, the heart, as I have indicated, was uplifted only to a medium extent.

When we were out of the London traffic and it was possible to converse without bumping into buses and pedestrians, I threw the meeting open for debate.

"You have not forgotten our telephone conversation of yestreen, Jeeves?"

"No, sir."

"You have the salient points docketed in your mind?"

"Yes, sir."

"Have you been brooding on them?"

"Yes, sir."

"Got a bite of any sort?"

"Not yet, sir."

"No, I hardly expected you would. These things always take time."

"Yes, sir."

"The core of the matter is," I said, twiddling the wheel to avoid a passing hen, "that in Roberta Wickham we are dealing with a girl of high and haughty spirit."

"Yes, sir."

"And girls of high and haughty spirit need kidding along. This cannot be done by calling them carrot-topped Jezebels."

"No, sir."

"I know if anyone called me a carrot-topped Jezebel, umbrage is the first thing I'd take. Who was Jezebel, by the way? The name seems familiar, but I can't place her."

"A character in the Old Testament, sir. A queen of Israel."

"Of course, yes. Be forgetting my own name next. Eaten by dogs, wasn't she?"

"Yes, sir."

"Can't have been pleasant for her."

"No, sir."

"Still, that's the way the ball rolls. Talking of being eaten by dogs, there's a dachshund at Brinkley who when you first meet him will give you the impression that he plans to convert you into a light snack between his regular meals. Pay no attention. It's all eyewash. His belligerent attitude is simply—"

"Sound and fury signifying nothing, sir?"

"That's it. Pure swank. A few civil words, and he will be grappling you . . . What's that expression I've heard you use?"

"Grappling me to his soul with hoops of steel, sir?"

"In the first two minutes. He wouldn't hurt a fly, but he has to put up a front because his name's Poppet. One can readily appreciate that when a dog hears himself addressed day in and day out as Poppet, he feels he must throw his weight about. His self-respect demands it."

"Precisely, sir."

"You'll like Poppet. Nice dog. Wears his ears inside out. Why do dachshunds wear their ears inside out?"

"I could not say, sir."

"Nor me. I've often wondered. But this won't do, Jeeves. Here we are, yakking about Jezebels and dachshunds, when we ought to be concentrating our minds on—"

I broke off abruptly. My eye had been caught by a wayside inn. Well, not actually so much by the wayside inn as by what was standing outside it—to wit, a scarlet roadster which I recognized instantly as the property of Bobbie Wickham. One saw what had happened. Driving back to Brinkley after a couple of nights with Mother, she had found the going a bit warm and had stopped off at this hostelry for a quick one. And a very sensible thing to do, too. Nothing picks one up more than a spot of sluicing on a hot summer afternoon.

I applied the brakes.

"Mind waiting here a minute, Jeeves?"

"Certainly, sir. You wish to speak to Miss Wickham?"

"Ah, you spotted her car?"

"Yes, sir. It is distinctly individual."

"Like its owner. I have a feeling that I may be able to accomplish something in the breach-healing way with a honeyed word or two. Worth trying, don't you think?"

"Unquestionably, sir."

"At a time like this one doesn't want to leave any avenue unturned."

The interior of the wayside inn—the Fox and Goose, not that it matters—was like the interiors of all wayside inns, dark and cool and smelling of beer, cheese, coffee, pickles and the sturdy English peasantry. Entering, you found yourself in a cozy nook with tankards on the walls and chairs and tables dotted hither and thither. On one of the chairs at one of the tables Bobbie was seated with a glass and a bottle of ginger ale before her.

"Good Lord, Bertie," she said as I stepped up and what-ho-ed. "Where did you spring from?"

I explained that I was on my way back to Brinkley from London in my car.

"Be careful someone doesn't pinch it. I'll bet you haven't taken out the keys."

"No, but Jeeves is there, keeping watch and ward, as you might say."

"Oh, you've brought Jeeves with you? I thought he was on his holiday."

"He very decently canceled it."

"Pretty feudal."

"Very. When I told him I needed him at my side, he didn't hesitate."

"What do you need him at your side for?"

The moment had come for the honeyed word. I lowered my voice to a confidential murmur, but on her inquiring if I had laryngitis raised it again.

"I had an idea that he might be able to do something."

"What about?"

"About you and Kipper," I said, and started to feel my way cautiously toward the core and center. It would be necessary, I knew, to pick my words with c., for with girls of high and haughty spirit you have to watch your step, especially if they have red hair, like Bobbie. If they think you're talking out of

105

turn, dudgeon ensues, and dudgeon might easily lead her to reach for the ginger-ale bottle and bean me with it. I don't say she would, but it was a possibility that had to be taken into account. So I sort of eased into the agenda.

"I must begin by saying that Kipper has given me a full eyewitness's—well, earwitness's, I suppose you'd say—report of that chat you and he had over the telephone, and no doubt you are saying to yourself that it would have been in better taste for him to have kept it under his hat. But you must remember that we were boys together, and a fellow naturally confides in a chap he was boys together with. Anyway, be that as it may, he poured out his soul to me, and he hadn't been pouring long before I was able to see that he was cut to the quick. His blood pressure was high, his eye rolled in what they call a fine frenzy, and he was death-where-is-thy-stinging like nobody's business."

I saw her quiver and kept a wary eye on the ginger-ale bottle. But even if she had raised it and brought it down on the Wooster bean, I couldn't have been more stunned than I was by the words that left her lips.

"The poor lamb!"

I had ordered a gin and tonic. I now spilled a portion of this.

"Did you say 'poor lamb'?"

"You bet I said poor lamb, though poor sap would perhaps be a better description. Just imagine him taking all that stuff I said seriously. He ought to have known I didn't mean it."

I groped for the gist.

"You were just making conversation?"

"Well, blowing off steam. For heaven's sake, isn't a girl allowed to blow off steam occasionally? I never dreamed it would really upset him. Reggie always takes everything so literally."

"Then is the position that the laughing love god is once more working at the old stand?"

"Like a beaver."

"In fact, to coin a phrase, you're sweethearts still?"

"Of course. I may have meant what I said at the time, but only for about five minutes."

I drew a deep breath and a moment later wished I hadn't, because I drew it while drinking the remains of my gin and tonic.

"Does Kipper know of this?" I said, when I had finished coughing.

"Not yet. I'm on my way to tell him."

I raised a point on which I particularly desired assurance.

"Then what it boils down to is: No wedding bells for me?"

"I'm afraid not."

"Quite all right. Anything that suits you."

"I don't want to get jugged for bigamy."

"No, one sees that. And your selection for the day is Kipper. I don't blame you. The ideal mate."

"Just the way I look at it. He's terrific, isn't he?"

"Colossal."

"I wouldn't marry anyone else if they came to me bringing apes, ivory and peacocks. Tell me what he was like as a boy."

"Oh, much the same as the rest of us."

"Nonsense."

"Except, of course, for rescuing people from burning buildings and saving blue-eyed children from getting squashed by runaway horses."

"He did that a lot?"

"Almost daily."

"Was he the Pride of the School?"

"Oh, rather."

"Not that it was much of a school to be the pride of, from what he tells me. A sort of Dotheboys Hall, wasn't it?"

"Conditions under Aubrey Upjohn were fairly tough. One's mind reverts particularly to the sausages on Sunday."

"Reggie was very funny about those. He said they were made not from contented pigs but from pigs which had expired, regretted by all, of glanders, the botts and tuberculosis."

"Yes, that would be quite a fair description of them, I suppose. You going?" I said, for she had risen.

"I can't wait another minute. I want to fling myself into Reggie's arms. If I don't see him soon, I shall pass out."

"I know how you feel. The chap in the 'Yeoman's Wedding Song' thought along those same lines, only the way he put it was 'Ding dong, ding dong, ding dong, I hurry along.' At one time I often used to render the number at village concerts, and there was a nasty Becher's Brook to get over when you got to 'For it is my wedding morning,' because you had to stretch out the 'mor' for about ten minutes, which tested the lung power severely. I remember the vicar once telling me—"

Here I was interrupted, as I'm so often interrupted when giving my views on the 'Yeoman's Wedding Song,' by her saying that she was dying to hear all about it but would rather wait till she could get it in my autobiography. We went out together, and I saw her off and returned to where Jeeves kept his vigil in the car, all smiles. I was all smiles, I mean, not Jeeves. The best he ever does is to let his mouth twitch slightly on one side, generally the left. I was in rare fettle, and the heart had touched a new high. I don't know anything that braces one up like finding you haven't got to get married after all.

"Sorry to keep you waiting, Jeeves," I said. "Hope you weren't bored?"

"Oh, no, sir, thank you. I was quite happy with my Spinoza."

"Eh?"

"The copy of Spinoza's *Ethics* which you kindly gave me some time ago."

"Oh, ah, yes, I remember. Good stuff?"

"Extremely, sir."

"I suppose that it turns out in the end that the butler did it.

Well, Jeeves, you'll be glad to hear that everything's under control."

"Indeed, sir?"

"Yes, rift in lute mended and wedding bells liable to ring out at any moment. She's changed her mind."

"*Varium et mutabile femina semper*, sir."

"I shouldn't wonder. And now," I said, climbing in and taking the wheel, "I'll unfold the tale of Wilbert and the cow-creamer, and if that doesn't make your knotted locks do a bit of starting from their spheres, I for one shall be greatly surprised."

• 12 •

Arriving at Brinkley in the quiet evenfall and putting the old machine away in the garage, I noticed that Aunt Dahlia's car was there and gathered from this that the aged relative was around and about once more. Nor was I in error. I found her in her boudoir getting outside a dish of tea and a crumpet. She greeted me with one of those piercing view-halloos which she had picked up on the hunting field in the days when she had been an energetic chivvier of the British fox. It sounded like a gas explosion and went through me from stem to stern. I've never hunted, myself, but I understand that half the battle is being able to make noises like some jungle animal with dyspepsia, and I believe that Aunt Dahlia in her prime could lift fellow members of the Quorn and Pytchley out of their saddles with a single yip, though separated from them by two plowed fields and a stretch of woodland.

"Hullo, ugly," she said. "Turned up again, have you?"

"Just this moment breasted the tape."

"Been to Herne Bay, young Herring tells me."

"Yes, to fetch Jeeves. How's Bonzo?"

"Spotty but cheerful. What did you want Jeeves for?"

"Well, as it turns out, his presence isn't needed, but I only discovered that when I was halfway here. I was bringing him along to meditate—no, it isn't meditate—to mediate, that's the word, between Bobbie Wickham and Kipper. You knew they were betrothed?"

"Yes, she told me."

"Did she tell you about shoving that thing in the *Times* saying she was engaged to me?"

"I was the first in whom she confided. I got a good laugh out of that."

"More than Kipper did, because it hadn't occurred to the cloth-headed young nitwit to confide in him. When he read the announcement, he reeled and everything went black. It knocked his faith in woman for a loop, and after seething for a while he sat down and wrote her a letter in the Thomas Otway vein."

"In the whose vein?"

"You are not familiar with Thomas Otway? Seventeenth-century dramatist, celebrated for making bitter cracks about the other sex. Wrote a play called *The Orphan,* which is full of them."

"So you do read something beside the comics?"

"Well, actually I haven't steeped myself to any great extent in Thos's output, but Kipper told me about him. He held the view that women are a mess, and Kipper passed this information on to Bobbie in this letter of which I speak. It was a snorter."

"And you never thought of explaining to him, I suppose?"

"Of course I did. But by that time she'd got the letter."

"Why didn't the idiot tell her not to open it?"

"It was his first move. 'I've found a letter from you here, precious,' she said. 'On no account open it, angel,' he said. So of course she opened it."

She pursed the lips, nodded the loaf, and ate a moody piece of crumpet.

"So that's why he's been going about looking like a dead fish. I suppose Roberta broke the engagement?"

"In a speech lasting five minutes without a pause for breath."

"And you brought Jeeves along to mediate?"

"That was the idea."

"But if things have gone as far as that . . ."

"You doubt whether even Jeeves can heal the rift?" I patted her on the topknot. "Dry the starting tear, old ancestor, it's healed. I met her at a pub on the way here, and she told me that almost immediately after she had flipped her lid in the manner described she had a change of heart. She loves him still with a passion that's more like boiling oil than anything, and when we parted she was tooling off to tell him so. By this time they must be like ham and eggs again. It's a great burden off my mind, because, having parted brass rag with Kipper, she announced her intention of marrying me."

"A bit of luck for you, I should have thought."

"Far from it."

"Why? You were crazy about the girl once."

"But no longer. The fever has passed, the scales have fallen from my eyes, and we're just good friends. The snag in this business of falling in love, aged relative, is that the parties of the first part so often get mixed up with the wrong parties of the second part, robbed of their cooler judgment by the parties of the second part's glamour. Put it like this: The male sex is divided into rabbits and non-rabbits and the female sex into dashers and dormice, and the trouble is that the male rabbit has a way of getting attracted by the female dasher (who would be fine for the male non-rabbit) and realizing too late that he ought to have been concentrating on some mild, gentle dormouse with whom he could settle down peacefully and nibble lettuce."

"The whole thing is, in short, a bit of a mix-up?"

"Exactly. Take me and Bobbie. I yield to no one in my appreciation of her *espièglerie*, but I'm one of the rabbits and always have been, while she is about as pronounced a dasher as ever dashed. What I like is the quiet life, and Roberta Wickham wouldn't recognize the quiet life if you brought it to her on a plate with watercress round it. She's all for not letting the sun go down without having started something calculated to stagger humanity. In a word, she needs the guiding hand, which is a thing I couldn't supply her with. Whereas from Kipper she will get it in abundance, he being one of those tough non-rabbits for whom it is child's play to make the little woman draw the line somewhere. That is why the union of these twain has my support and approval and why, when she told me all that in the pub, I felt like doing a buck-and-wing dance. Where is Kipper? I should like to shake him by the hand and pat his back."

"He went on a picnic with Wilbert and Phyllis."

The significance of this did not escape me.

"Tailing up stuff, eh? Right on the job, is he?"

"Wilbert is constantly under his eyes."

"And if ever a man needed to be constantly under an eye, it's the above kleptomaniac."

"The what?"

"Haven't you been told? Wilbert's a pincher."

"How do you mean, a pincher?"

"He pinches things. Everything that isn't nailed down is grist to his mill."

"Don't be an ass."

"I'm not being an ass. He's got Uncle Tom's cow-creamer."

"I know."

"You know?"

"Of course I know."

Her—what's the word? Phlegm, is it?—something beginning with a p—astounded me. I had expected to freeze her young, or, rather, middle-aged, blood and have her perm stand on end like quills upon the fretful porpentine, and she hadn't moved a muscle.

"Beshrew me," I said, "you take it pretty calmly."

"Well, what's there to get excited about? Tom sold him the thing."

"What?"

"Wilbert got in touch with him at Harrogate and put in his bid, and Tom phoned me to give it to him. Just shows how important that deal must be to Tom. I'd have thought he would rather have parted with his eyeteeth."

I drew a deep breath, this time fortunately unmixed with gin and tonic. I was profoundly stirred.

"You mean," I said, my voice quivering like that of a coloratura soprano, "that I went through that soul-shattering experience all for nothing?"

"Who's been shattering your soul, if any?"

"Ma Cream. By popping in while I was searching Wilbert's room for the loathsome object. Naturally I thought he'd swiped it and hidden it there."

"And she caught you?"

"Not once, but twice."

"What did she say?"

"She recommended that I take treatment from Roddy Glossop, of whose skill in ministering to the mentally afflicted she had heard such good reports. One sees what gave her the idea. I was halfway under the dressing table at the moment, and no doubt she thought it odd."

"Bertie! How absolutely priceless!"

The adjective "priceless" seemed to me an ill-chosen one, and I said so. But my words were lost in the gale of mirth into which she now exploded. I have never heard anyone laugh so heartily, not even Bobbie on the occasion when the rake jumped up and hit me on the tip of the nose.

"I'd have given fifty quid to have been there," she said, when she was able to get the vocal cords working. "Halfway under the dressing table, were you?"

"The second time. When we first foregathered, I was sitting on the floor with a chair round my neck."

"Like an Elizabethan ruff, as worn by Thomas Botway."

"Otway," I said stiffly. As I have mentioned, I like to get things right. And I was about to tell her that what I had hoped for from a blood relation was sympathy and condolence rather than this crackling of thorns under a pot, as it is sometimes called, when the door opened and Bobbie came in.

The moment I cast an eye on her, it seemed to me that there was something strange about her aspect. Normally, this beazel presents to the world the appearance of one who is feeling that if it isn't the best of all possible worlds, it's quite good enough to be going on with till a better one comes along. Verve, I mean, and animation and all that sort of thing. But now there was a listlessness about her, not the listlessness of the cat Augustus, but more that of the female in the picture in the Louvre, of whom Jeeves, on the occasion when he lugged me there to take a dekko at her, said that hers was the head upon which all the ends of the world are come. He drew my attention, I remember, to the weariness of the eyelids. I got just the same impression of weariness from Bobbie's eyelids.

Unparting her lips, which were set in a thin line as if she had just been taking a suck at a lemon, she said, "I came to get that book of Mrs. Cream's that I was reading, Mrs. Travers."

"Help yourself, child," said the ancestor. "The more people in this joint reading her stuff, the better. It all goes to help the composition."

"So you got here all right, Bobbie," I said. "Have you seen Kipper?"

I wouldn't say she snorted, but she certainly sniffed.

"Bertie," she said in a voice straight from the refrigerator, "will you do me a favor?"

"Of course. What?"

"Don't mention that rat's name in my presence," she said, and pushed off, the eyelids still weary.

She left me fogged and groping for the inner meaning, and I could see from Aunt Dahlia's goggling eyes that the basic idea hadn't got across with her either.

"Well!" she said. "What's all this? I thought you told me she loved young Herring with a passion like boiling oil."

"That was her story."

"The oil seems to have gone off the boil. Yes, sir, if that was the language of love, I'll eat my hat," said the blood relation, alluding, I took it, to the beastly straw contraption she wears when she does her gardening—concerning which I can only say that it is almost as foul as Uncle Tom's Sherlock Holmes deerstalker, which has frightened more crows than any other lid in Worcestershire. "They must have had another fight."

"It does look like it," I agreed, "and I don't understand how it can have happened, considering that she left me with the love light in her eyes, and can't have been back here more than about half an hour. One asks oneself what, in so short a time, can have changed a girl full of love and ginger ale into a girl who speaks of the adored object as 'that rat' and doesn't want to hear his name mentioned? These are deep waters. Should I send for Jeeves?"

"What on earth can Jeeves do?"

"Well, now you put it that way, I'm bound to admit that I don't know. It's just that one drops into the habit of sending for Jeeves whenever things have gone agley, if that's the word I'm thinking of. Scotch, isn't it? Agley, I mean. It sounds Scotch to me. However, passing lightly over that, the thing to do when you want the low-down is to go to the fountainhead and get it straight from the horse's mouth. Kipper can solve this mystery. I'll pop along and find him."

I was, however, spared the trouble of popping, for at this moment he entered left center.

"Oh, there you are, Bertie," he said. "I heard you were back. I was looking for you."

He had spoken in a low, husky sort of way, like a voice from the tomb, and I now saw that he was exhibiting all the earmarks of a man who has recently had a bomb explode in his vicinity. His shoulders sagged and his eyes were glassy. He looked, in short, like the fellow who hadn't started to take Old Doctor Gordon's Bile Magnesia, and I snapped into it without preamble. This was no time for being tactful and pretending not to notice.

"What's all this strained-relations stuff between you and Bobbie, Kipper?" I said, and when he said, "Oh, nothing," I rapped the table sharply and told him to cut out the coy stuff and come clean.

"Yes," said Aunt Dahlia. "What's happened, young Herring?"

I think that for a moment he was about to draw himself up with hauteur and say that he would prefer, if we didn't mind, not to discuss his private affairs, but when he was halfway up he caught Aunt Dahlia's eye and returned to position one. Aunt Dahlia's eye, while not in the same class as that of my Aunt Agatha, who is known to devour her young and conduct human sacrifices at the time of the full moon, has lots of authority. He subsided into a chair and sat there looking filleted.

"Well, if you must know," he said, "she's broken the engagement."

This didn't get us any farther. We had assumed as much. You don't go calling people rats if love still lingers.

"But it's only an hour or so," I said, "since I left her outside a hostelry called the Fox and Goose, and she had just been giving you a rave notice. What came unstuck? What did you do to the girl?"

"Oh, nothing."

117

"Come, come."

"Well, it was this way."

There was a pause here while he said that he would give a hundred quid for a stiff whisky and soda, but as this would have involved all the delay of ringing for Pop Glossop and having it fetched from the lowest bin, Aunt Dahlia would have none of it. In lieu of the desired refreshment she offered him a cold crumpet, which he declined, and told him to get on with it.

"Where I went wrong," he said, still speaking in that low, husky voice, as if he had been a ghost suffering from catarrh, "was in getting engaged to Phyllis Mills."

"What!" I cried.

"What!" cried Aunt Dahlia.

"Egad!" I said.

"What on earth did you do that for?" said Aunt Dahlia.

He shifted uneasily in his chair, like a man troubled with ants in the pants.

"It seemed a good idea at the time," he said. "Bobbie had told me on the telephone that she never wanted to speak to me again in this world or the next, and Phyllis had been telling me that, while she shrank from Wilbert Cream because of his murky past, she found him so magnetic that she knew she wouldn't be able to refuse him if he proposed, and I had been commissioned to stop him from proposing, so I thought the simplest thing to do was to get engaged to her myself. So we talked it over, and having reached a thorough understanding that it was simply a ruse and nothing binding on either side, we announced it to Cream."

"Very shrewd," said Aunt Dahlia. "How did he take it?"

"He reeled."

"Lot of reeling there's been in this business," I said. "You reeled, if you recollect, when you remembered you'd written that letter to Bobbie."

"And I reeled again when she suddenly appeared from nowhere just as I was kissing Phyllis."

118

I pursed the lips. Getting a bit French, this sequence, it seemed to me.

"There was no need for you to do that."

"No need, perhaps, but I wanted to make it look natural to Cream."

"Oh, I see. Driving it home, as it were?"

"That was the idea. Of course I wouldn't have done it if I'd known that Bobbie had changed her mind and wanted things to be as they were before that telephone conversation. But I didn't know. It's just one of life's little ironies. You get the same sort of thing in Thomas Hardy."

I knew nothing of this T. Hardy of whom he spoke, but I saw what he meant. It was like what's always happening in the novels of suspense, where the girl goes around saying "Had I but known."

"Didn't you explain?"

He gave me a pitying look.

"Have you ever tried explaining something to a redhaired girl who's madder than a wet hen?"

I took his point.

"What happened then?"

"Oh, she was very ladylike. Talked amiably of this and that till Phyllis had left us. Then she started in. She said she had raced here with a heart overflowing with love, longing to be in my arms, and a jolly surprise it was to find those arms squeezing the stuffing out of another and . . . oh, well, a lot more along those lines. The trouble is, she's always been a bit squiggle-eyed about Phyllis, because in Switzerland she held the view that we were a shade too matey. Nothing in it, of course."

"Just good friends?"

"Exactly."

"Well, if you want to know what I think—" said Aunt Dahlia.

But we never did get around to knowing what she thought, for at this moment Phyllis came in.

· 13 ·

GIVING THE WENCH the once-over as she entered, I found
myself well able to understand why Bobbie, on observing
her entangled with Kipper, had exploded with so loud a
report. Of course, I'm not, myself, an idealistic girl in love
with a member of the staff of the *Thursday Review* and never
have been, but if I were I know I'd get the megrims somewhat severely if I caught him in a clinch with anyone as per-
sonable as this stepdaughter of Aubrey Upjohn, for though
shaky on the I.Q., physically she was, I had to admit, a pip-
perino of the first water. Her eyes were considerably bluer
than the skies above, she was wearing a simple summer
dress which accentuated rather than hid the graceful out-
lines of her figure, if you know what I mean, and it was not
surprising that Wilbert Cream, seeing her, should have lost
no time in reaching for the book of poetry and making a
beeline with her to the nearest leafy glade.

"Oh, Mrs. Travers," she said, spotting Aunt Dahlia, "I've just been talking to Daddy on the telephone."

This took the old ancestor's mind right off the tangled affairs of the Kipper-Bobbie axis, to which a moment before she had been according her best attention, and I didn't wonder. With the prize-giving at Market Snodsbury Grammar School, a function at which all that was bravest and fairest in the neighborhood would be present, only two days away, she must have been getting pretty uneasy about the continued absence of the big shot slated to address the young scholars on ideals and life in the world outside. If you are on the board of governors of a school and have contracted to supply an orator for the great day of the year, you can be forgiven for feeling a trifle jumpy when you learn that the silver-tongued one has gadded off to the metropolis, leaving no word as to when he will be returning, if ever. For all she knew, Upjohn might have got the holiday spirit and be planning to remain burning up the boulevards indefinitely, and of course nothing gives a big beano a black eye more surely than the failure of the principal speaker to show up. So now she quite naturally blossomed like a rose in June and asked if the old son of a bachelor had mentioned anything about when he was coming back.

"He's coming back tonight. He says he hopes you haven't been worrying."

A snort of about the caliber of an explosion in an ammunition dump escaped my late father's sister.

"Oh, does he? Well, I've a piece of news for him. I *have* been worrying. What's kept him in London so long?"

"He's been seeing his lawyer about this libel action he's bringing against the *Thursday Review*."

I have often asked myself how many inches it was that Kipper leaped from his chair at these words. Sometimes I think it was ten, sometimes only six, but whichever it was, he unquestionably came up from the padded seat like an athlete competing in the sitting high jump event. Scarface McColl couldn't have risen more nippily.

"Against the *Thursday Review?*" said Aunt Dahlia. "That's your rag, isn't it, young Herring? What have they done to stir him up?"

"It's this book Daddy wrote about preparatory schools. He wrote a book about preparatory schools. Did you know he had written a book about preparatory schools?"

"Hadn't an inkling. Nobody tells me anything."

"Well, he wrote this book about preparatory schools. It was about preparatory schools."

"About preparatory schools, was it?"

"Yes, about preparatory schools."

"Thank God we've got that straightened out at last. I had a feeling we should get somewhere if we dug long enough. And—?"

"And the *Thursday Review* said something libelous about it, and Daddy's lawyer says the jury ought to give Daddy at least five thousand pounds. Because they libeled him. So he's been in London all this time seeing his lawyer. But he's coming back tonight. He'll be here for the prize-giving, and I've got his speech all typed out and ready for him. Oh, there's my precious Poppet," said Phyllis, as a distant barking reached the ears. "He's asking for his dinner, the sweet little angel. All right, darling, Mother's coming," she fluted, and buzzed off on the errand of mercy.

A brief silence followed her departure.

"I don't care what you say," said Aunt Dahlia at length in a defiant sort of way. "Brains aren't everything. She's a dear, sweet girl. I love her like a daughter, and to hell with anyone who calls her a half-wit. Why, hullo," she proceeded, seeing that Kipper was slumped back in his chair trying without much success to hitch up a drooping lower jaw. "What's eating you, young Herring?"

I could see that Kipper was in no shape for conversation, so I took it upon myself to explain.

"A certain stickiness has arisen, aged relative. You heard what P. Mills said before going to minister to Poppet. Those words tell the story."

"What do you mean?"

"The facts are readily stated. Upjohn wrote this slim volume, which, if you recall, was about preparatory schools, and in it, so Kipper tells me, said that the time spent in these establishments was the happiest of our lives. Ye Ed passed it on to Kipper for comment, and he, remembering the dark days at Malvern House, Bramley-on-Sea, when he and I were plucking the gowans fine there, slated it with no uncertain hand. Correct, Kipper?"

He found speech, if you could call making a noise like a buffalo taking its foot out of a swamp finding speech.

"But, dash it," he said, finding a bit more, "it was perfectly legitimate criticism. I didn't mince my words, of course—"

"It would be interesting to find out what these unminced words were," said Aunt Dahlia, "for among them there appear to have been one or two which seem likely to set your proprietor back five thousand of the best and brightest. Bertie, get your car out and go to Market Snodsbury station and see if the bookstall has a copy of this week's— No, wait, hold the line. Cancel that order. I shan't be a minute," she said, and went out, leaving me totally fogged as to what she was up to. What aunts are up to is never an easy thing to divine.

I turned to Kipper. "Bad show," I said.

From the way he writhed I gathered that he was feeling it could scarcely be worse.

"What happens when an editorial assistant on a weekly paper lets the bosses in for substantial libel damages?"

He was able to answer that one.

"He gets the push and, what's more, finds it pretty damned difficult to land another job. He's on the black list."

I saw what he meant. These birds who run weekly papers believe in watching the pennies. They like to get all that's coming to them, and when the stuff, instead of pouring in, starts pouring out as the result of an injudicious move on the part of a unit of the staff, what they do to that unit is plenty. I think Kipper's outfit was financed by some sort of board or syndicate, but boards and syndicates are just as sensitive about having to cough up as individual owners. As Kipper had indicated, they not only give the erring unit the heave-ho but pass the word round to the other boards and syndicates.

"Herring?" the latter say when Kipper comes seeking employment. "Isn't he the bimbo who took the bread out of the mouths of the *Thursday Review* people? Chuck the blighter out of the window and we want to see him bounce." If this action of Upjohn's went through, Kipper's chances of any sort of salaried post were meager, if not slim. It might be years before all was forgiven and forgotten.

"Selling pencils in the gutter is about the best I'll be able to look forward to," said Kipper, and he had just buried his face in his hands, as fellows are apt to do when contemplating a future that's a bit on the bleak side, when the door opened to reveal, not, as I had expected, Aunt Dahlia, but Bobbie.

"I got the wrong book," she said. "The one I wanted was—"

Then her eye fell on Kipper and she stiffened in every limb, rather like Lot's wife, who, as you probably know, did the wrong thing that time there was all that unpleasantness with the cities of the plain and got turned into a pillar of salt, though what was the thought behind this I've never been able to understand. Salt, I mean. Seems so bizarre somehow and not at all what you would expect.

"Oh!" she said haughtily, as if offended by this glimpse into the underworld, and even as she spoke a hollow groan burst from Kipper's interior and he raised an ashen face. And at the sight of that ashen f. the haughtiness went out of Roberta Wickham with a whoosh, to be replaced by all the old love, sympathy, womanly tenderness and what not, and

124

she bounded at him like a leopardess getting together with a lost cub.

"Reggie! Oh, Reggie! Reggie, darling, what is it?" she cried, her whole demeanor undergoing a marked change for the better. She was, in short, melted by his distress, as so often happens with the female sex. Poets have frequently commented on this. You are probably familiar with the one who said, "Oh, woman in our hours of ease tum tumty tiddly something please, when something something something brow, a something something something thou."

She turned on me with an animal snarl.

"What have you been doing to the poor lamb?" she demanded, giving me one of the nastiest looks seen that summer in the midland counties; and I had just finished explaining that it was not I but Fate or Destiny that had removed the sunshine from the poor lamb's life, when Aunt Dahlia returned. She had a slip of paper in her hand.

"I was right," she said. "I knew Upjohn's first move on getting a book published would be to subscribe to a press-cutting agency. I found this on the hall table. It's your review of his slim volume, young Herring, and having run an eye over it I'm not surprised that he's a little upset. I'll read it to you."

As might have been expected, this having been foreshadowed a good deal in one way and another, what Kipper had written was on the severe side, and as far as I was concerned it fell into the rare and refreshing fruit class. I enjoyed every minute of it. It concluded as follows:

"Aubrey Upjohn might have taken a different view of preparatory schools if he had done a stretch at the Dotheboys Hall conducted by him at Malvern House, Bramley-on-Sea, as we had the misfortune to do. We have not forgotten the sausages on Sunday, which were made not from contented pigs but from pigs which had expired, regretted by all, of glanders, the botts and tuberculosis."

Until this passage left the aged relative's lips Kipper had been sitting with the tips of his fingers together, nodding from time to time as much as to say, "Caustic, yes, but perfectly legitimate criticism," but on hearing this excerpt he did another of his sitting high jumps, lowering all previous records by several inches. It occurred to me as a passing thought that if all other sources of income failed, he had a promising future as an acrobat.

"But I never wrote that," he gasped.

"Well, it's here in cold print."

"Why, that's libelous!"

"So Upjohn and his legal eagle seem to feel. And I must say it reads like a pretty good five thousand pounds' worth to me."

"Let me look at that," yipped Kipper. "I don't understand this. No, half a second, darling. Not now. Later. I want to concentrate," he said, for Bobbie had flung herself on him and was clinging to him like the ivy on the old garden wall.

"Reggie!" she wailed. Yes, wail's the word. "It was me!"

"Eh?"

"That thing Mrs. Travers just read. You remember you showed me the proof at lunch that day and told me to drop it off at the office, as you had to rush along to keep a golf date. I read it again after you'd gone, and saw you had left out that bit about the sausages—accidentally, I thought—and it seemed to me so frightfully funny and clever that—well, I put it in at the end. I felt it just rounded the thing off."

• 14 •

THERE WAS silence for some moments, broken only by the sound of an aunt saying "Lord love a duck!" Kipper stood blinking, as I had sometimes seen him do at the boxing tourneys in which he indulged, when in receipt of a shrewd buffet on some tender spot like the tip of the nose. Whether or not the idea of taking Bobbie's neck in both hands and twisting it into a spiral floated through his mind, I cannot say, but if so it was merely the idle dream of a couple of seconds or so, for almost immediately love prevailed. She had described him as a lamb, and it was with all the mildness for which lambs are noted that he now spoke.

"Oh, I see. So that's how it was."

"I'm so sorry."

"Don't mention it."

"Can you ever forgive me?"

"Oh, rather."

"I meant so well."

"Of course you did."

"Will you really get into trouble about this?"

"There may be some slight unpleasantness."

"Oh Reggie!"

"Quite all right."

"I've ruined your life."

"Nonsense. The *Thursday Review* isn't the only paper in London. If they fire me, I'll accept employment elsewhere."

This scarcely squared with what he had told me about being black-listed, but I forbore to mention this, for I saw that his words had cheered Bobbie up considerably, and I didn't want to bung a spanner into her mood of *bien être*. Never does to dash the cup of happiness from a girl's lips when after plumbing the depths she has started to take a swig at it.

"Of course!" she said. "Any paper would be glad to have a valuable man like you."

"They'll fight like tigers for his services," I said, helping things along. "You don't find a chap like Kipper out of circulation for more than a day or so."

"You're so clever."

"Oh, thanks."

"I don't mean you, ass, I mean Reggie."

"Ah, yes. Kipper has what it takes, all right."

"All the same," said Aunt Dahlia, "I think, when Upjohn arrives, you had better do all you can to ingratiate yourself with him."

I got her meaning. She was recommending that grappling-to-the-soul-with-hoops-of-steel stuff.

"Yes," I said. "Exert the charm, Kipper, and there's a chance he might call the thing off."

"Bound to," said Bobbie. "Nobody can resist you, darling."

"Do you think so, darling?"

"Of course I do, darling."

"Well, let's hope you're right, darling. In the meantime," said Kipper, "if I don't get that whisky and soda soon, I shall disintegrate. Would you mind if I went in search of it, Mrs. Travers?"

"It's the very thing I was about to suggest myself. Dash along and drink your fill, my unhappy young stag at eve."

"I'm feeling rather like a restorative, too," said Bobbie.

"Me also," I said, swept along on the tide of the popular movement. "Though I would advise," I said, when we were outside, "making it port. More authority. We'll look in on Swordfish. He will provide."

We found Pop Glossop in his pantry polishing silver, and put in our order. He seemed a little surprised at the inrush of such a multitude, but on learning that our tongues were hanging out obliged with a bottle of the best, and after we had done a bit of tissue-restoring, Kipper, who had preserved a brooding silence since entering, rose and left us, saying that if we didn't mind he would like to muse apart for awhile. I saw Pop Glossop give him a sharp look as he went out, and I knew that Kipper's demeanor had roused his professional interest, causing him to scent in the young visitor a potential customer. These brain specialists are always on the job and never miss a trick.

Tactfully waiting till the door had closed, he said, "Is Mr. Herring an old friend of yours, Mr. Wooster?"

"Bertie."

"I beg your pardon. Bertie. You have known him for some time?"

"Practically from the egg."

"And is Miss Wickham a friend of his?"

"Reggie Herring and I are engaged, Sir Roderick," said Bobbie.

Her words seemed to seal the Glossop lips. He said, "Oh?" and began to talk about the weather and continued to do so until Bobbie, who since Kipper's departure had been exhibiting signs of restlessness, said she thought she would go and see how he was making out. Finding himself de-Wickhamed, he unsealed his lips without delay.

"I did not like to mention it before Miss Wickham, as she and Mr. Herring are engaged, for one is always loath to occasion anxiety, but that young man has a neurosis."

"He isn't always as dippy as he looked just now."

"Nevertheless—"

"And let me tell you something, Roddy. If you were as up against it as he is, you'd have a neurosis, too."

And feeling that it would do no harm to get his views on the Kipper situation, I unfolded the tale.

"So you see the posish," I concluded. "The only way he can avoid the fate that is worse than death—*viz.*, letting his employers get nicked for a sum beyond the dreams of avarice— is by ingratiating himself with Upjohn, which would seem to any thinking man a shot that's not on the board. I mean, he had four years with him at Malvern House and didn't ingratiate himself once, so it's difficult to see how he's going to start doing it now. It seems to me the thing's an impasse. French expression," I explained, "meaning that we're stymied good and proper with no hope of finding a formula."

To my surprise, instead of clicking the tongue and waggling the head gravely to indicate that he saw the stickiness of the dilemma, he chuckled fatly, as if having spotted an amusing side to the thing which had escaped me. Having done this, he blessed his soul, which was his way of saying "Gorblimey."

"It really is quite extraordinary, my dear Bertie," he said, "how associating with you restores my youth. Your lightest word seems to bring back old memories. I find myself recollecting episodes in the distant past which I have not thought of for years and years. It is as though you waved a magic wand of some kind. This matter of the problem confronting your friend Mr. Herring is a case in point. While you were telling me of his troubles, the mists shredded away, the hands of the clock turned back, and I was once again a young fellow in my early twenties, deeply involved in the strange affair of Bertha Simmons, George Lanchester and Bertha's father, old Mr. Simmons, who at that time resided in Putney. He was in the imported lard-and-butter business."

"The what was that strange affair again?"

He repeated the cast of characters, asked me if I would care for another drop of port, a suggestion with which I readily fell in, and proceeded.

"George, a young man of volcanic passions, met Bertha Simmons at a dance at Putney Town Hall in aid of the widows of deceased railway porters and became instantly enamored. And his love was returned. When he encountered Bertha next day in Putney High Street and, taking her off to a confectioner's for an ice cream, offered her with it his hand and heart, she accepted them enthusiastically. She said that when they were dancing together on the previous night something had seemed to go all over her, and he said he had had exactly the same experience."

"Twin souls, what?"

"A most accurate description."

"In fact, so far, so good."

"Precisely. But there was an obstacle, and a very serious one. George was a swimming instructor at the local baths, and Mr. Simmons had higher views for his daughter. He forbade the marriage. I am speaking, of course, of the days when fathers did forbid marriages. It was only when George saved him from drowning that he relented and gave the young couple his consent and blessing."

"How did that happen?"

"Perfectly simple. I took Mr. Simmons for a stroll on the river bank and pushed him in, and George, who was waiting in readiness, dived into the water and pulled him out. Naturally I had to undergo a certain amount of criticism of my clumsiness, and it was many weeks before I received another invitation to Sunday supper at Chatsworth, the Simmons residence—quite a privation in those days when I was a penniless medical student and perpetually hungry—but I was glad to sacrifice myself to help a friend, and the results, as far as George was concerned, were of the happiest. And what crossed my mind, as you were telling me of Mr. Herring's desire to ingratiate himself with Mr. Upjohn, was that a similar—is 'setup' the term you young fellows use?—would answer in his case. All the facilities are here at Brinkley Court. In my rambles about the grounds I have noticed a small but quite adequate lake, and . . . Well, there you have it, my dear Bertie. I throw it out, of course, merely as a suggestion."

His words left me all of a glow. When I thought how I had misjudged him in the days when our relations had been distant, I burned with shame and remorse. It seemed incredible that I could ever have looked on this admirable loony-doctor as the menace in the treatment. What a lesson, I felt, this should teach all of us, that a man may have a bald head and bushy eyebrows and still remain at heart a jovial sportsman and one of the boys. There was about an inch of the ruby juice nestling in my glass, and as he finished speaking I raised the beaker in a reverent toast. I told him he had hit the bull's eye and was entitled to a cigar or coconut according to choice.

"I'll go and take the matter up with my principals immediately."

"Can Mr. Herring swim?"

"Like several fishes."

"Then I see no obstacle in the path."

We parted with mutual expressions of good will, and it was only after I had emerged into the summer air that I remembered I hadn't told him that Wilbert had purchased, not pinched, the cow-creamer, and for a moment I thought of going back to apprise him. But I thought again, and didn't. First things first, I said to myself, and the item at the top of the agenda paper was the bringing of a new sparkle to Kipper's eyes. Later on, I told myself, would do, and carried on to where he and Bobbie were pacing the lawn with bowed heads. It would not be long, I anticipated, before I would be bringing those heads up with a jerk.

Nor was I in error. Their enthusiasm was unstinted. Both agreed unreservedly that if Upjohn had the merest spark of human feeling in him, which of course had still to be proved, the thing was in the bag.

"But you never thought this up yourself, Bertie," said Bobbie, always inclined to underestimate the Wooster shrewdness. "You've been talking to Jeeves."

"No, as a matter of fact, it was Swordfish who had the idea."

Kipper seemed surprised.

"You mean you told him about it?"

"I thought it the strategic move. Four heads are better than three."

"And he advised shoving Upjohn into the lake?"

"That's right."

"Rather a peculiar butler."

I turned this over in my mind.

"Peculiar? Oh, I don't know. Fairly run-of-the-mill, I should call him. Yes, more or less the usual type," I said.

· 15 ·

WITH SELF all eagerness and enthusiasm for the work in hand, straining at the leash, as you might say, and full of the will to win, it came as a bit of a damper when I found on the following afternoon that Jeeves didn't think highly of Operation Upjohn. I told him about it just before starting out for the tryst, feeling that it would be helpful to have his moral support, and was stunned to see that his manner was austere and even puff-faced. He was giving me a description at the time of how it felt to act as judge at a seaside bathing-belles contest, and it was with regret that I was compelled to break into this, for he had been holding me spellbound.

"I'm sorry, Jeeves," I said, consulting my watch, "but I shall have to be dashing off. Urgent appointment. You must tell me the rest later."

"At any time that suits you, sir."

"Are you doing anything for the next half hour or so?"

"No, sir."

"Not planning to curl up in some shady nook with a cigarette and Spinoza?"

"No, sir."

"Then I strongly advise you to come down to the lake and witness a human drama."

And in a few brief words I outlined the program and the events which had led up to it. He listened attentively and raised his left eyebrow a fraction of an inch.

"Was this Miss Wickham's idea, sir?"

"No. I agree that it sounds like one of hers, but actually it was Sir Roderick Glossop who suggested it. By the way, you were probably surprised to find him buttling here."

"It did occasion me a momentary astonishment, but Sir Roderick explained the circumstances."

"Fearing that if he didn't let you in on it, you might unmask him in front of Mrs. Cream?"

"No doubt, sir. He would naturally wish to take all precautions. I gathered from his remarks that he has not yet reached a definite conclusion regarding the mental condition of Mr. Cream."

"No, he's still observing. Well, as I say, it was from his fertile bean that the idea sprang. What do you think of it?"

"Ill-advised, sir, in my opinion."

I was amazed. I could hardly b. my e.

"Ill-advised?"

"Yes, sir."

"But it worked without a hitch in the case of Bertha Simmons, George Lanchester and old Mr. Simmons."

"Very possibly, sir."

"Then why this defeatist attitude?"

"It is merely a feeling, sir, due probably to my preference for finesse. I mistrust these elaborate schemes. One cannot depend on them. As the poet Burns says, the best laid plans of mice and men gang aft agley."

"Scotch, isn't it, that word?"

"Yes, sir."

"I thought as much. The 'gang' told the story. Why do Scotsmen say 'gang'?"

"I have no information, sir. They have not confided in me."

I was getting a bit peeved by now, not at all liking the sniffiness of his manner. I had expected him to speed me on my way with words of encouragement and uplift, not to go trying to blunt the keen edge of my zest like this. I was rather in the position of a child who runs to his mother hoping for approval and endorsement of something he's done, and is awarded instead a brusque kick in the pants. It was with a good deal of warmth that I came back at him.

"So you think the poet Burns would look askance at this enterprise of ours, do you? Well, you can tell him from me he's an ass. We've thought the thing out to the last detail. Miss Wickham asks Mr. Upjohn to come for a stroll with her. She leads him to the lake. I am standing on the brink, ostensibly taking a look at the fishes playing amongst the reeds. Kipper, ready to the last button, is behind a neighboring tree. On the cue "Oh, look!" from Miss Wickham, accompanied by business of pointing with girlish excitement at something in the water, Upjohn bends over to peer. I push, Kipper dives in, and there we are. Nothing can possibly go wrong."

"Just as you say, sir. But I still have that feeling."

The blood of the Woosters is hot, and I was about to tell him in set terms what I thought of his bally feeling, when I suddenly spotted what it was that was making him crab the act. The green-eyed monster had bitten him. He was miffed because he wasn't the brains behind this binge, the blueprints for it having been laid down by a rival. Even great men have these weaknesses. So I held back the acid crack I might have made and went off with a mere "Oh, yeah?" No sense in twisting the knife in the wound, I mean.

All the same, I remained a bit hot under the collar, because when you're all strung up and tense and all that, the last thing you want is people upsetting you by ringing in the poet Burns. I hadn't told him, but our plans had already nearly been wrecked at the outset by the unfortunate circumstance of Upjohn, while in the metropolis, having shaved his mustache, this causing Kipper to come within a toucher of losing his nerve and calling the whole thing off. The sight of that bare expanse or steppe of flesh beneath the nose, he said, did something to him, bringing back the days when he had so often found his blood turning to ice on beholding it. It had required quite a series of pep talks to revive his manly spirits.

However, there was good stuff in the lad, and though for a while the temperature of his feet had dropped sharply, threatening to reduce him to the status of a non-co-operative cat in an adage, at 3:30 Greenwich Mean Time he was at his post behind the selected tree, resolved to do his bit. He poked his head round the tree as I arrived, and when I waved a cheery hand at him, waved a fairly cheery hand at me. Though I only caught a glimpse of him, I could see that his upper lip was stiff.

There being no signs as yet of the female star and her companion, I deduced that I was a bit on the early side. I lit a cigarette and stood awaiting their entrance, and was pleased to note that conditions could scarcely have been better for the coming water fete. Too often on an English summer day you find the sun going behind the clouds and a nippy wind springing up from the northeast, but this afternoon was one of those still, sultry afternoons when the slightest movement brings the persp. in beads to the brow, an afternoon, in short, when it would be a positive pleasure to be shoved into a lake. "Most refreshing," Upjohn would say to himself as the cool water played about his limbs.

I was standing there running over the stage directions in my mind to see that I had got them all clear, when I beheld Wilbert Cream approaching, the dog Poppet curvetting about his ankles. On seeing me the hound rushed forward with uncouth cries, as was his wont, but on heaving along-side and getting a whiff of Wooster Number Five calmed down, and I was at liberty to attend to Wilbert, who I could see desired speech with me.

He was looking, I noticed, fairly green about the gills, and he conveyed the same suggestion of having just swallowed a bad oyster which I had observed in Kipper on his arrival at Brinkley. It was plain that the loss of Phyllis Mills, goofy though she unquestionably was, had hit him a shrewd wallop, and I presumed that he was coming to me for sympathy and heart balm, which I would have been only too pleased to dish out. I hoped, of course, that he would make it crisp and remove himself at an early date, for when the moment came for the balloon to go up I didn't want to be hampered by an audience. When you're pushing someone into a lake, nothing embarrasses you more than having the front seats filled up with goggling spectators.

It was not, however, on the subject of Phyllis that he proceeded to touch.

"Oh, Wooster," he said, "I was talking to my mother a night or two ago."

"Oh, yes?" I said, with a slight wave of the hand intended to indicate that if he liked to talk to his mother anywhere, all over the house, he had my approval.

"She tells me you are interested in mice."

I didn't like the trend the conversation was taking, but I preserved my aplomb.

"Why, yes, fairly interested."

"She says she found you trying to catch one in my bedroom!"

"Yes, that's right."

"Good of you to bother."

"Not at all. Always a pleasure."

"She says you seemed to be making a very thorough search of my room."

138

"Oh, well, you know, when one sets one's hand to the plow."

"You didn't find a mouse?"

"No, no mouse. Sorry."

"I wonder if by any chance you happened to find an eighteenth-century cow-creamer?"

"Eh?"

"A silver jug shaped like a cow."

"No. Why, was it on the floor somewhere?"

"It was in a drawer of the bureau."

"Ah, then I would have missed it."

"You'd certainly miss it now. It's gone."

"Gone?"

"Gone."

"You mean disappeared, as it were?"

"I do."

"Strange."

"Very strange."

"Yes, does seem extremely strange, doesn't it?"

I had spoken with all the old Wooster coolness, and I doubt if a casual observer would have detected that Bertram was not at his ease, but I can assure my public that he wasn't, by a wide margin. My heart had leaped in the manner popularized by Kipper Herring and Scarface McColl, crashing against my front teeth with a thud which must have been audible in Market Snodsbury. A far less astute man would have been able to divine what had happened. Not knowing the score, owing to having missed the latest stop-press news, and looking on the cow-creamer purely in the light of a bit of the swag collected by Wilbert in the course of his larcenous career, Pop Glossop, all zeal, had embarked on the search he had planned to make, and intuition, developed by years of hunt-the-slipper, had led him to the right spot. Too late I regretted sorely that, concentrating so tensely on Operation Upjohn, I had failed to place the facts before him. Had he but known about summed it up.

"I was going to ask you," said Wilbert, "if you think I should inform Mrs. Travers."

The cigarette I was smoking was fortunately one of the kind that make you nonchalant, so it was nonchalantly—or fairly nonchalantly—that I was able to reply.

"Oh, I wouldn't do that."

"Why not?"

"Might upset her."

"You consider her a sensitive plant?"

"Oh, very. Rugged exterior, of course, but you can't go by that. No, I'd just wait awhile, if I were you. I expect it'll turn out that the thing's somewhere you put it but didn't think you'd put it. I mean, you often put a thing somewhere and think you've put it somewhere else and then find you didn't put it somewhere else but somewhere. I don't know if you follow me?"

"I don't."

"What I mean is, just stick around and you'll probably find the thing."

"You think it will return?"

"I do."

"Like a homing pigeon?"

"That's the idea."

"Oh?" said Wilbert, and turned away to greet Bobbie and Upjohn, who had just arrived on the boathouse landing stage. I had found his manner a little peculiar, particularly that last "Oh?" but I was glad that there was no lurking suspicion in his mind that I had taken the bally thing. He might so easily have got the idea that Uncle Tom, regretting having parted with his ewe lamb, had employed me to recover it privily, this being the sort of thing, I believe, that collectors frequently do. Nevertheless, I was still much shaken, and I made a mental note to tell Roddy Glossop to slip it back among his effects at the earliest possible moment.

I shifted over to where Bobbie and Upjohn were standing, and, though up and doing with a heart for any fate, couldn't help getting that feeling you get at times like this of having swallowed a double portion of butterflies. My emotions were somewhat similar to those I had experienced when I first sang the "Yeoman's Wedding Song." In public, I mean, for of course I had long been singing it in my bath.

"Hullo, Bobbie," I said.

"Hullo, Bertie," she said.

"Hullo, Upjohn," I said.

The correct response to this would have been "Hullo, Wooster," but he blew his lines and merely made a noise like a wolf with its big toe caught in a trap. Seemed a bit restive, I thought, as if wishing he were elsewhere.

Bobbie was all girlish animation.

"I've been telling Mr. Upjohn about that big fish we saw in the lake yesterday, Bertie."

"Ah, yes, the big fish."

"It was a whopper, wasn't it?"

"Very well developed."

"I brought him down here to show it to him."

"Quite right. You'll enjoy the big fish, Upjohn."

I had been perfectly correct in supposing him to be restive. He did his wolf impersonation once more.

"I shall do nothing of the sort," he said, and you couldn't find a better word than "testily" to describe the way he spoke. "It is most inconvenient for me to be away from the house at this time. I am expecting a telephone call from my lawyer."

"Oh, I wouldn't bother about telephone calls from lawyers," I said heartily. "These legal birds never say anything worth listening to. Just gab gab gab. You'll never forgive yourself if you miss the big fish. You were saying, Upjohn?" I broke off courteously, for he had spoken.

"I am saying, Mr. Wooster, that both you and Miss Wickham are laboring under a singular delusion in supposing that I am interested in fish, whether large or small. I ought never to have left the house. I shall return there at once."

141

"Oh, don't go yet," I said.

"Wait for the big fish," said Bobbie.

"Bound to be along shortly," I said.

"At any moment now," said Bobbie.

Her eyes met mine, and I read in them the message she was trying to convey, *viz.*, that the time had come to act. There is a tide in the affairs of men which taken at the flood leads on to fortune. Not my own. Jeeves's. She bent over and pointed with an eager finger.

"Oh, look!" she cried.

This, as I had explained to Jeeves, should have been the cue for Upjohn to bend over, too, thus making it a simple task for me to do my stuff, but he didn't bend over an inch. And why? Because at this moment the goof Phyllis, suddenly appearing in our midst, said, "Daddy, dear, you're wanted on the telephone."

Upon which, standing not on the order of his going, Upjohn was off as if propelled from a gun. He couldn't have moved quicker if he had been the dachshund Poppet, who at this juncture was running round in circles, trying, if I read his thoughts aright, to work off the rather heavy lunch he had had earlier in the afternoon.

One began to see what the poet Burns had meant. I don't know anything that more promptly gums up a dramatic sequence than the sudden and unexpected exit of an important member of the cast at a crucial point in the proceedings. I was reminded of the time when we did *Charley's Aunt* at the Market Snodsbury Town Hall in aid of the local church-organ fund, and halfway through the second act, just when we were all giving of our best, Catsmeat Potter-Pirbright, who was playing Lord Fancourt Babberley, left the stage abruptly to attend to an unforeseen nosebleed.

As far as Bobbie and I were concerned, silence reigned, this novel twist in the scenario having wiped speech from our lips, as the expression is, but Phyllis continued vocal.

"I found this darling pussycat in the garden," she said, and for the first time I observed that she was bearing Augustus in her arms. He was looking a bit disgruntled, and one could readily see why. He wanted to catch up with his sleep and was being kept awake by the endearments she was murmuring in his ear.

She lowered him to the ground.

"I brought him here to talk to Poppet. Poppet loves cats, don't you, angel? Come and say how-d'you-do to the sweet pussykins, darling."

I shot a quick look at Wilbert Cream, to see how he was reacting to this. It was the sort of observation that might well have quenched the spark of love in his bosom, for nothing tends to cool the human heart more swiftly than baby talk. But, far from being revolted, he was gazing yearningly at her as if her words were music to his ears. Very odd, I felt, and I was just saying to myself that you never could tell, when I became aware of a certain liveliness in my immediate vicinity.

At the moment when Augustus touched ground and curling himself into a ball fell into a light doze, Poppet had completed his tenth lap and was preparing to start on his eleventh. Seeing Augustus, he halted in mid-stride, smiled broadly, turned his ears inside out, stuck his tail straight up at right angles to the parent body and bounded forward, barking merrily.

I could have told the silly ass his attitude was all wrong. Roused abruptly from slumber, the most easygoing cat is apt to wake up cross. Already Augustus had had much to endure from Phyllis, who had doubtless jerked him out of dreamland when scooping him up in the garden, and all this noise and heartiness breaking out just as he had dropped off again put the lid on his sullen mood. He spat peevishly, there was a sharp yelp, and something long and brown came shooting between my legs, precipitating itself and me into the depths. The waters closed about me, and for an instant I knew no more.

When I rose to the surface, I found that Poppet and I were not the only bathers. We had been joined by Wilbert Cream, who had dived in, seized the hound by the scruff of the neck, and was towing him at a brisk pace to the shore. And by one of those odd coincidences I was at this moment seized by the scruff of the neck myself.

"It's all right, Mr. Upjohn, keep quite cool, keep quite . . . What the hell are you doing here, Bertie?" said Kipper, for it was he. I may have been wrong, but it seemed to me that he spoke petulantly.

I expelled a pint or so of H_2O.

"You may well ask," I said, moodily detaching a water beetle from my hair. "I don't know if you know the meaning of the word 'agley,' Kipper, but that, to put it in a nutshell, is the way things have ganged."

· 16 ·

REACHING THE mainland some moments later and, accompanied by Bobbie, squelching back to the house like a couple of Napoleons squelching back from Moscow, we encountered Aunt Dahlia, who, wearing that hat of hers that looks like one of those baskets you carry fish in, was messing about in the herbaceous border by the tennis lawn. She gaped at us dumbly for perhaps five seconds, then uttered an ejaculation, far from suitable to mixed company, which she had no doubt picked up from a fellow Nimrod in her hunting days.

Having got this off the chest, she said, "What's been going on in this joint? Wilbert Cream came by here just now, soaked to the eyebrows, and now you two appear, leaking at every seam. Have you all been playing water polo with your clothes on?"

"Not so much water polo, more that seaside bathing-belles stuff," I said. "But it's a long story, and one feels that the cagey thing for Kipper and me to do now is to nip along and

145

get into some dry things, not to linger conferring with you, much," I added courteously, "as we always enjoy your conversation."

"The extraordinary thing is that I saw Upjohn not long ago, and he was as dry as a bone. How was that? Couldn't you get him to play with you?"

"He had to go and talk to his lawyer on the phone," I said, and leaving Bobbie to place the facts before her, we resumed our squelching. And I was in my room, having shed the moistened outer crust and substituted something a bit more *sec* in pale flannel, when there was a knock on the door. I flung wide the gates and found Bobbie and Kipper on the threshold.

The first thing I noticed about their demeanor was the strange absence of gloom, despondency and what not. I mean, considering that it was little more than a quarter of an hour since all our hopes and dreams had taken the knock, one would have expected their hearts to be bowed down with weight of woe, but their whole aspect was one of buck and optimism. It occurred to me as a possible solution that, with that bulldog spirit of never admitting defeat which has made Englishmen—and, of course, Englishwomen—what they are, they had decided to have another go along the same lines at some future date, and I asked if this was the case.

The answer was in the negative. Kipper said no, there was no likelihood of getting Upjohn down to the lake again, and Bobbie said that even if they did, it wouldn't be any good, because I would be sure to mess things up once more.

This stung me, I confess.

"How do you mean, mess things up?"

"You'd be bound to trip over your flat feet and fall in, as you did today."

"Pardon me," I said, preserving with an effort the polished suavity demanded from an English gentleman when chewing the rag with one of the other sex. "You're talking through the back of your fatheaded little neck. I did not trip over my flat feet. I was hurled into the depths by an Act of God, to wit, a totally unexpected dachshund getting between my legs. If you're going to blame anyone, blame the goof Phyllis, for bringing Augustus there and calling him in his hearing a sweet pussykins. Naturally it made him sore and disinclined to stand any lip from barking dogs."

"Yes," said Kipper, always the staunch pal. "It wasn't Bertie's fault, angel. Say what you will of dachshunds, their peculiar shape makes them the easiest breed of dog to trip over in existence. I feel that Bertie emerges without a stain on his character."

"I don't," said Bobbie. "Still, it doesn't matter."

"No, it doesn't really matter," said Kipper, "because your aunt has suggested a scheme that's just as good as the Lanchester-Simmons thing, if not better. She was telling Bobbie about the time when Boko Fittleworth was trying to ingratiate himself with your Uncle Percy, and you very sportingly offered to go and call your Uncle Percy a lot of offensive names, so that Boko, hovering outside the door, could come in and stick up for him, thus putting himself in solid with him. You probably remember the incident?"

I quivered. I remembered the incident all right.

"She thinks the same treatment would work with Upjohn, and I'm sure she's right. You know how you feel when you suddenly discover you've a real friend, a fellow who thinks you're terrific and won't hear a word said against you? It touches you. If you had anything in the nature of a prejudice against the chap, you change your opinion of him. You feel you can't do anything to injure such a sterling bloke. And that's how Upjohn is going to feel about me, Bertie, when I come in and lend him my sympathy and support as you stand there calling him all the names you can think of. You must have picked up dozens from your aunt. She used to hunt, and if you hunt, you have to know all the names there are, because people are always riding over hounds and

147

all that. Ask her to jot down a few of the best on a half-sheet of note paper."

"He won't need that," said Bobbie. "He's probably got them all tucked away in his mind."

"Of course. Learned them at her knee as a child. Well, that's the setup, Bertie. You wait your opportunity and corner Upjohn somewhere and tower over him—"

"As he crouches in his chair."

"—and shake your finger in his face and abuse him roundly. And when he's quailing beneath your scorn and wishing some friend in need would intervene and save him from this terrible ordeal, I come in, having heard all. Bobbie suggests that I knock you down, but I don't think I could do that. The recollection of our ancient friendship would make me pull my punch. I shall simply rebuke you. 'Wooster,' I shall say, 'I am shocked. Shocked and astounded. I cannot understand how you can talk like that to a man I have always respected and looked up to, a man in whose preparatory school I spent the happiest years of my life. You strangely forget yourself, Wooster.' Upon which you slink out, bathed in shame and confusion, and Upjohn thanks me brokenly and says if there is anything he can do for me, I have only to name it."

"I still think you ought to knock him down."

"Having endeared myself to him thus—"

"Much more box-office."

"Having endeared myself to him thus, I lead the conversation round to the libel suit."

"One good punch in the eye would do it."

"I say that I have seen the current issue of the *Thursday Review*, and I can quite understand him wanting to mulct the journal in substantial damages, but 'Don't forget, Mr. Upjohn,' I say, 'that when a weekly paper loses a chunk of money, it has to retrench, and the way it retrenches is by getting rid of the more junior members of its staff. You wouldn't want me to lose my job, would you, Mr. Upjohn?'

He starts. 'Are you on the staff of the *Thursday Review?*' he says. 'For the time being, yes,' I say. 'But if you bring that suit, I shall be selling pencils in the street.' This is the crucial moment. Looking into his eyes, I can see that he is thinking of that five thousand quid, and for an instant, quite naturally, he hesitates. Then his better self prevails. His eyes soften. They fill with tears. He clasps my hand. He tells me he could use five thousand quid as well as the next man, but no money in the world would make him dream of doing an injury to the fellow who championed him so stoutly against that louse Wooster, and the scene ends with our going off together to Swordfish's pantry for a drop of port, probably with our arms round each other's waists, and that night he writes a letter to his lawyer telling him to call the suit off. Any questions?"

"Not from me. It isn't as if he could find out that it was you who wrote that review. It wasn't signed."

"No, thank heaven for the editorial austerity that prevented that."

"I can't see a flaw in the scenario. He'll have to withdraw the suit."

"In common decency, one would think. The only thing that remains is to choose a time and place for Bertie to operate."

"No time like the present."

"But how do we locate Upjohn?"

"He's in Mr. Travers' study. I saw him through the French window."

"Excellent. Then, Bertie, if you're ready . . . "

It will probably have been noticed that during these exchanges I had taken no part in the conversation. This was because I was fully occupied with envisaging the horror that lay before me. I knew that it did lie before me, of course, for where the ordinary man would have met the suggestion they had made with a firm *nolle prosequi*, I was barred from doing

149

this by the code of the Woosters, which, as is pretty generally known, renders it impossible for me to let a pal down. If the only way of saving a boyhood friend from having to sell pencils in the street—though I should have thought that blood oranges would have been a far more lucrative line—was by wagging my finger in the face of Aubrey Upjohn and calling him names, that finger would have to be wagged and those names called. The ordeal would whiten my hair from the roots up and leave me a mere shell of my former self, but it was one that I must go through. Mine not to reason why, as the fellow said.

So I uttered a rather husky "Right ho" and tried not to think of how the Upjohn face looked without its mustache. For what chilled the feet most was the mental picture of that bare upper lip which he had so often twitched at me in what are called days of yore. Dimly, as we started off for the arena, I could hear Bobbie saying "My hero!" and Kipper asking anxiously if I was in good voice, but it would have taken a fat lot more than my hero-ing and solicitude about my vocal cords to restore tone to Bertram's nervous system. I was, in short, feeling like an inexperienced novice going up against the heavyweight champion when in due course I drew up at the study door, opened it and tottered in. I could not forget that an Aubrey Upjohn who for years had been looking strong parents in the eye and making them wilt, and whose toughness was a byword in Bramley-on-Sea, was not a man lightly to wag a finger in the face of.

Uncle Tom's study was a place I seldom entered during my visits to Brinkley Court, because when I did go there he always grabbed me and started to talk about old silver, whereas if he caught me in the open he often touched on other topics, and the way I looked at it was that there was no sense in sticking one's neck out. It was more than a year since I had been inside this sanctum, and I had forgotten how extraordinarily like its interior was to that of Aubrey Upjohn's lair at Malvern House. Discovering this now, and seeing Aubrey Upjohn seated at the desk as I had so often seen him sit on the occasions when he had sent for me to discuss some recent departure of mine from the straight and narrow path, I found what little was left of my *sang-froid* expiring with a pop. And at the same time I spotted the flaw in this scheme I had undertaken to sit in on—*viz.*, that you can't just charge into a room and start calling someone names out of a blue sky, as it were—you have to lead up to the thing. *Pourparlers,* in short, are of the essence.

So I said, "Oh, hullo," which seemed to me about as good a *pourparler* as you could have by way of an opener. I should imagine that those statesmen of whom I was speaking always edge into their conferences conducted in an atmosphere of the utmost cordiality in some such manner.

"Reading?" I said.

He lowered his book—one of Ma Cream's, I noticed—and flashed an upper lip at me.

"Your powers of observation have not led you astray, Wooster. I *am* reading."

"Interesting book?"

"Very. I am counting the minutes until I can resume its perusal undisturbed."

I'm pretty quick, and I at once spotted that the atmosphere was not of the utmost cordiality. He hadn't spoken matily, and he wasn't eying me matily. His whole manner seemed to suggest that he felt that I was taking up space in the room which could have been better employed for other purposes.

However, I persevered. "I see you've shaved off your mustache."

"I have. You do not feel, I hope, that I pursued a mistaken course?"

"Oh, no, rather not. I grew a mustache myself last year, but had to get rid of it."

"Indeed?"

"Public sentiment was against it."

"I see. Well, I should be delighted to hear more of your reminiscences, Wooster, but at the moment I am expecting a telephone call from my lawyer."

"I thought you'd had one."

"I beg your pardon?"

"When you were down by the lake, didn't you go off to talk to him?"

"I did. But when I reached the telephone, he had grown tired of waiting and had rung off. I should never have allowed Miss Wickham to take me away from the house."

"She wanted you to see the big fish."

"So I understood her to say."

"Talking of fish, you must have been surprised to find Kipper here."

"Kipper?"

"Herring."

"Oh, Herring," he said, and one spotted the almost total lack of animation in his voice. And conversation had started to flag, when the door flew open and the goof Phyllis bounded in, full of girlish excitement.

"Oh, Daddy," she burbled, "are you busy?"

"No, my dear."

"Can I speak to you about something?"

"Certainly. Goodbye, Wooster."

I saw what this meant. He didn't want me around. There was nothing for it but to ooze out through the French window, so I oozed, and had hardly got outside when Bobbie sprang at me like a leopardess.

"What on earth are you fooling about for like this, Bertie?" she stage-whispered. "All that rot about mustaches. I thought you'd be well into it by this time."

I pointed out that as yet Aubrey Upjohn had not given me a cue.

"You and your cues!"

"All right, me and my cues. But I've got to sort of lead the conversation in the right direction, haven't I?"

"I see what Bertie means, darling," said Kipper. "He wants—"

"A *point d'appui.*"

"A what?" said Bobbie.

"Sort of jumping-off place."

The beazel snorted.

"If you ask me, he's lost his nerve. I knew this would happen. The worm has got cold feet."

I could have crushed her by drawing her attention to the fact that worms don't have feet, cold or piping hot, but I had no wish to bandy words.

"I must ask you, Kipper," I said with frigid dignity, "to request your girl friend to preserve the decencies of debate. My feet are not cold. I am as intrepid as a lion and only too anxious to get down to brass tacks, but just as I was working round to the *res*, Phyllis came in. She said she had something she wanted to speak to him about."

Bobbie snorted again, this time in a despairing sort of way.

"She'll be there for hours. It's no good waiting."

"No," said Kipper. "May as well call it off for the moment. We'll let you know time and place of next fixture, Bertie."

"Oh, thanks," I said, and they drifted away.

And about a couple of minutes later, as I stood there brooding on Kipper's sad case, Aunt Dahlia came along. I was glad to see her. I thought she might possibly come across with aid and comfort, for though, like the female in the poem I was mentioning, she sometimes was inclined to be a toughish egg in hours of ease, she could generally be relied on to be there with the soothing solace when one had anything wrong with one's brow.

As she approached, I got the impression that her own brow had for some reason taken it on the chin. Quite a good deal of that upon-which-all-the-ends-of-the-earth-are-come stuff, it seemed to me.

Nor was I mistaken.

"Bertie," she said, heaving to beside me and waving a trowel in an overwrought manner, "do you know what?"

"No, what?"

"I'll tell you what," said the aged relative, rapping out a sharp monosyllable such as she might have uttered in her Quorn and Pytchley days on observing a unit of the pack of hounds chasing a rabbit. "That ass Phyllis has gone and got engaged to Wilbert Cream!"

·17·

HER WORDS gave me quite a wallop. I don't say I reeled, and
everything didn't actually go black, but I was shaken, as
what nephew would not have been. When a loved aunt has
sweated herself to the bone trying to save her godchild from
the clutches of a New York playboy and learns that all her
well-meant efforts have gone blue on her, it's only natural
for her late brother's son to shudder in sympathy.

"You don't mean that?" I said. "Who told you?"

"She did."

"In person?"

"In the flesh. She came skipping to me just now, clapping
her little hands and bleating about how very, very happy
she was, dear Mrs. Travers. The silly young geezer. I nearly
conked her one with my trowel. I'd always thought her half-
baked, but now I think they didn't even put her in the oven."

"But how did it happen?"

"Apparently that dog of hers joined you in the water."

"Yes, that's right, he took his dip with the rest of us. But what's that got to do with it?"

"Wilbert Cream dived in and saved him."

"He could have got ashore perfectly well under his own steam. In fact, he was already on his way, doing what looked like an Australian crawl."

"That wouldn't occur to a pinhead like Phyllis. To her Wilbert Cream is the man who rescued her dachshund from a watery grave. So she's going to marry him."

"But you don't marry fellows because they rescue dachshunds."

"You do, if you've a mentality like hers."

"Seems odd."

"And is. But that's how it goes. Girls like Phyllis Mills are an open book to me. For four years I was, if you remember, the proprietor and editress of a weekly paper for women." She was alluding to the periodical entitled *Milady's Boudoir*, to the Husbands And Brothers page of which I once contributed an article or "piece" on What The Well-Dressed Man Is Wearing. It had recently been sold to a mug up Liverpool way, and I have never seen Uncle Tom look chirpier than when the deal went through, he for those four years having had to foot the bills.

"I don't suppose," she continued, "that you were a regular reader, so for your information there appeared in each issue a short story, and in seventy per cent of those short stories the hero won the heroine's heart by saving her dog or her cat or her canary or whatever foul animal or bird she happened to possess. Well, Phyllis didn't write all those stories, but she easily might have done, for that's the way her mind works. When I say 'mind,'" said the blood relation, "I refer to the quarter-teaspoonful of brain which you might possibly find in her head if you sank an artesian well. Poor Jane!"

"Poor who?"

"Her mother. Jane Mills."

"Oh, ah, yes. She was a pal of yours, you told me."

"The best I ever had, and she was always saying to me 'Dahlia, old girl, if I pop off before you, for heaven's sake look after Phyllis and see that she doesn't marry some ghastly outsider. She's sure to want to. Girls always do, goodness knows why,' she said, and I knew she was thinking of her first husband, who was a heel to end all heels and a constant pain in the neck to her till one night he most fortunately walked into the river Thames while under the influence of the sauce and didn't come up for days. 'Do stop her,' she said, and I said 'Jane, you can rely on me.' And now this happens."

I endeavored to soothe. "You can't blame yourself."

"Yes, I can."

"It isn't your fault."

"I invited Wilbert Cream here."

"Merely from a wifely desire to do Uncle Tom a bit of good."

"And I let Upjohn stick around, always at her elbow egging her on."

"Yes, Upjohn's the bird I blame."

"Me, too."

"But for his—undue influence, do they call it?—Phyllis would have remained a bachelor or spinster or whatever it is. 'Thou art the man, Upjohn!' seems to me the way to sum it up. He ought to be ashamed of himself."

"And am I going to tell him so! I'd give a tenner to have Aubrey Upjohn here at this moment."

"You can get him for nothing. He's in Uncle Tom's study." Her face lit up.

"He is?" She threw her head back and inflated the lungs. "UPJOHN!" she boomed, rather like someone calling the cattle home across the sands of Dee, and I issued a kindly word of warning.

"Watch that blood pressure, old ancestor."

"Never you mind my blood pressure. You let it alone, and it'll leave you alone. UPJOHN!"

He appeared in the French window, looking cold and

157

severe, as I had so often seen him look when hobnobbing with him in his study at Malvern House, self not there as a willing guest but because I'd been sent for. ("I should like to see Wooster in my study immediately after morning prayers" was the formula.)

"Who is making that abominable noise? Oh, it's you, Dahlia."

"Yes, it's me."

"You wished to see me?"

"Yes, but not the way you're looking now. I'd have preferred you to have fractured your spine or at least to have broken a couple of ankles and got a touch of leprosy."

"My dear Dahlia!"

"I'm not your dear Dahlia. I'm a seething volcano. Have you seen Phyllis?"

"She has just left me."

"Did she tell you?"

"That she was engaged to Wilbert Cream? Certainly."

"And I suppose you're delighted?"

"Of course I am."

"Yes, of course you are! I can well imagine that it's your dearest wish to see that unfortunate muttonheaded girl become the wife of a man who lets off stink bombs in night clubs and pinches the spoons and has had three divorces already and who, if the authorities play their cards right, will end up cracking rocks in Sing Sing. That is, unless the loony-bin gets its bid in first. Just a Prince Charming, you might say."

"I don't understand you."

"Then you're an ass."

"Well, really!" said Aubrey Upjohn, and there was a dangerous note in his voice. I could see that the relative's manner, which was not affectionate, and her words, which lacked cordiality, were peeving him. It looked like an odds-on shot that in about another two ticks he would be giving her the Collect for the Day to write out ten times or even instructing her to bend over while he fetched his whangee. You can push these preparatory schoolmasters just so far.

"A fine way for Jane's daughter to end up. Mrs. Broadway Willie!"

"Broadway Willie?"

"That's what he's called in the circles in which he moves, into which he will now introduce Phyllis. 'Meet the moll,' he'll say, and then he'll teach her in twelve easy lessons how to make stink bombs, and the children, if and when, will be trained to pick people's pockets as they dandle them on their knee. And you'll be responsible, Aubrey Upjohn!"

I didn't like the way things were trending. Admittedly the aged relative was putting up a great show and it was a pleasure to listen to her, but I had seen Upjohn's lip twitch and that look of smug satisfaction come into his face which I had so often seen when he had been counsel for the prosecution in some case in which I was involved and had spotted a damaging flaw in my testimony. The occasion when I was on trial for having broken the drawing-room window with a cricket ball springs to the mind. It was plain to an eye as discerning as mine that he was about to put it across the old flesh and blood properly, making her wish she hadn't spoken. I couldn't see how, but the symptoms were all there.

I was right. That twitching lip had not misled me.

"If I might be allowed to make a remark, my dear Dahlia," he said, "I think we are talking at cross-purposes. You appear to be under the impression that Phyllis is marrying Wilbert's younger brother Wilfred, the notorious playboy whose escapades have caused the family so much distress and who, as you are correct in saying, is known to his disreputable friends as Broadway Willie. Wilfred, I agree, would make—and on three successive occasions has made—a most undesirable husband, but no one to my knowledge has ever spoken a derogatory word of Wilbert. I know few young men who are more generally respected. He is a member of the faculty of one of the greatest American universities, over in this country on his sabbatical. He teaches Romance languages."

Stop me if I've told you this before—I rather fancy I have—but once when I was up at Oxford and chatting on the riverbank with a girl called something that's slipped my mind, there was a sound of barking and a great hefty dog of the Hound of the Baskervilles type came galloping at me, obviously intent on mayhem, its whole aspect that of a dog that has no use for Woosters. And I was just commending my soul to God and thinking that this was where my new flannel trousers got about thirty bobs' worth of value bitten out of them, when the girl, waiting till she saw the whites of its eyes, with extraordinary presence of mind opened a colored Japanese umbrella in the animal's face. Upon which, with a startled exclamation it did three back somersaults and retired into private life.

And the reason I bring this up now is that, barring the somersaults, Aunt Dahlia's reaction to this communiqué was precisely that of the above hound to the Japanese umbrella. The same visible taken-abackness. She has since told me that her emotions were identical with those she had experienced when she was out with the Pytchley and riding over a plowed field in rainy weather and the horse of a sportslover in front of her suddenly kicked three pounds of wet mud into her face.

She gulped like a bulldog trying to swallow a sirloin steak many sizes too large for its thoracic cavity.

"You mean there are two of them?"

"Exactly."

"And Wilbert isn't the one I thought he was?"

"You have grasped the position of affairs to a nicety. You will appreciate now, my dear Dahlia," said Upjohn, speaking with the same unction, if that's the word, with which he had spoken when unmasking his batteries and presenting unshakable proof that yours was the hand, Wooster, which propelled this cricket ball, "that your concern, though doing you the greatest credit, has been needless. I could wish Phyllis no better husband. Wilbert has looks, brains, character—and excellent prospects," he added, rolling the words round his tongue like vintage port. "His father, I should imagine, would be worth at least twenty million dollars, and Wilbert is the elder son. Yes, most satisfactory, most . . . "

As he spoke, the telephone rang, and with a quick "Ha!" he shot back into the study like a homing rabbit.

· 18 ·

For perhaps a quarter of a minute after he had passed from the scene the aged relative stood struggling for utterance. At the end of this period she found speech.

"Of all the damn silly fatheaded things!" she vociferated, if that's the word. "With a million ruddy names to choose from, these ruddy Creams call one ruddy son Wilbert and the other ruddy son Wilfred, and both these ruddy sons are known as Willie. Just going out of their way to mislead the innocent bystander. You'd think people would have more consideration."

Again I begged her to keep an eye on her blood pressure and not get so worked up, and once more she brushed me off, this time with a curt request that I go and boil my head.

"You'd be worked up if you had just been scored off by Aubrey Upjohn, with that loathsome self-satisfied look on his face as if he'd been rebuking a pimply pupil at his beastly school for shuffling his feet in church."

"Odd, that," I said, struck by the coincidence. "He once rebuked me for that very reason. And I had pimples."

"Pompous ass!"

"Shows what a small world it is."

"What's he doing here, anyway? I didn't invite him."

"Bung him out. I took this point up with you before, if you remember. Cast him into outer darkness, where there is weeping and gnashing of teeth."

"I will, if he gives me any more of his lip."

"I can see you're in dangerous mood."

"You bet I'm in dangerous . . . My God! He's with us again!"

And A. Upjohn was indeed filtering through the French window. But he had lost the look of which the ancestor had complained, the one he was wearing now seeming to suggest that since last heard from something had occurred to wake the fiend that slept in him.

"Dahlia!" he—yes, better make it vociferated, once more. I'm pretty sure it's the word I want.

The fiend that slept in Aunt Dahlia was also up on its toes. She gave him a look which, if directed at an erring member of the personnel of the Quorn or Pytchly hound ensemble, would have had that member sticking his tail between his legs and resolving for the future to lead a better life.

"Now what?"

Just as Aunt Dahlia had done, Aubrey Upjohn struggled for utterance. Quite a bit of utterance-struggling there had been around these parts this summer afternoon.

"I have just been speaking to my lawyer on the telephone," he said, getting going after a short stage wait. "I had asked him to make inquiries and ascertain the name of the author of that libelous attack on me in the columns of the *Thursday Review*. He did so, and has now informed me that it was the work of my former pupil, Reginald Herring."

He paused at this point, to let us chew it over, and the heart sank. Mine, I mean. Aunt Dahlia's seemed to be carry-

163

ing on much as usual. She scratched her chin with her trowel, and said, "Oh, yes?"

Upjohn blinked as if he had been expecting something better than this in the way of sympathy and concern. "Is that all you can say?"

"That's the lot."

"Oh? Well, I am suing the paper for heavy damages, and, furthermore, I refuse to remain in the same house with Reginald Herring. Either he goes or I go."

There was the sort of silence which I believe cyclones drop into for a second or two before getting down to it and starting to give the populace the works. Throbbing? Yes, throbbing wouldn't be a bad word to describe it. Nor would electric, for the matter of that, and if you care to call it ominous, it will be all right with me. It was a silence of the type that makes the toes curl and sends a shiver down the spinal cord as you stand waiting for the bang. I could see Aunt Dahlia swelling slowly like a chunk of bubble gum, and a less prudent man than Bertram Wooster would have warned her again about her blood pressure.

"I beg your pardon?" she said.

He repeated the key words.

"Oh?" said the relative, and went off with a pop. I could have told Upjohn he was asking for it. Normally as genial a soul as ever broke biscuit, this aunt, when stirred, can become the haughtiest of *grandes dames* before whose wrath the stoutest quail, and she doesn't, like some, have to use a lorgnette to reduce the citizenry to pulp; she does it all with the naked eye. "Oh?" she said. "So you have decided to revise my guest list for me? You have the nerve, the—the—"

I saw she needed helping out.

"Audacity," I said, throwing her the line.

"The audacity to dictate to me who I shall have in my house." It should have been "whom," but I let it go.

"You have the—"

"Crust."

164

"—the immortal rind," she amended, and I had to admit it was stronger, "to tell me whom"—she got it right that time—"I may entertain at Brinkley Court and who"—wrong again—"I may not. Very well, if you feel unable to breathe the same air as my friends, you must please yourself. I believe the Bull and Bush in Market Snodsbury is quite comfortable."

"Well spoken of in the Automobile Guide," I said.

"I shall go there," said Upjohn. "I shall go there as soon as my things are packed. Perhaps you will be good enough to tell your butler to pack them."

He strode off, and she went into Uncle Tom's study, me following, she still snorting. She rang the bell.

Jeeves appeared.

"Jeeves?" said the relative, surprised. "I was ringing for—"

"It is Sir Roderick's afternoon off, madam."

"Oh? Well, would you mind packing Mr. Upjohn's things, Jeeves? He is leaving us."

"Very good, madam."

"And you can drive him to Market Snodsbury, Bertie."

"Right ho," I said, not much liking the assignment, but liking less the idea of endeavoring to thwart this incandescent aunt in her current frame of mind.

Safety First is the Wooster slogan.

· 19 ·

It isn't much of a run from Brinkley Court to Market Snodsbury, and I deposited Upjohn at the Bull and Bush and
started m-p-h-ing homeward in what you might call a trice.
We parted, of course, on rather distant terms, but the great
thing when you've got an Upjohn on your books is to part
and not be fussy about how it's done, and had it not been for
all this worry about Kipper, for whom I was now mourning
in spirit more than ever, I should have been feeling fine.

I could see no happy issue for him from the soup in which
he was immersed. No words had been exchanged between
Upjohn and self on the journey out, but the glimpses I had
caught of his face from the corner of the eye had told me
that he was grim and resolute, his supply of the milk of human kindness plainly short by several gallons. No hope, it
seemed to me, of turning him from his fell purpose.

I garaged the car and went to Aunt Dahlia's sanctum to
ascertain whether she had cooled off at all since I had left

her, for I was still anxious about that blood pressure of hers. One doesn't want aunts going up in a sheet of flame all over the place.

She wasn't there, having, I learned later, withdrawn to her room to bathe her temples with Eau de Cologne and do Yogi deep breathing, but Bobbie was, and not only Bobbie but Jeeves. He was handing her something in an envelope, and she was saying "Oh, Jeeves, you've saved a human life," and he was saying "Not at all, miss." The gist, of course, escaped me, but I had no leisure to probe into gists.

"Where's Kipper?" I asked, and was surprised to note that Bobbie was dancing round the room on the tips of her toes uttering animal cries, apparently ecstatic in their nature.

"Reggie?" she said, suspending the farmyard imitations for a moment. "He went for a walk."

"Does he know that Upjohn's found out he wrote that thing?"

"Yes, your aunt told him."

"Then we ought to be in conference."

"About Upjohn's libel action? It's all right about that. Jeeves has pinched his speech."

I could make nothing of this. It seemed to me that the beazel spoke in riddles.

"Have you an impediment in your speech, Jeeves?"

"No, sir."

"Then what, if anything, does the young prune mean?"

"Miss Wickham's allusion is to the typescript of the speech which Mr. Upjohn is to deliver tomorrow to the scholars of Market Snodsbury Grammar School, sir."

"She said you'd pinched it."

"Precisely, sir."

I started.

"You don't mean . . . ?"

"Yes, he does," said Bobbie, resuming the Ballet Russe movements. "Your aunt told him to pack Upjohn's bags, and

167

the first thing he saw when he smacked into it was the speech. He trousered it and brought it along to me."

I raised an eyebrow.

"Well, really, Jeeves!"

"I deemed it best, sir."

"And did you deem right!" said Bobbie, executing a Nijinsky whatever-it's-called. "Either Upjohn agrees to drop that libel suit or he doesn't get these notes, as he calls them, and without them he won't be able to utter a word. He'll have to come across with the price of the papers. Won't he, Jeeves?"

"He would appear to have no alternative, miss."

"Unless he wants to get up on that platform and stand there opening and shutting his mouth like a goldfish. We've got him cold."

"Yes, but half a second," I said.

I spoke reluctantly. I didn't want to damp the young ball of worsted in her hour of joy, but a thought had occurred to me.

"I see the idea, of course. I remember Aunt Dahlia telling me about this strange inability of Upjohn's to be silver-tongued unless he has the material in his grasp; but suppose he says he's ill and can't appear?"

"He won't."

"I would."

"But you aren't trying to get the Conservative Association of the Market Snodsbury division to choose you as their candidate at the coming by-election. Upjohn is, and it's vitally important for him to address the multitude tomorrow and make a good impression, because half the selection committee have sons at the school and will be there, waiting to judge for themselves how good he is as a speaker. Their last nominee stuttered, and they didn't discover it till the time came for him to dish it out to the constituents. They don't want to make a mistake this time."

"Yes, I get you now," I said. I remembered that Aunt Dahlia had spoken to me of Upjohn's political ambitions.

"So that fixes that," said Bobbie. "His future hangs on this speech, and we've got it and he hasn't. We take it from there."

"And what exactly is the procedure?"

"That's all arranged. He'll be ringing up any moment now, making inquiries. When he does, you step to the telephone and outline the position of affairs to him."

"Me?"

"That's right."

"Why me?"

"Jeeves deems it best."

"Well, really, Jeeves! Why not Kipper?"

"Mr. Herring and Mr. Upjohn are not on speaking terms, sir."

"So you can see what would happen if he heard Reggie's voice. He would hang up haughtily, and all the weary work to do again. Whereas he'll drink in your every word."

"But, dash it—"

"And, anyway, Reggie's gone for a walk and isn't available. I do wish you wouldn't always be so difficult, Bertie. Your aunt tells me it was just the same when you were a child. She'd want you to eat your cereal, and you would stick your ears back and be stubborn and non-co-operative, like Jonah's ass in the Bible."

I could not let this go uncorrected. It's pretty generally known that when at school I won a prize for Scripture Knowledge.

"Balaam's ass. Jonah was the chap who had the whale. Jeeves!"

"Sir?"

"To settle a bet, wasn't it Balaam's ass that entered the *nolle prosequi?*"

"Yes, sir."

169

"I told you so," I said to Bobbie, and would have continued grinding her into the dust, had not the telephone at this moment tinkled, diverting my mind from the point at issue. The sound sent a sudden chill through the Wooster limbs, for I knew what it portended.

Bobbie, too, was not unmoved.

"Hullo!" she said. "This, if I mistake not, is our client now. In you go, Bertie. Over the top and best of luck."

I have mentioned before that Bertram Wooster, chilled steel when dealing with the sterner sex, is always wax in a woman's hands, and the present case was no exception to the r. Short of going over Niagara Falls in a barrel, I could think of nothing I wanted to do less than chat with Aubrey Upjohn at this juncture, especially along the lines indicated, but having been requested by one of the delicately nurtured to take on the grim task, I had no option. I mean, either a chap's *preux* or he isn't, as the Chevalier Bayard used to say.

But as I approached the instrument and unhooked the thing you unhook, I was far from being at my most nonchalant, and when I heard Upjohn are-you-there-ing at the other end my manly spirit definitely blew a fuse. For I could tell by his voice that he was in the testiest of moods. Not even when conferring with me at Malvern House, Bramley-on-Sea, on the occasion when I put sherbet in the ink had I sensed in him a more marked stirred-upness.

"Hullo? Hullo? Hullo? Are you there? Will you kindly answer me? This is Mr. Upjohn speaking."

They always say that when the nervous system isn't all it should be the thing to do is to take a couple of deep breaths. I took six, which of course occupied a certain amount of time, and the delay noticeably increased his umbrage. Even at this distance one could spot what I believe is called the deleterious animal magnetism.

"Is this Brinkley Court?"

I could put him straight there. None other, I told him.

"Who are you?"

I had to think for a moment. Then I remembered.

"This is Wooster, Mr. Upjohn."

"Well, listen to me carefully, Wooster."

"Yes, Mr. Upjohn. How do you like the Bull and Bush? Everything pretty snug?"

"What did you say?"

"I was asking if you liked the Bull and Bush."

"Never mind the Bull and Bush."

"No, Mr. Upjohn."

"This is of vital importance. I wish to speak to the man who packed my things."

"Jeeves."

"What?"

"Jeeves."

"What do you mean by Jeeves?"

"Jeeves."

"You keep saying 'Jeeves' and it makes no sense. Who packed my belongings?"

"Jeeves."

"Oh, Jeeves is the man's name?"

"Yes, Mr. Upjohn."

"Well, he carelessly omitted to pack the notes for my speech at Market Snodsbury Grammar School tomorrow."

"No, really! I don't wonder you're sore."

"Saw whom?"

"Sore with an r."

"What?"

"No, sorry. I mean with an o-r-e."

"Wooster!"

"Yes, Mr. Upjohn?"

"Are you intoxicated?"

"No, Mr. Upjohn."

"Then you are driveling. Stop driveling, Wooster."

"Yes, Mr. Upjohn."

"Send for this man Jeeves immediately and ask him what he did with the notes for my speech."

"Yes, Mr. Upjohn."

"At once! Don't stand there saying 'Yes, Mr. Upjohn.'"

"No, Mr. Upjohn."

"It is imperative that I have them in my possession immediately."

"Yes, Mr. Upjohn."

Well, I suppose, looking at it squarely, I hadn't made much real progress and a not-too-close observer might quite possibly have got the impression that I had lost my nerve and was shirking the issue, but that didn't in my opinion justify Bobbie at this point in snatching the receiver from my grasp and bellowing the word "Worm!" at me.

"What did you call me?" said Upjohn.

"I didn't call you anything," I said. "Somebody called me something."

"I wish to speak to this man Jeeves."

"You do, do you?" said Bobbie. "Well, you're going to speak to me. This is Roberta Wickham, Upjohn. If I might have your kind attention for a moment."

I must say that, much as I disapproved in many ways of this carrot-topped Jezebel, as she was sometimes called, there was no getting away from it that she had mastered the art of talking to retired preparatory schoolmasters. The golden words came pouring out like syrup. Of course, she wasn't handicapped, as I had been, by having sojourned for some years beneath the roof of Malvern House, Bramley-on-Sea, and having at a malleable age associated with this old Frankenstein's monster when he was going good, but, even so, her performance deserved credit.

Beginning with a curt "Listen, Buster," she proceeded to sketch out with admirable clearness the salient points in the situation as she envisaged it, and judging from the loud buzzing noises that came over the wire, clearly audible to me though I was now standing in the background, it was evident that the nub was not escaping him. They were the

172

buzzing noises of a man slowly coming to the realization that a woman's hand had got him by the short hairs.

Presently they died away, and Bobbie spoke.

"That's fine," she said. "I was sure you'd come round to our view. Then I will be with you shortly. Mind there's plenty of ink in your fountain pen."

She hung up and legged it from the room, once more giving vent to those animal cries, and I turned to Jeeves as I had so often turned to him before when musing on the activities of the other sex.

"Women, Jeeves!"

"Yes, sir."

"Were you following all that?"

"Yes, sir."

"I gather that Upjohn, vowing . . . How does it go?"

"Vowing he would ne'er consent, consented, sir."

"He's withdrawing the suit."

"Yes, sir. And Miss Wickham prudently specified that he do so in writing."

"Thus avoiding all ranygazoo?"

"Yes, sir."

"She thinks of everything."

"Yes, sir."

"I thought she was splendidly firm."

"Yes, sir."

"It's the red hair that does it, I imagine."

"Yes, sir."

"If anyone had told me that I should live to hear Aubrey Upjohn addressed as 'Buster' . . . "

I would have spoken further, but before I could get under way the door opened, revealing Ma Cream, and Jeeves shimmered silently from the room. Unless expressly desired to remain, he always shimmers off when what is called the Quality arrives.

173

· 20 ·

THIS WAS the first time I had seen Ma Cream today, she having gone off around noon to lunch with some friends in Birmingham, and I would willingly not have seen her now, for something in her manner seemed to suggest that she spelled trouble. She was looking more like Sherlock Holmes than ever. Slap a dressing gown on her and give her a violin, and she could have walked straight into Baker Street and no questions asked.

Fixing me with a penetrating eye, she said, "Oh, there you are, Mr. Wooster. I was looking for you."

"You wished speech with me?"

"Yes. I wanted to say that now perhaps you'd believe me."

"I beg your pardon?"

"About that butler."

"What about him?"

"I'll tell you what about him. I'd sit down, if I were you. It's a long story."

I sat down. Glad to, as a matter of fact, for the legs were feeling weak.

"You remember I told you I mistrusted him from the first?"

"Oh, ah, yes. You did, didn't you?"

"I said he had a criminal face."

"He can't help his face."

"He can help being a crook and an imposter. Calls himself a butler, does he? The police could shake that story. He's no more a butler than I am."

I did my best. "But think of those references of his."

"I am thinking of them."

"He couldn't have stuck it out as major-domo to a man like Sir Roderick Glossop if he'd been dishonest."

"He didn't."

"But Bobbie said—"

"I remember very clearly what Miss Wickham said. She told me he had been with Sir Roderick Glossop for years."

"Well, then."

"You think that puts him in the clear?"

"Certainly."

"I don't, and I'll tell you why. Sir Roderick Glossop has a large clinic down in Somersetshire at a place called Chuffnell Regis, and a friend of mine is there. I wrote to her asking her to see Lady Glossop and get all the information she could about a former butler of hers named Swordfish. When I got back from Birmingham just now, I found a letter from her. She says that Lady Glossop told her she had never employed a butler called Swordfish. Try that one on for size."

I continued to do my best. The Woosters never give up. "You don't know Lady Glossop, do you?"

"Of course I don't, or I'd have written to her direct."

"Charming woman, but with a memory like a sieve. The sort who's always losing one glove at the theater. Naturally she wouldn't remember a butler's name. She probably thought all along it was Fotheringay or Binks or something. Very common, that sort of mental lapse. I was up at Oxford with a man called Robinson, and I was trying to think of his name the other day and the nearest I could get to it was Fosdyke. It only came back to me when I saw in the *Times* a few days ago that Herbert Robinson (26) of Grove Road, Ponder's End, had been had up at Bosher Street police court, charged with having stolen a pair of green-and-yellow checked trousers. Not the same chap, of course, but you get the idea. I've no doubt that one of these fine mornings Lady Glossop will suddenly smack herself on the forehead and cry 'Swordfish! Of *course!* And all this time I've been thinking of the honest fellow as Catbird!' "

She sniffed. And if I were to say that I liked the way she sniffed, I would be willfully deceiving my public. It was the sort of sniff Sherlock Holmes would have sniffed when about to clap the darbies on the chap who had swiped the Maharajah's ruby.

"Honest fellow, did you say? Then how do you account for this? I saw Willie just now, and he tells me that a valuable eighteenth-century cow-creamer that he bought from Mr. Travers is missing. And where is it, you ask? At this moment it is tucked away in Swordfish's bedroom in a drawer under his clean shirts."

In stating that the Woosters never give up, I was in error. These words caught me amidships and took all the fighting spirit out of me, leaving me a spent force.

"Oh, is it?" I said. Not good, but the best I could do.

"Yes, sir, that's where it is. Directly Willie told me the thing had gone, I knew where it had gone to. I went to this man Swordfish's room and searched it, and there it was. I've sent for the police."

Again I had that feeling of having been spiritually knocked base over apex. I gaped at the woman.

"You've sent for the police?"

"I have, and they're sending a sergeant. He ought to be here at any moment. And shall I tell you something? I'm going now to stand outside Swordfish's door, to see that

176

nobody tampers with the evidence. I'm not going to take any chances. I wouldn't want to say anything to suggest that I don't trust you implicitly, Mr. Wooster, but I don't like the way you've been sticking up for this fellow. You've been far too sympathetic with him for my taste."

"It's just that I think he may have yielded to sudden temptation and all that."

"Nonsense. He's probably been acting this way all his life. I'll bet he was swiping things as a small boy."

"Only biscuits."

"I beg your pardon?"

"Or crackers, you would call them, wouldn't you? He was telling me he occasionally pinched a cracker or two in his salad days."

"Well, there you are. You start with crackers and you end up with silver jugs. That's life," she said, and buzzed off to keep her vigil, leaving me kicking myself because I'd forgotten to say anything about the quality of mercy not being strained. It isn't, as I dare say you know, and a mention of this might just have done the trick.

I was still brooding on this oversight and wondering what was to be done for the best, when Bobbie and Aunt Dahlia came in, looking like a young female and an elderly female who were sitting on top of the world.

"Roberta tells me she has got Upjohn to withdraw the libel suit," said Aunt Dahlia. "I couldn't be more pleased, but I'm blowed if I can imagine how she did it."

"Oh, I just appealed to his better feelings," said Bobbie, giving me one of those significant glances. I got the message. The ancestor, she was warning me, must never learn that she had achieved her ends by jeopardizing the delivery of the Upjohn speech to the young scholars of Market Snodsbury Grammar School on the morrow. "I told him that the quality of mercy . . . What's the matter, Bertie?"

"Nothing. Just starting."

"What do you want to start for?"

177

"I believe Brinkley Court is open for starting in at about this hour, is it not? The quality of mercy, you were saying?"

"Yes. It isn't strained."

"I believe not."

"And in case you didn't know, it's twice bless'd and becomes the throned monarch better than his crown. I drove over to the Bull and Bush and put this to Upjohn, and he saw my point. So now everything's fine."

I uttered a hacking laugh.

"No," I said, in answer to a query from Aunt Dahlia. "I have not accidentally swallowed my tonsils, I was merely laughing hackingly. Ironical that the young blister should say that everything is fine, for at this very moment disaster stares us in the eyeball. I have a story to relate which I think you will agree falls into the fretful porpentine class," I said, and without further *pourparlers* I unshipped my tale.

I had anticipated that it would shake them to their foundation garments, and it did. Aunt Dahlia reeled like an aunt struck behind the ear with a blunt instrument, and Bobbie tottered like a redhaired girl who hadn't known it was loaded.

"You see the setup," I continued, not wanting to rub it in but feeling that they should be fully briefed. "Glossop will return from his afternoon off to find the awful majesty of the law waiting for him, complete with handcuffs. We can hardly expect him to accept an exemplary sentence without a murmur, so his first move will be to establish his innocence by revealing all. 'True,' he will say, 'I did pinch this bally cow-creamer, but merely because I thought Wilbert had pinched it and it ought to be returned to store,' and he will go on to explain his position in the house—all this, mind you, in front of Ma Cream. So what ensues? The sergeant removes the gyves from his wrists, and Ma Cream asks you if she may use your telephone for a moment, as she wishes to call her husband on long distance. Pop Cream listens attentively to the tale she tells, and when Uncle Tom looks in on him later, he finds him with folded arms and a forbidding scowl.

178

'Travers,' he says, 'The deal's off.' 'Off?' quavers Uncle Tom. 'Off,' says Cream. 'O-ruddy-double-f. I don't do business with guys whose wives bring in loony-doctors to observe my son.' A short while ago Ma Cream was urging me to try something on for size. I suggest that we do the same for this."

Aunt Dahlia had sunk into a chair and was starting to turn purple. Strong emotion always has this effect on her.

"The only thing left, it seems to me," I said, "is to put our trust in a higher power."

"You're right," said the relative, fanning her brow. "Go and fetch Jeeves, Roberta. And what you do, Bertie, is get out that car of yours and scour the countryside for Glossop. It may be possible to head him off. Come on, come on, let's have some service. What are you waiting for?"

I hadn't exactly been waiting. I'd only been thinking that the enterprise had more than a touch of looking for a needle in a haystack about it. You can't find loony-doctors on their afternoon off just by driving around Worcestershire in a car; you need bloodhounds and handkerchiefs for them to sniff at and all that professional stuff. Still, there it was.

"Right ho," I said. "Anything to oblige."

· 21 ·

AND, OF COURSE, as I had anticipated from the start, the thing was a washout. I stuck it out for about an hour and then, apprised by a hollow feeling in the midriff that the dinner hour was approaching, laid a course for home.

Arriving there, I found Bobbie in the drawing room. She had the air of a girl who was waiting for something, and when she told me that the cocktails would be coming along in a moment, I knew what it was.

"Cocktails, eh? I could do with one or possibly more," I said. "My fruitless quest has taken it out of me. I couldn't find Glossop anywhere. He must be somewhere, of course, but Worcestershire hid its secret well."

"Glossop?" she said, seeming surprised. "Oh, he's been back for ages."

She wasn't half as surprised as I was. The calm with which she spoke amazed me.

"Good Lord! This is the end."

"What is?"

"This is. Has he been pinched?"

"Of course not. He told them who he was and explained everything."

"Oh, gosh!"

"What's the matter? Oh, of course, I was forgetting. You don't know the latest developments. Jeeves solved everything."

"He did?"

"With a wave of the hand. It was so simple, really. One wondered why one hadn't thought of it oneself. On his advice, Glossop revealed his identity and said your aunt had got him down here to observe *you*."

I reeled, and might have fallen had I not clutched at a photograph on a near-by table of Uncle Tom in the uniform of the East Worcestershire Volunteers.

"No!" I said.

"And of course it carried immediate conviction with Mrs. Cream. Your aunt explained that she had been uneasy about you for a long time, because you were always doing extraordinary things like sliding down water pipes and keeping twenty-three cats in your bedroom and all that, and Mrs. Cream recalled the time when she had found you hunting for mice under her son's dressing table, so she quite agreed that it was high time you were under the observation of an experienced eye like Glossop's. She was greatly relieved when Glossop assured her that he was confident of effecting a cure. She said we must all be very, very kind to you. So everything's nice and smooth. It's extraordinary how things turn out for the best, isn't it?" she said, laughing merrily.

Whether I would or would not at this juncture have taken her in an iron grasp and shaken her till she frothed is a point on which I can make no definite pronouncement. The chivalrous spirit of the Woosters would probably have restrained me, much as I resented that merry laughter, but as it happened the matter was not put to the test, for at this moment Jeeves entered, bearing a tray on which were glasses and a

181

substantial shaker filled to the brim with the juice of the juniper berry. Bobbie drained her beaker with all possible speed and left us, saying that if she didn't get dressed she'd be late for dinner, and Jeeves and I were alone, like a couple of bimbos in one of those movies where two strong men stand face to face and might is the only law.

"Well, Jeeves," I said.

"Sir?"

"Miss Wickham has been telling me all."

"Ah, yes, sir."

"The words 'Ah, yes, sir' fall far short of an adequate comment on the situation. A nice—what is it? Begins with an i—im-something."

"Imbroglio, sir?"

"That's it. A nice imbroglio you've landed me in. Thanks to you . . ."

"Yes, sir."

"Don't say 'Yes, sir.' Thanks to you I have been widely publicized as off my rocker."

"Not widely, sir. Merely to your immediate circle now resident at Brinkley Court."

"You have held me up at the bar of world opinion as a man who has not got all his marbles."

"It was not easy to think of an alternative scheme, sir."

"And let me tell you," I said, and I meant this to sting, "it's amazing that you got away with it."

"Sir?"

"There's a flaw in your story that sticks out like a sore thumb."

"Sir?"

"It's no good standing there saying 'Sir,' Jeeves. It's obvious. The cow-creamer was in Glossop's bedroom. How did he account for that?"

"On my suggestion, sir, he explained that he had removed it from your room, where he had ascertained that you had hidden it after purloining it from Mr. Cream."

I started.

"You mean—" I, yes, thundered would be the word—"you mean that I am now labeled not only as a loony in a general sort of way but also as a klept-whatever-it-is?"

"Merely to your immediate circle now resident at Brinkley Court, sir."

"You keep saying that, and you must know it's the purest applesauce. You don't really think the Creams will maintain a tactful reserve? They'll dine out on it for years. Returning to America, they'll spread the story from the rockbound coasts of Maine to the Everglades of Florida, with the result that when I go over there again, keen looks will be shot at me at every house I go into and spoons counted before I leave. And do you realize that in a few shakes I've got to show up at dinner and have Mrs. Cream being very, very kind to me? It hurts the pride of the Woosters, Jeeves."

"My advice, sir, would be to fortify yourself for the ordeal."

"How?"

"There are always cocktails, sir. Should I pour you another?"

"You should."

"And we must always remember what the poet Longfellow said, sir."

"What was that?"

"Something attempted, something done, has earned a night's repose. You have the satisfaction of having sacrificed yourself in the interests of Mr. Travers."

He had found a talking point. He had reminded me of those postal orders, sometimes for as much as ten bob, which Uncle Tom had sent me in the Malvern House days. I softened. Whether or not a tear rose to my eye, I cannot say, but it may be taken as official that I softened.

"How right you are, Jeeves," I said.

Stiff Upper Lip, Jeeves

To
David Jasen

CHAPTER
ONE

I MARMALADED a slice of toast with something of a flourish, and I don't suppose I have ever come much closer to saying "Tra-la-la" as I did the lathering, for I was feeling in mid-season form this morning. God, as I once heard Jeeves put it, was in His heaven and all right with the world. (He added, I remember, some guff about larks and snails, but that is a side issue and need not detain us.)

It is no secret in the circles in which he moves that Bertram Wooster, though as glamorous as one could wish when night has fallen and the revels get under way, is seldom a ball of fire at the breakfast table. Confronted with the eggs and b., he tends to pick cautiously at them, as if afraid they may leap from the plate and snap at him. Listless about sums it up. Not much bounce to the ounce.

But today vastly different conditions had prevailed. All had been verve, if that's the word I want, and animation. Well, when I tell you that after sailing through a couple of sausages like a tiger of the jungle tucking into its luncheon coolie I was now, as indicated, about to tackle the toast and marmalade, I fancy I need say no more.

The reason for this improved outlook on the proteins and carbohydrates is not far to seek. Jeeves was back, earning his weekly envelope once more at the old stand. Her butler having come down with an ailment of some sort, my Aunt Dahlia, my good and deserving aunt, had borrowed him for a house party she was throwing at Brinkley Court, her Worcestershire residence, and he had been away for more than a week. Jeeves, of course, is a gentleman's gentleman, not a butler, but if the call comes, he can buttle with the best of them. It's in the blood. His Uncle Charlie is a butler, and no doubt he has picked up many a hint on technique from him.

He came in a little later to remove the debris, and I asked him if he had had a good time at Brinkley.

"Extremely pleasant, thank you, sir."

"More than I had in your absence. I felt like a child of tender years deprived of its Nannie. If you don't mind me calling you a Nannie."

"Not at all, sir."

Though, as a matter of fact, I was giving myself a slight edge, putting it that way. My Aunt Agatha, the one who eats broken bottles and turns into a werewolf at the time of the full moon, generally refers to Jeeves as my keeper.

"Yes, I missed you sorely, and had no heart for whooping it up with the lads at the Drones. From sport to sport they . . . how does that gag go?"

"Sir?"

188

"I heard you pull it once with reference to Freddie Widgeon, when one of his girls had given him the bird. Something about hurrying."

"Ah yes, sir. 'From sport to sport they hurry me, to stifle my regret—'"

"'And when they win a smile from me, they think that I forget.' That was it. Not your own, by any chance?"

"No, sir. An old English drawing-room ballad."

"Oh? Well, that's how it was with me. But tell me all about Brinkley. How was Aunt Dahlia?"

"Mrs. Travers appeared to be in her customary robust health, sir."

"And how did the party go off?"

"Reasonably satisfactorily, sir."

"Only reasonably?"

"The demeanor of Mr. Travers cast something of a gloom on the proceedings. He was low-spirited."

"He always is when Aunt Dahlia fills the house with guests. I've known even a single foreign substance in the woodwork to make him drain the bitter cup."

"Very true, sir, but on this occasion I think his despondency was due principally to the presence of Sir Watkyn Bassett."

"You don't mean that old crumb was there?" I said, Great-Scott-ing, for I knew that if there is one man for whose insides my Uncle Tom has the most vivid distaste, it is this Bassett. "You astound me, Jeeves."

"I, too, must confess to a certain surprise at seeing the gentleman at Brinkley Court, but no doubt Mrs. Travers felt it incumbent upon her to return his hospitality. You will recollect that Sir Watkyn recently entertained Mrs. Travers and yourself at Totleigh Towers."

I winced. Intending, I presumed, merely to refresh my

memory, he had touched an exposed nerve. There was some cold coffee left in the pot, and I took a sip to restore my equanimity.

"The word 'entertained' is not well chosen, Jeeves. If locking a fellow in his bedroom, as near as a toucher with gyves upon his wrists, and stationing the local police force on the lawn below to insure that he doesn't nip out of the window at the end of a knotted sheet is your idea of entertaining, it isn't mine, not by a jugful."

I don't know how well up you are in the Wooster archives, but if you have dipped into them to any extent, you will probably recall the sinister affair of Sir Watkyn Bassett and my visit to his Gloucestershire home. He and my Uncle Tom are rival collectors of what are known as objets d'art, and on one occasion he pinched a silver cow creamer, as the revolting things are called, from the relation by marriage, and Aunt Dahlia and self went to Totleigh to pinch it back, an enterprise which, though crowned with success, as the expression is, so nearly landed me in the jug that when reminded of that house of horror I still quiver like an aspen, if aspens are the things I'm thinking of.

"Do you ever have nightmares, Jeeves?" I asked, having got through with my bit of wincing.

"Not frequently, sir."

"Nor me. But when I do, the setup is always the same. I am back at Totleigh Towers with Sir W. Bassett, his daughter Madeline, Roderick Spode, Stiffy Byng, Gussie Fink-Nottle, and the dog Bartholomew, all doing their stuff, and I wake, if you will pardon the expression so soon after breakfast, sweating at every pore. Those were the times that . . . what, Jeeves?"

"Tried men's souls, sir."

"They certainly did—in spades. Sir Watkyn Bassett, eh?"

I said thoughtfully. "No wonder Uncle Tom mourned and would not be comforted. In his position I'd have been low-spirited myself. Who else were among those present?"

"Miss Bassett, sir, Miss Byng, Miss Byng's dog, and Mr. Fink-Nottle."

"Gosh! Practically the whole Totleigh Towers gang. Not Spode?"

"No, sir. Apparently no invitation had been extended to his lordship."

"His what?"

"Mr. Spode, if you recall, recently succeeded to the title of Lord Sidcup."

"So he did. I'd forgotten. But Sidcup or no Sidcup, to me he will always be Spode. There's a bad guy, Jeeves."

"Certainly a somewhat forceful personality, sir."

"I wouldn't want him in my orbit again."

"I can readily understand it, sir."

"Nor would I willingly foregather with Sir Watkyn Bassett, Madeline Bassett, Stiffy Byng, and Bartholomew. I don't mind Gussie. He looks like a fish and keeps newts in a glass tank in his bedroom, but one condones that sort of thing in an old schoolfellow, just as one condones in an old Oxford friend such as the Rev. H. P. Pinker the habit of tripping over his feet and upsetting things. How was Gussie? Pretty bobbish?"

"No, sir. Mr. Fink-Nottle, too, seemed to me low-spirited."

"Perhaps one of his newts had got tonsillitis or something."

"It is conceivable, sir."

"You've never kept newts, have you?"

"No, sir."

"Nor have I. Nor, to the best of my knowledge, have

191

Einstein, Jack Dempsey, and the Archbishop of Canterbury, to name but three others. Yet Gussie revels in their society and is never happier than when curled up with them. It takes all sorts to make a world, Jeeves."

"It does, indeed, sir. Will you be lunching in?"

"No, I've a date at the Ritz," I said, and went off to climb into the outer crust of the English gentleman.

As I dressed, my thoughts returned to the Bassetts, and I was still wondering why on earth Aunt Dahlia had allowed the pure air of Brinkley Court to be polluted by Sir Watkyn and associates when the telephone rang and I went into the hall to answer it.

"Bertie?"

"Oh, hullo, Aunt Dahlia."

There had been no mistaking that loved voice. As always when we converse on the telephone, it had nearly fractured my eardrum. This aunt was at one time a prominent figure in hunting circles, and when in the saddle, so I'm told, could make herself heard not only in the field or meadow where she happened to be but in several adjoining counties. Retired now from active fox chivying, she still tends to address a nephew in the tone of voice previously reserved for rebuking hounds for taking time off to chase rabbits.

"So you're up and about, are you?" she boomed. "I thought you'd be in bed, snoring your head off."

"It is a little unusual for me to be in circulation at this hour," I agreed, "but I rose today with the lark and, I think, the snail. Jeeves!"

"Sir?"

"Didn't you tell me once that snails were early risers?"

"Yes, sir. The poet Browning in his *Pippa Passes*, having established that the hour is seven A.M., goes on to say, 'The lark's on the wing, the snail's on the thorn.'"

"Thank you, Jeeves. I was right, Aunt Dahlia. When I

slid from between the sheets, the lark was on the wing, the snail on the thorn."

"What the devil are you babbling about?"

"Don't ask me; ask the poet Browning. I was merely apprising you that I was up betimes. I thought it was the least I could do to celebrate Jeeves' return."

"He got back all right, did he?"

"Looking bronzed and fit."

"He was in rare form here. Bassett was terrifically impressed."

I was glad to have this opportunity of solving the puzzle which had been perplexing me.

"Now there," I said, "you have touched on something I'd very much like to have information *re*. What on earth made you invite Pop Bassett to Brinkley?"

"I did it for the wife and kiddies."

I eh-what-ed. "You wouldn't care to amplify that?" I said. "It got past me to some extent."

"For Tom's sake, I mean," she replied with a hearty laugh that rocked me to my foundations. "Tom's been feeling rather low of late because of what he calls iniquitous taxation. You know how he hates to give up."

I did, indeed. If Uncle Tom had his way, the revenue authorities wouldn't get so much as a glimpse of his money.

"Well, I thought having to fraternize with Bassett would take his mind off it—show him that there are worse things in this world than income tax. Our doctor here gave me the idea. He was telling me about a thing called Hodgkin's disease that you cure by giving the patient arsenic. The principle's the same. That Bassett really is the limit. When I see you, I'll tell you the story of the black amber statuette. It's a thing he's just bought for his collection. He was showing it to Tom when he was here, gloating over it. Tom suffered agonies, poor old buzzard."

193

"Jeeves told me he was low-spirited."

"So would you be, if you were a collector and another collector you particularly disliked had got hold of a thing you'd have given your eyeteeth to have in your own collection."

"I see what you mean," I said, marveling, as I had often done before, that Uncle Tom could attach so much value to objects which I personally would have preferred not to be found dead in a ditch with. The cow creamer I mentioned earlier was one of them, being a milk jug shaped like a cow, of all ghastly ideas. I have always maintained fearlessly that the spiritual home of all these fellows who collect things is a padded cell in a loony bin.

"It gave Tom the worst attack of indigestion he's had since he was last lured into eating lobster. And talking of indigestion, I'm coming up to London for the day the day after tomorrow and shall require you to give me lunch."

I assured her that that should be attended to, and after the exchange of a few more civilities she rang off.

"That was Aunt Dahlia, Jeeves," I said, coming away from the machine.

"Yes, sir, I fancied I recognized Mrs. Travers' voice."

"She wants me to give her lunch the day after tomorrow. I think we'd better have it here. She's not keen on restaurant cooking."

"Very good, sir."

"What's this black amber statuette thing she was talking about?"

"It is a somewhat long story, sir."

"Then don't tell me now. If I don't rush, I shall be late for my date."

I reached for the umbrella and hat and was heading for the open spaces when I heard Jeeves give that soft cough of his and, turning, saw that a shadow was about to fall on what had been a day of joyous reunion. In the eye which he was fixing on me I detected the auntlike gleam which always means that he disapproves of something, and when he said in a soupy tone of voice "Pardon me, sir, but are you proposing to enter the Ritz Hotel in that hat?" I knew that the time had come when Bertram must show that iron resolution of his which has been so widely publicized.

In the matter of head-joy Jeeves is not in tune with modern progressive thought, his attitude being best described, perhaps, as hidebound, and right from the start I had been asking myself what his reaction would be to the blue Alpine hat with the pink feather in it which I had purchased in his absence. Now I knew. I could see at a g. that he wanted no piece of it and that the picture rising before his eyes of the young master parading London's West End with it perched on his bean was plainly one that he viewed with concern and looked askance at.

I, in sharp contradistinction, was all for this Alpine lid. With me, when I saw it in the shop, it had been a case of love at first sight. I was prepared to concede that it would have been more suitable for rural wear, but against this had to be set the fact that it unquestionably lent a diablerie to my appearance, and mine is an appearance that needs all the diablerie it can get. In my voice, therefore, as I replied, there was a touch of steel.

"Yes, Jeeves, I am."

"Very good, sir."

"You don't like this hat?"

"No, sir."

"Well, I do," I said rather cleverly, and went out with it tilted just that merest shade over the left eyebrow which makes all the difference.

CHAPTER
TWO

MY DATE at the Ritz was with Emerald Stoker, younger
offspring of that pirate of the Spanish Main, old Pop
Stoker, the character who once kidnapped me on board
his yacht with a view to making me marry his elder daughter
Pauline. Long story, I won't go into it now, merely saying
that the old fathead had got entirely the wrong angle on the
relations between his ewe lamb and myself, we being just
good friends, as the expression is. Fortunately it all ended
happily, with the popsy linked in matrimony with Marma-
duke, Lord Chuffnell, an ancient buddy of mine, and we're
still good friends. I put in an occasional weekend with her
and Chuffy, and when she comes to London on a shopping
binge or whatever it may be, I see to it that she gets her
calories. Quite natural, then, that when her sister Emerald

came over from America to study painting at the Slade, she should have asked me to keep an eye on her and give her lunch from time to time. Kindly old Bertram, the family friend.

I was a bit late, as I had foreshadowed, in getting to the tryst, and she was already there when I arrived. It struck me, as it did every time I saw her, how strange it is that members of a family can be so unlike each other—how different in appearance, I mean, Member A so often is from Member B, and for the matter of that Member B from Member C, if you follow what I'm driving at. Take the Stoker troupe, for instance. To look at them, you'd never have guessed they were united by ties of blood. Old Stoker resembled one of those fellows who play bit parts in gangster pictures; Pauline was of a beauty so radiant that strong men whistled after her in the street; while Emerald, in sharp contradistinction, was just ordinary, no different from a million other nice girls, except perhaps for a touch of the Pekingese about the nose and eyes and more freckles than you usually see.

I always enjoyed putting on the nose bag with her, for there was a sort of motherliness about her which I found restful. She was one of those soothing, sympathetic girls you can take your troubles to, confident of having your hand held and your head patted. I was still a bit ruffled about Jeeves and the Alpine hat and of course told her all about it, and nothing could have been in better taste than her attitude. She said it sounded as if Jeeves must be something like her father—she had never met him—Jeeves, I mean, not her father, whom of course she had met frequently—and she told me I had been quite right in displaying the velvet hand in the iron glove, or rather the other way around, isn't it, because it never did to let oneself be bossed. Her father, she said, always tried to boss everybody, and in her opinion one of these days some haughty spirit was going to haul off and poke him in the nose—which, she said, and I agreed with her, would do him all the good in the world.

I was so grateful for these kind words that I asked her if she would care to come to the theater on the following night, I knowing where I could get hold of a couple of tickets for a well-spoken-of musical, but she said she couldn't make it.

"I'm going down to the country this afternoon to stay with some people. I'm taking the four o'clock train at Paddington."

"Going to be there long?"

"About a month."

"At the same place all the time?"

"Of course."

She spoke lightly, but I found myself eyeing her with a certain respect. Myself, I've never found a host and hostess who could stick my presence for more than about a week. Indeed, long before that as a general rule the conversation at the dinner table is apt to turn on the subject of how good the train service to London is, those present obviously hoping wistfully that Bertram will avail himself of it. Not to mention the timetables left in your room with a large cross against the two thirty-five and the legend "Excellent train. Highly recommended."

"Their name's Bassett." I started visibly. "They live in Gloucestershire." I started visibly. "Their house is called—"

"Totleigh Towers?"

She started visibly, making three visible starts in all.

"Oh, do you know them? Well, that's fine. You can tell me about them."

This surprised me somewhat.

"Why, don't *you* know them?"

"I've only met Miss Bassett. What are the rest of them like?"

It was a subject on which I was a well-informed source, but I hesitated for a moment, asking myself if I ought to reveal to this frail girl what she was letting herself in for. Then I decided that the truth must be told and nothing held back. Cruel to hide the facts from her and allow her to go off to Totleigh Towers unprepared.

"The inmates of the leper colony under advisement," I said, "consist of Sir Watkyn Bassett, his daughter Madeline, his niece Stephanie Byng, a chap named Spode who recently took to calling himself Lord Sidcup, and Stiffy Byng's Aberdeen terrier Bartholomew, the last of whom you would do well to watch closely if he gets anywhere near your ankles, for he biteth like a serpent and stingeth like an adder. So you've met Madeline Bassett? What did you think of her?"

She seemed to weigh this. A moment or two passed before she surfaced again. When she spoke, it was with a spot of wariness in her voice.

"Is she a great friend of yours?"

"Far from it."

"Well, she struck me as a drip."

"She is a drip."

"Of course, she's very pretty. You have to hand her that."

I shook the loaf.

"Looks are not everything. I admit that any red-blooded sultan or pasha, if offered the opportunity of adding M. Bassett to the personnel of his harem, would jump to it without hesitation, but he would regret his impulsiveness before the end of the first week. She's one of those soppy girls, riddled from head to foot with whimsy. She holds the view that the stars are God's daisy chain, that rabbits are gnomes

199

in attendance on the Fairy Queen, and that every time a fairy blows its wee nose a baby is born, which, as we know, is not the case. She's a drooper."

"Yes, that's how she seemed to me. Rather like one of the love-sick maidens in *Patience*."

"Eh?"

"*Patience*. Gilbert and Sullivan. Haven't you ever seen it?"

"Oh yes, now I recollect. My Aunt Agatha made me take her son Thos to it once. Not at all a bad little show, I thought, though a bit highbrow. We now come to Sir Watkyn Bassett, Madeline's father."

"Yes, she mentioned her father."

"And well she might."

"What's he like?"

"One of those horrors from outer space. It may seem a hard thing to say of any man, but I would rank Sir Watkyn Bassett as an even bigger stinker than your father."

"Would you call Father a stinker?"

"Not to his face, perhaps."

"He thinks you're crazy."

"Bless his old heart."

"And you can't say he's wrong. Anyway, he's not so bad, if you rub him the right way."

"Very possibly, but if you think a busy man like myself has time to go rubbing your father, either with or against the grain, you are greatly mistaken. The word 'stinker,' by the way, reminds me that there is one redeeming aspect of life at Totleigh Towers—the presence in the neighboring village of the Rev. H. P. ('Stinker') Pinker, the local curate. You'll like him. He used to play football for England. But watch out for Spode. He's about eight feet high and has the sort of eye that can open an oyster at sixty paces. Take a line through gorillas you have met, and you will get the idea."

"You do seem to have some nice friends."

"No friends of mine. Though I'm fond of young Stiffy and am always prepared to clasp her to my bosom, provided she doesn't start something. But then she always does start something. I think that completes the roster. Oh no, Gussie. I was forgetting Gussie."

"Who's he?"

"Fellow I've known for years and years. He's engaged to Madeline Bassett. Chap named Gussie Fink-Nottle."

She uttered a sharp squeak.

"Does he wear horn-rimmed glasses?"

"Yes."

"And keep newts?"

"In great profusion. Why, do you know him?"

"I've met him. We met at a studio party."

"I didn't know he ever went to studio parties."

"He went to this one, and we talked most of the evening. I thought he was a lamb."

"You mean a fish."

"I don't mean a fish."

"He looks like a fish."

"He does not look like a fish."

"Well, have it your own way," I said tolerantly, knowing it was futile to attempt to reason with a girl who had spent an evening vis-à-vis Gussie Fink-Nottle and didn't think he looked like a fish. "So there you are, that's Totleigh Towers. Wild horses wouldn't drag me there, not that I suppose they would ever try, but you'll probably have a good enough time," I said, for I didn't wish to depress her unduly. "It's a beautiful place, and it isn't as if you were going there to pinch a cow creamer."

"To what a what?"

"Nothing, nothing. I was just thinking of something," I said, and turned the conv. to other topics.

She gave me the impression, when we parted, of being a bit pensive, which I could well understand, and I wasn't feeling too unpensive myself. There's a touch of the superstitious in my makeup, and the way the Bassett ménage seemed to be raising its ugly head, if you know what I mean, struck me as sinister. I had a . . . what's the word? . . . begins with a p . . . pre-something . . . presentiment, that's the baby . . . I had a presentiment that I was being tipped off by my guardian angel that Totleigh Towers was trying to come back into my life and that I would be well advised to watch my step and keep an eye skinned.

It was consequently a thoughtful Bertram Wooster who half an hour later sat toying with a stoup of malvoisie in the smoking room of the Drones Club. To the overtures of fellow members who wanted to hurry me from sport to sport I turned a deaf ear, for I wished to brood. And I was trying to tell myself that all this Totleigh Towers business was purely coincidental and meant nothing, when the smoking-room waiter slid up and informed me that a gentleman stood without, asking to have a speech with me. A clerical gentleman named Pinker, he said, and I gave another of my visible starts, the presentiment stronger on the wing than ever.

It wasn't that I had any objection to the sainted Pinker. I loved him like a b. We were up at Oxford together, and our relations have always been on strictly David and Jonathan lines. But, while technically not a resident of Totleigh Towers, he helped the Vicar vet the souls of the local yokels in the adjoining village of Totleigh-in-the-Wold, and that was near enough to it to make this sudden popping up of his deepen the apprehension I was feeling. It seemed to me that it only needed Sir Watkyn Bassett, Madeline Bassett, Roderick Spode, and the dog Bartholomew to saunter in, arm in arm, and I would have a full hand. My respect for my guardian angel's astuteness hit a new high. A gloomy bird, with a marked disposition to take the dark view and make one's flesh creep, but there was no gainsaying that he knew his stuff.

"Bung him in," I said dully, and in due season the Rev. H. P. Pinker lumbered across the threshold and, advancing with outstretched hand, tripped over his feet and upset a small table, his almost invariable practice when moving from spot to spot in any room where there's furniture.

CHAPTER
THREE

WHICH WAS ODD, when you came to think of it, because after representing his University for four years and his country for six on the football field, he still turns out for the Harlequins when he can get a Saturday off from saving souls, and when footballing is as steady on his pins as a hart or roe or whatever the animals are that don't trip over their feet and upset things. I've seen him a couple of times in the arena and was profoundly impressed by his virtuosity. Rugby football is more or less a sealed book to me, I never having gone in for it, but even I could see that he was good. The lissomeness with which he moved hither and thither was most impressive, as was his homicidal ardor when doing what I believe is called tackling. Like the Canadian Mounted Police, he always got his man, and when he did so the air was vibrant with the excited cries of morticians in the audience making bids for the body.

He's engaged to be married to Stiffy Byng, and his long years of football should prove an excellent preparation for setting up house with her. The way I look at it is that when a fellow has had plug-uglies in cleated boots doing a Shuffle-off-to-Buffalo on his face Saturday after Saturday since he was a slip of a boy, he must get to fear nothing, not even marriage with a girl like Stiffy, who from early childhood has seldom let the sun go down without starting some loony enterprise calculated to bleach the hair of one and all.

There was plenty and to spare of the Rev. H. P. Pinker. Even as a boy, I imagine, he must have burst seams and broken try-your-weight machines, and grown to man's estate he might have been Roderick Spode's twin brother. Purely in the matter of thews, sinews, and tonnage, I mean of course, for whereas Roderick Spode went about seeking whom he might devour and was a consistent menace to pedestrians and traffic, Stinker, though no doubt a fiend in human shape when assisting the Harlequins Rugby football club to dismember some rival troop of athletes, was in private life a gentle soul with whom a child could have played. In fact, I once saw a child doing so.

Usually when you meet this man of God, you find him beaming. I believe his merry smile is one of the sights of Totleigh-in-the-Wold, as it was of Magdalen College, Oxford, when we were up there together. But now I seemed to note in his aspect a certain gravity, as if he had just discovered schism in his flock or found a couple of choir boys smoking reefers in the churchyard. He gave me the impression of a two-hundred-pound curate with something on his mind besides his hair. Upsetting another table, he took a seat and said he was glad he had caught me.

"I thought I'd find you at the Drones."

"You have," I assured him. "What brings you to the metrop?"

"I came up for a Harlequins committee meeting."

"And how were they all?"

"Oh, fine."

"That's good. I've been worrying myself sick about the Harlequins committee. Well, how have you been keeping, Stinker?"

"I've been all right."

"Are you free for dinner?"

"Sorry, I've got to get back to Totleigh."

"Too bad. Jeeves tells me Sir Watkyn and Madeline and Stiffy have been staying with my aunt at Brinkley."

"Yes."

"Have they returned?"

"Yes."

"And how's Stiffy?"

"Oh, fine."

"And Bartholomew?"

"Oh, fine."

"And your parishioners? Going strong, I trust?"

"Oh yes, they're fine."

I wonder if anything strikes you about the slice of give-and-take I've just recorded. No? Oh, surely. I mean, here were we, Stinker Pinker and Bertram Wooster, buddies who had known each other virtually from the egg, and we were talking like a couple of strangers making conversation on a train. At least, he was, and more and more I became convinced that his bosom was full of the perilous stuff that weighs upon the heart, as I remember Jeeves putting it once.

I persevered in my efforts to uncork him.

"Well, Stinker," I said, "what's new? Has Pop Bassett given you that vicarage yet?"

This caused him to open up a bit. His manner became more animated.

"No, not yet. He doesn't seem able to make up his mind. One day he says he will, the next day he says he's not so sure, he'll have to think it over."

I frowned. I disapproved of this shilly-shallying. I could see how it must be throwing a spanner into Stinker's whole foreign policy, putting him in a spot and causing him alarm and despondency. He can't marry Stiffy on a curate's stipend, so they've got to wait till Pop Bassett gives him a vicarage, which he has in his gift. And while I personally, though fond of the young gumboil, would run a mile in tight shoes to avoid marrying Stiffy, I knew him to be strongly in favor of signing her up.

"Something always happens to put him off. I think he was about ready to close the deal before he went to stay at Brinkley, but most unfortunately I bumped into a valuable vase of his and broke it. It seemed to rankle rather."

I heaved a sigh. It's always what Jeeves would call most disturbing to hear that a chap with whom you have plucked the gowans fine, as the expression is, isn't making out as well as could be wished. I was all set to follow this Pinker's career with considerable interest, but the way things were shaping it began to look as if there wasn't going to be a career to follow.

"You move in a mysterious way your wonders to perform, Stinker. I believe you would bump into something if you were crossing the Gobi desert."

"I've never been in the Gobi desert."

"Well, don't go. It isn't safe. I suppose Stiffy's sore about this . . . what's the word? . . . Not vaseline. . . . Vacillation, that's it. She chafes, I imagine, at this vacillation on Bassett's part and resents him letting 'I dare not' wait upon 'I would,' like the poor cat in the adage. Not my own, that, by the way. Jeeves'. Pretty steamed up, isn't she?"

"She is rather."

"I don't blame her. Enough to upset any girl. Pop Bassett has no right to keep gumming up the course of true love like this."

"No."

"He needs a kick in the pants."

"Yes."

"If I were Stiffy, I'd put a toad in his bed or strychnine in his soup."

"Yes. And talking of Stiffy, Bertie—"

He broke off, and I eyed him narrowly. There could be no question to my mind that I had been right about that perilous stuff. His bosom was obviously chock full of it.

"There's something the matter, Stinker."

"No, there isn't. Why do you say that?"

"Your manner is strange. You remind me of a faithful dog looking up into its proprietor's face as if it were trying to tell him something. Are you trying to tell me something?"

He swallowed once or twice, and his color deepened, which took a bit of doing, for even when his soul is in repose he always looks like a clerical beetroot. It was as though the collar he buttons at the back was choking him. In a hoarse voice he said, "Bertie."

"Hullo?"

"Bertie."

"Still here, old man, and hanging on your lips."

"Bertie, are you busy just now?"

"Not more than usual."

"You could get away for a day or two?"

"I suppose one might manage it."

"Then can you come to Totleigh?"

"To stay with you, do you mean?"

"No, to stay at Totleigh Towers."

I stared at the man, wide-eyed as the expression is. Had it not been that I knew him to be abstemiousness itself, rarely indulging in anything stronger than a light lager, and not even that during Lent, I should have leaped to the conclusion that there beside me sat a curate who had been having a couple. My eyebrows rose till they nearly disarranged my front hair.

"Stay *where?* Stinker, you're not yourself, or you wouldn't be gibbering like this. You can't have forgotten the ordeal I passed through last time I went to Totleigh Towers."

"I know. But there's something Stiffy wants you to do for her. She wouldn't tell me what it was, but she said it was most important and that you would have to be on the spot to do it."

I drew myself up. I was cold and resolute.

"You're crazy, Stinker!"

"I don't see why you say that."

"Then let me explain where your whole scheme falls to the ground. To begin with, is it likely that after what has passed between us Sir Watkyn B. would issue an invitation to one who has always been to him a pain in the neck to end all pains in the neck? If ever there was a man who was all in favor of me taking the high road while he took the low road, it is this same Bassett. His idea of a happy day is one spent with at least a hundred miles between him and Bertram."

"Madeline would invite you, if you sent her a wire asking if you could come for a day or two. She never consults Sir

Watkyn about guests. It's an understood thing that she has anyone she wants to at the house."

This I knew to be true, but I ignored the suggestion and proceeded remorselessly.

"In the second place, I know Stiffy. A charming girl whom, as I was telling Emerald Stoker, I am always prepared to clasp to my bosom—at least I would be if she wasn't engaged to you—but one who is a cross between a ticking bomb and a poltergeist. She lacks that balanced judgment which we like to see in girls. She gets ideas, and if you care to call them bizarre ideas, it will be all right with me. I need scarcely remind you that when I last visited Totleigh Towers she egged you on to pinch Constable Eustace Oates' helmet, the one thing a curate should shrink from doing if he wishes to rise to heights in the Church. She is, in short, about as loony a young shrimp as ever wore a windswept hairdo. What this commission is that she has in mind for me we cannot say, but going by the form book I see it as something totally unfit for human consumption. Didn't she even hint at its nature?"

"No. I asked, of course, but she said she would rather keep it under her hat till she saw you."

"She won't see me."

"You won't come to Totleigh?"

"Not within fifty miles of the sewage dump."

"She'll be terribly disappointed."

"You will administer spiritual solace. That's your job. Tell her these things are sent to try us."

"She'll probably cry."

"Nothing better for the nervous system. It does something, I forget what, to the glands. Ask any well-known Harley Street physician."

I suppose he saw that my iron front was not to be shaken,

for he made no further attempt to sell the idea to me. With a sigh that seemed to come up from the soles of the feet, he rose, said goodbye, knocked over the glass from which I had been refreshing myself, and withdrew.

Knowing how loath Bertram Wooster always is to let a pal down and fail him in his hour of need, you are probably thinking that this distressing scene had left me shaken, but as a matter of fact it had bucked me up like a day at the seaside.

Let's just review the situation. Ever since breakfast my guardian angel had been scaring the pants off me by practically saying in so many words that Totleigh Towers was all set to re-enter my life, and it was now clear that what he had in mind had been the imminence of this plea to me to go there, he feeling that in a weak moment I might allow myself to be persuaded against my better judgment. The peril was now past. Totleigh Towers had made its spring and missed by a mile, and I no longer had a thing to worry about. It was with a light heart that I joined a group of pleasure-seekers who were playing darts and cleaned them up with effortless skill. Three o'clock was approaching when I left the club en route for home, and it must have been getting on for half past when I hove alongside the apartment house where I have my abode.

There was a cab standing outside, laden with luggage. From its window Gussie Fink-Nottle's head was poking out, and I remember thinking once again how mistaken Emerald Stoker had been about his appearance. Seeing him steadily, if not whole, I could detect in his aspect no trace of the lamb, but he was looking so like a halibut that if he hadn't been wearing horn-rimmed spectacles, a thing halibuts seldom do, I might have supposed myself to be gazing on something AWOL from a fishmonger's slab.

I gave him a friendly yodel, and he turned the spectacles in my direction.

"Oh, hullo, Bertie," he said, "I've just been calling on you. I left a message with Jeeves. Your aunt told me to tell you she's coming to London the day after tomorrow and she wants you to give her lunch."

"Yes, she was on the phone to that effect this morning. I suppose she thought you'd forget to notify me. Come in and have some orange juice," I said, for it is to that muck that he confines himself with making whoopee.

He looked at his watch, and his eyes lost the gleam that always comes into them when orange juice is mentioned.

"I wish I could, but I can't," he sighed. "I should miss my train. I'm off to Totleigh on the four o'clock at Paddington."

"Oh, really? Well, look out for a friend of yours, who'll be on it. Emerald Stoker."

"Stoker? Stoker? Emerald Stoker?"

"Girl with freckles. American. Looks like a Pekingese of the better sort. She tells me she met you at a studio party the other day, and you talked about newts."

His face cleared.

"Of course, yes. Now I've placed her. I didn't get her name that day. Yes, we had a long talk about newts. She used to keep them herself as a child, only she called them guppies. A most delightful girl. I shall enjoy seeing her again. I don't know when I've met a girl who attracted me more."

"Except, of course, Madeline."

His face darkened. He looked like a halibut that's taken offense at a rude remark from another halibut.

"Madeline! Don't talk to me about Madeline! Madeline makes me sick!" he hissed. "Paddington!" he shouted to the charioteer, and was gone with the wind, leaving me gaping after him, all of a twitter.

CHAPTER
FOUR

AND I'LL tell you why I was all of a t. My critique of her when chatting with Emerald Stoker will have shown how allergic I was to this Bassett beazel. She was scarcely less of a pain in the neck to me than I was to her father or Roderick Spode. Nevertheless, there was a grave danger that I might have to take her for better or for worse, as the book of rules puts it.

The facts may be readily related. Gussie, enamored of the Bassett, would have liked to let her in on the way he felt, but every time he tried to do so his nerve deserted him and he found himself babbling about newts. At a loss to know how to swing the deal, he got the idea of asking me to plead his cause, and when I pleaded it, the Bassett, as pronounced a fathead as ever broke biscuit, thought I was pleading mine. She said she was so so sorry to cause me pain, but her heart belonged to Gussie. Which would have been fine, had she not gone on to say that if anything should ever happen to make her revise her conviction that he was a king among men and she was compelled to give him the heave-ho, I was the next in line, and while she could never love me with the same fervor she felt for Gussie, she would do her best to make me happy. I was, in a word, in the position of a Vice-President of the United States of America who, while feeling that he is all right so far, knows that he will be for it at a moment's notice if anything goes wrong with the man up top.

Little wonder, then, that Gussie's statement that Madeline made him sick smote me like a ton of bricks and had me indoors and bellowing for Jeeves before you could say what ho. As had so often happened before, I felt that my only course was to place myself in the hands of a higher power.

"Sir?" he said, manifesting himself.

"A ghastly thing has happened, Jeeves! Disaster looms."

"Indeed, sir? I am sorry to hear that."

There's one thing you have to give Jeeves credit for. He lets the dead past bury its d. He and the young master may have had differences about Alpine hats with pink feathers in them, but when he sees the y. m. on the receiving end of the slings and arrows of outrageous fortune, he sinks his dudgeon and comes through with the feudal spirit at its best. So now, instead of being cold and distant and aloof, as a lesser man would have been, he showed the utmost agitation and concern. That is to say, he allowed one eyebrow to rise perhaps an eighth of an inch, which is as far as he ever goes in the way of expressing emotion.

"What would appear to be the trouble, sir?"

215

I sank into a chair and mopped the frontal bone. Not for many a long day had I been in such a doodah.

"I've just seen Gussie Fink-Nottle."

"Yes, sir. Mr. Fink-Nottle was here a moment ago."

"I met him outside. He was in a cab. And do you know what?"

"No, sir."

"I happened to mention Miss Bassett's name, and he said—follow this closely, Jeeves—he said—I quote—'Don't talk to me about Madeline. Madeline makes me sick.' Close quotes."

"Indeed, sir?"

"Those are not the words of love."

"No, sir."

"They are the words of a man who for some reason not disclosed is fed to the front teeth with the adored object. I hadn't time to go into the matter, because a moment later he was off like a scalded cat to Paddington, but it's pretty clear there must have been a rift in the what-d' you-call-it. Begins with an l."

"Would lute be the word for which you are groping, sir?"

"Possibly. I don't know that I'd care to bet on it."

"The poet Tennyson speaks of the little rift within the lute, that by and by will make the music mute and ever widening slowly silence all."

"Then lute it is. And we know what's going to happen if this particular lute goes phut."

We exchanged significant glances. At least, I gave him a significant glance, and he looked like a stuffed frog, his habit when being discreet. He knows just how I'm situated as regards M. Bassett, but naturally we don't discuss it except by going into the sig-glance-stuffed-frog routine. I mean, you can't talk about a thing like that. I don't know if it would actually come under the head of speaking lightly of a woman's name, but it wouldn't be seemly, and the Woosters are sticklers for seemliness. So, for that matter, are the Jeeveses.

"What ought I to do, do you think?"

"Sir?"

"Don't stand there saying 'Sir?' You know as well as I do that a situation has arisen which calls for the immediate coming of all good men to the aid of the party. It is of the essence that Gussie's engagement does not spring a leak. Steps must be taken."

"It would certainly seem advisable, sir."

"But what steps? I ought, of course, to hasten to the seat of war and try to start the dove of peace going into its act—have a bash, in other words, at seeing what a calm, kindly man of the world can do to bring the young folks together, if you get what I mean."

"I apprehend you perfectly, sir. Your role, as I see it, would be that of what the French call the *raisonneur*."

"You're probably right. But mark this. Apart from the fact that the mere thought of being under the roof of Totleigh Towers again is one that freezes the gizzard, there's another snag. I was talking to Stinker Pinker just now, and he says that Stiffy Byng has something she wants me to do for her. Well, you know the sort of thing Stiffy generally wants people to do. You recall the episode of Constable Oates' helmet?"

"Very vividly, sir."

"Oates had incurred her displeasure by reporting to her Uncle Watkyn that her dog Bartholomew had spilled him off his bicycle, causing him to fall into a ditch and sustain bruises and contusions, and she persuaded Harold Pinker, a man in holy orders who buttons his collar at the back, to pinch his helmet for her. And that was comparatively mild for Stiffy. There are no limits, literally none, to what she can think of when she gives her mind to it. The imagination boggles at the thought of what she may be cooking up for me."

"Certainly you may be pardoned for feeling apprehensive, sir."

"So there you are. I'm on the horns of . . . what are those things you get on the horns of?"

"Dilemmas, sir."

"That's right. I'm on the horns of a dilemma. Shall I, I ask myself, go and see what I can accomplish in the way of running repairs on the lute, or would it be more prudent to stay put and let nature take its course, trusting to Time, the great healer, to do its stuff?"

"If I might make a suggestion, sir?"

"Press on, Jeeves."

"Would it not be possible for you to go to Totleigh Towers but to decline to carry out Miss Byng's wishes?"

I weighed this. It was, I could see, a thought.

"Issue a *nolle prosequi*, you mean? Tell her to go and boil her head?"

"Precisely, sir."

I eyed him reverently.

"Jeeves," I said, "as always, you have found the way. I'll wire Miss Bassett asking if I can come, and I'll wire Aunt Dahlia that I can't give her lunch, as I'm leaving town. And I'll tell Stiffy that whatever she has in mind, she gets no service and cooperation from me. Yes, Jeeves, you've hit it. I'll go to Totleigh, though the flesh creeps at the prospect. Pop Bassett will be there. Spode will be there. Stiffy will be there. The dog Bartholomew will be there. It makes one wonder why so much fuss has been made about those half-a-league half-a-league half-a-league-onward bimbos who rode into the Valley of Death. They weren't going to find Pop Bassett at the other end. Ah well, let us hope for the best."

"The only course to pursue, sir."

"Stiff upper lip, Jeeves, what?"

"Indubitably, sir. That, if I may say so, is the spirit."

CHAPTER
FIVE

As STINKER had predicted, Madeline Bassett placed no obstacle in the way of my visiting Totleigh Towers. In response to my invitation-cadging missive she gave me the green light, and an hour or so after her telegram had arrived Aunt Dahlia rang up from Brinkley, full of eagerness to ascertain what the hell, she having just received my wire saying that owing to absence from the metropolis I would be unable to give her the lunch for which she had been budgeting.

Her call came as no surprise. I had anticipated that there might be a certain liveliness on the Brinkley front. The old flesh and blood is a genial soul who loves her Bertram dearly, but she is a woman of imperious spirit. She dislikes having her wishes thwarted, and her voice came booming at me like a pack of hounds in full cry.

"Bertie, you foul young blot on the landscape?"

"Speaking."

"I got your telegram."

"I thought you would. Very efficient, the gramming service."

"What do you mean, you're leaving town? You never leave town except to come down here and wallow in Anatole's cooking."

Her allusion was to her peerless French chef, at the mention of whose name the mouth starts watering automatically. God's gift to the gastric juices I have sometimes called him.

"Where are you going?"

My mouth having stopped watering, I said I was going to Totleigh Towers, and she uttered an impatient snort.

"There's something wrong with this blasted wire. It sounded as if you were saying you were going to Totleigh Towers."

"I am."

"To Totleigh *Towers?*"

"I leave this afternoon."

"What in the world made them invite you?"

"They didn't. I invited myself."

"You mean you're deliberately seeking the society of Sir Watkyn Bassett? You must be more of an ass than even I have ever thought you. And I speak as a woman who has just had the old bounder in her hair for more than a week."

I saw her point, and hastened to explain.

"I admit Pop Bassett is a bit above the odds," I said, "and unless one is compelled by circumstances it is always wisest not to stir him, but a sharp crisis has been precipitated in my affairs. All is not well between Gussie Fink-Nottle and Madeline Bassett. Their engagement is tottering toward the melting pot, and you know what that engagement means to me. I'm going down there to try to heal the rift."

"What can you do?"

"My role, as I see it, will be that of what the French call the *raisonneur*."

"And what does that mean?"

"Ah, there you have me, but that's what Jeeves says I'll be."

"Are you taking Jeeves with you?"

"Of course. Do I ever stir foot without him?"

"Well, watch out, that's all I say to you; watch out. I happen to know that Bassett is making overtures to him."

"How do you mean, overtures?"

"He's trying to steal him from you."

I reeled, and might have fallen, had I not been sitting at the time.

"Incredulous!"

"If you mean incredible, you're wrong. I told you how he had fallen under Jeeves' spell when he was here. He used to follow him with his eyes as he buttled, like a cat watching a duck, as Anatole would say. And one morning I heard him making him a definite proposition. Well? What's the matter with you? Have you fainted?"

I told her that my momentary silence had been due to the fact that her words had stunned me, and she said she didn't see why, knowing Bassett, I should be so surprised.

"You can't have forgotten how he tried to steal Anatole. There isn't anything to which that man won't stoop. He has no conscience whatsoever. When you get to Totleigh, go and see someone called Plank and ask him what he thinks of Sir Watkyn ruddy Bassett. He chiseled this poor devil Plank out of a . . . Oh, hell!" said the aged relative as a voice intoned "Thur-ree minutes," and she hung up, having made my flesh creep as nimbly as if she had been my guardian angel, on whose talent in that direction I have already touched.

222

It was still creeping with undiminished gusto as I steered the sports model along the road to Totleigh-in-the-Wold that afternoon. I was convinced, of course, that Jeeves would never dream of severing relations with the old firm, and when urged to do so by this blighted Bassett would stop his ears like the deaf adder, which, as you probably know, made a point of refusing to hear the voice of the charmer, charm he never so wisely. But the catch is that you can be convinced about a thing and nevertheless get pretty jumpy when you muse on it, and it was in no tranquil mood that I eased the Arab steed through the gates of Totleigh Towers and fetched up at the front door.

I don't know if you happen to have come across a hymn, the chorus of which goes

> *Tum tumty tumty tumty*
> *Tum tiddly om pom isle,*
> *Where every prospect pleases*
> *And only man is vile*

or words to that effect, but the description would have fitted Totleigh Towers like the paper on the wall. Its façade, its spreading grounds, rolling parkland, smoothly shaven lawns and what not were all just like Mother makes, but what percentage was there in that, when you knew what was waiting for you inside? It's never a damn bit of use a prospect pleasing if the gang that goes with it lets it down.

This lair of old Bassett's was one of the fairly stately homes of England—not a showplace like the joints you read about with three hundred and sixty-five rooms, fifty-two staircases, and twelve courtyards, but definitely not a bungalow. He had bought it furnished some time previously from a Lord Somebody who needed cash, as so many do these days.

Not Pop Bassett, though. In the evening of his life he had more than a sufficiency. It would not be going too far, indeed, to describe him as stinking rich. For a great part of his adult life he had been a metropolitan police magistrate, and in that capacity once fined me five quid for a mere lighthearted peccadillo on Boat Race Night, when a mild reprimand would more than have met the case. It was shortly after this that a relative died and left him a vast fortune. That, at least, was the story given out. What really happened, of course, was that all through his years as a magistrate he had been trousering the fines, amassing the stuff in sackfuls. Five quid here, five quid there, it soon mounts up.

We had made goodish going on the road, and it wasn't more than about four-forty when I rang the front-door bell. Jeeves took the car to the stables, and the butler—Butterfield was his name, I remembered—led me to the drawing room.

"Mr. Wooster," he said, loosing me in.

I was not surprised to find tea in progress, for I had heard the clinking of cups. Madeline Bassett was at the controls, and she extended a drooping hand to me.

"Bertie! How nice to see you."

I can well imagine that a casual observer, if I had confided to him my qualms at the idea of being married to this girl, would have raised his eyebrows and been at a loss to understand, for she was undeniably an eyeful, being slim, svelte, and bountifully equipped with golden hair and all the fixings. But where the casual observer would have been making his bloomer was in overlooking that squashy soupiness of hers, that subtle air she had of being on the point of talking baby talk. She was the sort of girl who puts her hands over a husband's eyes, as he is crawling in to breakfast with a morning head, and says, "Guess who?"

I once stayed at the residence of a newly married pal of mine, and his bride had had carved in large letters over the fireplace in the drawing room, where it was impossible to miss it, the legend "Two Lovers Built This Nest," and I can still recall the look of dumb anguish in the other half of the sketch's eyes every time he came in and saw it. Whether Madeline Bassett, on entering the marital state, would go to such an awful extreme, one could not say, but it seemed most probable, and I resolved that when I started trying to reconcile her and Gussie, I would not scamp my work but would give it everything I had.

"You know Mr. Pinker," she said, and I perceived that Stinker was present. He was safely wedged in a chair and hadn't, as far as I could see, upset anything yet, but he gave me the impression of a man who was crouching for the spring and would begin to operate shortly. There was a gateleg table laden with muffins and cucumber sandwiches, which I foresaw would attract him like a magnet.

On seeing me, he had started visibly, dropping a plate with half a muffin on it, and his eyes had widened. I knew what he was thinking, of course. He supposed that my presence must be due to a change of heart. Rejoice with me, for I have found the sheep which was lost, he was no doubt murmuring to himself. I mourned in spirit a bit for the poor fish, knowing what a nasty knock he had coming to him when he got on to it that nothing was going to induce me to undertake whatever the foul commission might be that Stiffy had earmarked for me. On that point I was resolved to be firm, no matter what spiritual agonies he and she suffered in the process. I had long since learned that the secret of a happy and successful life was to steer clear of any project masterminded by that young scourge of the species.

The conversation that followed was what you might

call . . . I've forgotten the word, but it begins with a d. I mean, with Stinker within earshot Madeline and I couldn't get down to brass tacks, so we just chewed the fat . . . desultory, that's the word I wanted. We just chewed the fat in a desultory way. Stinker said he was there to talk over the forthcoming school treat with Sir Watkyn, and I said, "Oh, is there a school treat coming up?" And Madeline said it was taking place the day after tomorrow and owing to the illness of the vicar Mr. Pinker would be in sole charge, and Stinker winced a bit, as if he didn't like the prospect much.

Madeline asked if I had had a nice drive down, and I said, "Oh, splendid." Stinker said Stiffy would be so pleased I had come, and I smiled one of my subtle smiles. And then Butterfield came in and said Sir Watkyn could see Mr. Pinker now, and Stinker oozed off. And the moment the door had closed behind curate and butler, Madeline clasped her hands, gave me one of those squashy looks, and said:

"Oh, Bertie, you should not have come here. I had not the heart to deny your pathetic request—I knew how much you yearned to see me again, however briefly, however hopelessly—but was it *wise?* Is it not merely twisting the knife in the wound? Will it not simply cause you needless pain to be near me, knowing we can never be more than just good friends? It is useless, Bertie. You must not hope. I love Augustus."

Her words, as you may well imagine, were music to my e. She wouldn't, I felt, have come out with anything as definite as this if there had been a really serious spot of trouble between her and Gussie. Obviously that crack of his about her making him sick had been a mere passing what-d'-you-call-it, the result of some momentary attack of the pip caused possibly by her saying he smoked too much or something of the sort. Anyway, whatever it was that had rifted the lute was now plainly forgotten and forgiven, and I was saying to myself that, the way things looked, I ought to be able to duck out of here immediately after breakfast tomorrow, when I noticed that a look of pain had spread over her map and that the eyes were dewy.

"It makes me so sad to think of your hopeless love, Bertie," she said, adding something which I didn't quite catch about moths and stars. "Life is so tragic, so cruel. But what can I do?"

"Not a thing," I said heartily. "Just carry on regardless."

"But it breaks my heart."

And with these words she burst into what are sometimes called uncontrollable sobs. She sank into her chair, covering her face with her hands, and it seemed to me that the civil thing to do was to pat her head. This project I now carried out, and I can see, looking back, that it was a mistake. I remember Monty Bodkin of the Drones, who once patted a weeping female on the head, unaware that his betrothed was standing in his immediate rear, drinking the whole thing in, telling me that the catch in this head-patting routine is that, unless you exercise the greatest care, you forget to take your hand off. You just stand there resting it on the subject's bean, and this is apt to cause spectators to purse their lips.

Monty fell into this error and so did I. And the lip-pursing was attended to by Spode, who chanced to enter at this moment. Seeing the popsy bathed in tears, he quivered from stem to stern.

"Madeline!" he yipped. "What's the matter?"

"It is nothing, Roderick, nothing," she replied chokingly.

She buzzed off, no doubt to bathe her eyes, and Spode pivoted round and gave me a penetrating look. He had grown a bit, I noticed, since I had last seen him, being now about nine foot seven. In speaking of him to Emerald Stoker I had, if you remember, compared him to a gorilla, and what I had had in mind had been the ordinary run-of-the-mill gorilla, not the large economy size. What he was looking like now was King Kong. His fists were clenched, his eyes glittered, and the dullest observer could have divined that it was in no sunny spirit that he was regarding Bertram.

CHAPTER
SIX

To EASE the strain, I asked him if he would have a cucumber sandwich, but with an impassioned gesture he indicated that he was not in the market for cucumber sandwiches, though I could have told him, for I had found them excellent, that he was passing up a good thing.

"A muffin?"

No, not a muffin, either. He seemed to be on a diet.

"Wooster," he said, his jaw muscles moving freely, "I can't make up my mind whether to break your neck or not."

"Not" would have been the way my vote would have been cast, but he didn't give me time to say so.

"I was amazed when I heard from Madeline that you had had the effrontery to invite yourself here. Your motive, of course, was clear. You have come to try to undermine her faith in the man she loves and sow doubts in her mind. Like a creeping snake," he added, and I was interested to learn that this was what snakes did. "You had not the elementary decency, when she had made her choice, to accept her decision and efface yourself. You hoped to win her away from Fink-Nottle."

Feeling that it was about time I said something, I got as far as "I," but he shushed me with another of those impassioned gestures. I couldn't remember when I'd met anyone so resolved on hogging the conversation.

"No doubt you will say that your love was so overpowering that you could not resist the urge to tell her of it and plead with her. Utter nonsense. Despicable weakness. Let me tell you, Wooster, that I have loved that girl for years and years, but never by word or look have I so much as hinted it to her. It was a great shock to me when she became engaged to this man Fink-Nottle, but I accepted the situation because I thought that that was where her happiness lay. Though stunned, I kept—"

"A stiff upper lip?"

"—my feelings to myself. I sat—"

"Like Patience on a monument."

"—tight, and said nothing that would give her a suspicion of how I felt. All that mattered was that she should be happy. If you ask me if I approve of Fink-Nottle as a husband for her, I admit frankly that I do not. To me he seems to possess all the qualities that go to make the perfect pill, and I may add that my opinon is shared by her father. But he is the man she has chosen and I abide by her choice. I do not crawl behind Fink-Nottle's back and try to prejudice her against him."

"Very creditable."

"What did you say?"

I said I had said it did him credit. Very white of him, I said I thought it.

"Oh? Well, I suggest to you, Wooster, that you follow my example. And let me tell you that I shall be watching you closely, and I shall expect to see less of this head-stroking you were doing when I came in. If I don't, I'll—"

Just what he proposed to do he did not reveal, though I was able to hazard a guess, for at this moment Madeline returned. Her eyes were pinkish and her general aspect down among the wines and spirits.

"I will show you your room, Bertie," she said in a pale, saintlike voice, and Spode gave me a warning look.

"Be careful, Wooster, be very careful," he said as we went out.

Madeline seemed surprised.

"Why did Roderick tell you to be careful?"

"Ah, that we shall never know. Afraid I might slip on the parquet floor, do you think?"

"He sounded as if he was angry with you. Had you been quarreling?"

"Good heavens, no. Our talk was conducted throughout in an atmosphere of the utmost cordiality."

"I thought he might be annoyed at your coming here."

"On the contrary. Nothing could have exceeded the warmth of his 'Welcome to Totleigh Towers.' "

"I'm so glad. It would pain me so much if you and he were . . . Oh, there's Daddy."

We had reached the upstairs corridor, and Sir Watkyn Bassett was emerging from his room, humming a light air. It died on his lips as he saw me, and he stood staring at me aghast. He reminded me of one of those fellows who spend the night in haunted houses and are found next morning dead to the last drop with a look of awful horror on their faces.

"Oh, Daddy," said Madeline. "I forgot to tell you. I asked Bertie to come here for a few days."

Pop Bassett swallowed painfully.

"When you say a few days—?"

"At least a week, I hope."

"Good God!"

"If not longer."

"Great heavens!"

"There is tea in the drawing room, Daddy."

"I need something stronger than tea," said Pop Bassett in a low, husky voice, and he tottered off, a broken man. The sight of his head disappearing as he made for the lower regions where the snootful awaited him brought to my mind a poem I used to read as a child. I've forgotten most of it, but it was about a storm at sea and the punch line ran " 'We are lost,' the captain shouted, as he staggered down the stairs."

"Daddy seems upset about something," said Madeline.

"He did convey that impression," I said, speaking austerely, for the old blister's attitude had offended me. I could make allowances for him, because naturally a man of regular habits doesn't like suddenly finding Woosters in his midst, but I did feel that he might have made more of an effort to bear up. Think of the Red Indians, Bassett, I would have said to him, had we been on better terms, pointing out that they were never in livelier spirits than when being cooked on both sides at the stake.

This painful encounter, following so quickly on my conversation, if you could call it a conversation, with Spode, might have been expected to depress me, but this was far from being the case. I was so uplifted by the official news that all was well between M. Bassett and G. Fink-Nottle that I gave it little thought. It's never, of course, the ideal setup to come to stay at a house where your host shudders to the depths of his being at the mere sight of you and is compelled to rush to where the bottles are and get a restorative, but the Woosters can take the rough with the s., and the bonging of the gong for dinner some little time later found me in excellent fettle. It was to all intents and purposes with a song on my lips that I straightened my tie and made my way to the trough.

Dinner is usually the meal at which you catch Bertram at his best, and certainly it's the meal I always most enjoy. Many of my happiest hours have been passed in the society of the soup, the fish, the pheasant or whatever it may be, the soufflé, the fruits in their season, and the spot of port to follow. They bring out the best in me. "Wooster," those who know me have sometimes said, "may be a pretty total loss during the daytime hours, but plunge the world in darkness, switch on the soft lights, uncork the champagne, and shove a dinner into him, and you'd be surprised."

But if I am to sparkle and charm all and sundry, I make one proviso—viz., that the company be congenial. And anything less congenial than the co. on this occasion I have seldom encountered. Sir Watkyn Bassett, who was plainly still much shaken at finding me on the premises, was very far from being the jolly old squire who makes the party go from the start. Beyond shooting glances at me over his glasses, blinking as if he couldn't bring himself to believe I was real, and looking away with a quick shudder, he contributed little or nothing to what I have heard Jeeves call the feast of reason and the flow of soul. Add Spode, strong and silent, Madeline Bassett, mournful and drooping, Gussie, also apparently mournful, and Stiffy, who seemed to be in a kind of daydream, and you had something resembling a wake of the less rollicking type.

Somber, that's the word I was trying to think of. The atmosphere was somber. The whole binge might have been a scene from one of those Russian plays my Aunt Agatha sometimes makes me take her son Thos to at the Old Vic in order to improve his mind, which, as is widely known, can do with all the improvement that's coming to it.

It was toward the middle of the meal that, feeling that it was about time somebody said something, I drew Pop Bassett's attention to the table's centerpiece. In any normal house it would have been a bowl of flowers or something on that order, but this being Totleigh Towers it was a small black figure carved of some material I couldn't put a name to. It was so gosh-awful in every respect that I presumed it must be something he had collected recently. My Uncle Tom is always coming back from sales with similar eyesores.

"That's new, isn't it?" I said, and he started violently. I suppose he'd just managed to persuade himself that I was merely a mirage and had been brought up with a round turn on discovering that I was there in the flesh.

"That thing in the middle of the table that looks like the end man in a minstrel show. It's something you got since . . . er . . . since I was here last, isn't it?"

Tactless of me, I suppose, to remind him of that previous visit of mine, and I oughtn't to have brought it up, but these things slip out.

"Yes," he said, having paused for a moment to shudder. "It is the latest addition to my collection."

"Daddy bought it from a man named Plank who lives not far from here at Hockley-cum-Meston," said Madeline.

234

"Attractive little bijou," I said. It hurt me to look at it, but I felt that nothing was to be lost by giving him the old oil. "Just the sort of thing Uncle Tom would like to have. By Jove," I said, remembering, "Aunt Dahlia was speaking to me about it on the phone yesterday, and she told me Uncle Tom would give his eyeteeth to have it in his collection. I'm not surprised. It looks valuable."

"It's worth a thousand pounds," said Stiffy, coming out of her coma and speaking for the first time.

"As much as that? Golly!" Amazing, I was thinking, that magistrates could get to be able to afford expenditure on that scale just by persevering through the years fining people and sticking to the money. "What is it? Soapstone?"

I had said the wrong thing.

"Amber," Pop Bassett snapped, giving me the sort of look he had given me in heaping measure on the occasion when I had stood in the dock before him at Bosher Street Police Court. "Black amber."

"Of course, yes. That's what Aunt Dahlia said, I recall. She spoke very highly of it, let me tell you, extremely highly."

"Indeed?"

"Oh, absolutely."

I had been hoping that this splash of dialogue would have broken the ice, so to speak, and started us off kidding back and forth like the guys and dolls in one of those old-world salons you read about. But no. Silence fell again, and eventually, at long last, the meal came to an end, and two minutes later I was on my way to my room, where I proposed to pass the rest of the evening with an Erle Stanley Gardner I'd brought with me. No sense, as I saw it, in going and mixing with the mob in the drawing room and having Spode glare at me and Pop Bassett sniff at me and Madeline Bassett as likely as not sing old English folk songs at me till bedtime. I was aware that in executing this quiet sneak I was being guilty of a social gaffe which would have drawn raised eyebrows from the author of a book of etiquette, but the great lesson we learn from life is to know when and when not to be in the center of things.

CHAPTER
SEVEN

I HAVEN'T mentioned it till now, having been all tied up with other matters, but during dinner, as you may well imagine, something had been puzzling me not a little—the mystery, to wit, of what on earth had become of Emerald Stoker.

At that lunch of ours she had told me in no uncertain terms that she was off to Totleigh on the four o'clock train that afternoon, and, however leisurely its progress, it must have got there by this time, because Gussie had traveled on it and he had fetched up at the joint all right. But I could detect no sign of her on the premises. It seemed to me, sifting the evidence, that only one conclusion could be arrived at—that she had been pulling the Wooster leg.

But why? With what motive? That was what I was asking

myself as I sneaked up the stairs to where Erle Stanley Gardner awaited me. If you had cared to describe me as perplexed and bewildered, you would have been perfectly correct.

Jeeves was in my room when I got there, going about his gentleman's gentlemanly duties, and I put my problem up to him.

"Did you ever see a film called *The Vanishing Lady*, Jeeves?"

"No, sir. I rarely attend cinematographic performances."

"Well, it was about a lady who vanished, if you follow what I mean, and the reason I bring it up is that a female friend of mine has apparently disappeared into thin air, leaving not a wrack behind, as I once heard you put it."

"Highly mysterious, sir."

"You said it. I seek in vain for a solution. When I gave her lunch yesterday, she told me she was off on the four o'clock train to go and stay at Totleigh Towers, and the point I want to drive home is that she hasn't arrived. You remember the day I lunched at the Ritz?"

"Yes, sir. You were wearing an Alpine hat."

"There is no need to dwell on the Alpine hat, Jeeves."

"No, sir."

"If you really want to know, several fellows at the Drones asked me where I had got it."

"No doubt with a view to avoiding your hatter, sir."

I saw that nothing was to be gained by bandying words. I turned the conversation to a pleasanter and less controversial subject.

"Well, Jeeves, you'll be glad to hear that everything's all right."

"Sir?"

"About that lute we were speaking of. No rift. Sound as a bell. I have it straight from the horse's mouth that Miss

Bassett and Gussie are sweethearts still. The relief is stupendous."

I hadn't expected him to clap his hands and leap about, because of course he never does, but I wasn't prepared for the way he took this bit of hot news. He failed altogether to string along with my jocund mood.

"I fear, sir, that you are too sanguine. Miss Bassett's attitude may well be such as you have described, but on Mr. Fink-Nottle's side, I am sorry to say, there exists no little dissatisfaction and resentment."

The smile which had been splitting my face faded. It's never easy to translate what Jeeves says into basic English, but I had been able to grab this one off the bat, and what I believe the French call a *frisson* went through me like a dose of salts.

"You mean she's a sweetheart still, but he isn't?"

"Precisely, sir. I encountered Mr. Fink-Nottle in the stable yard as I was putting away the car, and he confided his troubles to me. His story occasioned me grave uneasiness."

Another *frisson* passed through my frame. I had the unpleasant feeling you get sometimes that centipedes in large numbers are sauntering up and down your spinal column. I feared the worst.

"But what's happened?" I faltered, if faltered's the word.

"I regret to inform you, sir, that Miss Bassett has insisted on Mr. Fink-Nottle adopting a vegetarian diet. His mood is understandably disgruntled and rebellious."

I tottered. In my darkest hour I had never anticipated anything as bad as this. You wouldn't think it to look at him, because he's small and shrimplike and never puts on weight, but Gussie loves food. Watching him tucking into his rations at the Drones, a tapeworm would raise its hat respectfully, knowing that it was in the presence of a master.

Cut him off, therefore, from the roasts and boileds and particularly from cold steak and kidney pie, a dish of which he is inordinately fond, and you turned him into something fit for treasons, stratagems, and spoils, as the fellow said— the sort of chap who would break an engagement as soon as look at you. At the moment of my entry I had been about to light a cigarette, and now the lighter fell from my nerveless hand.

"She's made him become a *vegetarian?*"

"So Mr. Fink-Nottle informed me, sir."

"No chops?"

"No, sir."

"No steaks?"

"No, sir."

"Just spinach and similar garbage?"

"So I gather, sir."

"But why?"

"I understand that Miss Bassett has recently been reading the life of the poet Shelley, sir, and has become converted to his view that the consumption of flesh foods is unspiritual. The poet Shelley held strong opinions on this subject."

I picked up the lighter in a sort of trance. I was aware that Madeline B. was as potty as they come in the matter of stars and rabbits and what happened when fairies blew their wee noses, but I had never dreamed that her goofiness would carry her to such lengths as this. But as the picture rose before my eyes of Gussie at the dinner table picking with clouded brow at what had unquestionably looked like spinach, I knew that his story must be true. No wonder Gussie in agony of spirit had said that Madeline made him sick. Just so might a python at a zoo have spoken of its keeper, had the latter suddenly started feeding it cheese straws in lieu of the daily rabbit.

"But this is frightful, Jeeves!"

"Certainly somewhat disturbing, sir."

"If Gussie is seething with revolt, anything may happen."

"Yes, sir."

"Is there nothing we can do?"

"It might be possible for you to reason with Miss Bassett, sir. You would have a talking point. Medical research has established that the ideal diet is one in which animal and vegetable foods are balanced. A strict vegetarian diet is not recommended by the majority of doctors, as it lacks sufficient protein and in particular does not contain the protein which is built up of the amino acids required by the body. Competent observers have traced some cases of mental disorder to this shortage."

"You'd tell her that?"

"It might prove helpful, sir."

"I doubt it," I said, blowing a despondent smoke ring. "I don't think it would sway her."

"Nor on consideration do I, sir. The poet Shelley regarded the matter from the humanitarian standpoint rather than that of bodily health. He held that we should show reverence for other life-forms, and it is his views that Miss Bassett has absorbed."

A hollow groan escaped me.

"Curse the poet Shelley! I hope he trips over a loose shoelace and breaks his ruddy neck."

"Too late, sir. He is no longer with us."

"Blast all vegetables!"

"Yes, sir. Your concern is understandable. I may mention that the cook expressed herself in a somewhat similar vein when I informed her of Mr. Fink-Nottle's predicament. Her heart melted in sympathy with his distress."

I was in no mood to hear about cooks' hearts, soluble

or otherwise, and I was about to say so when he proceeded.

"She instructed me to apprise Mr. Fink-Nottle that if he were agreeable to visiting the kitchen at some late hour when the household had retired for the night, she would be happy to supply him with cold steak and kidney pie."

It was as if the sun had come smiling through the clouds or the long shot on which I had placed my wager had nosed its way past the opposition in the last ten yards and won by a short head. For the peril that had threatened to split the Bassett–Fink-Nottle axis had been averted. I knew Gussie from soup to nuts. Cut him off from the proteins and the amino acids, and you soured his normally amiable nature, turning him into a sullen hater of his species who asked nothing better than to bite his n. and dearest and bite them good. But give him this steak and kidney pie outlet, thus allowing him to fulfill what they call his legitimate aspirations, and chagrin would vanish and he would become his old lovable self once more. The dark scowl would be replaced by the tender simper, the acid crack by the honeyed word, and all would be hotsy-totsy once more with his love life. My bosom swelled with gratitude to the cook whose quick thinking had solved the problem and brought home the bacon.

"Who is she, Jeeves?"

"Sir?"

"This life-saving cook. I shall want to give her a special mention in my evening prayers."

"She is a woman of the name of Stoker, sir."

"*Stoker?* Did you say Stoker?"

"Yes, sir."

"Odd!"

"Sir?"

"Nothing. Just a rather strange coincidence. Have you told Gussie?"

242

"Yes, sir. I found him most cooperative. He plans to present himself in the kitchen shortly after midnight. Cold steak and kidney pie is, of course, merely a palliative—"

"On the contrary. It's Gussie's favorite dish. I've known him to order it even on curry day at the Drones. He loves the stuff."

"Indeed, sir? That is very gratifying."

"Gratifying is the word. What a lesson this teaches us, Jeeves—never to despair, never to throw in the towel and turn our face to the wall, for there is always hope."

"Yes, sir. Would you be requiring anything further?"

"Not a thing, thanks. My cup runneth over."

"Then I will be saying good night, sir."

"Good night, Jeeves."

After he had gone, I put in about half an hour on my Erle Stanley Gardner, but I found rather a difficulty in following the thread and keeping my attention on the clues. My thoughts kept straying to this epoch-making cook. Strange, I felt, that her name should be Stoker. Some relation, perhaps.

I could picture the woman so exactly. Stout, red-faced, spectacled, a little irritable, perhaps, if interrupted when baking a cake or thinking out a sauce, but soft as butter at heart. No doubt something in Gussie's wan aspect had touched her ("That boy needs feeding up, poor little fellow"), or possibly she was fond of goldfish and had been drawn to him because he reminded her of them. Or she may have been a Girl Guide. At any rate, whatever the driving motive behind her day's good deed, she had deserved well of Bertram, and I told myself that a thumping tip should reward her on my departure. Purses of gold should be scattered, and with a lavish hand.

I was musing thus and feeling more benevolent every minute, when who should blow in but Gussie in person, and

I had been right in picturing his aspect as wan. He wore the unmistakable look of a man who has been downing spinach for weeks.

I took it that he had come to ask me what I was doing at Totleigh Towers, a point on which he might naturally be supposed to be curious, but that didn't seem to interest him. He plunged without delay into as forceful a denunciation of the vegetable world as I've ever heard, oddly enough being more bitter about Brussels sprouts and broccoli than about spinach, which I would have expected him to feature. It was some considerable time before I could get a word in, but when I did my voice dripped with sympathy.

"Yes, Jeeves was telling me about that," I said, "and my heart bled for you."

"And so it jolly well ought to have done—in buckets—if you've a spark of humanity in you," he retorted warmly. "Words cannot describe the agonies I've suffered, particularly when staying at Brinkley Court."

I nodded. I knew just what an ordeal it must have been. With Aunt Dahlia's peerless chef wielding the skillet, the last place where you want to be on a vegetarian diet is Brinkley. Many a time when enjoying the old relative's hospitality I've regretted that I had only one stomach to give to the evening's bill of fare.

"Night after night I had to refuse Anatole's unbeatable eatables, and when I tell you that two nights in succession he gave us those Mignonettes de Poulet Petit Duc of his and on another occasion his Timbales de Ris de Veau Toulousaine, you will appreciate what I went through."

It being my constant policy to strew a little happiness as I go by, I hastened to point out the silver lining in the c's.

"Your sufferings must have been terrible," I agreed. "But courage, Gussie. Think of the cold steak and kidney pie."

I had struck the right note. His drawn face softened.

244

"Jeeves told you about that?"

"He said the cook had it all ready and waiting for you, and I remember thinking at the time that she must be a pearl among women."

"That is not putting it at all too strongly. She's an angel in human shape. I spotted her solid merits the moment I saw her."

"You've seen her?"

"Of course I've seen her. You can't have forgotten that talk we had when I was in the cab, about to start off for Paddington. Though why you should have got the idea that she looks like a Pekingese is more than I can imagine."

"Eh? Who?"

"Emerald Stoker. She doesn't look in the least like a Pekingese."

"What's Emerald Stoker got to do with it?"

He seemed surprised.

"Didn't she tell you?"

"Tell me what?"

"That she was on her way here to take office as the Totleigh Towers cook."

I goggled. I thought for a moment that the privations through which he was passing must have unhinged this newt fancier's brain.

"Did you say *cook?*"

"I'm surprised she didn't tell you. I suppose she felt that you weren't to be trusted to keep her secret. She would, of course, have spotted you as a babbler from the outset. Yes, she's the cook all right."

"But *why* is she the cook?" I said, getting down to the *res* in that direct way of mine.

"She explained that fully to me on the train. It appears that she's dependent on a monthly allowance from her father in New York, and normally she gets by reasonably comfortably on this. But early this month she was unfortunate in her investments on the turf. Sunny Jim in the three o'clock at Kempton Park."

I recalled the horse to which he referred. Only prudent second thoughts had kept me from having a bit on it myself.

"The animal ran sixth in a field of seven and she lost her little all. She was then faced with the alternative of applying to her father for funds, which would have necessitated a full confession of her rash act, or of seeking some gainful occupation which would tide her over till, as she put it, the United States Marines arrived."

"She could have touched me or her sister Pauline."

"My good ass, a girl like that doesn't borrow money. Much too proud. She decided to become a cook. She tells me she didn't hesitate more than about thirty seconds before making her choice."

I wasn't surprised. To have come clean to the paternal parent would have been to invite hell of the worst description. Old Stoker was not the type of father who laughs indulgently when informed by a daughter that she has lost her chemise and foundation garments at the races. I don't suppose he has ever laughed indulgently in his life. I've never seen him even smile. Apprised of his child's goings-on, he would unquestionably have blown his top and reduced her to the level of a fifth-rate power. I have been present on occasions when the old gawd-help-us was going good, and I can testify that his boiling point is low. Quite rightly had she decided that silence was best.

It was quite a load off my mind to be able to file away the Emerald Stoker mystery in my casebook as solved, for I dislike being baffled and the thing had been weighing on me, but there were one or two small points to be cleared up.

"How did she happen to come to Totleigh?"

"I must have been responsible for that. During our talk at that studio party, I remember mentioning that Sir Watkyn was in the market for a cook, and I suppose I must have given her his address, for she applied for the post and got it. These American girls have such enterprise."

"Is she enjoying her job?"

"Thoroughly, according to Jeeves. She's teaching the butler rummy."

"I hope she skins him to the bone."

"No doubt she will when he is sufficiently advanced to play for money. And she tells me she loves to cook. What's her cooking like?"

I could answer that. She had once or twice given me dinner at her flat, and the browsing had been impeccable.

"It melts in the mouth."

"It hasn't melted in mine," said Gussie bitterly. "Ah well," he added, a softer light coming into his eyes, "there's always that steak and kidney pie."

And on this happier note he took his departure.

CHAPTER
EIGHT

IT WAS pretty late when I finished the perusal of my Erle
Stanley Gardner and later when I woke from the light doze
into which I had fallen on closing the volume. Totleigh
Towers had long since called it a day, and all was still
throughout the house except for a curious rumbling noise
proceeding from my interior. After bending an ear to this
for a while, I was able to see what was causing it. I had fed
sparsely at the dinner table, with the result that I had become as hungry as dammit.

I don't know if you have had the same experience, but a
thing I've always found about myself is that it takes very
little to put me off my feed. Let the atmosphere at lunch or
dinner be what you might call difficult, and my appetite
tends to dwindle. I've often had this happen when breaking

bread with my Aunt Agatha, and it had happened again at tonight's meal. What with the strain of constantly catching Pop Bassett's eye and looking hastily away and catching Spode's and looking hastily away and catching Pop's again, I had done far less than justice to Emerald Stoker's no doubt admirable offerings. You read stories sometimes where someone merely toys with his food or even pushes away his plate untasted, and that substantially was what I had done. So now this strange hollow feeling, as if some hidden hand had scooped out my insides with a tablespoon.

This imperative demand for sustenance had probably been coming on during my Erle Stanley Gardnering, but I had been so intent on trying to keep tab on the murder gun and the substitute gun and the gun which Perry Mason had buried in the shrubbery that I hadn't noticed it. Only now had the pangs of hunger really started to throw their weight about, and more and more clearly as they did so there rose before my eyes the vision of that steak and kidney pie which was lurking in the kitchen, and it was as though I could hear a soft voice calling to me, "Come and get it."

It's odd how often you find that out of evil cometh good, as the expression is. Here was a case in point. I had always thought of my previous visit to Totleigh Towers as a total loss. I saw now that I had been wrong. It had been an ordeal testing the nervous system to the utmost, but there was one thing about it to be placed on the credit side of the ledger. I allude to the fact that it had taught me the way to the kitchen. The route lay down the stairs, through the hall, into the dining room, and through the door at the end of the last named. Beyond the door I presumed that there was some sort of passage or corridor and then you were in the steak and kidney pie zone. A simple journey, not to be compared for complexity with some I had taken at night in my time.

With the Woosters to think is to act, and scarcely more than two minutes later I was on my way.

It was dark on the stairs and just as dark, if not darker, in the hall. But I was making quite satisfactory progress and was about halfway through the latter when an unforeseen hitch occurred. I bumped into a human body, the last thing I had expected to encounter en route, and for an instant . . . well, I won't say that everything went black, because everything was black already, but I was considerably perturbed. My heart did one of those spectacular leaps Nijinsky used to do in the Russian Ballet, and I was conscious of a fervent wish that I could have been elsewhere.

Elsewhere, however, being just where I wasn't, I had no option but to grapple with this midnight marauder, and when I did so I was glad to find that he was apparently one who had stunted his growth by smoking as a boy. There was a shrimplike quality about him which I found most encouraging. It seemed to me that it would be an easy task to throttle him into submission, and I was getting down to it with a hearty goodwill when my hand touched what were plainly spectacles and at the same moment a stifled "Hey, look out for my glasses!" told me my diagnosis had been all wrong. This was no thief in the night but an old crony with whom in boyhood days I had often shared my last bar of milk chocolate.

"Oh, hullo, Gussie," I said. "Is that you? I thought you were a burglar."

There was a touch of asperity in his voice as he replied: "Well, I wasn't."

"No, I see that now. Pardonable mistake, though, you must admit."

"You nearly gave me heart failure."

"I, too, was somewhat taken aback. No one more surprised than the undersigned when you suddenly popped up. I thought I had a clear track."

"Where to?"

"Need you ask? The steak and kidney pie. If you've left any."

"Yes, there's quite a bit left."

"Was it good?"

"Delicious."

"Then I think I'll be getting along. Good night, Gussie. Sorry you were troubled."

Continuing on my way, I think I must have lost my bearings a little. Shaken, no doubt, by the recent encounter. These get-togethers take their toll. At any rate, to cut a long story s., what happened was that as I felt my way along the wall I collided with what turned out to be a grandfather clock, for the existence of which I had not budgeted, and it toppled over with a sound like the delivery of several tons of coal through the roof of a conservatory. Glass crashed, pulleys and things parted from their moorings, and as I stood trying to separate my heart from the front teeth in which it had become entangled, the lights flashed on and I beheld Sir Watkyn Bassett.

It was a moment fraught with embarrassment. It's bad enough to be caught by your host prowling about his house after hours even when said host is a warm admirer and close personal friend, and I have, I think, made it clear that Pop Bassett was not one of my fans. He could barely stand the sight of me by daylight, and I suppose I looked even worse to him at one o'clock in the morning.

My feeling of having been slapped between the eyes with a custard pie was deepened by the spectacle of his dressing

251

gown. He was a small man . . . you got the impression, seeing him, that when they were making magistrates there wasn't enough material left over when they came to him . . . and for some reason not easy to explain it nearly always happens that the smaller the ex-magistrate, the louder the dressing gown. His was a bright-purple number with yellow frogs, and I am not deceiving my public when I say that it smote me like a blow, rendering me speechless.

Not that I'd have felt chatty even if he had been upholstered in something quiet in dark blue. I don't believe you can ever be completely at your ease in the company of someone before whom you've stood in the dock saying "Yes, your worship" and "No, your worship" and being told by him that you're extremely lucky to get off with a fine and not fourteen days without the option. This is particularly so if you have just smashed a grandfather clock whose welfare is no doubt very near his heart. At any rate, be that as it may, he was the one to open the conversation, not me.

"Good God!" he said, speaking with every evidence of horror. "You!"

A thing I never know, and probably never will, is what to say when somebody says "You!" to me. A mild "Oh, hullo" was the best I could do on this occasion, and I felt at the time it wasn't good. Better, of course, than "What ho, there, Bassett!" but nevertheless not good.

"Might I ask what you are doing here at this hour, Mr. Wooster?"

Well, I might have laughed a jolly laugh and replied, "Upsetting grandfather clocks," keeping it light, as it were, if you know what I mean, but something told me it wouldn't go so frightfully well. I had what amounted to an inspiration.

"I came down to get a book. I'd finished my Erle Stanley

Gardner and I couldn't seem to drop off to sleep, so I came to see if I couldn't pick up something from your shelves. And in the dark I bumped into the clock."

"Indeed?" he said, putting a wealth of sniffiness into the word. A thing about this undersized little son of a bachelor I ought to have mentioned earlier is that during his career on the bench he was one of those unpleasant sarcastic magistrates who get themselves so disliked by the criminal classes. You know the type. Their remarks are generally printed in the evening papers with the word "laughter" after them in brackets, and they count the day lost when they don't make some unfortunate pickpocket or some wretched drunk and disorderly feel like a piece of cheese. I know that on the occasion when we stood face to face in Bosher Street Police Court he convulsed the audience with three solid yaks at my expense in the first two minutes, bathing me in confusion. "Indeed?" he said. "Might I inquire why you were conducting your literary researches in the dark? It would surely have been well within the scope of even your limited abilities to press a light switch."

He had me there, of course. The best I could say was that I hadn't thought of it, and he sniffed a nasty sniff, as much as to suggest that I was just the sort of dead-from-the-neck-up dumb brick who wouldn't have thought of it. He then turned to the subject of the clock, one which I would willingly have left unventilated. He said he had always valued it highly, it being more or less the apple of his eye.

"My father bought it many years ago. He took it everywhere with him."

Here again I might have lightened things by asking him if his parent wouldn't have found it simpler to have worn a wristwatch, but I felt once more that he was not in the mood.

253

"My father was in the diplomatic service and was constantly transferred from one post to another. He was never parted from the clock. It accompanied him in perfect safety from Rome to Vienna, from Vienna to Paris, from Paris to Washington, from Washington to Lisbon. One would have said it was indestructible. But it had still to pass the supreme test of encountering Mr. Wooster, and that was too much for it. It did not occur to Mr. Wooster . . . one cannot think of everything . . . that light may be obtained by pressing a light switch, so he—"

Here he broke off, not so much because he had finished what he had to say as because at this point in the conversation I sprang on to the top of a large chest which stood some six or seven feet distant from the spot where we were chewing the fat. I may have touched the ground once while in transit, but not more than once and that once not willingly. A cat on hot bricks could not have moved with greater nippiness.

My motives in doing so were founded on a solid basis. Toward the later stages of his observations on the clock I had gradually become aware of a curious sound, as if someone in the vicinity was gargling mouthwash, and looking about me I found myself gazing into the eyes of the dog Bartholomew, which were fixed on me with the sinister intentness which is characteristic of this breed of animal. Aberdeen terriers, possibly owing to their heavy eyebrows, always seem to look at you as if they were in the pulpit of the church of some particularly strict Scottish sect and you were a parishioner of dubious reputation sitting in the front row of the stalls.

Not that I noticed his eyes very much, my attention being riveted on his teeth. He had an excellent set and was baring them, and all I had ever heard of his tendency to bite first

254

and ask questions afterwards passed through my mind in a flash. Hence the leap for life. The Woosters are courageous, but they do not take chances.

Pop Bassett was plainly nonplussed, and it was only when his gaze, too, fell upon Bartholomew that he abandoned what must have been his original theory—that Bertram had cracked under the strain and would do well to lose no time in seeing a good mental specialist. He eyed Bartholomew coldly and addressed him as if he had been up before him in his police court.

"Go away, sir! Lie down, sir! Go away!" he said, rasping, if that's the word.

Well, I could have told him that you can't talk to an Aberdeen terrier in that tone of voice for, except perhaps for Doberman pinschers, there is no breed of dog quicker to take offense.

"Really, the way my niece allows this infernal animal to roam at large about the—"

"House" I suppose he was about to say, but the word remained unspoken. It was a moment for rapid action, not for speech. The gargling noise had increased in volume, and Bartholomew was flexing his muscles and getting under way. He moved, he stirred, he seemed to feel the rush of life along his keel, as the fellow said, and Pop Bassett, with a lissomeness of which I would not have suspected him, took to himself the wings of the dove and floated down beside me on the chest. Whether he clipped a second or two off my time I cannot say, but I rather think he did.

"This is intolerable!" he said as I moved courteously to make room for him, and I could see the thing from his point of view. All he asked from life, now that he had made his pile, was to be as far away as possible from Bertram Wooster, and here he was cheek by jowl, as you might say, on a rather uncomfortable chest with him. A certain peevishness was inevitable.

"Not too good," I agreed. "Unquestionably open to criticism, the animal's behavior."

"He must be off his head. He knows me perfectly well. He sees me every day."

"Ah," I said, putting my finger on the weak spot in his argument, "but I don't suppose he's ever seen you in that dressing gown."

I had been too outspoken. He let me see at once that he had taken umbrage.

"What's wrong with my dressing gown?" he demanded hotly.

"A bit on the bright side, don't you think?"

"No, I do not."

"Well, that's how it would strike a high-strung dog."

I paused here to chuckle softly, and he asked what the devil I was giggling about. I put him abreast.

"I was merely thinking that I wish we *could* strike the high-strung dog. The trouble on these occasions is that one is always weaponless. It was the same some years ago when an angry swan chased self and friend on to the roof of a sort of boathouse building at my Aunt Agatha's place in Hertfordshire. Nothing would have pleased us better than to bung a brick at the bird, or slosh him with a boathook, but we had no brick and were short of boathooks. We had to wait till Jeeves came along, which he eventually did in answer to our cries. It would have thrilled you to have seen Jeeves on that occasion. He advanced dauntlessly and—"

"Mr. Wooster!"

"Speaking."

"Kindly spare me your reminiscences."

"I was merely saying—"

"Well, don't."

Silence fell. On my part, a wounded silence, for all I'd tried to do was take his mind off things with entertaining chitchat. I moved an inch or two away from him in a marked manner. The Woosters do not force their conversation on the unwilling.

All this time Bartholomew had been trying to join us, making a series of energetic springs. Fortunately Providence in its infinite wisdom had given Scotties short legs, and though full of the will to win he could accomplish nothing constructive. However much an Aberdeen terrier may bear 'mid snow and ice a banner with the strange device Excelsior, he nearly always has to be content with dirty looks and the sharp, passionate bark.

Some minutes later my fellow rooster came out of the silence. No doubt the haughtiness of my manner had intimidated him, for there was a mildness in his voice which had not been there before.

"Mr. Wooster."

I turned coldly.

"Were you addressing me, Bassett?"

"There must be something we can do."

"You might fine the animal five pounds."

"We cannot stay here all night."

"Why not? What's to stop us?"

This held him. He relapsed into silence once more. And we were sitting there like a couple of Trappist monks when a voice said "Well, for heaven's sake!" and I perceived that Stiffy was with us.

Not surprising, of course, that she should have turned up sooner or later. If Scotties come, I ought to have said to myself, can Stiffy be far behind?

CHAPTER
NINE

CONSIDERING THAT so substantial a part of her waking
hours is devoted to thrusting innocent bystanders into the
soup, Stiffy is far prettier than she has any right to be. She's
on the small side—petite, I believe, is the technical term—
and I have always felt that when she and Stinker walk up
the aisle together, if they ever do, their disparity in height
should be good for a laugh or two from the ringside pews.
The thought has occurred to me more than once that the
correct response for Stinker to make, when asked by the
M.C. if he is prepared to take this Stephanie to be his
wedded wife, would be "Why, certainly, what there is of
her."

"What on earth do you two think you're doing?" she inquired, not unnaturally surprised to see her uncle and an

old friend in our current position. "And why have you been upsetting the furniture?"

"That was me," I said. "I bumped into the grandfather clock. I'm as bad as Stinker, aren't I, bumping into things, ha-ha."

"Less of the ha-ha," she riposted warmly. "And don't mention yourself in the same breath as my Harold. Well, that doesn't explain why you're sitting up there like a couple of buzzards on a treetop."

Pop Bassett intervened, speaking at his sniffiest. Her comparison of him to a buzzard, though perfectly accurate, seemed to have piqued him.

"We were savagely attacked by your dog."

"Not so much attacked," I said, "as given nasty looks. We didn't vouchsafe him time to attack us, deeming it best to get out of his sphere of influence before he could settle down to work. He's been trying to get at us for the last two hours; at least it seems like two hours."

She was quick to defend the dumb chum.

"Well, how can you blame the poor angel? Naturally he thought you were international spies in the pay of Moscow. Prowling about the house at this time of night. I can understand Bertie doing it, because he was dropped on the head as a baby, but I'm surprised at you, Uncle Watkyn. Why don't you go to bed?"

"I shall be delighted to go to bed," said Pop Bassett stiffly, "if you will remove this animal. He is a public menace."

"Very high-strung," I put in. "We were remarking on it only just now."

"He's all right, if you don't go out of your way to stir him up. Get back to your basket, Bartholomew, you bounder," said Stiffy, and such was the magic of her personality that the hound turned on its heel without a word and passed into the night.

Pop Bassett climbed down from the chest and directed a fishy magisterial look at me.

"Good night, Mr. Wooster. If there is any more of my furniture you wish to break, pray consider yourself at perfect liberty to indulge your peculiar tastes," he said, and he, too, passed into the night.

Stiffy looked after him with a thoughtful eye.

"I don't believe Uncle Watkyn likes you, Bertie. I noticed the way he kept staring at you at dinner, as if appalled. Well, I don't wonder your arrival hit him hard. It did me. I've never been so surprised in my life as when you suddenly bobbed up like a corpse rising to the surface of a sheet of water. Harold told me he had pleaded with you to come here but nothing would induce you. What made you change your mind?"

In my previous sojourn at Totleigh Towers circumstances had compelled me to confide in this young prune my position as regarded her cousin Madeline, so I had no hesitation now in giving her the lowdown.

"I learned that there was trouble between Madeline and Gussie, due, I have since been informed, to her forcing him to follow in the footsteps of the poet Shelley and become a vegetarian, and I felt that I might accomplish something as a *raisonneur*."

"As a whatonneur?"

"I thought that would be a bit above your head. It's a French expression meaning, I believe, though I would have to check with Jeeves, a calm kindly man of the world who intervenes when a rift has occurred between two loving hearts and brings them together again. Very essential in the present crisis."

"You mean that if Madeline hands Gussie the pink slip, she'll marry you?"

"That, broadly, is the strength of it. And while I admire and respect Madeline, I'm all against the idea of having her smiling face peeping at me over the coffeepot for the rest of my life. So I came here to see what I could do."

"Well, you couldn't have come at a better moment. Now you're here, you can get cracking on that job Harold told you I want you to do for me."

I saw that the time had come for some prompt in-the-bud-nipping.

"Include me out. I won't touch it. I know you and your jobs."

"But this is something quite simple. You can do it on your head. And you'll be bringing sunshine and happiness into the life of a poor slob who can do with a bit of both. Were you ever a Boy Scout?"

"Not since early boyhood."

"Then you've lots of leeway to make up in the way of kind deeds. This'll be a nice start for you. The facts are as follows."

"I don't want to hear them."

"You would prefer that I recalled Bartholomew and told him to go on where he left off?"

She had what Jeeves had called a talking point.

"Very well. Tell me all. But briefly."

"It won't take long, and then you can be off to beddy-bye. You remember that little black statuette thing on the table at dinner?"

"Ah yes, the eyesore."

"Uncle Watkyn bought it from a man called Plank."

"So I gathered."

"Well, do you know what he paid him for it?"

"A thousand quid, didn't you say?"

"No, I didn't. I said it was worth that. But he got it out of this poor blighter Plank for a fiver."

"You're kidding."

"No, I'm not. He paid him five pounds. He makes no secret of it. When we were at Brinkley, he was showing the thing to Mr. Travers and telling him all about it . . . how he happened to see it on Plank's mantelpiece and spotted how valuable it was and told Plank it was worth practically nothing but he would give him five pounds for it because he knew how hard up he was. He gloated over how clever he had been, and Mr. Travers writhed like an egg whisk."

I could well believe it. If there's one thing that makes a collector spit blood, it's hearing about another collector getting a bargain.

"How do you know Plank was hard up?"

"Well, would he have let the thing go for a fiver if he wasn't?"

"Something in that."

"You can't say Uncle Watkyn isn't a dirty dog."

"I would never dream of saying he isn't—and always has been—the dirtiest of dogs. It bears out what I have frequently maintained—that there are no depths to which magistrates won't stoop. I don't wonder you look askance. Your Uncle Watkyn stands revealed as a chiseler of the lowest type. But nothing to be done about it, of course."

"I don't know so much about that."

"Why, have you tried doing anything?"

"In a sort of way. I arranged that Harold should preach a very strong sermon on Naboth's Vineyard. Not that I suppose you've ever heard of Naboth's Vineyard."

I bridled. She had offended my amour-propre.

"I doubt if there's a man in London and the home counties who has the facts relating to Naboth's Vineyard more thoroughly at his fingertips than me. The news may not have reached you, but when at school I once won a prize for Scripture Knowledge."

"I bet you cheated."

"Not at all. Sheer merit. Did Stinker cooperate?"

"Yes, he thought it was a splendid idea and went about sucking throat pastilles for a week, so as to be in good voice. The setup was the same as the play in *Hamlet*. You know. With which to catch the conscience of the king and all that."

"Yes, I see the strategy all right. How did it work out?"

"It didn't. Harold lives in the cottage of Mrs. Bootle, the postman's wife, where they only have oil lamps, and the sermon was on a table with a lamp on it, and he bumped into the table and upset the lamp and it burned the sermon and he hadn't time to write it out again, so he had to dig out something on another topic from the old stockpile. He was terribly disappointed."

I pursed my lips, and was on the point of saying that of all the web-footed muddlers in existence H. P. Pinker took the well-known biscuit, when it occurred to me that it might possibly hurt her feelings, and I desisted. The last thing I wanted was to wound the child, particularly when I remembered that crack of hers about recalling Bartholomew.

"So we've got to handle the thing another way, and that's where you come in."

I smiled a tolerant smile.

"I can see where you're heading," I said. "You want me to go to your Uncle Watkyn and slip a jack under his better self. 'Play the game, Bassett,' you want me to say; 'let conscience be your guide, Bassett,' trying to drive it into his nut how wrong it is to put over a fast one on the widow and the orphan. I am assuming for purposes of argument that

263

Plank is an orphan, though possibly not a widow. But, my misguided young shrimp, do you really suppose that Pop Bassett looks on me as a friend and counselor to whom he is always willing to lend a ready ear? You yourself were stressing only a moment ago how allergic he was to the Wooster charm. It's no good me talking to him."

"I don't want you to."

"Then what do you want me to do?"

"I want you to pinch the thing and return it to Plank, who will then sell it to Mr. Travers at a proper price. The idea of Uncle Watkyn only giving him a fiver for it! We can't have him getting away with raw work like that. He needs a sharp lesson."

I smiled another tolerant smile. The young boll weevil amused me. I was thinking how right I had been in predicting that any job assigned by her to anyone would be unfit for human consumption.

"Well, really, Stiffy!"

The quiet rebuke in my voice ought to have bathed her in shame and remorse, but it didn't. She came back at me strongly.

"I don't know what you're Well-really-ing about. You're always pinching things, aren't you? Policemen's helmets and things like that."

I inclined the bean. It was true that I had once lived in Arcady.

"There is," I was obliged to concede, "a certain substance in what you say. I admit that in my time I may have removed a lid or two from the upper stories of members of the constabulary—"

"Well, then."

"—but only on Boat Race Night and when the heart was younger than it is as of even date. It was an episode of the sort that first brought me and your Uncle Watkyn together. But you can take it from me that the hot blood has cooled and I'm a reformed character. My answer to your suggestion is no."

"No?"

"N-ruddy-o," I said, making it clear to the meanest intelligence. "Why don't you pinch the thing yourself?"

"It wouldn't be any good. I couldn't take it to Plank. I'm confined to barracks. Bartholomew bit the butler, and the sins of the Scotty are visited upon its owner. I do think you might reconsider, Bertie."

"Not a hope."

"You're a blighter!"

"But a blighter who knows his own mind and is not to be shaken by argument or plea, however specious."

She was silent for a space. Then she gave a little sigh.

"Oh, dear," she said. "And I did hope I wouldn't have to tell Madeline about Gussie."

I gave another of those visible starts of mine. I've seldom heard words I liked the sound of less. Fraught with sinister significance they seemed to me.

"Do you know what happened tonight, Bertie? I was roused from sleep about an hour ago, and what do you think roused me? Stealthy footsteps, no less. I crept out of my room, and I saw Gussie sneaking down the stairs. All was darkness, of course, but he had a little torch and it shone on his spectacles. I followed him. He went to the kitchen. I peered in, and there was the cook shoveling cold steak and kidney pie into him like a stevedore loading a grain ship. And the thought flashed into my mind that if Madeline heard of this, she would give him the bum's rush before he knew what had hit him."

"But a girl doesn't give a fellow the bum's rush just be-

265

cause she's told him to stick to the sprouts and spinach and she hears that he's been wading into the steak and kidney pie," I said, trying to reassure myself but not getting within several yards of it.

"I bet Madeline would."

And so, thinking it over, did I. You can't judge goofs like Madeline Bassett by ordinary standards. What the normal popsy would do and what she would do in any given circumstances were two distinct and separate things. I had not forgotten the time when she had severed relations with Gussie purely because through no fault of his own he got stinko when about to present the prizes at Market Snodsbury Grammar School.

"You know how high her ideals are. Yes, sir, if someone were to drop an incautious word to her about tonight's orgy, those wedding bells would not ring out. Gussie would be at liberty, and she would start looking about her for somebody else to fill the vacant spot. I really think you'll have to reconsider that decision of yours, Bertie, and do just this one more bit of pinching."

"Oh, my sainted aunt!"

I spoke as harts do when heated in the chase and panting for cooling streams. It would have been plain to a far less astute mind than mine that this blighted Byng had got me by the short hairs and was in a position to dictate tactics and strategy.

Blackmail, of course, but the gentler sex loves blackmail. Not once but on several occasions has my aunt Dahlia bent me to her will by threatening that if I didn't play ball she would bar me from her table, thus dashing Anatole's lunches and dinners from my lips. Show me a delicately nurtured female, and I will show you a ruthless Napoleon of Crime prepared without turning a hair to put the screws on some unfortunate male whose services she happens to be in need of. There ought to be a law.

"It looks as if the die were cast," I said reluctantly.

"It is," she assured me.

"You're really adamant?"

"Couldn't be more so. My heart bleeds for Plank, and I'm going to see that justice is done."

"Right ho, then. I'll have a crack at it."

"That's my little man. The whole thing's so frightfully easy and simple. All you have to do is lift the thing off the dining-room table and smuggle it over to Plank. Think how his face'll light up when you walk in on him with it. 'My hero!' I expect he'll say."

And with a laugh which, though silvery, grated on my ear like a squeaking slate pencil she buzzed off.

CHAPTER
TEN

PROCEEDING TO my room and turning in between the sheets,
I composed myself for sleep, but I didn't get a lot of it and
what I did get was much disturbed by dreams of being
chased across difficult country by sharks, some of them looking like Stiffy, some like Sir Watkyn Bassett, others like the
dog Bartholomew. When Jeeves came shimmering in next
morning with the breakfast tray, I lost no time in supplying
him with full information *re* the harrow I found myself the
toad under.

"You see the posish, Jeeves," I concluded. "When the
loss of the thing is discovered and the hue and cry sets in,
who will be the immediate suspect? Wooster, Bertram. My
name in this house is already mud, and the men up top will
never think of looking further for the guilty party. On the

other hand, if I refuse to sit in, Stiffy will consider herself scorned, and we all know what happens when you scorn a woman. She'll tell Madeline Bassett that Gussie has been at the steak and kidney pie, and ruin and desolation will ensue. I see no way of beating the game."

To my surprise, instead of raising an eyebrow the customary eighth of an inch and saying "Most disturbing, sir," he came within an ace of smiling. That is to say, the left corner of his mouth quivered almost imperceptibly before returning to position one.

"You cannot accede to Miss Byng's request, sir."

I took an astonished sip of coffee. I couldn't follow his train of thought. It seemed to me that he couldn't have been listening.

"But if I don't, she'll squeal to the FBI."

"No, sir, for the lady will be forced to admit that it is physically impossible for you to carry out her wishes. The statuette is no longer at large. It has been placed in Sir Watkyn's collection room behind a stout steel door."

"Good Lord! How do you know?"

"I chanced to pass the dining room, sir, and inadvertently overheard a conversation between Sir Watkyn and his lordship."

"Call him Spode."

"Very good, sir. Mr. Spode was observing to Sir Watkyn that he had not at all liked the interest you displayed in the figurine at dinner last night."

"I was just giving Pop B the old salve in the hope of sweetening the atmosphere a bit."

"Precisely, sir, but your statement that the object was 'just the sort of thing Uncle Tom would like to have' made a deep impression on Mr. Spode. Remembering the unfortunate episode of the cow creamer, which did so much to mar the pleasantness of your previous visit to Totleigh Towers, he informed Sir Watkyn that he had revised his original view that you were here to attempt to lure Miss Bassett from Mr. Fink-Nottle, and that he was now convinced that your motive in coming to the house had to do with the figurine, and that you were planning to purloin it on Mr. Travers' behalf. Sir Watkyn, who appeared much moved, accepted the theory in toto, all the more readily because of an encounter which he said he had had with you in the early hours of this morning."

I nodded.

"Yes, we got together in the hall at, I suppose, about one A.M. I had gone down to see if I could get a bit of that steak and kidney pie."

"I quite understand, sir. It was an injudicious thing to do, if I may say so, but the claims of steak and kidney pie are of course paramount. It was immediately after this that Sir Watkyn fell in with Mr. Spode's suggestion that the statuette be placed under lock and key in the collection room. I presume that it is now there, and when it is explained to Miss Byng that only by means of burglars' tools or a flask of trinitrotoluol could you obtain access to it and that neither of these is in your possession, I am sure the lady will see reason and recede from her position."

Only the circumstance of my being in bed at the moment kept me from dancing a few carefree steps.

"You speak absolute sooth, Jeeves. This lets me out."

"Completely, sir."

"Perhaps you wouldn't mind going and explaining the position of affairs to Stiffy now. You can tell the story so much better than I could, and she ought to be given the lowdown as soon as possible. I don't know where she is at this time of day, but you'll find her messing about somewhere, I've no doubt."

"I saw Miss Byng in the garden with Mr. Pinker, sir. I think she was trying to prepare him for his approaching ordeal."

"Eh?"

"If you recall, sir, owing to the temporary indisposition of the vicar, Mr. Pinker will be in sole charge of the school treat tomorrow, and he views the prospect with not unnatural qualms. There is a somewhat lawless element among the schoolchildren of Totleigh-in-the-Wold, and he fears the worst."

"Well, tell Stiffy to take a couple of minutes off from the pep talk and listen to your communiqué."

"Very good, sir."

He was absent quite a time—so long, in fact, that I was dressed when he returned.

"I saw Miss Byng, sir."

"And—"

"She is still insistent that you restore the statuette to Mr. Plank."

"She's cuckoo. I can't get into the collection room."

"No, sir, but Miss Byng can. She informs me that not long ago Sir Watkyn chanced to drop his key, and she picked it up and omitted to apprise him. Sir Watkyn had another key made, but the original remains in Miss Byng's possession."

I clutched the brow.

"You mean she can get into the room any time she feels like it?"

"Precisely, sir. Indeed, she has just done so."

And so saying he fished the eyesore from an inner pocket and handed it to me.

"Miss Byng suggests that you take the object to Mr.

Plank after luncheon. In her droll way she said the meal—I quote her words—would put the necessary stuffing into you and nerve you for the . . . It is somewhat early, sir, but shall I get you a little brandy?"

"Not a little, Jeeves," I said. "Fetch the cask."

I don't know how Emerald Stoker was with brush and palette, never having seen any of her output, but she unquestionably had what it takes where cooking was concerned, and any householder would have been glad to sign her up for the duration. The lunch she provided was excellent, everything most toothsome.

But with this ghastly commission of Stiffy's on the agenda paper, I had little appetite for her offerings. The brow was furrowed, the manner distrait, the stomach full of butterflies.

"Jeeves," I said as he accompanied me to my car at the conclusion of the meal, speaking rather peevishly, perhaps, for I was not my usual sunny self, "doesn't it strike you as odd that, with infant mortality so rife, a girl like Stiffy should have been permitted to survive into the early twenties? Some mismanagement there. What's the tree I read about somewhere that does you in if you sit under it?"

"The upas tree, sir."

"She's a female upas tree. It's not safe to come near her. Disaster on every side is what she strews. And another thing. It's all very well for her to say . . . glibly?"

"Or airily, sir. The words are synonymous."

"It's all very well for her to say glibly or airily, 'Take this blasted eyesore to Plank,' but how do I find him? I can't go rapping on every door in Hockley-cum-Meston, saying, 'Excuse me, are you Plank?' It'd be like looking for a needle in a haystack."

"A very colorful image, sir. I appreciate your difficulty.

I would suggest that you proceed to the local post office and institute inquiries there. Post-office officials invariably have information at their disposal as to the whereabouts of dwellers in the vicinity."

He had not erred. Braking the car in the Hockley-cum-Meston High Street, I found that the post office was one of those shops you get in villages, where, in addition to enjoying the postal facilities, you can purchase cigarettes, pipe tobacco, wool, lollipops, string, socks, boots, overalls, picture postcards, and bottles containing yellow nonalcoholic drinks, probably fizzy. In answer to my query, the old lady behind the counter told me I would find Plank up at the big house with the red shutters about half a mile further back along the road. She seemed a bit disappointed that information was all I was after and that I had no intention of buying a pair of socks or a ball of string, but she bore up philosophically, and I toddled back to the car.

I remembered the house she had spoken of, having passed it on my way. Imposing mansion with a lot of land. This Plank, I took it, would be some sort of laborer on the estate. I pictured him as a sturdy, gnarled old fellow whose sailor son had brought home the eyesore from one of his voyages, and neither of them had had the foggiest that it was valuable. "I'll put it on the mantelpiece, Dad," no doubt the son had said. "It'll look well up there." To which the old gaffer had replied, "Aye, lad, gormed if 'twon't look gradely on the mantelpiece." Or words to that effect. I can't do the dialect, of course. So they had shoved it on the mantelpiece, and then along had come Sir Watkyn Bassett with his smooth city ways and made suckers out of parent and offspring. Happening all the time, that sort of thing.

I reached the house and was about to knock on the door

when there came bustling up an elderly gentleman with a square face, much tanned, as if he had been sitting out in the sun quite a lot without his parasol.

"Oh, there you are," he said. "Hope I haven't kept you waiting. We were having football practice, and I lost track of the time. Come in, my dear fellow, come in."

I need scarcely say that this exuberant welcome to one who, whatever his merits, was a total stranger warmed my heart quite a good deal. It was with the feeling that his attitude did credit to Gloucestershire hospitality that I followed him through a hall liberally besprinkled with the heads of lions, leopards, gnus, and other fauna into a room with French windows opening on the front garden. Here he left me while he went off to fetch drinks, his first question having been, Would I care for one for the tonsils, to which I had replied with considerable enthusiasm that I would. When he returned, he found me examining the photographs on the wall. The one on which my eye was resting at the moment was a school football group, and it was not difficult to spot the identity of the juvenile delinquent holding the ball and sitting in the middle.

"You?" I said.

"That's me," he replied. "My last year at school. I skippered the side that season. That's old Scrubby Willoughby sitting next to me. Fast-wing three-quarter, but never would learn to give the reverse pass."

"He wouldn't?" I said, shocked. I hadn't the remotest what he was talking about, but he had said enough to show me that this Willoughby must have been a pretty dubious character, and when he went on to tell me that poor old Scrubby had died of cirrhosis of the liver in the Federal

Malay States, I wasn't really surprised. I imagine these fellows who won't learn to give the reverse pass generally come to a fairly sticky end.

"Chap on my other side is Smiler Todd, prop forward."

"Prop forward, eh?"

"And a very good one. Played for Cambridge later on. You fond of Rugger?"

"I don't think I know him."

"Rugby football."

"Oh, ah. No, I've never gone in for it."

"You haven't?"

"No."

"Good God!"

I could see that I had sunk pretty low in his estimation, but he was a host and managed to fight down the feeling of nausea with which my confession had afflicted him.

"I've always been mad keen on Rugger. Didn't get much of it after leaving school, as they stationed me in West Africa. Tried to teach the natives there the game, but had to give it up. Too many deaths, with the inevitable subsequent blood feuds. Retired now and settled down here. I'm trying to make Hockley-cum-Meston the best football village in these parts, and I will say for the lads that they're coming on nicely. What we need is a good prop forward, and I can't find one. But you don't want to hear all this. You want to know about my Brazilian expedition."

"Oh, have you been to Brazil?"

I seemed to have said the wrong thing, as one so often does. He stared.

"Didn't you know I'd been to Brazil?"

"Nobody tells me anything."

"I should have thought they'd have briefed you at the

275

office. Seems silly to send a reporter all the way down here without telling him what they're sending him for."

I'm pretty astute, and I saw there had been a mix-up somewhere.

"Were you expecting a reporter?"

"Of course I was. Aren't you from the *Daily Express*?"

"Sorry, no."

"I thought you must be the chap who was coming to interview me about my Brazilian explorations."

"Oh, you're an explorer?"

Again I had said the wrong thing. He was plainly piqued.

"What did you think I was? Does the name Plank mean nothing to you?"

"Is your name Plank?"

"Of course it is."

"Well, what a very odd coincidence," I said, intrigued. "I'm looking for a character called Plank. Not you, somebody else. The bimbo I want is a sturdy tiller of the soil, probably gnarled, with a sailor son. As you have the same name as him, you'll probably be interested in the story I'm about to relate. I have here," I said, producing the black amber thing, "a whatnot."

He gaped at it.

"Where did you get that? That's the bit of native sculpture I picked up on the Congo and sold to Sir Watkyn Bassett."

I was amazed.

"*You* sold it to him?"

"Certainly."

"Well, shiver my timbers!"

I was conscious of a Boy Scoutful glow. I liked this Plank, and I rejoiced that it was in my power to do him as good a turn as anyone had ever done anybody. God bless Bertram Wooster, I felt he'd be saying in another couple of ticks. For the first time I was glad that Stiffy had sent me on this mission.

"Then I'll tell you what," I said. "If you'll just give me five pounds——"

I broke off. He was looking at me with a cold, glassy stare, as no doubt he had looked at the late lions, leopards, and gnus whose remains were to be viewed on the walls of the outer hall. Fellows at the Drones who have tried to touch Oofy Prosser, the club millionaire, for a trifle to see them through till next Wednesday have described him to me as looking just like that.

"Oh, so that's it!" he said, and even Pop Bassett could not have spoken more nastily. "I've got your number now. I've met your sort all over the world. You won't get any five pounds, my man. You sit where you are and don't move. I'm going to call the police."

"It will not be necessary, sir," said a respectful voice, and Jeeves entered through the French window.

CHAPTER
ELEVEN

His ADVENT drew from me a startled goggle and, I rather think, a cry of amazement. Last man I'd expected to see, and how he had got here defeated me. I've sometimes felt that he must dematerialize himself like those fellows in India—fakirs, I think they're called—who fade into thin air in Bombay and turn up five minutes later in Calcutta or points west with all the parts reassembled.

Nor could I see how he had divined that the young master was in sore straits and in urgent need of his assistance, unless it was all done by what I believe is termed telepathy. Still, here he was, with his head bulging at the back and on his face that look of quiet intelligence which comes from eating lots of fish, and I welcomed his presence. I knew from experience what a wizard he was at removing the oppressed from the soup, and the soup was what I was at this point in my affairs deeply immersed in.

"Major Plank?" he said.

Plank, too, was goggling.

"Who on earth are you?"

"Chief Inspector Witherspoon, sir, of Scotland Yard. Has this man been attempting to obtain money from you?"

"Just been doing that very thing."

"As I suspected. We have had our eye on him for a long time but till now have never been able to apprehend him in the act."

"Notorious crook, is he?"

"Precisely, sir. He is a confidence man of considerable eminence in the underworld who makes a practice of calling at houses and extracting money from their owners with some plausible story."

"He does more than that. He pinches things from people and tries to sell them. Look at that statuette he's holding. It's a thing I sold to Sir Watkyn Bassett, who lives at Totleigh-in-the-Wold, and he had the cool cheek to come here and try to sell it to me for five pounds."

"Indeed, sir? With your permission I will impound the object."

"You'll need it as evidence?"

"Exactly, sir. I shall now take him to Totleigh Towers and confront him with Sir Watkyn."

"Yes, do. That'll teach him. Nasty hangdog look the fellow's got. I suspected from the first he was wanted by the police. Had him under observation for a long time, have you?"

"For a very long time, sir. He is known to us at the Yard as Alpine Joe, because he always wears an Alpine hat."

"He's got it with him now."

"He never moves without it."

"You'd think he'd have the sense to adopt some rude disguise."

"You would indeed, sir, but the mental processes of a man like that are hard to follow."

"Then there's no need for me to phone the local police?"

"None, sir. I will take him into custody."

"You wouldn't like me to hit him over the head first with a Zulu knobkerrie?"

"Unnecessary, sir."

"It might be safer."

"No, sir, I am sure he will come quietly."

"Well, have it your own way. But don't let him give you the slip."

"I will be very careful, sir."

"And shove him into a dungeon with dripping walls and see to it that he is well gnawed by rats."

"Very good, sir."

What with all the stuff about reverse passes and prop forwards, plus the strain of seeing gentlemen's personal gentlemen appear from nowhere and of having to listen to that loose talk about Zulu knobkerries, the Wooster bean was not at its best as we moved off, and there was nothing in the way of conversational give-and-take until we had reached my car, which I had left at the front gate.

"Chief Inspector *who?*" I said, recovering a modicum of speech as we arrived at our objective.

"Witherspoon, sir."

"Why Witherspoon? On the other hand," I added, for I like to look on both sides of a thing, "why not Witherspoon? However, that is not germane to the issue and can be reserved for discussion later. The real point—the nub—the thing that should be threshed out immediately—is how on earth do you come to be here?"

"I anticipated that my arrival might occasion you a certain surprise, sir. I hastened after you directly I learned of the revelation Sir Watkyn had made to Miss Byng, for I foresaw that your interview with Major Plank would be embarrassing, and I hoped to be able to intercept you before you could establish communication with him."

Practically all of this floated past me.

"How do you mean, the revelation Pop Bassett made to Stiffy?"

"It occurred shortly after luncheon, sir. Miss Byng informs me that she decided to approach Sir Watkyn and make a last appeal to his better feelings. As you are aware, the matter of the statuette has always been one that affected her deeply. She thought that if she reproached Sir Watkyn with sufficient vehemence, something constructive might result. Greatly to her astonishment, she had hardly begun to speak when Sir Watkyn, chuckling heartily, asked her if she could keep a secret. He then revealed that there was no foundation for the story he had told Mr. Travers and that in actual fact he had paid Major Plank a thousand pounds for the object."

It took me perhaps a quarter of a minute to sort all this out.

"A thousand quid?"

"Yes, sir."

"Not a fiver?"

"No, sir."

"You mean he lied to Uncle Tom?"

"Yes, sir."

"What on earth did he do that for?"

281

I thought he would say he hadn't a notion, but he didn't.

"I think Sir Watkyn's motive was obvious, sir."

"Not to me."

"He acted from a desire to exasperate Mr. Travers. Mr. Travers is a collector, and collectors are never pleased when they learn that a rival collector has acquired at an insignificant price an objet d'art of great value."

It penetrated. I saw what he meant. The discovery that Pop Bassett had got hold of a thousand-quid thingummy for practically nothing would have been gall and w. to Uncle Tom. Stiffy had described him as writhing like an egg whisk, and I could well believe it. It must have been agony for the poor old buster.

"You've hit it, Jeeves. It's just what Pop Bassett would do. Nothing would please him better than to spoil Uncle Tom's day. What a man, Jeeves!"

"Yes, sir."

"Would you like to have a mind like his?"

"No, sir."

"Nor me. It just shows how being a magistrate saps the moral fiber. I remember thinking as I stood before him in the dock that he had a shifty eye and that I wouldn't trust him as far as I could throw an elephant. I suppose all magistrates are like that."

"There may be exceptions, sir."

"I doubt it. Twisters, every one of them. So my errand was . . . what, Jeeves?"

"Bootless, sir."

"Bootless? It doesn't sound right, but I suppose you know. Well, I wish the news you've just sprung could have broken before I presented myself chez Plank. I would have been spared a testing ordeal."

"I can appreciate the nervous strain you must have undergone, sir. It is unfortunate that I was not able to arrive earlier."

"How did you arrive at all? That's what's puzzling me. You can't have walked."

"No, sir. I borrowed Miss Byng's car. I left it some little distance down the road and proceeded to the house on foot. Hearing voices, I approached the French window and listened and was thus enabled to intervene at the crucial moment."

"Very resourceful."

"Thank you, sir."

"I should like to express my gratitude. And when I say gratitude, I mean heartfelt gratitude."

"Not at all, sir. It was a pleasure."

"But for you, Plank would have had me in the local calaboose in a matter of minutes. Who is he, by the way? I got the impression that he was an explorer of sorts."

"Yes, sir."

"Pretty far-flung, I gathered."

"Extremely, sir. He has recently returned from an expedition into the interior of Brazil. He inherited the house where he resides from a deceased godfather. He breeds cocker spaniels, suffers somewhat from malaria, and eats only nonfattening protein bread."

"You seem to have got him taped all right."

"I made inquiries at the post office, sir. The person behind the counter was most informative. I also learned that Major Plank is an enthusiast on Rugby football and is hoping to make Hockley-cum-Meston invincible on the field."

"Yes, so he was telling me. You aren't a prop forward, are you, Jeeves?"

"No, sir. Indeed, I do not know what the term signifies."

"I don't, either, except that it's something a team has to have if it's hoping to do down the opposition at Rugby football. Plank, I believe, has searched high and low for one, but his errand has been bootless. Rather sad, when you come to think of it. All that money, all those cocker spaniels, all that protein bread, but no prop forward. Still, that's life."

"Yes indeed, sir."

I slid behind the steering wheel and told him to hop in.

"But I was forgetting. You've got Stiffy's car. Then I'll be driving on. The sooner I get this statuette thing back into her custody, the better."

He didn't shake his head, because he never shakes his head, but he raised the southeast corner of a warning eyebrow.

"If you will pardon the suggestion, sir, I think it would be more advisable for me to take the object to Miss Byng. It would scarcely be prudent for you to enter the environs of Totleigh Towers with it on your person. You might encounter his lordship . . . I should say Mr. Spode."

I Well-I'll-be-dashed. He had surprised me.

"Surely you aren't suggesting that he would frisk me?"

"I think it highly possible, sir. In the conversation which I overheard, Mr. Spode gave me the impression of being prepared to stop at nothing. If you will give me the object, I will see that Miss Byng restores it to the collection room at the earliest possible moment.

I mused, but not for long. I was only too pleased to get rid of the beastly thing.

"Very well, if you say so. Here you are. Though I think you're wronging Spode."

"I think not, sir."

And blow me tight if he wasn't right. Scarcely had I

steered the car into the stable yard when a solid body darkened the horizon, and there was Spode, looking like Chief Inspector Witherspoon about to make a pinch.

"Wooster!" he said.

"Speaking," I said.

"Get out of that car," he said. "I'm going to search it."

CHAPTER
TWELVE

I WAS conscious of a thrill of thankfulness for Jeeves' prescience, if prescience is the word I want. I mean that uncanny knack he has of peering into the future and forming
his plans and schemes well ahead of time. But for his
thoughtful diagnosis of the perils that lay before me, I
should at this juncture have been deep in the mulligatawny
and no hope of striking for the shore. As it was, I was able
to be nonchalant, insouciant, and debonair. I was like the
fellow I once heard Jeeves speak of who was armed so
strong in honesty that somebody's threats passed by him as
the idle wind, which he respected not. I think if Spode had
been about three feet shorter and not so wide across the
shoulders, I would have laughed a mocking laugh and quite
possibly have flicked my cambric handkerchief in his face.

He was eyeing me piercingly, little knowing what an ass he was going to feel before yonder sun had set.

"I have just searched your room."

"You have? You surprise me. Looking for something, were you?"

"You know what I'm looking for. That amber statuette you said your uncle would be so glad to have."

"Oh, that? I understood it was in the collection room."

"Who told you that?"

"A usually well-informed source."

"Well, it is no longer in the collection room. Somebody has removed it."

"Most extraordinary."

"And when I say 'somebody,' I mean a slimy sneak thief of the name of Wooster. The thing isn't in your bedroom, so if it is not in your car, you must have it on you. Turn out your pockets."

I humored his request, largely influenced by the fact that there was so much of him. A Singer midget would have found me far less obliging. The contents having been placed before him, he snorted in a disappointed way, as if he had hoped for better things, and dived into the car, opening drawers and looking under cushions. And Stiffy, coming along at this moment, drank in his vast trouser seat with a curious eye.

"What goes on?" she asked.

This time I did laugh that mocking laugh. It seemed to be indicated.

"You know that black eyesore thing that was on the dinner table? Apparently it's disappeared, and Spode has got the extraordinary idea that I've pinched it and am holding it . . . what's the word . . . not incognito . . . incommunicado, that's it. He thinks I'm holding it incommunicado."

"He does?"

"So he says."

"Man must be an ass."

Spode wheeled around, flushed with his excesses. I was pleased to see that while looking under the seat he had got a bit of oil on his nose. He eyed Stiffy bleakly.

"Did you call me an ass?"

"Certainly I did. I was taught by a long series of governesses always to speak the truth. The idea of accusing Bertie of taking that statuette."

"It does sound silly," I agreed. "Bizarre is perhaps the word."

"The thing's in Uncle Watkyn's collection room."

"It is not in the collection room."

"Who says so?"

"I say so."

"Well, I say it is. Go and look, if you don't believe me. Stop that, Bartholomew, you blighted dog!" bellowed Stiffy, abruptly changing the subject, and she hastened off on winged feet to confer with the hound, who had found something in, I presumed, the last stages of decay and was rolling on it. I could follow her train of thought. Scotties at their best are niffy. Add to their natural bouquet the aroma of a dead rat or whatever it was, and you have a mixture too rich for the human nostril. There was a momentary altercation, and Bartholomew, cursing a good deal, as was natural, was hauled off tubwards.

A minute or two later Spode returned with most of the stuffing removed from his person.

"I seem to have done you an injustice, Wooster," he said, and I was amazed that he had it in him to speak so meekly.

288

The Woosters are always magnanimous. We do not crush the vanquished beneath the iron heel.

"Oh, was the thing there all right?"

"Er—yes. Yes, it was."

"Ah well, we all make mistakes."

"I could have sworn it had gone."

"But wasn't the door locked?"

"Yes."

"Reminds you of one of those mystery stories, doesn't it, where there's a locked room with no windows, and blowed if one fine morning you don't find a millionaire inside with a dagger of Oriental design sticking in his wishbone. You've got some oil on your nose."

"Oh, have I?" he said, feeling.

"Now you've got it on your cheek. I'd go and join Bartholomew in the bathtub if I were you."

"I will. Thank you, Wooster."

"Not at all, Spode, or, rather, Sidcup. Don't spare the soap."

I suppose there's nothing that braces one more thoroughly than the spectacle of the forces of darkness stubbing their toe, and the heart was light as I made my way to the house. What with this and what with that, it was as though a great weight had rolled off me. Birds sang, insects buzzed, and I felt that what they were trying to say was "All is well. Bertram has come through."

But a thing I've often noticed is that when I've got something off my mind, it pretty nearly always happens that Fate sidles up and shoves on something else, as if curious to see how much the traffic will bear. It went into its act on the present occasion. Feeling that I needed something else to worry about, it spat on its hands and got down to it, allowing Madeline Bassett to corner me as I was passing through the hall.

Even if she had been her normal soupy self, she would have been the last person I wanted to have a word with, but this she was far from being. Something had happened to remove the droopiness, and her eyes had a gleam in them which filled me with a nameless fear. She was obviously all steamed up for some reason, and it was plain that what she was about to say was not going to make the last of the Woosters clap his hands in glee and start chanting hosannas like the Cherubim and Seraphim, if I've got the names right. A moment later she revealed what it was that was eating her, dishing it out without what I believe is called preamble.

"I am furious with Augustus!" she said, and my heart stood still. It was as if the Totleigh Towers specter, if there was one, had laid an icy hand on it.

"Why, what's happened?"

"He was very rude to Roderick."

This seemed incredible. Nobody but an all-in wrestling champion would be rude to a fellow as big as Spode.

"Surely not?"

"I mean he was very rude *about* Roderick. He said he was sick and tired of seeing him clumping about the place as if it belonged to him, and hadn't he got a home of his own, and if Daddy had an ounce more sense than a billiard ball he would charge him rent. He was most offensive."

My h. stood stiller. It is not stretching the facts to say that I was appalled and all of a doodah. It just showed, I was telling myself, what a vegetarian diet can do to a chap, changing him in a flash from a soft-boiled to a hard-boiled egg. I have no doubt the poet Shelley's circle noticed the same thing with the poet Shelley.

I tried to pour oil on the troubled w's.

"Probably just kidding, don't you think?"

"No, I don't."

"He didn't say it with a twinkle in his eye?"

"No."

"Nor with a light laugh?"

"No."

"You might not have noticed it. Very easy to miss, these light laughs."

"He meant every word he said."

"Then it was probably just a momentary spasm of what-d'you-call-it. Irritability. We all have them."

She ground a tooth or two. At least, it looked as if that was what she was doing.

"It was nothing of the kind. He was harsh and bitter, and he has been like that for a long time. I noticed it first at Brinkley. One morning we had walked in the meadows and the grass was all covered with little wreaths of mist, and I said, Didn't he sometimes feel that they were the elves' bridal veils, and he said sharply, 'No, never,' adding that he had never heard such a silly idea in his life."

Well, of course, he was perfectly correct, but it was no good pointing that out to a girl like Madeline Bassett.

"And that evening we were watching the sunset, and I said sunsets always made me think of the Blessed Damozel leaning out from the gold bar of heaven, and he said, 'Who?' and I said, 'The Blessed Damozel,' and he said, 'Never heard of her.' And he said that sunsets made him sick and so did the Blessed Damozel and he had a pain in his inside."

I saw that the time had come to be a *raisonneur*.

"This was at Brinkley?"

"Yes."

"I see. After you had made him become a vegetarian. Are you sure," I said, raisonneuring like nobody's business, "that you were altogether wise in confining him to spinach and what not? Many a proud spirit rebels when warned off the proteins. And I don't know if you know it, but medical research has established that the ideal diet is one in which animal and vegetable foods are balanced. It's something to do with the something acids required by the body."

I won't say she actually snorted, but the sound she uttered was certainly on the border line of the snort.

"What nonsense!"

"It's what doctors say."

"Which doctors?"

"Well-known Harley Street physicians."

"I don't believe it. Thousands of people are vegetarians and enjoy perfect health."

"Bodily health, yes," I said, cleverly seizing on the debating point. "But what of the soul? If you suddenly steer a fellow off the steaks and chops, it does something to his soul. My Aunt Agatha once made my Uncle Percy be a vegetarian, and his whole nature became soured. Not," I was forced to admit, "that it wasn't fairly soured already, as anyone's would be who was in constant contact with my Aunt Agatha. I bet you'll find that that's all that's wrong with Gussie. He simply wants a mutton chop or two under his belt."

"Well, he's not going to have them. And if he continues to behave like a sulky child, I shall know what to do about it."

I remember Stinker Pinker telling me once that toward the end of his time at Oxford he was down in Bethnel Green spreading the light and a costermonger kicked him in the stomach. He said it gave him a strange, confused, dreamlike feeling, and that's what these ominous words of M. Bassett's gave me now. She had spoken them from between teeth which, if not actually clenched, were the next thing to it, and it was as if the substantial boot of a vendor of blood oranges and bananas had caught me squarely in the solar plexus.

"Er—what will you do about it?"

"Never mind."

I put out a cautious feeler.

"Suppose . . . not that it's likely to happen, of course . . . but suppose Gussie, maddened by abstinence, were to go off and tuck into . . . well, to take an instance at random, cold steak and kidney pie, what would be the upshot?"

I had never supposed that she had it in her to give anyone a piercing look, but that is what she gave me now. I don't think even Aunt Agatha's eyes have bored more deeply into me.

"Are you telling me, Bertie, that Augustus has been eating steak and kidney pie?"

"Good heavens, no. It was just a thingummy."

"I don't understand you."

"What do they call questions that aren't really questions? Begins with an h. Hypothetical, that's the word. It was just a hypothetical question."

"Oh? Well, the answer to it is that if I found that Augustus had been eating the flesh of animals slain in anger, I would have nothing more to do with him," she said, and she biffed off, leaving me a spent force and a mere shell of my former self.

CHAPTER
THIRTEEN

THE FOLLOWING day dawned bright and fair. At least I suppose it did. I didn't see it dawning myself, having dropped off into a troubled slumber some hours before it got its nose down to it, but when the mists of sleep cleared and I was able to attend to what was going on, sunshine was seeping through the window and the ear detected the chirping of about seven hundred and fifty birds, not one of whom, unlike me, appeared to have a damn thing on his or her mind. As carefree a bunch as I've ever struck, and it gave me the pip to listen to them, for melancholy had marked me for her own, as the fellow said, and all this buck and heartiness simply stepped up the gloom in which my yesterday's chat with Madeline Bassett had plunged me.

As may well be imagined, her obiter dicta, as I believe they're called, had got right in amongst me. This, it was plain, was no mere lovers' tiff, to be cleaned up with a couple of tears and a kiss or two, but a real Class A rift which, if prompt steps were not taken through the proper channels, would put the lute right out of business and make it as mute as a drum with a hole in it. And the problem of how those steps were to be taken defeated me. Two iron wills had clashed. On the one hand we had Madeline's strong anti-flesh-food bias, on the other Gussie's firm determination to get all the cuts off the joint that were coming to him. What, I asked myself, would the harvest be, and I was still shuddering at the thought of what the future might hold when Jeeves trickled in with the morning cup of tea.

"Eh?" I said absently as he put it on the table. Usually I spring at the refreshing fluid like a seal going after a slice of fish. Preoccupied, if you know what I mean. Or distrait, if you care to put it that way.

"I was saying that we are fortunate in having a fine day for the school treat, sir."

I sat up with a jerk, upsetting the cuppa as deftly as if I'd been the Rev. H. P. Pinker.

"Is it today?"

"This afternoon, sir."

I groaned one of those hollow ones.

"It needed but this, Jeeves."

"Sir?"

"The last straw. I'd enough on my mind already."

"There is something disturbing you, sir?"

"You're right there is. Hell's foundations are quivering. What do you call it when a couple of nations start off by being all palsy-walsy and then begin calling each other ticks and bounders?"

"Relations have deteriorated would be the customary phrase, sir."

"Well, relations have deteriorated between Miss Bassett

and Gussie. He, as we know, was already disgruntled, and now she's disgruntled, too. She has taken exception to a derogatory crack he made about the sunset. She thinks highly of sunsets, and he told her they made him sick. Can you believe this?"

"Quite readily, sir. Mr. Fink-Nottle was commenting to me on the sunset yesterday evening. He said it looked so like a slice of underdone beef that it tortured him to see it. One can appreciate his feelings."

"I dare say, but I wish he'd keep them to himself. He also appears to have spoken disrespectfully of the Blessed Damozel. Who's the Blessed Damozel, Jeeves? I don't seem to have heard of her."

"The heroine of a poem by the late Dante Gabriel Rossetti, sir. She leaned out from the gold bar of heaven."

"Yes, I gathered that. That much was specified."

"Her eyes were deeper than the depths of waters stilled at even. She had three lilies in her hand, and the stars in her hair were seven."

"Oh, were they? Well, be that as it may, Gussie said she made him sick, too, and Miss Bassett's as sore as a sunburned neck."

"Most disturbing, sir."

"Disturbing is the word. If things go on the way they are, no bookie would give odds of less than a hundred to eight on this betrothal lasting another week. I've seen betrothals in my time, many of them, but never one that looked more likely to come apart at the seams than that of Augustus Fink-Nottle and Madeline, daughter of Sir Watkyn and the late Lady Bassett. The suspense is awful. Who was the chap I remember reading about somewhere, who had a sword hanging over him attached to a single hair?"

"Damocles, sir. It is an old Greek legend."

"Well, I know just how he must have felt. And with this on my mind, I'm expected to attend a ruddy school treat. I won't go."

"Your absence may cause remark, sir."

"I don't care. They won't get a smell of me. I'm oiling out, and let them make of it what they will."

Apart from anything else, I was remembering the story I had heard Pongo Twistleton tell one night at the Drones, illustrative of how unbridled passions are apt to become at these binges. Pongo got mixed up once in a school treat down in Somersetshire, and his description of how in order to promote a game called "Is Mr. Smith at Home?" he had had to put his head in a sack and allow the younger generation to prod him with sticks had held the smoking room spellbound. At a place like Totleigh, where even on normal days human life was not safe, still worse excesses were to be expected. The glimpse or two I had had of the local Dead End kids had told me how tough a bunch they were and how sedulously they should be avoided by the man who knew what was good for him.

"I shall nip over to Brinkley in the car and have lunch with Uncle Tom. You at my side, I hope?"

"Impossible, I fear, sir. I have promised to assist Mr. Butterfield in the tea tent."

"Then you can tell me all about it."

"Very good, sir."

"If you survive."

"Precisely, sir."

It was a nice easy drive to Brinkley, and I got there well in advance of the luncheon hour. Aunt Dahlia wasn't there, having, as foreshadowed, popped up to London for the day, and Uncle Tom and I sat down alone to a repast in Anatole's best vein. Over the Suprême de Foie Gras au Champagne and the Neige aux Perles des Alpes I placed him in possession of the facts relating to the black amber statuette thing, and his relief at learning that Pop Bassett hadn't got a thousand-quid objet d'art for a fiver was so profound and the things he said about Pop B so pleasing to the ear that by the time I started back my dark mood had become sensibly lightened and optimism had returned to its throne.

After all, I reminded myself, it wasn't as if Gussie was going to be indefinitely under Madeline's eye. In due season he would buzz back to London and there would be able to tuck into the beefs and muttons till his ribs squeaked, confident that not a word of his activities would reach her. The effect of this would be to refill him with sweetness and light, causing him to write her loving letters which would carry him along till she emerged from this vegetarian phase and took up stamp collecting or something. I know the other sex and their sudden enthusiasms. They get these crazes and wallow in them for a while, but they soon become fed up and turn to other things. My Aunt Agatha once went in for politics, but it only took a few meetings at which she got the bird from hecklers to convince her that the cagey thing to do was to stay at home and attend to her fancy needlework, giving the whole enterprise a miss.

It was getting on for what is called the quiet evenfall when I dropped anchor at Totleigh Towers. I did my usual sneak to my room, and I had been there a few minutes when Jeeves came in.

"I saw you arrive, sir," he said, "and I thought you might be in need of refreshment."

298

I assured him that his intuition had not led him astray, and he said he would bring me a whiskey-and-s. immediately.

"I trust you found Mr. Travers in good health, sir."

I was able to reassure him there.

"He was a bit low when I blew in, but on receipt of my news about the whatnot blossomed like a flower. It would have done you good to have heard what he had to say about Pop Bassett. And talking of Pop Bassett, how did the school treat go off?"

"I think the juvenile element enjoyed the festivities, sir."

"How about you?"

"Sir?"

"You were all right? They didn't put your head in a sack and prod you with sticks?"

"No, sir. My share in the afternoon's events was confined to assisting in the tea tent."

"You speak lightly, Jeeves, but I've known some dark work to take place in school treat tea tents."

"It is odd that you should say that, sir, for it was while partaking of tea that a lad threw a hard-boiled egg at Sir Watkyn."

"And hit him?"

"On the left cheekbone, sir. It was most unfortunate."

I could not subscribe to this.

"I don't know why you say 'unfortunate.' Best thing that could have happened, in my opinion. The very first time I set eyes on Pop Bassett, in the picturesque environment of Bosher Street Police Court, I remember saying to myself that there sat a man to whom it would do all the good in the world to have hard-boiled eggs thrown at him. One of my crowd on that occasion, a lady accused of being drunk and disorderly and resisting the police, did, on receipt of her sentence, throw her boot at him, but with a poor aim, succeeding only in beaning the magistrate's clerk. What's the boy's name?"

"I could not say, sir. His actions were cloaked in anonymity."

"A pity. I would have liked to reward him by sending camels bearing apes, ivory, and peacocks to his address. Did you see anything of Gussie in the course of the afternoon?"

"Yes, sir. Mr. Fink-Nottle, at Miss Bassett's insistence, played a large part in the proceedings and was, I am sorry to say, somewhat roughly handled by the younger revelers. Among other vicissitudes that he underwent, a child entangled its all-day sucker in his hair."

"That must have annoyed him. He's fussy about his hair."

"Yes, sir, he was visibly incensed. He detached the sweetmeat and threw it from him with a good deal of force, and by ill luck it struck Miss Byng's dog on the nose. Affronted by what he presumably mistook for an unprovoked assault, the animal bit Mr. Fink-Nottle in the leg."

"Poor old Gussie!"

"Yes, sir."

"Still, into each life some rain must fall."

"Precisely, sir. I will go and bring your whiskey-and-soda."

He had scarcely gone when Gussie blew in, limping a little but otherwise showing no signs of what Jeeves had called the vicissitudes he had undergone. He seemed, indeed, above rather than below his usual form, and I remember the phrase "the bulldog breed" passed through my mind. If Gussie was a sample of young England's stamina and fortitude, it seemed to me that the country's future was secure. It is not every nation that can produce sons capable of grinning, as he was doing, so shortly after being bitten by Aberdeen terriers.

"Oh, there you are, Bertie," he said. "Jeeves told me you were back. I looked in to borrow some cigarettes."

"Go ahead."

"Thanks," he said, filling his case. "I'm taking Emerald Stoker for a walk."

"You're *what?*"

"Or a row on the river. Whichever she prefers."

"But, Gussie—"

"Oh, before I forget. Pinker is looking for you. He says he wants to see you about something important."

"Never mind about Stinker. You can't take Emerald Stoker for walks."

"Can't I? Watch me."

"But—"

"Sorry, no time to talk now. I don't want to keep her waiting. So long; I must be off."

He left me plunged in thought, and not agreeable thought either. I think I have made it clear to the meanest i. that my whole future depended on Augustus Fink-Nottle sticking to the straight and narrow path and not blotting his copybook, and I could not but feel that by taking Emerald Stoker for walks he was skidding off the straight and narrow path and blotting his c. in no uncertain manner. That, at least, was, I was pretty sure, how an idealistic beazel like Madeline Bassett, already rendered hot under the collar by his subversive views on sunsets and Blessed Damozels, would regard it. It is not too much to say that when Jeeves returned with the whiskey-and-s., he found me all of a twitter and shaking on my stem.

I would have liked to put him abreast of this latest development, but, as I say, there are things we don't discuss, so

I merely drank deep of the flowing bowl and told him that Gussie had just been a pleasant visitor.

"He tells me Stinker Pinker wants to see me about something."

"No doubt with reference to the episode of Sir Watkyn and the hard-boiled egg, sir."

"Don't tell me it was Stinker who threw it."

"No, sir, the miscreant is believed to have been a lad in his early teens. But the young fellow's impulsive action has led to unfortunate consequences. It has caused Sir Watkyn to entertain doubts as to the wisdom of entrusting a vicarage to a curate incapable of maintaining order at a school treat. Miss Byng, while confiding this information to me, appeared greatly distressed. She had supposed—I quote her verbatim—that the thing was in the bag, and she is naturally much disturbed."

I drained my glass and lit a moody gasper. If Totleigh Towers wanted to turn me into a cynic, it was going the right way about it.

"There's a curse on this house, Jeeves. Broken blossoms and shattered hopes wherever you look. It seems to be something in the air. The sooner we're out of here, the better. I wonder if we couldn't—"

I had been about to add "make our getaway tonight," but at this moment the door flew open and Spode came bounding in, wiping the words from my lips and causing me to raise an eyebrow or two. I resented this habit he was developing of popping up out of a trap at me every other minute like a Demon King in pantomime, and only the fact that I couldn't think of anything restrained me from saying something pretty stinging. As it was, I wore the mask and spoke with the suavity of the perfect host.

"Ah, Spode. Come on in and take a few chairs," I said,

and was on the point of telling him that we Woosters kept open house, when he interrupted me with the uncouth abruptness so characteristic of these human gorillas. Roderick Spode may have had his merits, though I had never been able to spot them, but his warmest admirer couldn't have called him couth.

CHAPTER
FOURTEEN

"HAVE YOU seen Fink-Nottle?" he said.

I didn't like the way he spoke or the way he was looking. The lips, I noted, were twitching, and the eyes glittered with what I believe is called a baleful light. It seemed pretty plain to me that it was in no friendly spirit that he was seeking Gussie, so I watered down the truth a bit, as the prudent man does on these occasions.

"I'm sorry, no. I've only just got back from my uncle's place over Worcestershire way. Some urgent family business came up and I had to go and attend to it, so unfortunately missed the school treat. A great disappointment. You haven't seen Gussie, have you, Jeeves?"

He made no reply, possibly because he wasn't there. He generally slides discreetly off when the young master is entertaining the quality, and you never see him go. He just evaporates.

"Was it something important you wanted to see him about?"

"I want to break his neck."

My eyebrows, which had returned to normal, rose again. I also, if I remember rightly, pursed my lips.

"Well, really, Spode! Is this not becoming a bit thick? It's not so long ago that you were turning over in your mind the idea of breaking mine. I think you should watch yourself in this matter of neck-breaking and check the urge before it gets too strong a grip on you. No doubt you say to yourself that you can take it or leave it alone, but isn't there the danger of the thing becoming habit-forming? Why do you want to break Gussie's neck?"

He ground his teeth—at least that's what I think he did to them—and was silent for a space. Then, though there wasn't anyone within earshot but me, he lowered his voice.

"I can speak frankly to you, Wooster, because you, too, love her."

"Eh? Who?" I said. It should have been "whom," I suppose, but that didn't occur to me at the time.

"Madeline, of course."

"Oh, Madeline?"

"As I told you, I have always loved her, and her happiness is very dear to me. It is everything to me. To give her a moment's pleasure, I would cut myself in pieces."

I couldn't follow him there, but before I could go into the question of whether girls enjoy seeing people cut themselves in pieces he had resumed.

"It was a great shock to me when she became engaged to this man Fink-Nottle, but I accepted the situation because I

305

thought that that was where her happiness lay. Though stunned, I kept silent."

"Very white."

"I said nothing that would give her a suspicion of how I felt."

"Very pukka."

"It was enough for me that she should be happy. Nothing else mattered. But when Fink-Nottle turns out to be a libertine—"

"Who—Gussie?" I said, surprised. "The last chap I'd have attached such a label to. Pure as the driven s., I'd have thought, if not purer. What makes you think Gussie's a libertine?"

"The fact that less than ten minutes ago I saw him kissing the cook," said Spode through the teeth which I'm pretty sure he was grinding, and he dived out of the door and was gone.

How long I remained motionless, like a ventriloquist's dummy whose ventriloquist has gone off to the local and left it sitting, I cannot say. Probably not so very long, for when life returned to the rigid limbs and I legged it for open spaces to try to find Gussie and warn him of this V-shaped depression which was coming his way, Spode was still in sight. He was disappearing in a nor'-nor'easterly direction, so, not wanting to hobnob with him again while he was in this what you might call difficult mood, I pushed off sou'-sou'west and found that I couldn't have set my course more shrewdly. There was a sort of yew alley or rhododendron walk or some such thing confronting me, and as I entered it I saw Gussie. He was standing in a kind of trance, and his fatheadedness in standing when he ought to have been running like a rabbit smote me like a blow and lent an extra emphasis to the "Hoy!" with which I accosted him.

He turned, and as I approached him I noted that he seemed even more braced than when last seen. The eyes behind the horn-rimmed spectacles gleamed with a brighter light, and a smile wreathed his lips. He looked like a fish that's just learned that its rich uncle in Australia has pegged out and left it a packet.

"Ah, Bertie," he said, "we decided to go for a walk, not a row. We thought it might be a little chilly on the water. What a beautiful evening, Bertie, is it not?"

I couldn't see eye to eye with him there.

"It strikes you as that, does it? It doesn't me."

He seemed surprised.

"In what respect do you find it not up to sample?"

"I'll tell you in what respect I find it not up to sample. What's all this I hear about you and Emerald Stoker? Did you kiss her?"

The Soul's Awakening expression on his face became intensified. Before my revolted eyes, Augustus Fink-Nottle definitely smirked.

"Yes, Bertie, I did, and I'll do it again if it's the last thing I do. What a girl, Bertie! So kind, so sympathetic. She's my idea of a thoroughly womanly woman, and you don't see many of them around these days. I hadn't time when I was in your room to tell you about what happened at the school treat."

"Jeeves told me. He said Bartholomew bit you."

"And how right he was. The bounder bit me to the bone. And do you know what Emerald Stoker did? Not only did she coo over me like a mother comforting a favorite child, but she bathed and bandaged my lacerated leg. She was a ministering angel, the nearest thing to Florence Nightingale

307

you could hope to find. It was shortly after she had done the swabbing and bandaging that I kissed her."

"Well, you shouldn't have kissed her."

Again he showed surprise. He had thought it, he said, a pretty sound idea.

"But you're engaged to Madeline."

I had hoped with these words to start his conscience working on all twelve cylinders, but something seemed to have gone wrong with the machinery, for he remained as calm and unmoved as the fish on ice he so closely resembled.

"Ah, Madeline," he said, "I was about to touch on Madeline. Shall I tell you what's wrong with Madeline Bassett? No heart. That's where she slips up. Lovely to look at, but nothing *here*," he said, tapping the left side of his chest. "Do you know how she reacted to that serious flesh wound of mine? She espoused Bartholomew's cause. She said the whole thing was my fault. She accused me of having teased the little blister. In short, she behaved like a louse. How different from Emerald Stoker. Do you know what Emerald Stoker did?"

"You told me."

"I mean in addition to binding up my wounds. She went straight off to the kitchen and cut me a package of sandwiches. I have them here," said Gussie, exhibiting a large parcel and eyeing it reverently. "Ham," he added in a voice that throbbed with emotion. "She made them for me with her own hands, and I think it was her thoughtfulness even more than her divine sympathy that showed me that she was the only girl in the world for me. The scales fell from my eyes, and I saw that what I had once felt for Madeline had been just a boyish infatuation. What I feel for Emerald Stoker is the real thing. In my opinion she stands alone, and I shall be glad if you will stop going about the place saying that she looks like a Pekingese."

"But, Gussie—"

He silenced me with an imperious wave of the ham sandwiches.

"It's no good your saying 'But, Gussie.' The trouble with you, Bertie, is that you haven't got it in you to understand true love. You're a mere butterfly flitting from flower to flower and sipping, like Freddie Widgeon and the rest of the half-wits of whom the Drones Club is far too full. A girl to you is just the plaything of an idle hour, and anything in the nature of a grand passion is beyond you. I'm different. I have depth. I'm a marrying man."

"But you can't marry Emerald Stoker."

"Why not? We're twin souls."

I thought for a moment of giving him a word portrait of old Stoker, to show him the sort of father-in-law he would be getting if he carried through the project he had in mind, but I let it go. Reason told me that a fellow who for months had been expecting to draw Pop Bassett as a father-in-law was not going to be swayed by an argument like that. However frank my description of him, Stoker could scarcely seem anything but a change for the better.

I stood there at a loss, and was still standing there at a loss, when I heard my name called and, looking behind me, saw Stinker and Stiffy. They were waving hands and things, and I gathered that they had come to thresh out with me the matter of Sir Watkyn Bassett and the hard-boiled egg.

The last thing I would have wished at this crucial point in my affairs was an interruption, for all my faculties should have been concentrated on reasoning with Gussie and trying to make him see the light, but it has often been said of Bertram Wooster that when a buddy in distress is drawn to his attention he forgets self. No matter what his commitments elsewhere, the distressed buddy has only to beckon and he is with him. With a brief word to Gussie that I would be

309

back at an early date to resume our discussion, I hurried to where Stiffy and Stinker stood.

"Talk quick," I said. "I'm in conference. Too long to tell you all about it, but a serious situation has arisen. As, according to Jeeves, one has with you. From what he told me, I gathered that the odds against Stinker clicking as regards that vicarage have lengthened. More letting-I-dare-not-wait-upon-I-would-ness on Pop Bassett's part, he gave me to understand. Too bad."

"Of course, one can see it from Sir Watkyn's point of view," said Stinker, who, if he has a fault besides bumping into furniture and upsetting it, is always far too tolerant in his attitude toward the dregs of humanity. "He thinks that if I'd drilled the distinction between right and wrong more vigorously into the minds of the Infants Bible Class, the thing wouldn't have happened."

"I don't see why not," said Stiffy.

Nor did I. In my opinion, no amount of Sunday afternoon instruction would have been sufficient to teach a growing boy not to throw hard-boiled eggs at Sir Watkyn Bassett.

"But there's nothing I can do about it, is there?" I said.

"You bet there is," said Stiffy. "We haven't lost all hope of sweetening him. The great thing is to let his nervous system gradually recover its poise, and what we came to see you about, Bertie, was to tell you on no account to go near him till he's had a chance to simmer down. Don't seek him out. Leave him alone. The sight of you does something to him."

"No more than the sight of him does to me," I riposted warmly. I resented the suggestion that I had nothing better to do with my time than fraternize with ex-magistrates. "Certainly I'll avoid his society. It'll be a pleasure. Is that all?"

"That's all."

"Then I'll be getting back to Gussie," I said, and was starting to move off, when Stiffy uttered a sharp squeak.

"Gussie! That reminds me. There's something I wanted to tell him, something of vital concern to him, and I can't think how it slipped my mind. Gussie," she called, and Gussie, seeming to wake abruptly from a daydream, blinked and came over. "What are you doing hanging about here, Gussie?"

"Who, me? I was discussing something with Bertie, and he said he'd be back, when at liberty, to go into it further."

"Well, let me tell you that you've no time for discussing things with Bertie."

"Eh?"

"Or for saying 'Eh?' I met Roderick just now, and he asked me if I knew where you were, because he wants to tear you limb from limb, owing to his having seen you kiss the cook."

Gussie's jaw fell with a dull thud.

"You never told me that," he said to me, and one spotted the note of reproach in his voice.

"No, sorry, I forgot to mention it. But it's true. You'd better start coping. Run like a hare, is my advice."

He took it. Standing not on the order of his going, as the fellow said, he dashed off as if shot from a gun and was making excellent time when he was brought up short by colliding with Spode, who had at that moment entered left center.

CHAPTER
FIFTEEN

IT'S ALWAYS disconcerting to have even as small a chap as
Gussie take you squarely in the midriff, as I myself can
testify, having had the same experience down in Washington
Square during a visit to New York. Washington Square is
bountifully supplied with sad-eyed Italian kids who whiz to
and fro on roller skates, and one of them, proceeding on his
way with lowered head, rammed me in the neighborhood of
the third waistcoat button at a high rate of m.p.h. It gave
me a strange where-am-I feeling, and I imagine Spode's sen-
sations were somewhat similar. His breath escaped him in a
sharp "Oof!" and he swayed like some forest tree beneath
the woodman's ax. But unfortunately Gussie had paused to
sway, too, and this gave Spode time to steady himself on
even keel and regroup his forces. Reaching out a hamlike

hand, he attached it to the scruff of Gussie's neck and said, "Ha!"

"Ha!" is one of those things it's never easy to find the right reply to—it resembles "You!" in that respect—but Gussie was saved the necessity of searching for words by the fact that he was being shaken like a cocktail in a manner that precluded speech, if precluded is the word I want. His spectacles fell off and came to rest near where I was standing. I picked them up with a view to returning them to him when he had need of them, which I could see would not be immediately.

As this Fink-Nottle was a boyhood friend, with whom, as I have said, I had frequently shared my last bar of milk chocolate, and as it was plain that if someone didn't intervene pretty soon he was in danger of having all his internal organs shaken into a sort of macédoine or hash, the thought of taking some steps to put an end to this distressing scene naturally crossed my mind. The problem presenting several points of interest was, of course, what steps to take. My tonnage was quite insufficient to enable me to engage Spode in hand-to-hand conflict, and I toyed with the idea of striking him on the back of the head with a log of wood. But this project was rendered null and void by the fact that there were no logs of wood present. These yew alleys or rhododendron walks provide twigs and fallen leaves but nothing in the shape of logs capable of being used as clubs. And I had just decided that something might be accomplished by leaping on Spode's back and twining my arms around his neck when I heard Stiffy cry, "Harold!"

One gathered what she was driving at. Gussie was no particular buddy of hers, but she was a tenderhearted young prune and one always likes to save a fellow creature's life, if possible. She was calling on Stinker to get into the act and

313

save Gussie's. And a quick look at him showed me that he was at a loss to know how to proceed. He stood there passing a finger thoughtfully over his chin, like a cat in an adage.

I knew what was stopping him getting action. It was not . . . it's on the tip of my tongue . . . begins with a p . . . I've heard Jeeves use the word . . . pusillanimity, that's it, meaning broadly that a fellow is suffering from a pronounced case of cold feet . . . it was not, as I was saying when I interrupted myself, pusillanimity that held him back. Under normal conditions lions could have taken his correspondence course, and had he encountered Spode on the football field, he would have had no hesitation in springing at his neck and twisting it into a lover's knot. The trouble was that he was a curate, and the brass hats of the Church look askance at curates who swat parishioners. Sock your flock, and you're sunk. So now he shrank from intervening, and when he did intervene, it was merely with the soft word that's supposed to turn away wrath.

"I say, you know, what?" he said.

I could have told him he was approaching the thing from the wrong angle. When a gorilla like Spode is letting his angry passions rise, there is little or no percentage in the mild remonstrance. Seeming to realize this, he advanced to where the blighter was now, or so it appeared, trying to strangle Gussie and laid a hand on his shoulder. Then, seeing that this, too, achieved no solid results, he pulled. There was a rending sound, and the clutching hand relaxed its grip.

I don't know if you've ever tried detaching a snow leopard of the Himalayas from its prey—probably not, as most people don't find themselves out that way much—but if you did, you would feel fairly safe in budgeting for a show of annoyance on the animal's part. It was the same with Spode. Incensed at what I suppose seemed to him this unwarrantable interference with his aims and objects, he hit Stinker on the nose, and all the doubts that had been bothering that man of God vanished in a flash.

I should imagine that if there's one thing that makes a fellow forget that he's in holy orders, it's a crisp punch on the beezer. A moment before, Stinker had been all concern about the disapproval of his superiors in the cloth, but now, as I read his mind, he was saying to himself, "To hell with my superiors in the cloth," or however a curate would put it; "let them eat cake."

It was a superb spectacle while it lasted, and I was able to understand what people meant when they spoke of the Church Militant. A good deal to my regret, it did not last long. Spode was full of the will to win, but Stinker had the science. It was not for nothing that he had added a boxing blue to his football blue when at the old Alma Mater. There was a brief mix-up, and the next thing one observed was Spode on the ground, looking like the corpse which had been in the water several days. His left eye was swelling visibly, and a referee could have counted a hundred over him without eliciting a response.

Stiffy, with a brief "At-a-boy," led Stinker off, no doubt to bathe his nose and stanch the vital flow, which was considerable, and I handed Gussie his glasses. He stood twiddling them in a sort of trance, and I made a suggestion which I felt was in his best interests.

"Not to presume to dictate, Gussie, but wouldn't it be wise to remove yourself before Spode comes to? From what I know of him, I think he's one of those fellows who wake up cross."

I have seldom seen anyone move quicker. We were out of the yew alley, if it was a yew alley, or the rhododendron walk, if that's what it was, almost before the words had left my lips. We continued to set a good pace, but eventually we slowed up a bit and he was able to comment on the recent scene.

"That was a ghastly experience, Bertie," he said.

"Can't have been at all pleasant," I agreed.

"My whole past life seemed to flash before me."

"That's odd. You weren't drowning."

"No, but the principle's the same. I can tell you I was thankful when Pinker made his presence felt. What a splendid chap he is."

"One of the best."

"That's what today's Church needs—more curates capable of hauling off and letting fellows like Spode have it where it does most good. One feels so safe when he's around."

I put a point which seemed to have escaped his notice.

"But he won't always be around. He has Infants Bible Classes and Mothers Meetings and all that sort of thing to occupy his time. And don't forget that Spode, though crushed to earth, will rise again."

His jaw sagged a bit.

"I never thought of that."

"If you take my advice, you'll clear out and go underground for a while. Stiffy would lend you her car."

"I believe you're right," he said, adding something about out of the mouths of babes and sucklings, which I thought a bit offensive. "I'll leave this evening."

"Without saying goodbye."

"Of course without saying goodbye. No, don't go that way. Keep bearing to the left. I want to go to the kitchen garden. I told Em I'd meet her there."

"You told *who?*"

"Emerald Stoker. Who did you think I meant? She had

to go to the kitchen garden and gather beans and things for tonight's dinner."

And there, sure enough, she was with a large basin in her hands, busy about her domestic duties.

"Here's Bertie, Em," said Gussie, and she whisked round, spilling a bean or two.

I was disturbed to see how every freckle on her face lit up as she looked at him, as if she were gazing on some lovely sight, which was far from being the case. In me she didn't seem much interested. A brief "Hullo, Bertie" appeared to cover it as far as I was concerned, her whole attention being earmarked for Gussie. She was staring at him as a mother might have stared at a loved child who had shown up at the home after a clash with one of the neighborhood children. Until then I had been too agitated to notice how disheveled his encounter with Spode had left him, but I now saw that his general appearance was that of something that has been passed through a wringer.

"What . . . *what* have you been doing to yourself?" She ejaculated, if that's the word. "You look like a devastated area."

"Inevitable in the circs," I said. "He's been having a spot of unpleasantness with Spode."

"Is that the man you were telling me about? The human gorilla?"

"That's the one."

"What happened?"

"Spode tried to shake the stuffing out of him."

"You poor precious lambkin," said Emerald, addressing Gussie, not me. "Gosh, I wish I had him here for a minute. I'd teach him!"

And by what I have always thought an odd coincidence her wish was granted. A crashing sound like that made by a herd of hippopotami going through the reeds on a river-bank attracted my notice and I beheld Spode approaching at the rate of knots with the obvious intention of resuming at as early a date as possible his investigations into the color of Gussie's insides which Stinker's intervention had compelled him to file under the head of unfinished business. In predicting that this menace in the treatment, though crushed to earth, would rise again, I had been perfectly correct.

There seemed to me a strong resemblance in the new-comer's manner to that of those Assyrians who, so we learn from sources close to them, came down like a wolf on the fold with their cohorts all gleaming with purple and gold. He could have walked straight into their camp, and they would have laid down the red carpet for him, recognizing him instantly as one of the boys.

But where the Assyrians had had the bulge on him was that they weren't going to find in the fold a motherly young woman with strong wrists and a basin in her hands. This basin appeared to be constructed of some thickish form of china, and as Spode grabbed Gussie and started to go into the old shaking routine it descended on the back of his head with what some call a dull and others a sickening thud. It broke into several fragments, but by that time its mission had been accomplished. His powers of resistance sapped, no doubt, by his recent encounter with the Rev. H. P. Pinker, Spode fell to earth he knew not where and lay there looking peaceful. I remember thinking at the time that this was not his lucky day, and it just showed, I thought, that it's always a mistake to be a louse in human shape, as he had been from birth, because sooner or later retribution is bound to overtake you. As I recall Jeeves putting it once, the mills of God grind slowly, but they grind exceeding small, or words to that effect.

For a space Emerald Stoker stood surveying her handiwork with a satisfied smile on her face, and I didn't blame her for looking a bit smug, for she had unquestionably fought the good fight. Then suddenly, with a quick "Oh, golly," she was off like a nymph surprised while bathing, and a moment later I understood what had caused this mobility. She had seen Madeline Bassett approaching, and no cook likes to have to explain to her employer why she has been bonneting her employer's guests with china basins.

As Madeline's eyes fell on the remains, they widened to the size of golf balls and she looked at Gussie as if he had been a mass murderer she wasn't very fond of.

"What have you been doing to Roderick?" she demanded.

"Eh?" said Gussie.

"I said, What have you done to Roderick?"

Gussie adjusted his spectacles and shrugged a shoulder.

"Oh, that? I merely chastised him. The fellow had only himself to blame. He asked for it, and I had to teach him a lesson."

"You brute!"

"Not at all. He had the option of withdrawing. He must have foreseen what would happen when he saw me remove my glasses. When I remove my glasses, those who know what's good for them take to the hills."

"I hate you, I hate you!" cried Madeline, a thing I didn't know anyone ever said except in the second act of a musical comedy.

"You do?" said Gussie.

"Yes, I do. I loathe you."

"Then, in that case," said Gussie, "I shall now eat a ham sandwich."

And this he proceeded to do with a sort of wolfish gusto

319

that sent cold shivers down my spine, and Madeline shrieked sharply.

"This is the end!" she said, another thing you don't often hear.

When things between two once loving hearts have hotted up to this extent, it is always the prudent course for the innocent bystander to edge away, and this I did. I started back to the house, and in the drive I met Jeeves. He was at the wheel of Stiffy's car. Beside him, looking like a Scotch elder rebuking sin, was the dog Bartholomew.

"Good evening, sir," he said. "I have been taking this little fellow to the veterinary surgeon. Miss Byng was uneasy because he bit Mr. Fink-Nottle. She was afraid he might have caught something. I am glad to say the surgeon has given him a clean bill of health."

"Jeeves," I said. "I have a tale of horror to relate."

"Indeed, sir?"

"The lute is mute," I said, and as briefly as possible put him in possesion of the facts. When I had finished, he agreed that it was most disturbing.

"But I fear there is nothing to be done, sir."

I reeled. I have grown so accustomed to seeing Jeeves solve every problem, however sticky, that this frank confession of his inability to deliver the goods unmanned me.

"You're baffled?"

"Yes, sir."

"At a loss?"

"Precisely, sir. Possibly at some future date a means of adjusting matters will occur to me, but at the moment, I regret to say, I can think of nothing. I am sorry, sir."

I shrugged the shoulders. The iron had entered into my soul, but the upper lip was stiff.

"It's all right, Jeeves. Not your fault if a thing like this

320

lays you a stymie. Drive on, Jeeves," I said, and he drove on. The dog Bartholomew gave me an unpleasantly superior look as they moved off, as if asking me if I were saved.

I pushed along to my room, the only spot in this joint of terror where anything in the nature of peace and quiet was to be had, not that even there one got much of it. The fierce rush of life at Totleigh Towers had got me down, and I wanted to be alone.

I suppose I must have sat there for more than half an hour, trying to think what was to be done for the best, and then, out of what I have heard Jeeves describe as the welter of emotions, one coherent thought emerged, and that was that if I didn't shortly get a snifter, I would expire in my tracks. It was now the cocktail hour, and I knew that, whatever his faults, Sir Watkyn Bassett provided apéritifs for his guests. True, I had promised Stiffy that I would avoid his society, but I had not anticipated then that this emergency would arise. It was a straight choice between betraying her trust and perishing where I sat, and I decided on the former alternative.

I found Pop Bassett in the drawing room with a well-laden tray at his elbow and hurried forward, licking my lips. To say that he looked glad to see me would be overstating it, but he offered me a life saver and I accepted it gratefully. An awkward silence of about twenty minutes followed, and then, just as I had finished my second and was fishing for the olive, Stiffy entered. She gave me a quick reproachful look, and I could see that her trust in Bertram's promises would never be the same again, but it was to Pop Bassett that she directed her attention.

"Hullo, Uncle Watkyn."

"Good evening, my dear."

"Having a spot before dinner?"

"I am."

"You think you are," said Stiffy, "but you aren't, and I'll tell you why. There isn't going to be any dinner. The cook's eloped with Gussie Fink-Nottle."

CHAPTER
SIXTEEN

I WONDER if you have ever noticed a rather peculiar thing—viz., how differently the same news item can affect two different people? I mean, you tell something to Jones and Brown, let us say, and while Jones sits plunged in gloom and looking licked to a splinter, Brown gives three rousing cheers and goes into a buck-and-wing dance. And the same thing is true of Smith and Robinson. Often struck me as curious, that has.

It was so now. Listening to the recent heated exchanges between Madeline Bassett and Gussie hadn't left me what you might call optimistic, but the heart bowed down with weight of woe to weakest hope will cling, as the fellow said, and I had tried to tell myself that their mutual love, though admittedly having taken it on the chin at the moment, might eventually get cracking again, causing all to be forgotten and forgiven. I mean to say, remorse has frequently been known to set in after a dustup between a couple of troth plighters, with all that Sorry-I-was-cross and Can-you-ever-forgive-me stuff, and love, after being down in the cellar for a time with no takers, perks up and carries on again as good as new. Oh, blessings on the falling out that all the more endears is the way I heard Jeeves put it once.

But at Stiffy's words this hope collapsed as if it had been struck on the back of the head with a china basin containing beans, and I sank forward in my chair, the face buried in the hands. It is always my policy to look on the bright side, but in order to do this you have to have a bright side to look on, and under existing conditions there wasn't one. This, as Madeline Bassett would have said, was the end. I had come to this house as a *raisonneur* to bring the young folks together, but however much of a *raisonneur* you are, you can't bring young folks together if one of them elopes with somebody else. You are not merely hampered but shackled. So now, as I say, I sank forward in my chair, the f. buried in the h.

To Pop Bassett, on the other hand, this bit of front-page news had plainly come as rare and refreshing fruit. My face being buried as stated, I couldn't see if he went into a buck-and-wing dance, but I should think it highly probable that he did a step or two, for when he spoke you could tell from the timbre of his voice that he was feeling about as pepped up as a man can feel without bursting.

One could understand his fizziness, of course. Of all the prospective sons-in-law in existence, Gussie, with the possible exception of Bertram Wooster, was the one he would have chosen last. He had viewed him with concern from the start, and if he had been living back in the days when fathers called the shots in the matter of their daughters' marriages, would have forbidden the banns without a second thought.

Gussie once told me that when he, Gussie, was introduced to him, Bassett, as the fellow who was to marry his, Bassett's, offspring, he, Bassett, had stared at him with his jaw dropping and then in a sort of strangled voice had said, "*What!*" Incredulously, if you see what I mean, as if he were hoping that they were just playing a jolly practical joke on him and that in due course the real chap would jump out from behind a chair and say, "April fool!" And when he, Bassett, at last got on to it that there was no deception and that Gussie was really what he had drawn, he went off into a corner and sat there motionless, refusing to speak when spoken to.

Little wonder, then, that Stiffy's announcement had bucked him up like a dose of Doctor Somebody's Tonic Swamp Juice, which acts directly on the red corpuscles and imparts a gentle glow.

"Eloped?" he gurgled.

"That's right."

"With the cook?"

"With none other. That's why I said there wasn't going to be any dinner. We shall have to make do with hard-boiled eggs, if there are any left over from the treat."

The mention of hard-boiled eggs made Pop Bassett wince for a moment, and one could see that his thoughts had flitted back to the tea tent, but he was far too happy to allow sad memories to trouble him for long. With a wave of the hand he dismissed dinner as something that didn't matter one way or the other. The Bassetts, the wave suggested, could rough it if they had to.

"Are you sure of your facts, my dear?"

"I met them as they were starting off. Gussie said he hoped I wouldn't mind him borrowing my car."

"You reassured him, I trust?"

"Oh, yes. I said, 'That's all right, Gussie. Help yourself.' "

"Good girl. Good girl. An excellent response. Then they have really gone?"

"With the wind."

"And they plan to get married?"

"As soon as Gussie can get a special license. You have to apply to the Archbishop of Canterbury, and I'm told he stings you for quite a bit. "

"Money well spent."

"That's how Gussie feels. He told me he was dropping the cook at Bertie's aunt's place and then going on to London to confer with the Archbish. He's full of zeal."

This extraordinary statement that Gussie was landing Emerald Stoker on Aunt Dahlia brought my head up with a jerk. I found myself speculating on how the old flesh and blood was going to take the intrusion, and it gave me rather an awed feeling to think how deep Gussie's love for his Em must be, to make him face such fearful risks. The aged relative has a strong personality and finds no difficulty, when displeased, in reducing the object of her displeasure to a spot of grease in a matter of minutes. I am told that sportsmen whom in her hunting days she had occasion to rebuke for riding over hounds were never the same again and for months would go about in a sort of stupor, starting at sudden noises.

My head being now up, I was able to see Pop Bassett, and I found that he was regarding me with an eye so benevolent that I could hardly believe that this was the same ex-magistrate with whom I had so recently been hobnobbing, if you can call it hobnobbing when a couple of fellows sit in a couple of chairs for twenty minutes without saying a word to each other. It was plain that joy had made him the friend of all the world, even to the extent of allowing him to look at Bertram without a shudder. He was more like something out of Dickens than anything human.

"Your glass is empty, Mr. Wooster," he cried buoyantly. "May I refill it?"

I said he might. I had had two, which is generally my limit, but with my aplomb shattered as it was I felt that a third wouldn't hurt. Indeed, I would have been willing to go even more deeply into the thing. I once read about a man who used to drink twenty-six martinis before dinner, and the conviction was beginning to steal over me that he had had the right idea.

"Roderick tells me," he proceeded, as sunny as if a crack of his had been greeted with laughter in court, "that the reason you were unable to be with us at the school treat this afternoon was that urgent family business called you to Brinkley Court. I trust everything turned out satisfactorily?"

"Oh yes, thanks."

"We all missed you, but business before pleasure, of course. How was your uncle? You found him well, I hope?"

"Yes, he was fine."

"And your aunt?"

"She had gone to London."

"Indeed? You must have been sorry not to have seen her. I know few women I admire more. So hospitable. So breezy. I have seldom enjoyed anything more than my recent visit to her house."

I think his exuberance would have led him to continue in the same strain indefinitely, but at this point Stiffy came out of the thoughtful silence into which she had fallen. She had been standing there regarding him with a speculative eye, as if debating within herself whether or not to start some-

327

thing, and now she gave the impression that her mind was made up.

"I'm glad to see you so cheerful, Uncle Watkyn. I was afraid my news might have upset you."

"Upset me!" said Pop Bassett incredulously. "Whatever put that idea in your head?"

"Well, you're short one son-in-law."

"It is precisely that that has made this the happiest day of my life."

"Then you can make it the happiest of mine," said Stiffy, striking while the iron was h. "By giving Harold that vicarage."

Most of my attention, as you may well imagine, being concentrated on contemplating the soup in which I was immersed, I cannot say whether or not Pop Bassett hesitated, but if he did, it was only for an instant. No doubt for a second or two the vision of that hard-boiled egg rose before him and he was conscious again of the resentment he had been feeling at Stinker's failure to keep a firm hand on the junior members of his flock, but the thought that Augustus Fink-Nottle was not to be his son-in-law drove the young cleric's shortcomings from his mind. Filled with the milk of human kindness so nearly to the brim that you could almost hear it sloshing about inside him, he was in no shape to deny anyone anything. I really believe that if at this point in the proceedings I had tried to touch him for a fiver, he would have parted without a cry.

"Of course, of course, of course, of course," he said, caroling like one of Jeeves' larks on the wing. "I am sure that Pinker will make an excellent vicar."

"The best," said Stiffy. "He's wasted as a curate. No scope. Running under wraps. Unleash him as a vicar, and he'll be the talk of the established church. He's as hot as a pistol."

"I have always had the highest opinion of Harold Pinker."

"I'm not surprised. All the nibs feel the same. They know he's got what it takes. Very sound on doctrine and can preach like a streak."

"Yes, I enjoy his sermons. Manly and straightforward."

"That's because he's one of these healthy outdoor open-air men. Muscular Christianity, that's his dish. He used to play football for England."

"Indeed?"

"He was what's called a prop forward."

"Really?"

At the words "prop forward" I had, of course, started visibly. I hadn't known that that's what Stinker was, and I was thinking how ironical life could be. I mean to say, there was Plank searching high and low for a forward of this nature, saying to himself that he would pretty soon have to give up the hopeless quest, and here was I in a position to fill the bill for him but, owing to the strained condition of our relations, unable to put him on to this good thing. Very sad, I felt, and the thought occurred to me, as it had often done before, that one ought to be kind even to the very humblest, because you never know when they may not come in useful.

"Then may I tell Harold that the balloon's going up?" said Stiffy.

"I beg your pardon?"

"I mean it's official about this vicarage?"

"Certainly, certainly, certainly."

"Oh, Uncle Watkyn! How can I thank you?"

"Quite all right, my dear," said Pop Bassett, more Dickensy than ever. "And now," he went on, parting from his moorings and making for the door, "you will excuse me, Stephanie, and you, Mr. Wooster. I must go to Madeline and—"

"Congratulate her?"

"I was about to say dry her tears."

"If any."

"You think she will not be in a state of dejection?"

"Would any girl be, who's been saved by a miracle from having to marry Gussie Fink-Nottle?"

"True. Very true," said Pop Bassett, and he was out of the room like one of those wing three-quarters who, even if they can't learn to give the reverse pass, are fast.

If there had been any uncertainty as to whether Sir Watkyn Bassett had done a buck-and-wing dance, there was none about Stiffy doing one now. She pirouetted freely, and the dullest eye could discern that it was only the fact that she hadn't one on that kept her from strewing roses from her hat. I had seldom seen a young shrimp so above herself. And I, having Stinker's best interests at heart, packed all my troubles in the old kit bag for the time being and rejoiced with her. If there's one thing Bertram Wooster is and always has been nippy at, it's forgetting his personal worries when a pal is celebrating some stroke of good fortune.

For some time Stiffy monopolized the conversation, not letting me get a word in edgeways. Women are singularly gifted in this respect. The frailest of them has the lung power of a gramophone record and the flow of speech of a Regimental Sergeant Major. I have known my Aunt Agatha to go on calling me names long after you would have supposed that both breath and inventiveness would have given out.

Her theme was the stupendous bit of good luck which was about to befall Stinker's new parishioners, for they would be getting not only the perfect vicar, a saintly character who would do the square thing by their souls, but in addition the sort of vicar's wife you dream about. It was only when she paused after drawing a picture of herself doling out soup to the deserving poor and asking in a gentle voice after their rheumatism that I was able to rise to a point of order. In the midst of all the joyfulness and backslapping a sobering thought had occurred to me.

"I agree with you," I said, "that this would appear to be the happy ending, and I can quite see how you have arrived at the conclusion that it's the maddest, merriest day of all the glad new year, but there's something you ought to give a thought to, and it seems to me you're overlooking it."

"What's that? I didn't think I'd missed anything."

"This promise of Pop Bassett's to give you the vicarage."

"All in order, surely? What's your kick?"

"I was only thinking that, if I were you, I'd get it in writing."

This stopped her as if she had bumped into a prop forward. The ecstatic animation faded from her face, to be replaced by the anxious look and the quick chewing of the lower lip. It was plain that I had given her food for thought.

"You don't think Uncle Watkyn would double-cross us?"

"There are no limits to what your foul Uncle Watkyn can do, if the mood takes him," I responded gravely. "I wouldn't trust him an inch. Where's Stinker?"

"Out on the lawn, I think."

"Then get hold of him and bring him here and have Pop Bassett embody the thing in the form of a letter."

"I suppose you know you're making my flesh creep?"

"Merely pointing out the road to safety."

She mused awhile, and the lower lip got a bit more chewing done to it.

"All right," she said at length. "I'll fetch Harold."

"And it wouldn't hurt to bring a couple of lawyers, too," I said as she whizzed past me.

It was about five minutes later, as I was falling into a reverie and brooding once more on the extreme stickiness of my affairs, that Jeeves came in and told me I was wanted on the telephone.

CHAPTER
SEVENTEEN

I PALED beneath my tan.

"Who is it, Jeeves?"

"Mrs. Travers, sir."

Precisely what I had feared. It was, as I have indicated, an easy drive from Totleigh Towers to Brinkley Court, and in his exhilarated state Gussie would no doubt have kept a firm foot on the accelerator and given the machine all the gas at his disposal. I presumed that he and girl friend must have just arrived and that this telephone call was Aunt Dahlia what-the-helling. Knowing how keenly the old bean resented being made the recipient of anything in the nature of funny business, into which category Gussie's butting in uninvited with his Em in attendance would unquestionably fall, I braced myself for the coming storm with as much fortitude as I could muster.

You might say, of course, that his rash act was no fault of mine and had nothing to do with me, but it's practically routine for aunts to blame nephews for everything that happens. It seems to be what nephews are for. It was only by an oversight, I have always felt, that my Aunt Agatha omitted to hold me responsible a year or two ago when her son, young Thos, nearly got sacked from the scholastic institution which he attends for breaking out at night in order to go and shy for coconuts at the local amusement park.

"How did she seem, Jeeves?"

"Sir?"

"Did she give you the impression that she was splitting a gusset?"

"Not particularly, sir. Mrs. Travers' voice is always robust. Would there be any reason why she should be splitting the gusset to which you refer?"

"You bet there would. No time to tell you now, but the skies are darkening and the air is full of V-shaped depressions off the coast of Iceland."

"I am sorry, sir."

"Nor are you the only one. Who was the fellow—or fellows, for I believe there was more than one—who went into the burning fiery furnace?"

"Shadrach, Meshach, and Abednego, sir."

"That's right. The names were on the tip of my tongue. I read about them when I won my Scripture Knowledge prize at school. Well, I know just how they must have felt. Aunt Dahlia?" I said, for I had now reached the instrument.

I had been expecting to have my ear scorched with well-chosen words, but to my surprise she seemed in merry mood. There was no suggestion of recrimination in her voice.

"Hullo there, you young menace to western civilization," she boomed. "How are you? Still ticking over?"

"To a certain extent. And you?"

"I'm fine. Did I interrupt you in the middle of your tenth cocktail?"

"My third," I corrected. "I usually stay steady at two, but Pop Bassett insisted on replenishing my glass. He's a bit above himself at the moment and very much the master of the revels. I wouldn't put it past him to have an ox roasted whole in the marketplace, if he can find an ox."

"Stinko, is he?"

"Not perhaps stinko, but certainly effervescent."

"Well, if you can suspend your drunken orgy for a minute or two, I'll tell you the news from home. I got back from London a quarter of an hour ago, and what do you think I found waiting on the mat? That newt-collecting freak Spink-Bottle, accompanied by a girl who looks like a Pekingese with freckles."

I drew a deep breath and embarked on my speech for the defense. If Bertram was to be put in the right light, now was the moment. True, her manner so far had been affable and she had given no sign of being about to go off with a bang, but one couldn't be sure that that wasn't because she was just biding her time. It's never safe to dismiss aunts lightly at times like this.

"Yes," I said, "I heard he was on his way, complete with freckled human Pekingese. I am sorry, Aunt Dahlia, that you should have been subjected to this unwarrantable intrusion, and I would like to make it abundantly clear that it was not the outcome of any advice or encouragement from me. I was in total ignorance of his intentions. Had he confided in me his purpose of inflicting his presence on you, I should have—"

Here I paused, for she had asked me rather brusquely to put a sock in it.

335

"Stop babbling, you ghastly young gas bag. What's all this silver-tongued orator stuff about?"

"I was merely expressing my regret that you should have been subjected—"

"Well, don't. There's no need to apologize. I couldn't be more pleased. I admit that I'm always happier when I don't have Spink-Bottle breathing down the back of my neck and taking up space in the house which I require for other purposes, but the girl was as welcome as manna in the wilderness."

Having won that prize for Scripture Knowledge I was speaking of, I had no difficulty in grasping her allusion. She was referring to an incident which occurred when the children of Israel were crossing some desert or other and were sorely in need of refreshment, rations being on the slender side. And they were just saying to one another how well a spot of manna would go down and regretting that there was none in the quartermaster's stores when blowed if a whole wad of the stuff didn't descend from the skies, just making their day.

Her words had of course surprised me somewhat, and I asked her why Emerald Stoker had been as welcome as manna in the w.

"Because her arrival brought sunshine into a stricken home. There couldn't have been a smoother piece of timing. You didn't see Anatole when you were over here this afternoon, did you?"

"No. Why?"

"I was wondering if you had noticed anything wrong with him. Shortly after you left, he developed a *mal au foie* or whatever he called it and took to his bed."

"I'm sorry."

"So was Tom. He was looking forward gloomily to a

dinner cooked by the kitchen maid, who, though a girl of many sterling merits, always adopts the scorched-earth policy when preparing a meal, and you know what his digestion's like. Conditions looked dark, and then Spink-Bottle suddenly revealed that this Pekingese of his was an experienced chef, and she's taken over. Who is she? Do you know anything about her?"

I was, of course, able to supply the desired information.

"She's the daughter of a well-to-do American millionaire called Stoker, who, I imagine, will be full of strange oaths when he hears she's married Gussie, the latter being, as you will concede, not everybody's cup of tea."

"So he isn't going to marry Madeline Bassett?"

"No, the fixture has been scratched."

"That's definite, is it?"

"Yes."

"You can't have been much success as a *raisonneur*."

"No."

"Well, I think she'll make Spink-Bottle a good wife. Seems a very nice girl."

"Few better."

"But this leaves you in rather a spot, doesn't it? If Madeline Bassett is now at large, won't she expect you to fill in?"

"That, aged relative, is the fear that haunts me."

"Has Jeeves nothing to suggest?"

"He says he hasn't. But I've known him on previous occasions to be temporarily baffled and then suddenly to wave his magic wand and fix everything up. So I haven't entirely lost hope."

"No, I expect you'll wriggle out of it somehow, as you always do. I wish I had a fiver for every time you've been within a step of the altar rails and have managed to escape

337

unscathed. I remember you telling me once that you had faith in your star."

"Quite. Still, it's no good trying to pretend that peril doesn't loom. It looms like the dickens. The corner in which I find myself is tight."

"And you would like to get that way, too, I suppose? All right, you can get back to your orgy when I've told you why I rang you up."

"Haven't you?" I said, surprised.

"Certainly not. You don't catch me wasting time and money chatting with you about your amours. Here is the nub. You know that black amber thing of Bassett's?"

"The statuette? Of course."

"I want to buy it for Tom. I've come into a bit of money. The reason I went to London today was to see my lawyer about a legacy someone's left me. Old school friend, if that's of any interest to you. It works out at about a couple of thousand quid, and I want you to get that statuette for me."

"It's going to be pretty hard to get away with it."

"Oh, you'll manage. Go as high as fifteen hundred pounds, if you have to. I suppose you couldn't just slip it in your pocket? It would save a lot of overhead. But probably that's asking too much of you, so tackle Bassett and get him to sell it."

"Well, I'll do my best. I know how much Uncle Tom covets that statuette. Rely on me, Aunt Dahlia."

"That's my boy."

I returned to the drawing room in somewhat pensive mood, for my relations with Pop Bassett were such that it was going to be embarrassing trying to do business with him, but I was relieved that the aged relative had dismissed the idea of purloining the thing. Surprised, too, as well as relieved, because the stern lesson association with her over

338

the years has taught me is that when she wants to do a loved husband a good turn, she is seldom fussy about the methods employed at that end. It was she who had initiated, if that's the word I want, the theft of the cow creamer, and you would have thought she would have wanted to save money on the current deal. Her view has always been that if a collector pinches something from another collector, it doesn't count as stealing, and of course there may be something in it. Pop Bassett, when at Brinkley, would unquestionably have looted Uncle Tom's collection, had he not been closely watched. These collectors have about as much conscience as the smash-and-grab fellows for whom the police are always spreading dragnets.

I was musing along these lines and trying to think what would be the best way of approaching Pop, handicapped as I would be by the fact that he shuddered like a jelly in a high wind every time he saw me and preferred when in my presence to sit and stare before him without uttering, when the door opened and Spode came in.

CHAPTER
EIGHTEEN

THE FIRST THING that impressed itself on the senses was that
he had about as spectacular a black eye as you could meet
with in a month of Sundays, and I found myself at a momentary loss to decide how it was best to react to it. I mean,
some fellows with bunged-up eyes want sympathy, others
prefer that you pretend that you've noticed nothing unusual
in their appearance. I came to the conclusion that it was
wisest to greet him with a careless "Ah, Spode," and I did
so, though I suppose, looking back, that "Ah, Sidcup"
would have been more suitable; and it was as I spoke that
I became aware that he was glaring at me in a sinister
manner with the eye that wasn't closed. I have spoken of
these eyes of his as being capable of opening an oyster at
sixty paces, and even when only one of them was functioning

the impact of his gaze was disquieting. I have known my Aunt Agatha's gaze to affect me in the same way.

"I was looking for you, Wooster," he said.

He uttered the words in the unpleasant rasping voice which had once kept his followers on the jump. Before succeeding to his new title, he had been one of those Dictators who were fairly common at one time in the metropolis and had gone about with a mob of underlings wearing black shorts and shouting "Heil, Spode!" or words along those general lines. He gave it up when he became Lord Sidcup, but he was still apt to address all and sundry as if he were ticking off some erring member of his entourage whose shorts had got a patch on them.

"Oh, were you?" I said.

"I was." He paused for a moment, continuing to give me the eye; then he said, "So!"

"So!" is another of those things like "You!" and "Ha!" which it's never easy to find the right answer to. Nothing in the way of a comeback suggested itself to me, so I merely lit a cigarette in what I intended to be a nonchalant manner, though I may have missed it by a considerable margin, and he proceeded.

"So I was right!"

"Eh?"

"In my suspicions."

"Eh?"

"They have been confirmed."

"Eh?"

"Stop saying 'Eh?' you miserable worm, and listen to me."

I humored him. You might have supposed that having so recently seen him knocked base over apex by the Rev. H. P. Pinker and subsequently laid out cold by Emerald Stoker and her basin of beans I would have regarded him with contempt as pretty small-time stuff and rebuked him sharply for calling me a miserable worm, but the idea never so much as crossed my mind. He had suffered reverses, true, but they had left him with his spirit unbroken and the muscles of his brawny arms just as much like iron bands as they had always been, and the way I looked at it was that if he wanted me to go easy on the word "Eh?" he had only to say so.

Continuing to pierce me with the eye that was still on duty, he said, "I happened to be passing through the hall just now."

"Oh?"

"I heard you talking on the telephone."

"Oh?"

"You were speaking to your aunt."

"Oh?"

"Don't keep saying 'Oh?' blast you."

Well, these restrictions were making it a bit hard for me to hold up my end of the conversation, but there seemed nothing to be done about it. I maintained a rather dignified silence, and he resumed his remarks.

"Your aunt was urging you to steal Sir Watkyn's amber statuette."

"She wasn't!"

"Pardon me. I thought you would try to deny the charge, so I took the precaution of jotting down your actual words. The statuette was mentioned and you said, 'It's going to be pretty hard to get away with it.' She then presumably urged you to spare no effort, for you said, 'Well, I'll do my best. I know how much Uncle Tom covets that statuette. Rely on me, Aunt Dahlia.' What the devil are you gargling about?"

"Not gargling," I corrected. "Laughing lightly. Because you've got the whole thing wrong, though I must say the way you've managed to record the dialogue does you a good deal of credit. Do you use shorthand?"

"How do you mean I've got it wrong?"

"Aunt Dahlia was asking me to try to buy the thing from Sir Watkyn."

He snorted and said "Ha!" and I thought it a bit unjust that he should say "Ha!" if I wasn't allowed to say "Eh?" and "Oh?" There should always be a certain give-and-take in these matters, or where are you?

"Do you expect me to believe that?"

"Don't you believe it?"

"No, I don't. I'm not an ass."

This, of course, was a debatable point, as I once heard Jeeves describe it, but I didn't press it.

"I know that aunt of yours," he proceeded. "She would steal the filling of your back teeth if she thought she could do it without detection." He paused for a moment, and I knew that he was thinking of the cow creamer. He had always—and, I must admit, not without reason—suspected the old flesh and blood of being the motive force behind its disappearance, and I imagine it had been a nasty knock to him that nothing could be proved. "Well, I strongly advise you, Wooster, not to let her make a cat's-paw of you this time, because if you're caught, as you certainly will be, you'll be for it. Don't think that Sir Watkyn will hush the thing up to avoid a scandal. You'll go to prison, that's where you'll go. He dislikes you intensely, and nothing would please him more than to be able to give you a long stretch without the option."

I thought this showed a vindictive spirit in the old warthog, and one that I deplored, but I felt it would be injudicious to say so. I merely nodded understandingly. I was thankful that there was no danger of this contingency, as

343

Jeeves would have called it, arising. Strong in the knowledge that nothing would induce me to pinch their ruddy statuette, I was able to remain calm and nonchalant, or as calm and nonchalant as you can be when a fellow eight foot six in height with one eye bunged up and the other behaving like an oxyacetylene blowpipe is glaring at you.

"Yes, sir," said Spode, "it'll be chokey for you."

And he was going on to say that he would derive great pleasure from coming on visiting days and making faces at me through the bars, when Pop Bassett returned.

But a very different Bassett from the fizzy rejoicer who had exited so short a while before. Then he had been all buck and beans, as any father would have been whose daughter was not going to marry Gussie Fink-Nottle. Now his face was drawn and his general demeanor that of an incautious luncher who discovers when there is no time to draw back that he has swallowed a rather too elderly oyster.

"Madeline tells me," he began. Then he saw Spode's eye and broke off. It was the sort of eye which, even if you have a lot on your mind, you can't help noticing. "Good gracious, Roderick," he said, "did you have a fall?"

"Fall, my foot," said Spode; "I was socked by a curate."

"Good heavens! What curate?"

"There's only one in these parts, isn't there?"

"You mean you were assaulted by Mr. Pinker? You astound me, Roderick."

Spode spoke with genuine feeling.

"Not half as much as he astounded *me*. He was more or less of a revelation to me, I don't mind telling you, because I didn't know curates had left hooks like that. He's got a knack of feinting you off balance and then coming in with a sort of corkscrew punch which it's impossible not to admire. I must get him to teach it to me some time."

"You speak as though you bore him no animosity."

"Of course I don't. A very pleasant little scrap with no ill feeling on either side. I've nothing against Pinker. The one I've got it in for is the cook. She beaned me with a china basin. From behind, of all unsporting things. If you'll excuse me, I'll go and have a word with that cook."

He was so obviously looking forward to telling Emerald Stoker what he thought of her that it gave me quite a pang to have to break it to him that his errand would be bootless.

"You can't," I pointed out. "She is no longer with us."

"Don't be an ass. She's in the kitchen, isn't she?"

"I'm sorry, no. She's eloped with Gussie Fink-Nottle. A wedding has been arranged and will take place as soon as the Archbish of Canterbury lets him have a special license."

Spode reeled. He had only one eye to stare at me with, but he got all the mileage out of it that was possible.

"Is that true?"

"Absolutely."

"Well, that makes up for everything. If Madeline's back in circulation . . . Thank you for telling me, Wooster, old chap."

"Don't mention it, Spode, old man, or, rather, Lord Sidcup, old man."

For the first time, Pop Bassett appeared to become aware that the slight, distinguished-looking young fellow standing on one leg by the sofa was Bertram.

"Mr. Wooster," he said. Then he stopped, swallowed once or twice, and groped his way to the table where the drinks were. His manner was feverish. Having passed a liberal snootful down the hatch, he was able to resume. "I have just seen Madeline."

"Oh yes?" I said courteously. "How is she?"

"Off her head, in my opinion. She says she is going to marry you."

Well, I had more or less steeled myself to something along

345

these lines, so except for quivering like a stricken blanc-mange and letting my lower jaw fall perhaps six inches I betrayed no sign of discomposure, in which respect I differed radically from Spode, who reeled for the second time and uttered a cry like that of a cinnamon bear that has stubbed its toe on a passing rock.

"You're joking!"

Pop Bassett shook his head regretfully. His face was haggard.

"I wish I were, Roderick. I am not surprised that you are upset. I feel the same myself. I am distraught. I can see no light on the horizon. When she told me, it was as if I had been struck by a thunderbolt."

Spode was staring at me, aghast. Even now, it seemed, he was unable to take in the full horror of the situation. There was incredulity in his one good eye.

"But she can't marry *that!*"

"She seems resolved to."

"But he's worse than that fish-faced blighter."

"I agree with you. Far worse. No comparison."

"I'll go and talk to her," said Spode, and left us before I could express my resentment at being called *that*.

It was perhaps fortunate that only half a minute later Stiffy and Stinker entered, for if I had been left alone with Pop Bassett, I would have been hard put to it to hit on a topic of conversation calculated to interest, elevate, and amuse.

346

CHAPTER
NINETEEN

STINKER'S NOSE, as was only to be expected, had swollen a good deal since last heard from, but he seemed in excellent spirits, and Stiffy couldn't have been merrier and brighter. Both were obviously thinking in terms of the happy ending, and my heart bled freely for the unfortunate young slobs. I had observed Pop Bassett closely while Spode was telling him about Stinker's left hook, and what I had read on his countenance had not been encouraging.

These patrons of livings with vicarages to bestow always hold rather rigid views as regards the qualifications they demand from the curates they are thinking of promoting to fields of higher activity, and left hooks, however adroit, are not among them. If Pop Bassett had been a fight promoter on the lookout for talent and Stinker a promising novice anxious to be put on his next program for a six-round preliminary bout, he would no doubt have gazed on him with a kindly eye. As it was, the eye he was now directing at him was as cold and bleak as if my old crony had been standing before him in the dock, charged with having moved pigs without a permit or failed to abate a smoky chimney. I could see trouble looming, and I wouldn't have risked a bet on the happy e. even at the most liberal odds.

The stickiness of the atmosphere, so patent to my keener sense, had not communicated itself to Stiffy. No voice was whispering in her ear that she was about to be let down with a thud which would jar her to the back teeth. She was all smiles and viv-whatever-the-word is, plainly convinced that the signing on the dotted line was now a mere formality.

"Here we are, Uncle Watkyn," she said, beaming freely.

"So I see."

"I've brought Harold."

"So I perceive."

"We've talked it over, and we think we ought to have the thing embodied in the form of a letter."

Pop Bassett's eye grew colder and bleaker, and the feeling I had that we were all back in Bosher Street Police Court deepened. Nothing, it seemed to me, was needed to complete the illusion except a magistrate's clerk with a cold in the head, a fug you could cut with a knife, and a few young barristers hanging about hoping for dock briefs.

"I fear I do not understand you," he said.

"Oh, come, Uncle Watkyn, you know you're brighter than that. I'm talking about Harold's vicarage."

"I was not aware that Mr. Pinker had a vicarage."

"The one you're going to give him, I mean."

"Oh?" said Pop Bassett, and I have seldom heard an "Oh?" that had a nastier sound. "I have just seen Roderick," he added, getting down to the *res*.

At the mention of Spode's name Stiffy giggled, and I could have told her it was a mistake. There is a time for girlish frivolity and a time when it is misplaced. It had not escaped my notice that Pop Bassett had begun to swell like one of those curious circular fish you catch down in Florida, and in addition to this he was rumbling as I imagine volcanos do before starting in on the neighboring householders and making them wish they had settled elsewhere.

But even now Stiffy seemed to have no sense of impending doom. She uttered another silvery laugh. I've noticed this slowness in getting hep to atmospheric conditions in other girls. The young of the gentler sex never appear to realize that there are moments when the last thing required by their audience is the silvery laugh.

"I'll bet he had a shiner."

"I beg your pardon?"

"Was his eye black?"

"It was."

"I thought it would be. Harold's strength is as the strength of ten, because his heart is pure. Well, how about that embodying letter? I have a fountain pen. Let's get the show on the road."

I was expecting Pop Bassett to give an impersonation of a bomb falling on an ammunition dump, but he didn't. Instead, he continued to exhibit that sort of chilly stiffness which you see in magistrates when they're fining people five quid for boyish peccadilloes.

"You appear to be under a misapprehension, Stephanie," he said in the metallic voice he had once used when addressing the prisoner Wooster. "I have no intention of entrusting Mr. Pinker with a vicarage."

Stiffy took it big. She shook from windswept hairdo to shoe sole, and if she hadn't clutched at Stinker's arm might have taken a toss. One could understand her emotion. She

349

had been coasting along, confident that she had it made, and suddenly out of a blue and smiling sky these words of doom. No doubt it was the suddenness and unexpectedness of the wallop that unmanned her, if you can call it unmanning when it happens to a girl. I suppose she was feeling very much as Spode had felt when Emerald Stoker's basin had connected with his occiput. Her eyes bulged, and her voice came out in a passionate squeak.

"But, Uncle Watkyn! You promised!"

I could have told her she was wasting her breath trying to appeal to the old buzzard's better feelings, because magistrates, even when ex, don't have any. The tremolo in her voice might have been expected to melt what is usually called a heart of stone, but it had no more effect on Pop Bassett than the chirping of the household canary.

"Provisionally only," he said. " I was not aware, when I did so, that Mr. Pinker had brutally assaulted Roderick."

At these words Stinker, who had been listening to the exchanges in a rigid sort of way, creating the illusion that he had been stuffed by a good taxidermist, came suddenly to life, though, as all he did was make a sound like the last drops of water going out of a bathtub, it was hardly worth the trouble and expense. He succeeded, however, in attracting Pop Bassett's attention, and the latter gave him the eye.

"Yes, Mr. Pinker?"

It was a moment or two before Stinker followed up the gurgling noise with speech. And even then it wasn't much in the way of speech. He said: "I—er—He—er—"

"Proceed, Mr. Pinker."

"It was—I mean it wasn't—"

"If you could make yourself a little plainer, Mr. Pinker, it would be of great assistance to our investigations into the matter under discussion. I must confess to finding you far from lucid."

It was the type of crack he had been accustomed in the old Bosher Street days to seeing in print with "laughter" after it in brackets, but on this occasion it fell flatter than a Dover sole. It didn't get a snicker out of me, or out of Stinker, who merely knocked over a small china ornament and turned a deeper vermilion, while Stiffy came back at him in great shape.

"There's no need to talk like a magistrate, Uncle Watkyn."

"I beg your pardon?"

"In fact, it would be better if you stopped talking at all and let me explain. What Harold's trying to tell you is that he didn't brutally assault Roderick; Roderick brutally assaulted him."

"Indeed? That was not the way I heard the story."

"Well, it's the way it happened."

"I am perfectly willing to hear your version of the deplorable incident."

"All right, then. Here it comes. Harold was cooing to Roderick like a turtledove, and Roderick suddenly hauled off and plugged him squarely on the beezer. If you don't believe me, take a look at it. The poor angel spouted blood like a Versailles fountain. Well, what would you have expected Harold to do? Turn the other nose?"

"I would have expected him to remember his position as a clerk in holy orders. He should have complained to me, and I would have seen to it that Roderick made ample apology."

A sound like the shot heard round the world rang through the room. It was Stiffy snorting.

"Apology!" she cried, having got the snort out of her system. "What's the good of apologies? Harold took the only possible course. He sailed in and laid Roderick out cold, as anyone would have done in his place."

351

"Anyone who had not his cloth to think of."

"For goodness' sake, Uncle Watkyn, a fellow can't be thinking of cloth all the time. It was an emergency. Roderick was murdering Gussie Fink-Nottle."

"And Mr. Pinker *stopped* him? Great heavens!"

There was a pause while Pop Bassett struggled with his feelings. Then Stiffy, as Stinker had done with Spode, had a shot at the honeyed word. She had spoken of Stinker cooing to Spode like a turtledove, and if memory served me aright that was just how he had cooed, and it was of a cooing turtledove that she now reminded me. Like most girls, she can always get a melting note into her voice if she thinks there's any percentage to be derived from it.

"It's not like you, Uncle Watkyn, to go back on your solemn promise."

I could have corrected her there. I would have thought it was just like him.

"I can't believe it's really you who's doing this cruel thing to me. It's so unlike you. You have always been so kind to me. You have made me love and respect you. I have come to look on you as a second father. Don't louse the whole thing up now."

A powerful plea, which with any other man would undoubtedly have brought home the bacon. With Pop Bassett it didn't get to first base. He had been looking like a man with no bowels—of compassion, I mean of course—and he went on looking like one.

"If by that peculiar expression you intend to imply that you are expecting me to change my mind and give Mr. Pinker this vicarage, I must disappoint you. I shall do no such thing. I consider that he has shown himself unfit to be a vicar, and I am surprised that after what has occurred he can reconcile it with his conscience to continue his duties as a curate."

352

Strong stuff, of course, and it drew from Stinker what may have been a hollow groan or may have been a hiccup. I myself looked coldly at the old egg, and I rather think I curled my lip, though I should say it was very doubtful if he noticed my scorn, for his attention was earmarked for Stiffy. She had turned almost as scarlet as Stinker, and I heard a distinct click as her front teeth met. It was through these teeth (clenched) that she spoke.

"So that's how you feel about it?"

"It is."

"Your decision is final?"

"Quite final."

"Nothing will move you?"

"Nothing."

"I see," said Stiffy, having chewed the lower lip for a space in silence. "Well, you'll be sorry."

"I disagree with you."

"You will. Just wait. Bitter remorse is coming to you, Uncle Watkyn. Never underestimate the power of a woman," said Stiffy, and with a choking sob—though there again it may have been a hiccup—she rushed from the room.

She had scarcely left us when Butterfield entered, and Pop Bassett eyed him with the ill-concealed petulance with which men of testy habit eye butlers who butt in at the wrong moment.

"Yes, Butterfield? What is it, what is it?"

"Constable Oates desires a word with you, sir."

"Who?"

"Police Constable Oates, sir."

"What does he want?"

"I gather that he has a clue to the identity of the boy who threw a hard-boiled egg at you, sir."

The words acted on Pop Bassett as I'm told the sound of

bugles acts on war-horses, not that I've ever seen a war-horse. His whole demeanor changed in a flash. His face lit up, and there came into it the sort of look you see on the faces of bloodhounds when they settle down to the trail. He didn't actually say "Whoopee!" but that was probably because the expression was not familiar to him. He was out of the room in a matter of seconds, Butterfield lying some lengths behind, and Stinker, who had been replacing a framed photograph which he had knocked off a neighboring table, addressed me in what you might call a hushed voice.

"I say, Bertie, what do you think Stiffy meant when she said that?"

I, too, had been speculating as to what the young pipsqueak had had in mind. A sinister thing to say, it seemed to me. Those words "just wait" had had an ominous ring. I weighed his question gravely.

"Difficult to decide," I said. "It may be one thing or it may be another."

"She has such an impulsive nature."

"Very impulsive."

"It makes me uneasy."

"Why you? Pop B's the one who ought to be feeling uneasy. Knowing her as I do, if I were in his place—"

The sentence I had begun would, if it had come to fruition, have concluded with the words "I'd pack a few necessaries in a suitcase and go to Australia," but as I was about to utter them I chanced to glance out of the window and they froze on my lips.

The window looked on the drive, and from where I was standing I got a good view of the front steps, and when I saw what was coming up those front steps, my heart leaped from its base.

It was Plank. There was no mistaking that square, tanned

face and that purposeful walk of his. And when I reflected that in about a couple of ticks Butterfield would be showing him into the drawing room where I stood and we would meet once more, I confess that I was momentarily at a loss to know how to proceed.

My first thought was to wait till he had got through the front door and then nip out of the window, which was conveniently open. That, I felt, was what Napoleon would have done. And I was just about to get the show on the road, as Stiffy would have said, when I saw the dog Bartholomew come sauntering along, and I knew that I would be compelled to revise my strategy from the bottom up. You can't go climbing out of windows under the eyes of an Aberdeen terrier so prone as Bartholomew was always to think the worst. In due season, no doubt, he would learn that what he had taken for a burglar escaping with the swag had been in reality a harmless guest of the house and would be all apologies, but by that time my lower slopes would be as full of holes as a Swiss cheese.

Falling back on my second line of defense, I slid behind the sofa with a muttered "Not a word to a soul, Stinker. Chap I don't want to meet," and was nestling there like a turtle in its shell, when the door opened.

CHAPTER
TWENTY

IT'S PRETTY generally recognized at the Drones Club and elsewhere that Bertram Wooster is a man who knows how to keep the chin up and the upper lip stiff, no matter how rough the going may be. Beneath the bludgeonings of Fate, his head is bloody but unbowed, as the fellow said. In a word, he can take it.

But I must admit that as I crouched in my haven of refuge I found myself chafing not a little. Life at Totleigh Towers, as I mentioned earlier, had got me down. There seemed no way of staying put in the darned house. One was either soaring like an eagle on to the top of chests or whizzing down behind sofas like a diving duck, and apart from the hustle and bustle of it all that sort of thing wounds the spirit and does no good to the trouser crease. And so, as I say, I chafed.

I was becoming increasingly bitter about this man Plank and the tendency he seemed to be developing of haunting me like a family specter. I couldn't imagine what he was doing here. Whatever the faults of Totleigh Towers, I had supposed that, when there, one would at least be free from his society. He had an excellent home in Hockley-cum-Meston, and one sought in vain for an explanation of why the hell he didn't stay in it.

My disapproval extended to the personnel of the various native tribes he had encountered in the course of his explorations. On his own showing, he had for years been horning in uninvited on the aborigines of Brazil, the Congo, and elsewhere, and not one of them apparently had had the enterprise to get after him with a spear or to say it with poisoned darts from the family blowpipe. And these were fellows who called themselves savages. Savages, forsooth! The savages in the books I used to read in my childhood would have had him in the obituary column before he could say "What ho," but with the ones you get nowadays it's all slackness and laissez-faire. Can't be bothered. Leave it to somebody else. Let George do it. One sometimes wonders what the world's coming to.

From where I sat, my range of vision was necessarily a bit restricted, but I was able to see a pair of Empire-building brogue shoes, so I assumed that when the door had opened it was Butterfield showing him in, and this surmise was confirmed a moment later when he spoke. His was a voice which, once heard, lingers in the memory.

"Afternoon," he said.

"Good afternoon," said Stinker.

"Warm day."

"Very warm."

"What's been going on here? What are all those tents and swings and things in the park?"

357

Stinker explained that the annual school treat had only just concluded, and Plank expressed his gratification at having missed it. School treats, he said, were dashed dangerous things, always to be avoided by the shrewd, as they were only too apt to include competitions for bonny babies.

"Did you have a competition for bonny babies?"

"Yes, we did, as a matter of fact. The mothers always insist on it."

"The mothers are the ones you want to watch out for," said Plank. "I'm not saying the little beasts aren't bad enough themselves, dribbling out of the side of their mouths at you and all that sort of thing, but it's the mothers who constitute the really grave peril. Look," he said, and I think he must at this point have pulled up a trouser leg. "See that scar on my calf? That's what I got in Peru once for being fool enough to let myself be talked into judging a competition for bonny babies. The mother of one of the Honorably Mentioneds spiked me in the leg with a native dagger as I was stepping down from the judge's stand after making my speech. Hurt like sin, I can assure you, and still gives me a twinge when the weather's wet. Fellow I know is fond of saying that the hand that rocks the cradle rules the world. Whether this is so or not I couldn't tell you, but it certainly knows how to handle a Peruvian dagger."

I found myself revising to some extent the rather austere opinion I had formed of the slackness and lack of ginger of the modern native. The males might have lost their grip in recent years, but the female element, it seemed, still had the right stuff in them, though of course, where somebody like Plank is concerned, a stab in the fleshy part of the leg is only a step in the right direction, merely scratching the surface as you might say.

Plank continued chatty. "You live in these parts?" he said.

358

"Yes, I live in the village."

"Totleigh?"

"Yes."

"Don't run a Rugger club in Totleigh, do you?"

Stinker replied in the negative. The Totleigh-in-the-Wold athletes, he said, preferred the Association code, and Plank, probably shuddering, said, "Good God!"

"You ever played Rugger?"

"A little."

"You should take it up seriously. No finer sport. I'm trying to make the Hockley-cum-Meston team the talk of Gloucestershire. I coach the boys daily, and they're coming along very nicely, very nicely indeed. What I need is a good prop forward."

What he got was Pop Bassett, who came bustling in at this moment. He Good-afternoon-Plank-ed, and Plank responded in suitable terms.

"Very nice of you to look me up, Plank," said Pop. "Will you have something to drink?"

"Ah," said Plank, and you could see that he meant it.

"I would ask you to stay to dinner, but unfortunately one of my guests has eloped with the cook."

"Dashed sensible of him, if he was going to elope with anyone. Very hard to find these days, cooks."

"It has of course completely disorganized our domestic arrangements. Neither my daughter nor my niece is capable of preparing even the simplest meal."

"You'll have to go to the pub."

"It seems the only solution."

"If you were in West Africa, you could drop in and take potluck with a native chief."

"I am not in West Africa," said Pop Bassett, speaking, I thought, a little testily, and I could understand him feeling a bit miffed. It's always annoying when you're up against it and people tell you what a jolly time you could be having if you weren't and how topping everything would be if you were somewhere where you aren't.

"I dined out a good deal in West Africa," said Plank. "Capital dinners some of those fellows used to give me, I remember, though there was always the drawback that you could never be sure the main dish wasn't one of their wives' relations, broiled over a slow fire and disguised in some native sauce. Took the edge off your appetite, unless you were feeling particularly peckish."

"So I would be disposed to imagine."

"All a matter of taste, of course."

"Quite. Was there something you particularly wished to see me about, Plank?"

"No, nothing that I can think of."

"Then if you will excuse me, I will be getting back to Madeline."

"Who's Madeline?"

"My daughter. Your arrival interrupted me in a serious talk I was having with her."

"Something wrong with the girl?"

"Something extremely wrong. She is contemplating making a disastrous marriage."

"All marriages are disastrous," said Plank, who gave one the impression, reading between the lines, that he was a bachelor. "They lead to bonny babies, and bonny babies lead to bonny-baby competitions. I was telling this gentleman here of an experience I had in Peru and showing him the scar on my leg, the direct result of being ass enough to judge one of these competitions. Would you care to see the scar on my leg?"

"Some other time, perhaps."

"Any time that suits you. Why is this marriage you say she's contemplating so disastrous?"

"Because Mr. Wooster is not a suitable husband for her."

"Who's Mr. Wooster?"

"The man she wishes to marry. A typical young wastrel of the type so common nowadays."

"I used to know a fellow called Wooster, but I don't suppose it can be the same chap, because my Wooster was eaten by a crocodile on the Zambesi the other day, which rather rules him out. All right, Bassett, you pop back to the girl and tell her from me that if she's going to start marrying every Tom, Dick, and Harry she comes across, she ought to have her head examined. If she'd seen as many native chiefs' wives as I have, she wouldn't be wanting to make such an ass of herself. Dickens of a life they lead, those women. Nothing to do but grind maize meal and have bonny babies. Right ho, Bassett, don't let me keep you."

There came the sound of a closing door as Pop Bassett sped on his way, and Plank turned his attention to Stinker. He said: "I didn't tell that old ass, because I didn't want him sticking around in here talking his head off, but as a matter of fact I did come about something special. Do you happen to know where I can find a chap called Pinker?"

"My name's Pinker."

"Are you sure? I thought Bassett said it was Wooster."

"No, Wooster's the one who's going to marry Sir Watkyn's daughter."

"So he is. It all comes back to me now. I wonder if you can be the fellow I want. The Pinker I'm after is a curate."

"I'm a curate."

"You are? Yes, by Jove, you're perfectly right. I see your collar buttons at the back. You're not H. P. Pinker by any chance?"

"Yes."

"Prop forward for Oxford and England a few years ago?"

"Yes."

"Well, would you be interested in becoming a vicar?"

There was a crashing sound, and I knew that Stinker in his emotion must have upset his customary table. After a while he said in a husky voice that the one thing he wanted was to get his hooks on a vicarage or words to that effect, and Plank said he was glad to hear it.

"My chap at Hockley-cum-Meston is downing tools now that his ninetieth birthday is approaching, and I've been scouring the countryside for a spare. Extraordinarily difficult the quest has been, because what I wanted was a vicar who was a good prop forward, and it isn't often you find a parson who knows one end of a football from the other. I've never seen you play, I'm sorry to say, because I've been abroad so much, but with your record you must obviously be outstanding. So you can take up your duties as soon as old Bellamy goes into storage. When I get home, I'll embody the thing in the form of a letter."

Stinker said he didn't know how to thank him, and Plank said that was all right, no need of any thanks.

"I'm the one who ought to be grateful. We're all right at halfback and three-quarters, but we lost to Upper Bleaching last year simply because our prop forward proved a broken reed. This year we'll show 'em. Amazing bit of luck finding you, and I could never have done it if it hadn't been for a friend of mine, a Chief Inspector Witherspoon of Scotland Yard. He phoned me just now and told me you were to be found at Totleigh-in-the-Wold. He said if I called at Totleigh Towers, they would give me your address. Extraordinary how these Scotland Yard fellows nose things out. The result of years of practice, I suppose. What was that noise?"

Stinker said he had heard nothing.

362

"Sort of gasping noise. Seemed to come from behind that sofa. Take a look."

I was aware for a moment of Stinker's face peering down at me; then he turned away.

"There's nothing behind the sofa," he said, very decently imperiling his immortal soul by falsifying the facts on behalf of a pal.

"Thought it might be a dog being sick," said Plank.

And I suppose it had sounded rather like that. The revelation of Jeeves' black treachery had shaken me to my foundations, causing me to forget that in the existing circs silence was golden. A silly thing to do, of course, to gasp like that, but, dash it, if for years you have nursed a gentleman's personal gentleman in your bosom and out of a blue sky you find that he has deliberately sicced Brazilian explorers on to you, I maintain that you're fully entitled to behave like a dog in the throes of nausea. I could make nothing of his scurvy conduct and was so stunned that for a minute or two I lost the thread of the conversation. When the mists cleared, Plank was speaking, and the subject had been changed.

"I wonder how Bassett is getting on with that daughter of his. Do you know anything of this chap Wooster?"

"He's one of my best friends."

"Bassett doesn't seem too fond of him."

"No."

"Ah well, we all have our likes and dislikes. Which of the two girls is this Madeline he was speaking of? I've never met them, but I've seen them around. Is she the little squirt with the large blue eyes?"

I should imagine Stinker didn't care overmuch for hearing his loved one described as a little squirt, though reason must have told him that that was precisely what she was, but he replied without heat.

"No, that's Sir Watkyn's niece, Stephanie Byng."

"Byng? Now why does that name seem to ring a bell? Oh yes, of course. Old Johnny Byng, who was with me on one of my expeditions. Red-haired fellow; haven't seen him for years. He was bitten by a puma, poor chap, and they tell me he still hesitates in a rather noticeable manner before sitting down. Stephanie Byng, eh? You know her, of course?"

"Very well."

"Nice girl?"

"That's how she seems to me, and if you don't mind, I'll be going and telling her the good news."

"What good news?"

"About the vicarage."

"Oh, ah, yes. You think she'll be interested?"

"I'm sure she will. We're going to be married."

"Good God! No chance of getting out of it?"

"I don't want to get out of it."

"Amazing! I once hitchhiked all the way from Johannesburg to Cape Town to avoid getting married, and here you are seeming quite pleased at the prospect. Oh well, no accounting for tastes. All right, you run along. And I suppose I'd better have a word with Bassett before I leave. Fellow bores me stiff, but one has to be civil."

The door closed and silence fell, and after waiting a few minutes, just in case, I felt it was safe to surface. And I had just done so and was limbering up the limbs, which had become somewhat cramped, when the door opened and Jeeves came in carrying a tray.

CHAPTER
TWENTY-ONE

"Good evening, sir," he said. "Would you care for an appetizer? I was obliging Mr. Butterfield by bringing them. He is engaged at the moment in listening at the door of the room where Sir Watkyn is in conference with Miss Bassett. He tells me he is compiling his memoirs and never misses an opportunity of gathering suitable material."

I gave the man one of my looks. My face was cold and hard, like a school treat egg. I can't remember a time when I've been fuller of righteous indignation.

"What I want, Jeeves, is not a slab of wet bread with a dead sardine on it—"

"Anchovy, sir."

"Or anchovy. I am in no mood to split straws. I require an explanation, and a categorical one, at that."

"Sir?"

"You can't evade the issue by saying 'Sir?' Answer me this, Jeeves, with a simple yes or no. Why did you tell Plank to come to Totleigh Towers?"

I thought the query would crumple him up like a damp sock, but he didn't so much as shuffle a foot.

"My heart was melted by Miss Byng's tale of her misfortunes, sir. I chanced to encounter the young lady and found her in a state of considerable despondency as the result of Sir Watkyn's refusal to bestow a vicarage on Mr. Pinker. I perceived immediately that it was within my power to alleviate her distress. I had learned at the post office at Hockley-cum-Meston that the incumbent there was retiring shortly, and being cognizant of Major Plank's desire to strengthen the Hockley-cum-Meston forward line, I felt that it would be an excellent idea to place him in communication with Mr. Pinker. In order to be in a position to marry Miss Byng, Mr. Pinker requires a vicarage, and in order to compete successfully with rival villages in the football arena, Major Plank is in need of a vicar with Mr. Pinker's wide experience as a prop forward. Their interests appeared to me to be identical."

"Well, it worked all right. Stinker has clicked."

"He is to succeed Mr. Bellamy as incumbent at Hockley-cum-Meston?"

"As soon as Bellamy calls it a day."

"I am very happy to hear it, sir."

I didn't reply for a while, being obliged to attend to a sudden touch of cramp. This ironed out, I said, still icy: "You may be happy, but I haven't been for the last quarter of an hour or so, nestling behind the sofa and expecting Plank at any moment to unmask me. It didn't occur to you to envisage what would happen if he met me?"

"I was sure that your keen intelligence would enable you

to find a means of avoiding him, sir, as indeed it did. You concealed yourself behind the sofa?"

"On all fours."

"A very shrewd maneuver on your part, if I may say so, sir. It showed a resource and swiftness of thought which it would be difficult to overpraise."

My iciness melted. It is not too much to say that I was mollified. It's not often that I'm given the old oil in this fashion, most of my circle, notably my Aunt Agatha, being more prone to the slam than the rave. And it was only after I had been savoring that "keen intelligence" gag, if savoring is the word I want, for some moments that I suddenly remembered that marriage with Madeline Bassett loomed ahead, and I gave a start so visible that he asked me if I was feeling unwell.

I shook the loaf.

"Physically, no, Jeeves. Spiritually, yes."

"I do not quite understand you, sir."

"Well, here is the news, and this is Bertram Wooster reading it. I'm going to be married."

"Indeed, sir?"

"Yes, Jeeves, married. The banns are as good as up."

"Would it be taking a liberty if I were to ask——"

"Who to? You don't need to ask. Gussie Fink-Nottle has eloped with Emerald Stoker, thus creating a . . . what is it?"

"Would vacuum be the word you are seeking, sir?"

"That's right. A vacuum which I shall have to fill. Unless you can think of some way of getting me out of it."

"I will devote considerable thought to the matter, sir."

"Thank you, Jeeves," I said, and would have spoken further, but at this moment I saw the door opening and speechlessness supervened. But it wasn't, as I had feared, Plank; it was only Stiffy.

"Hullo, you two," she said. "I'm looking for Harold."

I could see at a g. that Jeeves had been right in describing her demeanor as despondent. The brow was clouded and the general appearance that of an overwrought soul. I was glad to be in a position to inject a little sunshine into her life. Pigeonholing my own troubles for future reference, I said: "He's looking for you. He has a strange story to relate. You know Plank?"

"What about him?"

"I'll tell you what about him. Plank to you hitherto has been merely a shadowy figure who hangs out at Hockley-cum-Meston and sells black amber statuettes to people, but he has another side to him."

She betrayed a certain impatience.

"If you think I'm interested in Plank—"

"Aren't you?"

"No, I'm not."

"You will be. He has, as I was saying, another side to him. He is a landed proprietor with vicarages in his gift, and, to cut a long story down to a short-short, as one always likes to do when possible, he has just given one to Stinker."

I had been right in supposing that the information would have a marked effect on her dark mood. I have never actually seen a corpse spring from its bier and start being the life and soul of the party, but I should imagine that its deportment would closely resemble that of this young Byng as the impact of my words came home to her. A sudden light shot into her eyes, which, as Plank had correctly said, were large and blue, and an ecstatic "Well, Lord love a duck!" escaped her. Then doubts seemed to creep in, for the eyes clouded over again.

"Is this true?"

"Absolutely official."

"You aren't pulling my leg?"

I drew myself up rather haughtily.

"I wouldn't dream of pulling your leg. Do you think Bertram Wooster is the sort of chap who thinks it funny to raise people's hopes, only to . . . what, Jeeves?"

"Dash them to the ground, sir."

"Thank you, Jeeves."

"Not at all, sir."

"You may take this information as coming straight from the mouth of the stable cat. I was present when the deal went through. Behind the sofa, but present."

She still seemed at a loss.

"But I don't understand. Plank has never met Harold."

"Jeeves brought them together."

"Did you, Jeeves?"

"Yes, miss."

"At-a-boy!"

"Thank you, miss."

"And he's really given Harold a vicarage?"

"The vicarage of Hockley-cum-Meston. He's embodying it in the form of a letter tonight. At the moment there's a vicar still vicking, but he's infirm and old and wants to turn it up as soon as they can put on an understudy. The way things look, I should imagine that we shall be able to unleash Stinker on the Hockley-cum-Meston souls in the course of the next few days."

My simple words and earnest manner had resolved the last of her doubts. The misgivings she may have had as to whether this was the real ginger vanished. Her eyes shone more like twin stars than anything, and she uttered animal cries and danced a few dance steps. Presently she paused and put a question.

"What's Plank like?"

"How do you mean, what's he like?"

"He hasn't a beard, has he?"

"No, no beard."

369

"That's good, because I want to kiss him, and if he had a beard, it would give me pause."

"Dismiss the notion," I urged, for Plank's psychology was an open book to me. The whole trend of that confirmed bachelor's conversation had left me with the impression that he would find it infinitely preferable to be spiked in the leg with a native dagger than to have popsies covering his up-turned face with kisses. "He'd have a fit."

"Well, I must kiss somebody. Shall I kiss you, Jeeves?"

"No, thank you, miss."

"You, Bertie?"

"I'd rather you didn't."

"Then I've a good mind to go and kiss Uncle Watkyn, louse of the first water though he has recently shown him-self."

"How do you mean, recently?"

"And having kissed him I shall tell him the news and taunt him vigorously with having let a good thing get away from him. I shall tell him that when he declined to avail himself of Harold's services he was like the Indian."

I did not get her drift.

"What Indian?"

"The base one my governesses used to make me read about, the poor simp whose hand . . . How does it go, Jeeves?"

"Threw a pearl away richer than all his tribe, miss."

"That's right. And I shall tell him I hope the vicar he does get will be a weed of a man who has a chronic cold in the head and bleats. Oh, by the way, talking of Uncle Wat-kyn reminds me. I shan't have any use for this now."

And so speaking she produced the black amber eyesore from the recesses of her costume like a conjurer taking a rabbit out of a hat.

CHAPTER
TWENTY-TWO

IT WAS as if she had suddenly exhibited a snake of the lowest order. I gazed at the thing, appalled. It needed but this to put the frosting on the cake.

"Where did you get that?" I asked in a voice that was low and trembled.

"I pinched it."

"What on earth did you do that for?"

"Perfectly simple. The idea was to go to Uncle Watkyn and tell him he wouldn't get it back unless he did the square thing by Harold. Power politics, don't they call it, Jeeves?"

"Or blackmail, miss."

"Yes, or blackmail, I suppose. But you can't be too nice in your methods when you're dealing with the Uncle Watkyns of this world. But now that Plank has eased the situation and made our paths straight, of course I shan't need it, and I suppose the shrewd thing is to return it to store before its absence is noted. Go and put it in the collection room, Bertie. Here's the key."

I recoiled as if she had offered me the dog Bartholomew. Priding myself as I do on being a *preux chevalier*, I like to oblige the delicately nurtured when it's feasible, but there are moments when only a *nolle prosequi* will serve, and I recognized this as one of them. The thought of making the perilous passage she was suggesting gave me goose pimples.

"I'm not going near the ruddy collection room. With my luck, I'd find your Uncle Watkyn there, arm in arm with Spode, and it wouldn't be too easy to explain what I was doing there and how I'd got in. Besides, I can't go roaming about the place with Plank on the premises."

She laughed one of those silvery ones, a practice to which, as I have indicated, she was far too much addicted.

"Jeeves told me about you and Plank. Very funny."

"I'm glad you think so. We personally were not amused."

Jeeves, as always, found the way.

"If you will give the object to me, miss, I will see that it is restored to its place."

"Thank you, Jeeves. Well, goodbye all. I'm off to find Harold," said Stiffy, and she withdrew, dancing on the tips of her toes.

I shrugged a shoulder.

"Women, Jeeves!"

"Yes, sir."

"What a sex!"

"Yes, sir."

"Do you remember something I said to you about Stiffy on our previous visit to Totleigh Towers?"

"Not at the moment, no, sir."

"It was on the occasion when she landed me with Police Constable Oates' helmet just as my room was about to be searched by Pop Bassett and his minions. Dipping into the future, I pointed out that Stiffy, who is pure padded cell from the foundations up, was planning to marry the Rev. H. P. Pinker, himself as pronounced a goop as ever preached about the Hivites and Hittites, and I speculated, if you recall, as to what their offspring, if any, would be like."

"Ah yes, sir, I recollect now."

"Would they, I asked myself, inherit the combined loopiness of two such parents?"

"Yes, sir, you were particularly concerned, I recall, for the well-being of the nurses, governesses, private-school masters, and public-school masters who would assume the charge of them."

"Little knowing that they were coming up against something hotter than mustard. Exactly. The thought still weighs heavy upon me. However, we haven't leisure to go into the subject now. You'd better take that ghastly object back where it belongs without delay."

"Yes, sir. If it were done when 'twere done, then 'twere well it were done quickly," he said, making for the door, and I thought, as I had so often thought before, how neatly he put these things.

It seemed to me that the time had now come to adopt the strategy which I had had in mind right at the beginning—viz., to make my getaway via the window. With Plank at large in the house and likely at any moment to come winging back to where the drinks were, safety could be obtained only by making for some distant yew alley or rhododendron walk and remaining ensconced there till he had blown over. I hastened to the window, accordingly, and picture my chagrin and dismay on finding that Bartholomew, instead of continuing his stroll, had decided to take a siesta on the grass immediately below. I had actually got one leg over the sill before he was drawn to my attention. In another half jiffy I should have dropped on him as the gentle rain from heaven upon the spot beneath.

I had no difficulty in recognizing the situation as what the French call an *impasse,* and as I stood pondering what to do for the best, footsteps sounded without, and feeling that 'twere well it were done quickly I made for the sofa once more, lowering my previous record by perhaps a split second.

I was surprised, as I lay nestling in my little nook, by the complete absence of dialogue that ensued. Hitherto, all my visitors had started chatting from the moment of their entry, and it struck me as odd that I should now be entertaining a couple of deaf-mutes. Peeping cautiously out, however, I found that I had been mistaken in supposing that I had with me a brace of guests. It was Madeline alone who had blown in. She was heading for the piano, and something told me that it was her intention to sing old folk songs, a pastime to which, as I have indicated, she devoted not a little of her leisure. She was particularly given to indulge in this nuisance when her soul had been undergoing an upheaval and required soothing, as of course it probably did at this juncture.

My fears were realized. She sang two in rapid succession, and the thought that this sort of thing would be a permanent feature of our married life chilled me to the core. I've always been what you might call allergic to old folk songs, and the older they are, the more I dislike them.

Fortunately, before she could start on a third she was interrupted. Clumping footsteps sounded, the door handle turned, heavy breathing made itself heard, and a voice said,

"Madeline!" Spode's voice, husky with emotion. "Madeline," he said, "I've been looking for you everywhere."

"Oh, Roderick! How is your eye?"

"Never mind my eye," said Spode. "I didn't come here to talk about eyes."

"They say a piece of beefsteak reduces the swelling."

"Nor about beefsteaks. Sir Watkyn has told me the awful news about you and Wooster. Is it true you're going to marry him?"

"Yes, Roderick, it is true."

"But you can't love a half-baked, half-witted ass like Wooster," said Spode, and I thought the remark extremely offensive. Pick your words more carefully, Spode, I might have said, rising and confronting him. However, for one reason and another I didn't, but continued to nestle, and I heard Madeline sigh, unless it was the draft under the sofa.

"No, Roderick, I do not love him. He does not appeal to the essential me. But I feel it is my duty to make him happy."

"Tchah!" said Spode, or something that sounded like that. "Why on earth do you want to go about making worms like Wooster happy?"

"He loves me, Roderick. You must have seen that dumb, worshiping look in his eyes as he gazes at me."

"I've something better to do than peer into Wooster's eyes. Though I can well imagine they look dumb. We've got to have this thing out, Madeline."

"I don't understand you, Roderick."

"You will."

"Ouch!"

I think on the cue "You will" he must have grabbed her by the wrist, for the word "Ouch!" had come through strong

375

and clear, and this suspicion was confirmed when she said he was hurting her.

"I'm sorry, sorry," said Spode. "But I refuse to allow you to ruin your life. You can't marry this man Wooster. I'm the one you're going to marry."

I was with him heart and soul, as the expression is. Nothing would ever make me really fond of Roderick Spode, but I liked the way he was talking. A little more of this, I felt, and Bertram would be released from his honorable obligations. I wished he had thought of taking this firm line earlier.

"I've loved you since you were so high."

Not being able to see him, I couldn't ascertain how high that was, but I presumed he must have been holding his hand not far from the floor. A couple of feet, would you say? About that, I suppose.

Madeline was plainly moved. I heard her gurgle.

"I know, Roderick, I know."

"You guessed my secret?"

"Yes, Roderick. How sad life is."

Spode declined to string along with her in this view.

"Not a bit of it. Life's fine. At least, it will be if you give this blighter Wooster the push and marry me."

"I have always been devoted to you, Roderick."

"Well, then?"

"Give me time to think."

"Carry on. Take all the time you need."

"I don't want to break Bertie's heart."

"Why not? Do him good."

"He loves me so dearly."

"Nonsense. I don't suppose he has ever loved anything in his life except a dry martini."

"How can you say that? Did he not come here because he found it impossible to stay away from me?"

"No, he jolly well didn't. Don't let him fool you on that point. He came here to pinch that black amber statuette of your father's."

"What!"

"That's what. In addition to being half-witted, he's a low thief."

"It can't be true!"

"Of course it's true. His uncle wants the thing for his collection. I heard him plotting with his aunt on the telephone not half an hour ago. 'It's going to be pretty hard to get away with it,' he was saying, 'but I'll do my best. I know how much Uncle Tom covets that statuette.' He's always stealing things. The very first time I met him, in an antique shop in the Brompton Road, he as near as a toucher got away with your father's umbrella."

A monstrous charge, and one which I can readily refute. He and Pop Bassett and I were, I concede, in the antique shop in the Brompton Road to which he had alluded, but the umbrella sequence was purely one of those laughable misunderstandings. Pop Bassett had left the blunt instrument propped against a seventeenth-century chair, and what caused me to take it up was the primeval instinct which makes a man without an umbrella, as I happened to be that morning, reach out unconsciously for the nearest one in sight, like a flower turning to the sun. The whole thing could have been explained in two words, but they hadn't let me say even one, and the slur had been allowed to rest on me.

"You shock me, Roderick!" said Madeline.

"Yes, I thought it would make you sit up."

"If this is really so, if Bertie is really a thief—"

"Well?"

"Naturally I will have nothing more to do with him. But I can't believe it."

"I'll go and fetch Sir Watkyn," said Spode. "Perhaps you'll believe him."

For several minutes after he had clumped out, Madeline must have stood in a reverie, for I didn't hear a sound out of her. Then the door opened, and the next thing that came across was a cough which I had no difficulty in recognizing.

CHAPTER
TWENTY-THREE

IT WAS that soft cough of Jeeves' which always reminds me
of a very old sheep clearing its throat on a distant mountain-
top. He coughed it at me, if you remember, on the occasion
when I first swam into his ken wearing the Alpine hat. It
generally signifies disapproval, but I've known it to occur
also when he's about to touch on a topic of a delicate nature.
And when he spoke, I knew that that was what he was going
to do now, for there was a sort of hushed note in his voice.

"I wonder if I might have a moment of your time, miss?"

"Of course, Jeeves."

"It is with reference to Mr. Wooster."

"Oh, yes?"

"I must begin by saying that I chanced to be passing the
door when Lord Sidcup was speaking to you and inadvert-

ently overheard his lordship's observations on the subject of Mr. Wooster. His lordship has a carrying voice. And I find myself in a somewhat equivocal position, torn between loyalty to my employer and a natural desire to do my duty as a citizen."

"I don't understand you, Jeeves," said Madeline, which made two of us.

He coughed again.

"I am anxious not to take a liberty, miss, but if I may speak frankly—"

"Please do."

"Thank you, miss. His lordship's words seemed to confirm a rumor which is circulating in the servants' hall that you are contemplating a matrimonial union with Mr. Wooster. Would it be indiscreet of me if I were to inquire if this is so?"

"Yes, Jeeves, it is quite true."

"If you will pardon me for saying so, I think you are making a mistake."

Well spoken, Jeeves, you are on the right lines, I was saying to myself, and I hoped he was going to rub it in. I waited anxiously for Madeline's reply, a little afraid that she would draw herself to her full height and dismiss him from her presence. But she didn't. She merely said again that she didn't understand him.

"If I might explain, miss. I am loath to criticize my employer, but I feel that you should know that he is a kleptomaniac."

"What!"

"Yes, miss. I had hoped to be able to preserve his little secret, as I have always done hitherto, but he has now gone to lengths which I cannot countenance. In going through his effects this afternoon I discovered this small black figure, concealed beneath his underwear."

I heard Madeline utter a sound like a dying soda-water siphon.

"But that belongs to my father!"

"If I may say so, nothing belongs to anyone if Mr. Wooster takes a fancy to it."

"Then Lord Sidcup was right?"

"Precisely, miss."

"He said Mr. Wooster tried to steal my father's umbrella."

"I heard him, and the charge was well founded. Umbrellas, jewelry, statuettes—they are all grist to Mr. Wooster's mill. I do not think he can help it. It is a form of mental illness. But whether a jury would take that view, I cannot say."

Madeline went into the soda-siphon routine once more.

"You mean he might be sent to prison?"

"It is a contingency that seems to me far from remote."

Again I felt that he was on the right lines. His trained senses told him that if there's one thing that puts a girl off marrying a chap, it is the thought that the honeymoon may be spoiled at any moment by the arrival of inspectors at the love nest, come to scoop him in for larceny. No young bride likes that sort of thing, and you can't blame her if she finds herself preferring to team up with someone like Spode, who, though a gorilla in fairly human shape, is known to keep strictly on the right side of the law. I could almost hear Madeline's thoughts turning in this direction, and I applauded Jeeves' sound grip on the psychology of the individual, as he calls it.

Of course, I could see that all this wasn't going to make my position in the Bassett home any too good, but there are times when only the surgeon's knife will serve. And I had the sustaining thought that if ever I got out from behind this sofa, I could sneak off to where my car waited champing at the bit and drive off Londonwards without stopping to say goodbye and thanks for a delightful visit. This would obviate—is it obviate?—all unpleasantness.

Madeline continued shaken.

"Oh dear, oh dear!" she said.

"Yes, miss."

"This has come as a great shock."

"I can readily appreciate it, miss."

"Have you known of this long?"

"Ever since I entered Mr. Wooster's employment."

"Oh dear, oh dear! Well, thank you, Jeeves."

"Not at all, miss."

I think Jeeves must have shimmered off after this, for silence fell and nothing happened except that my nose began to tickle. I would have given ten quid to have been able to sneeze, but this of course was outside the range of practical politics. I just crouched there, thinking of this and that, and after quite a while the door opened once more, this time to admit something in the nature of a mob scene. I could see three pairs of shoes and deduced that they were those of Spode, Pop Bassett, and Plank. Spode, it will be recalled, had gone to fetch Pop, and Plank presumably had come along for the ride, hoping no doubt for something moist at journey's end.

Spode was the first to speak, and his voice rang with the triumph that comes into the voices of suitors who have caught a dangerous rival bending.

"Here we are," he said. "I've brought Sir Watkyn to support my statement that Wooster is a low sneak thief who goes about snapping up everything that isn't nailed down. You agree, Sir Watkyn?"

"Of course I do, Roderick. It's only a month or so ago that he and that aunt of his stole my cow creamer."

"What's a cow creamer?" asked Plank.

"A silver cream jug, one of the gems of my collection."

"They got away with it, did they?"

"They did."

"Ah," said Plank. "Then in that case I think I'll have a whiskey-and-soda."

Pop Bassett was warming to his theme. His voice rose above the hissing of Plank's siphon.

"And it was only by the mercy of Providence that Wooster didn't make off with my umbrella that day in the Brompton Road. If that young man has one defect more marked than another, it is that he appears to be totally ignorant of the distinction between *meum* and *tuum*. He came up before me in my court once, I remember, charged with having stolen a policeman's helmet, and it is a lasting regret to me that I merely fined him five pounds."

"Mistaken kindness," said Spode.

"So I have always felt, Roderick. A sharper lesson might have done him all the good in the world."

"Never does to let these fellows off lightly," said Plank. "I had a servant chap in Mozambique who used to help himself to my cigars, and I foolishly overlooked it because he assured me he had got religion and everything would be quite all right from now on. And it wasn't a week later that he skipped out, taking with him a box of Havanas and my false teeth, which he sold to one of the native chiefs in the neighborhood. Cost me a case of trade gin and two strings of beads to get them back. Severity's the only thing. The iron hand. Anything else is mistaken for weakness."

Madeline gave a sob; at least it sounded like a sob.

"But, Daddy."

"Well?"

"I don't think Bertie can help himself."

"My dear child, it is precisely his habit of helping himself to everything he can lay his hands on that we are criticizing."

"I mean, he's a kleptomaniac."

"Eh? Who told you that?"

"Jeeves."

"That's odd. How did the subject come up?"

"He told me when he gave me this. He found it in Bertie's room. He was very worried about it."

There was a spot of silence—of a stunned nature, I imagine. Then Pop Bassett said "Good heavens!" and Spode said "Good Lord!" and Plank said "Why, that's that little thingummy I sold you, Bassett, isn't it?" Madeline gave another sob, and my nose began to tickle again.

"Well, this is astounding!" said Pop. "He found it in Wooster's room, you say?"

"Concealed beneath his underwear."

Pop Bassett uttered a sound like the wind going out of a dying duck.

"How right you were, Roderick! You said his motive in coming here was to steal this. But how he got into the collection room I cannot understand."

"These fellows have their methods."

"Seems to be a great demand for that thing," said Plank. "There was a young slab of damnation with a criminal face round at my place only yesterday trying to sell it to me."

"Wooster!"

"No, it wasn't Wooster. My fellow's name was Alpine Joe."

"Wooster would naturally adopt a pseudonym."

"I suppose he would. I never thought of that."

"Well, after this—" said Pop Bassett.

"Yes, after this," said Spode, "you're certainly not going

384

to marry the man, Madeline. He's worse than Fink-Nottle."

"Who's Fink-Nottle?" asked Plank.

"The one who eloped with Stoker," said Pop.

"Who's Stoker?" asked Plank. I don't think I've ever came across a fellow with a greater thirst for information.

"The cook."

"Ah yes. I remember you telling me. Knew what he was doing, that chap. I'm strongly opposed to anyone marrying anybody, but if you're going to marry someone, you unquestionably save something from the wreck by marrying a woman who knows what to do with a joint of beef. There was a fellow I knew in the Federated Malay States who—"

It would probably have been a diverting anecdote, but Spode didn't let him get on with it any further. Addressing Madeline, he said: "What you're going to do is marry me, and I don't want any argument. How about it, Madeline?"

"Yes, Roderick. I will be your wife."

Spode uttered a whoop which made my nose tickle worse than ever.

"That's the stuff! That's how I like to hear you talk! Come on out into the garden. I have much to say to you."

I imagine that at this juncture he must have folded her in his embrace and hustled her out, for I heard the door close. And as it did so Pop Bassett uttered a whoop somewhat similar in its intensity to the one that had proceeded from the Spode lips. He was patently boomps-a-daisy, and one could readily understand why. A father whose daughter, after nearly marrying Gussie Fink-Nottle and then nearly marrying me, sees the light and hooks on to a prosperous member of the British aristocracy is entitled to rejoice. I didn't like Spode and would have been glad at any time to see a Peruvian matron spike him in the leg with her dagger, but there was no denying that he was hot stuff matrimonially.

"Lady Sidcup!" said Pop, rolling the words round his tongue like vintage port.

"Who's Lady Sidcup?" asked Plank, anxious, as always, to keep abreast.

"My daughter will shortly be. One of the oldest titles in England. That was Lord Sidcup who has just left us."

"I thought his name was Roderick."

"His Christian name is Roderick."

"Ah!" said Plank. "Now I've got it. Now I have the whole picture. Your daughter was to have married someone called Fink-Nottle?"

"Yes."

"Then she was to have married this chap Wooster or Alpine Joe, as the case may be?"

"Yes."

"And now she's going to marry Lord Sidcup?"

"Yes."

"Clear as crystal," said Plank. "I knew I should get it threshed out in time. Simply a matter of concentration and elimination. You approve of this marriage? As far," he added, "as one can approve of any marriage?"

"I most certainly do."

"Then I think this calls for another whiskey-and-soda."

"I will join you," said Pop Bassett.

It was at this point, unable to hold it back any longer, that I sneezed.

"I knew there was something behind that sofa," said Plank, rounding it and subjecting me to the sort of look he had once given native chiefs who couldn't grasp the rules of Rugby football. "Odd sounds came from that direction. Good God, it's Alpine Joe."

"It's Wooster!"

"Who's Wooster? Oh, you told me, didn't you? What steps do you propose to take?"

"I have rung for Butterfield."

"Who's Butterfield?"

"My butler."

"What do you want a butler for?"

"To tell him to bring Oates."

"Who's Oates?"

"Our local policeman. He is having a glass of whiskey in the kitchen."

"Whiskey!" said Plank thoughtfully, and, as if reminded of something, went to the side table.

The door opened.

"Oh, Butterfield, will you tell Oates to come here."

"Very good, Sir Watkyn."

"Bit out of condition, that chap," said Plank, eyeing Butterfield's retreating back. "Wants a few games of Rugger to put him in shape. What are you going to do about this Alpine Joe fellow? You going to charge him?"

"I certainly am. No doubt he assumed that I would shrink from causing a scandal, but he was wrong. I shall let the law take its course."

"Quite right. Soak him to the utmost limit. You're a Justice of the Peace, aren't you?"

"I am, and intend to give him twenty-eight days in the second division."

"Or sixty? Nice round number, sixty. You couldn't make it six months, I suppose?"

"I fear not."

"No, I imagine you have a regular tariff. Ah, well, twenty-eight days is better than nothing."

"Police Constable Oates," said Butterfield in the doorway.

CHAPTER
TWENTY-FOUR

I DON'T know why it is, but there's something about being hauled off to a police bin that makes you feel a bit silly. At least, that's how it always affects me. I mean, there you are, you and the arm of the law, toddling along side by side, and you feel that in a sense he's your host and you ought to show an interest and try to draw him out. But it's so difficult to hit on anything in the nature of an exchange of ideas, and conversation never really flows. I remember at my private school, the one I won a prize for Scripture Knowledge at, the Rev. Aubrey Upjohn, the top brass, used to take us one by one for an educational walk on Sunday afternoons, and I always found it hard to sparkle when my turn came to step out at his side. It was the same on this occasion, when I accompanied Constable Oates to the village coop. It's no good my pretending the thing went with a swing, because it didn't.

Probably if I'd been one of the topnotchers, about to do a ten-year stretch for burglary or arson or what not, it would have been different, but I was only one of the small fry who get twenty-eight days in the second division, and I couldn't help thinking the officer was looking down on me. Not actually sneering, perhaps, but aloof in his manner, as if feeling I wasn't much for a cop to get his teeth into.

And, of course, there was another thing. Speaking of my earlier visit to Totleigh Towers, I mentioned that when Pop Bassett immured me in my room, he stationed the local police force on the lawn below to see that I didn't nip out of the window. That local police force was this same Oates, and as it was raining like the dickens at the time, no doubt the episode had rankled. Only a very sunny constable can look with an indulgent eye on the fellow responsible for his getting the nastiest cold in the head of his career.

At any rate, he showed himself now a man of few words, though good at locking people up in cells. There was only one at the Totleigh-in-the-Wold emporium, and I had it all to myself, a cozy little apartment with a window, not barred but too small to get out of, a grille in the door, a plank bed, and that rather powerful aroma of drunks and disorderlies which you always find in these homes from home. Whether it was superior or inferior to the one they had given me at Bosher Street, I was unable to decide. Not much in it either way, it seemed to me.

To say that when I turned in on the plank bed I fell into a dreamless sleep would be deceiving my public. I passed a somewhat restless night. I could have sworn, indeed, that I didn't drop off at all, but I suppose I must have done, because the next thing I knew sunlight was coming through the window and mine host was bringing me breakfast.

I got outside it with an appetite unusual with me at such an early hour, and at the conclusion of the meal I fished out an old envelope and did what I have sometimes done before when the bludgeonings of Fate were up and about to any extent—viz., make a list of Credits and Debits, as I believe Robinson Crusoe used to. The idea being to see whether I was ahead of or behind the game at moment of going to press.

The final score worked out as follows:

CREDIT	DEBIT
Not at all a bad breakfast, that. Coffee quite good. I was surprised.	Don't always be thinking of your stomach, you jailbird.
Who's a jailbird?	You're a jailbird.
Well, yes, I suppose I am, if you care to put it that way. But I am innocent. My hands are clean.	More than your face is.
Not looking my best, what?	You look like something the cat brought in.
A bath will put that right.	And you'll get one in prison.
You really think it'll come to that?	Well, you heard what Pop Bassett said.
I wonder what it's like, doing twenty-eight days? Hitherto, I've always just come for the night.	You'll hate it. It'll bore you stiff.
I don't know so much. They give you a cake of soap and a hymnbook, don't they?	What's the good of a cake of soap and a hymnbook?

I'll be able to whack up some sort of
indoor game with them. And don't
forget that I've not got to marry
Madeline Bassett. Let's hear what
you have to say to that.

And the Debit account didn't utter. I had baffled it.

Yes, I felt, as I hunted around in case there might be a
crumb of bread which I had overlooked, that amply com-
pensated me for the vicissitudes I was undergoing. And I
had been musing along these lines for a while, getting more
and more reconciled to my lot, when a silvery voice spoke,
making me jump like a startled grasshopper. I couldn't think
where it was coming from at first and speculated for a moment on the possibility of it being my guardian angel,
though I had always thought of him, I don't know why, as
being of the male sex. Then I saw something not unlike a
human face at the grille, and a closer inspection told me
that it was Stiffy.

I Hullo-there-ed cordially and expressed some surprise at
finding her on the premises.

"I wouldn't have thought Oates would have let you in.
It isn't Visitors Day, is it?"

She explained that the zealous officer had gone up to the
house to see her Uncle Watkyn and that she had sneaked in
when he had legged it.

"Oh, Bertie," she said, "I wish I could slip you in a file."

"What would I do with a file?"

"Saw through the bars, of course, ass."

"There aren't any bars."

"Oh, aren't there? That's a difficulty. We'll have to let
it go, then. Have you had breakfast?"

"Just finished."

"Was it all right?"

391

"Fairly toothsome."

"I'm glad to hear that, because I'm weighed down with remorse."

"You are? Why?"

"Use the loaf. If I hadn't pinched that statuette thing, none of this would have happened."

"Oh, I wouldn't worry."

"But I do worry. Shall I tell Uncle Watkyn that you're innocent, because I was the guilty party? You ought to have your name cleared."

I put the bee on this suggestion with the greatest promptitude.

"Certainly not. Don't dream of it."

"But don't you want your name cleared?"

"Not at the expense of you taking the rap."

"Uncle Watkyn wouldn't send me to chokey."

"I dare say not, but Stinker would learn all and would be shocked to the core."

"Coo! I didn't think of that."

"Think of it now. He wouldn't be able to help asking himself if it was a prudent move for a vicar to link his lot with yours. Doubts, that's what he'd have, and qualms. It isn't as if you were going to be a gangster's moll. The gangster would be all for you swiping everything in sight and would encourage you with word and gesture, but it's different with Stinker. When he marries you, he'll want you to take charge of the parish funds. Apprise him of the facts, and he won't have an easy moment."

"I see what you mean. Yes, you have a point there."

"Picture his jumpiness if he found you near the Sunday offertory bag. No, secrecy and silence is the only course."

She sighed a bit, as if her conscience was troubling her, but she saw the force of my reasoning.

"I suppose you're right, but I do hate the idea of you doing time."

"There are compensations."

"Such as?"

"I am saved from the scaffold."

"The —? Oh, I see what you mean. You get out of marrying Madeline."

"Exactly, and, as I remember telling you once, I am implying nothing derogatory to Madeline when I say that the thought of being united to her in bonds of holy wedlock was one that gave your old friend shivers down the spine. The fact is in no way to her discredit. I should feel just the same about marrying many of the world's noblest women. There are certain females whom one respects, admires, reveres, but only from a distance, and it is to this group that Madeline belongs."

And I was about to develop this theme, with possibly a reference to those folk songs, when a gruff voice interrupted our tête-à-tête, if you can call a thing a tête-à-tête when the two of you are on opposite sides of an iron grille. It was Constable Oates, returned from his excursion. Stiffy's presence displeased him, and he spoke austerely.

"What's all this?" he demanded.

"What's all what?" riposted Stiffy with spirit, and I remember thinking that she rather had him there.

"It's against regulations to talk to the prisoner, miss."

"Oates," said Stiffy, "you're an ass."

This was profoundly true, but it seemed to annoy the officer. He resented the charge, and said so, and Stiffy said she didn't want any backchat from him.

"You road-company rozzers make me sick. I was only trying to cheer him up."

It seemed to me that the officer gave a bitter snort, and a moment later he revealed why he had done so.

"It's me that wants cheering up," he said morosely. "I've just seen Sir Watkyn, and he says he isn't pressing the charge."

"What!" I cried.

"What!" yipped Stiffy.

"That's what," said the constable, and you could see that while there was sunshine above, there was none in his heart. I could sympathize with him, of course. Naturally nothing makes a member of the force sicker than to have a criminal get away from him. He was in rather the same position as some crocodile on the Zambesi or some puma in Brazil would have been if it had earmarked Plank for its lunch and seen him skin up a high tree.

"Shackling the police, that's what I call it," he said, and I think he spat on the floor. I couldn't see him, of course, but I was aware of a spitlike sound.

Stiffy whooped, well pleased, and I whooped myself, if I remember correctly. For all the bold front I had been putting up, I had never in my heart really liked the idea of rotting for twenty-eight days in a dungeon cell. Prison is all right for a night, but you don't want to go overdoing the thing.

"Then what are we waiting for?" said Stiffy. "Get a move on, officer. Fling wide those gates."

Oates flung them, not attempting to conceal his chagrin and disappointment, and I passed with Stiffy into the great world outside the prison walls.

"Goodbye, Oates," I said as we left, for one always likes to do the courteous thing. "It's been nice meeting you. How are Mrs. Oates and the little ones?"

His only reply was a sound like a hippopotamus taking

its foot out of the mud on a riverbank, and I saw Stiffy frown, as though his manner offended her.

"You know," she said as we reached the open spaces, "we really ought to do something about Oates, something that would teach him that we're not put into this world for pleasure alone. I can't suggest what offhand, but if we put our heads together, we could think of something. You ought to stay on, Bertie, and help me bring his ginger hairs in sorrow to the grave."

I raised an eyebrow.

"As the guest of your Uncle Watkyn?"

"You could muck in with Harold. There's a spare room at that cottage place of his."

"Sorry, no."

"You won't stay on?"

"I will not. I intend to put as many miles as possible in as short a time as possible between Totleigh-in-the-Wold and myself. And it's no good your using that expression 'lily-livered poltroon,' because I am adamant."

She made what I believe is called a *moue*. It's done by pushing the lips out and drawing them in again.

"I thought it wouldn't be any use asking you. No spirit, that's your trouble; no enterprise. I'll have to get Harold to do it."

And as I stood shuddering at the picture her words conjured up, she pushed off, exhibiting dudgeon. And I was still speculating as to what tureen of soup she was planning to land the sainted Pinker in and hoping that he would have enough sense to stay out of it, when Jeeves drove up in the car, a welcome sight.

"Good morning, sir," he said. "I trust you slept well."

"Fitfully, Jeeves. Those plank beds are not easy on the fleshy parts."

"So I would be disposed to imagine, sir. And your disturbed night has left you ruffled, I am sorry to see. You are far from *soigné*."

I could, I suppose, have said something about "Way down upon the *soigné* river," but I didn't. My mind was occupied with deeper thoughts. I was in pensive mood.

"You know, Jeeves," I said, "one lives and learns."

"Sir?"

"I mean, this episode has been a bit of an eye-opener to me. It has taught me a lesson. I see now what a mistake one makes in labeling someone as a ruddy Gawd-help-us just because he normally behaves like a ruddy Gawd-help-us. Look closely, and we find humanity in the unlikeliest places."

"A broad-minded view, sir."

"Take this Sir W. Bassett. In my haste, I have always penciled him in as a hellhound without a single redeeming quality. But what do I find? He has this softer side to him. Having got Bertram out on a limb, he does not, as one would have expected, proceed to saw it off but tempers justice with mercy, declining to press the charge. It has touched me a good deal to discover that under that forbidding exterior there lies a heart of gold. Why are you looking like a stuffed frog, Jeeves? Don't you agree with me?"

"Not altogether, sir, when you attribute Sir Watkyn's leniency to sheer goodness of heart. There were inducements."

"I don't dig you, Jeeves."

"I made it a condition that you be set at liberty, sir."

My inability to dig him became intensified. He seemed to me to be talking through the back of his neck, the last thing you desire in a personal attendant.

"How do you mean, condition? Condition of what?"

"Of my entering his employment, sir. I should mention that during my visit to Brinkley Court Sir Watkyn very kindly expressed appreciation of the manner in which I performed my duties and made me an offer to leave your service and enter his. This offer, conditional upon your release, I have accepted."

The police station at Totleigh-in-the-Wold is situated in the main street of that village, and from where we were standing I had a view of the establishments of a butcher, a baker, a grocer, and a publican licensed to sell tobacco, ales, and spirits. And as I heard these words, this butcher, this baker, this grocer, and this publican seemed to pirouette before my eyes as if afflicted with St. Vitus's dance.

"You're leaving me?" I gasped, scarcely able to b. my e.

The corner of his mouth twitched. He seemed to be about to smile but of course thought better of it.

"Only temporarily, sir."

Again I was unable to dig him.

"Temporarily?"

"I think it more than possible that after perhaps a week or so differences will arise between Sir Watkyn and myself, compelling me to resign my position. In that event, if you are not already suited, sir, I shall be most happy to return to your employment."

I saw all. It was a ruse, and by no means the worst of them. His brain enlarged by constant helpings of fish, he had seen the way and found a formula acceptable to all parties. The mists cleared from before my eyes, and the butcher, the baker, the grocer, and the publican licensed to sell tobacco, ales, and spirits switched back again to what is called the status quo.

A rush of emotion filled me.

"Jeeves," I said, and if my voice shook, what of it? We

Woosters are but human. "You stand alone. Others abide our question, but you don't, as the fellow said. I wish there was something I could do to repay you."

He coughed that sheeplike cough of his.

"There does chance to be a favor it is within your power to bestow, sir."

"Name it, Jeeves. Ask of me what you will, even unto half my kingdom."

"If you could see your way to abandoning your Alpine hat, sir."

I ought to have seen it coming. That cough should have told me. But I hadn't, and the shock was severe. I don't mind admitting that for an instant I reeled.

"You would go as far as that?" I said, chewing the lower lip.

"It was merely a suggestion, sir."

I took the hat off and gazed at it. The morning sunlight played on it, and it had never looked so blue, its feather so pink.

"I suppose you know you're breaking my heart?"

"I am sorry, sir."

I sighed. But, as I have said, the Woosters can take it.

"Very well, Jeeves. So be it."

I gave him the hat. It made me feel like a father reluctantly throwing his child from the sledge to divert the attention of the pursuing wolf pack, as I believe happens all the time in Russia in the winter months, but what would you?

"You propose to burn this Alpine hat, Jeeves?"

"No, sir. To present it to Mr. Butterfield. He thinks it will be of assistance to him in his courtship."

"His what?"

"Mr. Butterfield is courting a widowed lady in the village, sir."

This surprised me.

"But surely he was a hundred and four last birthday?"

"He is well stricken in years, yes, sir, but nevertheless—"

"There's life in the old dog yet?"

"Precisely, sir."

My heart melted. I ceased to think of self. It had just occurred to me that in the circumstances I would be unable to conclude my visit by tipping Butterfield. The hat would fill that gap.

"All right, Jeeves, give him the lid, and heaven speed his wooing. You might tell him that from me."

"I will make a point of doing so. Thank you very much, sir."

"Not at all, Jeeves."

Jeeves and the Tie
That Binds

1

As I SLID into my chair at the breakfast table and started to deal with the toothsome eggs and bacon which Jeeves had given of his plenty, I was conscious of a strange exhilaration, if I've got the word right. Pretty good the setup looked to me. Here I was, back in the old familiar headquarters, and the thought that I had seen the last of Totleigh Towers, of Sir Watkyn Bassett, of his daughter Madeline and above all of the unspeakable Spode, or Lord Sidcup as he now calls himself, was like the medium dose for adult of one of those patent medicines which tone the system and impart a gentle glow.

"These eggs, Jeeves," I said. "Very good. Very tasty."

"Yes, sir?"

"Laid, no doubt, by contented hens. And the coffee, perfect. Nor must I omit to give a word of praise to the bacon. I wonder if you notice anything about me this morning."

"You seem in good spirits, sir."

"Yes, Jeeves, I am happy today."

"I am very glad to hear it, sir."

"You might say I'm sitting on top of the world with a rainbow round my shoulder."

"A most satisfactory state of affairs, sir."

"What's the word I've heard you use from time to time —begins with eu?"

"Euphoria, sir?"

"That's the one. I've seldom had a sharper attack of euphoria. I feel full to the brim of Vitamin B. Mind you, I don't know how long it will last. Too often it is when one feels fizziest that the storm clouds begin doing their stuff."

"Very true, sir. Full many a glorious morning have I seen flatter the mountain tops with sovereign eye, kissing with golden face the meadows green, gilding pale streams with heavenly alchemy, Anon permit the basest clouds to ride with ugly rack on his celestial face and from the forlorn world his visage hide, stealing unseen to west with this disgrace."

"Exactly," I said. I couldn't have put it better myself. "One always has to budget for a change in the weather. Still, the thing to do is to keep on being happy while you can."

"Precisely, sir. Carpe diem, the Roman poet Horace advised. The English poet Herrick expressed the same sentiment when he suggested that we should gather rosebuds while we may. Your elbow is in the butter, sir."

"Oh, thank you, Jeeves."

Well, all right so far. Off to a nice start. But now we come to something which gives me pause. In recording the latest installment of the Bertram Wooster Story, a task at which I am about to have a pop, I don't see how I can avoid delving into the past a good deal, touching on events which took place in previous installments and explaining who's who and what happened when and where and why, and this will make it heavy going for those who have been with me from the start. "Old hat," they will cry, or, if French, *"Déjà vu."*

On the other hand, I must consider the new customers. I can't just leave the poor perishers to try to puzzle things out for themselves. If I did, the exchanges in the present case would run somewhat as follows.

SELF: The relief I felt at having escaped from Totleigh Towers was stupendous.

NEW C: What's Totleigh Towers?

SELF: For one thing, it had looked odds on that I should have to marry Madeline.

NEW C: Who's Madeline?

SELF: Gussie Fink-Nottle, you see, had eloped with the cook.

NEW C: Who's Gussie Fink-Nottle?

SELF: But most fortunately Spode was in the offing and he scooped her up, saving me from the scaffold.

NEW C: Who's Spode?

You see. Hopeless. Confusion would be rife, as one might put it. The only way out that I can think of is to ask the old gang to let their attention wander for a bit—there are heaps of things they can be doing: washing the car, solving the crossword puzzle, taking the dog for a run—while I place the facts before the newcomers.

Briefly, then, owing to circumstances I needn't go into, Madeline Bassett, daughter of Sir Watkyn Bassett of Totleigh Towers, Glos., had long been under the impression that I was hopelessly in love with her and had given me to understand that if ever she had occasion to return her betrothed, Gussie Fink-Nottle, to store, she would marry me. Which wouldn't have fitted in with my plans at all, she, though physically in the pin-up class, being as mushy a character as ever broke biscuit, convinced that the stars are God's daisy chain and that every time a fairy blows its wee nose a baby is born. The last thing, as you can well imagine, one would want about the home.

So when Gussie unexpectedly eloped with the cook, it looked as though Bertram was for it. If a girl thinks you're in love with her and says she will marry you, you can't very well voice a preference for being dead in a ditch. Not, I mean, if you want to regard yourself as a *preux chevalier,* as the expression is, which is always my aim.

But just as I was about to put in my order for sackcloth and ashes, up, as I say, popped Spode, now going about under the alias of Lord Sidcup. He had loved her since she was so high but had never got around to mentioning it, and when he did so now, they clicked immediately. And the thought that she was safely out of circulation and no longer a menace was possibly the prime ingredient in my current euphoria.

I think that makes everything clear to the meanest intelligence, does it not? Right ho, so we can go ahead. Where were we? Ah yes, I had just told Jeeves that I was sitting on top of the world with a rainbow round my shoulder, but expressing a doubt as to whether this state of things would last—and how well founded that doubt proved to be, for scarcely a forkful of eggs and b later it was borne in upon me that life was not the grand sweet song I had supposed it to be, but, as you might say, stern and earnest and full of bumps.

"Was I mistaken, Jeeves," I said, making idle conversation as I sipped my coffee, "or as the mists of sleep shredded away this morning did I hear your typewriter going?"

"Yes, sir. I was engaged in composition."

"A dutiful letter to Charlie Silversmith?" I said, alluding to his uncle who held the post of butler at Deverill Hall, where we had once been pleasant visitors. "Or possibly a lyric in the manner of the bloke who advocates gathering rosebuds?"

"Neither, sir. I was recording the recent happenings at Totleigh Towers for the club book."

And here, dash it, I must once more ask what I may call the old sweats to let their attention wander while I put the new arrivals abreast.

Jeeves, you must know (I am addressing the new arrivals), belongs to a club for butlers and gentleman's gentlemen round Curzon Street way, and one of the rules there is that every member must contribute to the club book the latest information concerning the fellow he's working for, the idea being to inform those seeking employment of the sort of thing they will be taking on. If a member is contemplating signing up with someone, he looks him up in the club book, and if he finds that he puts out crumbs for the birdies every morning and repeatedly saves golden-haired children from being run over by automobiles, he knows he is on a good thing and has no hesitation in accepting office. Whereas if the book informs him that the fellow habitually kicks starving dogs and generally begins the day by throwing the breakfast porridge at his personal attendant, he is warned in time to steer clear of him.

Which is all very well, and one follows the train of thought, but in my opinion such a book is pure dynamite and ought not to be permitted. There are, Jeeves has informed me, eleven pages in it about me, and what will the harvest be, I ask him, if it falls into the hands of my Aunt Agatha, with whom my standing is already low? She spoke her mind freely enough some years ago when—against my personal wishes—I was found with twenty-three cats in my bedroom, and again when I was accused—unjustly, I need hardly say—of having marooned A. B. Filmer, the Cabinet Minister, on an island in her lake. To what heights of eloquence would she not soar, if informed of my vicissitudes at Totleigh Towers? The imagination boggled, Jeeves, I tell him.

To which he replies that it won't fall into the hands of my Aunt Agatha, she not being likely to drop in at the Junior Ganymede, which is what his club is called, and there the matter rests. His reasoning is specious, and although he has more or less succeeded in soothing my tremors, I still can't help feeling uneasy, and my manner, as I addressed him now, had quite a bit of agitation in it.

"Good Lord!" I ejaculated, if ejaculated is the word I want. "Are you really writing up that Totleigh business?"

"Yes, sir."

"All the stuff about my being supposed to have pinched old Bassett's amber statuette?"

"Yes, sir."

"And the night I spent in a prison cell? Is this necessary? Why not let the dead past bury its dead? Why not forget all about it?"

"Impossible, sir."

"Why impossible? Don't tell me you can't forget things. You aren't an elephant."

I thought I had him there, but no.

"It is my membership in the Junior Ganymede which restrains me from obliging you, sir. The rules with reference to the club book are very strict and the penalty for omitting to contribute to it severe. Actual expulsion has sometimes resulted."

"I see," I said. I could appreciate that this put him in quite a spot, the feudal spirit making him wish to do the square thing by the young master, while a natural disinclination to get bunged out of a well-loved club urged him to let the young master boil his head. The situation seemed to me to call for what is known as a compromise.

"Well, couldn't you water the thing down a bit? Omit one or two of the juicier episodes?"

"I fear not, sir. The full facts are required. The committee insists on this."

I suppose I ought not at this point to have expressed a hope that his blasted committee would trip over banana skins and break their ruddy necks, for I seemed to detect on his face a momentary look of pain. But he was broadminded and condoned it.

"Your chagrin does not surprise me, sir. One can, how-

ever, understand their point of view. The Junior Ganymede club book is a historic document. It has been in existence more than eighty years."

"It must be the size of a house."

"No, sir, the records are in several volumes. The present
one dates back some twelve years. And one must remember
that it is not every employer who demands a great deal of
space."

"Demands!"

"I should have said 'requires.' As a rule, a few lines
suffice. Your eighteen pages are quite exceptional."

"Eighteen? I thought it was eleven."

"You are omitting to take into your calculations the report of your misadventures at Totleigh Towers, which I
have nearly completed. I anticipate that this will run to
approximately seven. If you will permit me, sir, I will pat
your back."

He made this kindly offer because I had choked on a
swallow of coffee. A few pats and I was myself again and
more than a little incensed, as always happens when we are
discussing his literary work. Eighteen pages, I mean to say,
and every page full of stuff calculated, if thrown open to
the public, to give my prestige the blackest of eyes. Conscious of a strong desire to kick the responsible parties in
the seat of the pants, I spoke with a generous warmth.

"Well, I call it monstrous. There's no other word for it.
Do you know what that blasted committee of yours is inviting? Blackmail, that's what it's inviting. Let some man of
ill will get his hooks on that book, and what'll be the upshot? Ruin, Jeeves, that's what'll be the upshot."

I don't know if he drew himself to his full height, because I was lighting a cigarette at the moment and wasn't
looking, but I think he must have done so, for his voice,
when he spoke, was the chilly voice of one who has drawn
himself to his full height.

409

"There are no men of ill will in the Junior Ganymede, sir."

I contested this statement hotly.

"That's what *you* think. How about Brinkley?" I said, my allusion being to a fellow the agency had sent me some years previously when Jeeves and I had parted company temporarily because he didn't like me playing the banjolele. "He's a member, isn't he?"

"A country member, sir. He rarely comes to the club. In passing, sir, his name is not Brinkley, it is Bingley."

I waved an impatient cigarette holder. I was in no mood to split straws. Or is it hairs?

"His name is not of the essence, Jeeves. What *is* of the e is that he went off on his afternoon out, came back in an advanced state of intoxication, set the house on fire and tried to dismember me with a carving knife."

"A most unpleasant experience, sir."

"Having heard noises down below, I emerged from my room and found him wrestling with the grandfather clock, with which he appeared to have had a difference. He then knocked over a lamp and leaped up the stairs at me, complete with cutlass. By a miracle I avoided becoming the late Bertram Wooster, but only by a miracle. And you say there are no men of ill will in the Junior Ganymede club. Tchah!" I said. It is an expression I don't often use, but the situation seemed to call for it.

Things had become difficult. Angry passions were rising and dudgeon bubbling up a bit. It was fortunate that at this juncture the telephone should have tootled, causing a diversion.

"Mrs. Travers, sir," said Jeeves, having gone to the instrument.

2

I HAD ALREADY divined who was at the other end of the wire, my good and deserving Aunt Dahlia having a habit of talking on the telephone with the breezy vehemence of a hog-caller in the western states of America calling his hogs to come and get it. She got this way through hunting a lot in her youth with the Quorn and the Pytchley. What with people riding over hounds, and hounds taking time off to chase rabbits, a girl who hunts soon learns to make herself audible. I believe that she, when in good voice, could be heard in several adjoining counties.

I stepped to the telephone, well pleased. There are few males or females whose society I enjoy more than that of this genial sister of my late father, and it was quite a time since we had foregathered. She lives near the town of Market Snodsbury in Worcestershire and sticks pretty closely to the rural seat, while I, as Jeeves had just recorded in the club book, had had my time rather full elsewhere of late. I was smiling sunnily as I took up the receiver. Not much good, of course, as she couldn't see me, but it's the spirit that counts.

"Hullo, aged relative."

"Hullo to you, you young blot. Are you sober?"

I felt a natural resentment at being considered capable of falling under the influence of the sauce at ten in the morning, but I reminded myself that aunts will be aunts.

Show me an aunt, I've often said, and I will show you someone who doesn't give a hoot how much her obiter dicta may wound a nephew's sensibilities. With a touch of hauteur I reassured her on the point she had raised and asked her in what way I could serve her.

"How about lunch?"

"I'm not in London. I'm at home. And you can serve me, as you call it, by coming here. Today, if possible."

"Your words are music to my ears, old ancestor. Nothing could tickle me pinker," I said, for I am always glad to accept her hospitality and to renew my acquaintance with the unbeatable eatables dished up by her superb French chef, Anatole, God's gift to the gastric juices. I have often regretted that I have but one stomach to put at his disposal. "Staying how long?"

"As long as you like, my beamish boy. I'll let you·know when the time comes to throw you out. The great thing is to get you here."

I was touched, as who would not have been, by the eagerness she showed for my company. Too many of my circle are apt when inviting me to their homes to stress the fact that they are only expecting me for the weekend and to dwell with too much enthusiasm on the excellence of the earlier trains back to the metropolis on Monday morning. The sunny smile widened an inch or two.

"Awfully good of you to have me, old blood relation."

"It is, rather."

"I look forward to seeing you."

"Who wouldn't?"

"Each minute will seem like an hour till we meet. How's Anatole?"

"Greedy young pig, always thinking of Anatole."

"Difficult to help it. The taste lingers. How is his art these days?"

"At its peak."

"That's good."

"Ginger says his output has been a revelation to him."

I asked her to repeat this. It had sounded to me just as if she had said "Ginger says his output has been a revelation to him," and I knew this couldn't be the case. It turned out, however, that it was.

"Ginger?" I said, not abreast.

"Harold Winship. He told me to call him Ginger. He's staying here. He says he's a friend of yours, which he would scarcely admit unless he knew it could be proved against him. You do know him, don't you? He speaks of having been at Oxford with you."

I uttered a joyful cry, and she said if I did it again, she would sue me, it having nearly cracked her eardrum. A notable instance of the pot calling the kettle black, as the old saying has it, she having been cracking mine since the start of the proceedings.

"Know him?" I said. "You bet I know him. We were like . . . Jeeves!"

"Sir?"

"Who were those two fellows?"

"Sir?"

"Greek, if I remember correctly. Always mentioned when the subject of bosom pals comes up."

"Would you be referring to Damon and Pythias, sir?"

"That's right. We were like Damon and Pythias, old ancestor. But what's he doing *chez* you? I wasn't aware that you and he had ever met."

"We hadn't. But his mother was an old school friend of mine."

"I see."

"And when I heard he was standing for Parliament in the by-election at Market Snodsbury, I wrote to him and told him to make my house his base. Much more comfortable than dossing at a pub."

"Oh, you've got a by-election at Market Snodsbury, have you?"

"Under full steam."

"And Ginger's one of the candidates?"

"The Conservative one. You seem surprised."

"I am. You might say stunned. I wouldn't have thought it was his dish at all. How's he doing?"

"Difficult to say so far. Anyway, he needs all the help he can get, so I want you to come and canvass for him."

This made me chew the lower lip for a moment. One has to exercise caution at a time like this, or where is one?

"What does it involve?" I asked guardedly. "I shan't have to kiss babies, shall I?"

"Of course you won't, you abysmal chump."

"I've always heard that kissing babies entered largely into these things."

"Yes, but it's the candidate who does it, poor blighter. All you have to do is go from house to house urging the inmates to vote for Ginger."

"Then rely on me. Such an assignment should be well within my scope. Old Ginger!" I said, feeling emotional. "It will warm the what-d'you-call-its of my heart to see him again."

"Well, you'll have the opportunity of hotting them up this very afternoon. He's gone to London for the day and wants you to lunch with him."

"Does he? Egad! That's fine. What time?"

"One-thirty."

"At what spot?"

"Barribault's grillroom."

"I'll be there. Jeeves," I said, hanging up, "you remember Ginger Winship, who used to play Damon to my Pythias?"

"Yes, indeed, sir."

"They've got an election on at Market Snodsbury, and he's standing in the Conservative interest."

"So I understood madam to say, sir."

"Oh, you caught her remarks?"

"With little or no difficulty, sir. Madam has a penetrating voice."

"It does penetrate, doesn't it?" I said, massaging the ear I had been holding to the receiver. "Good lung power."

"Extremely, sir."

"I wonder whether she ever sang lullabies to me in my cradle. If so, it must have scared me cross-eyed, giving me the illusion that the boiler had exploded. However, that is not germane to the issue, which is that we leave for her abode this afternoon. I shall be lunching with Ginger. In my absence, pack a few socks and toothbrushes, will you?"

"Very good, sir," he replied, and we did not return to the subject of the club book.

3

I<small>T WAS</small> with no little gusto and animation that some hours later I set out for the tryst. This Ginger was one of my oldest buddies, not quite so old as Kipper Herring or Catsmeat Potter-Pirbright, with whom I had plucked the gowans fine at prep school, public school and university, but definitely ancient. Our rooms at Oxford had been adjacent, and it would not be too much to say that from the moment he looked in to borrow a syphon of soda water we became more like brothers than anything, and this state of things had continued after we had both left the seat of learning.

For quite a while he had been a prominent member of the Drones Club, widely known for his effervescence and vivacity, but all of a sudden he had tendered his resignation and gone to live in the country, oddly enough at Steeple Bumpleigh in Essex, where my Aunt Agatha has her lair. This, somebody told me, was due to the circumstance that he had got engaged to a girl of strong character who disapproved of the Drones Club. You get girls like that every now and then, and in my opinion they are best avoided.

Well, naturally, this had parted us. He never came to London, and I, of course, never went to Steeple Bumpleigh. You don't catch me going anywhere near Aunt Agatha unless I have to. No sense in sticking one's neck out. But I had missed him sorely. Oh for the touch of a vanished hand is how you might put it.

Arriving at Barribault's, I found him in the lobby where you have the pre-luncheon gargle before proceeding to the grillroom, and after the initial What-ho-ing and What-a-time-since-we-met-ing, inevitable when two vanished hands who haven't seen each other for ages reestablish contact, he asked me if I would like one for the tonsils.

"I won't join you," he said. "I'm not actually on the wagon, I have a little light wine at dinner now and then, but my fiancée wants me to stay off cocktails. She says they harden the arteries."

If you are about to ask me if this didn't make me purse the lips a bit, I can assure you that it did. It seemed to point to his having gone and got hitched up with a popsy totally lacking in the proper spirit, and it bore out what I had been told about her being a girl of strong character. No one who wasn't could have dashed the cup from his lips in this manner. She had apparently made him like it, too, for he had spoken of her not with the sullen bitterness of one crushed beneath the iron heel but with devotion in every syllable. Plainly he had got it up his nose and didn't object to being bossed.

How different from me, I reflected, that time when I was engaged to my Uncle Percy's bossy daughter, Florence Craye. It didn't last long, because she gave me the heave-ho and got betrothed to a fellow called Gorringe who wrote vers libre, but while it lasted I felt like one of those Ethiopian slaves Cleopatra used to push around, and I chafed more than somewhat. Whereas Ginger obviously hadn't even started to chafe. It isn't difficult to spot when a fellow's chafing, and I could detect none of the symptoms. He seemed to think that putting the presidential veto on cocktails showed what an angel of mercy the girl was, always working with his good at heart.

417

The Woosters do not like drinking alone, particularly with a critical eye watching them to see if their arteries are hardening, so I declined the proffered snort—reluctantly, for I was athirst—and came straight to the main item on the agenda paper. On my way to Barribault's I had, as you may suppose, pondered deeply on this business of him standing for Parliament, and I wanted to know the motives behind the move. It looked cockeyed to me.

"Aunt Dahlia tells me you are staying with her in order to be handy to Market Snodsbury while giving the electors there the old oil," I said.

"Yes, she very decently invited me. She was at school with my mother."

"So she told me. How do you like it there?"

"It's a wonderful place."

"Grade A. Gravel soil, main drainage, spreading grounds and Company's own water. And, of course, Anatole's cooking."

"Ah!" he said, and I think he would have bared his head, only he hadn't a hat on. "Very gifted, that man."

"A wizard," I agreed. "His dinners must fortify you for the tasks you have to face. How's the election coming along?"

"All right."

"Kissed any babies lately?"

"Ah!" he said again, this time with a shudder. I could see that I had touched an exposed nerve. "What blighters babies are, Bertie, dribbling, as they do, at the side of the mouth. Still, it has to be done. My agent tells me to leave no stone unturned if I want to win the election."

"But why do you want to win the election? I'd have thought you wouldn't have touched Parliament with a ten-foot pole," I said, for I knew the society there was very mixed. "What made you commit this rash act?"

"My fiancée wanted me to," he said, and as his lips

418

framed the word "fiancée" his voice took on a sort of tremolo like that of a male turtledove cooing to a female turtledove. "She thought I ought to be carving out a career for myself."

"Do you want a career?"

"Not much, but she insisted."

The uneasiness I had felt when he told me the beazel had made him knock off cocktails deepened. His every utterance rendered it more apparent to an experienced man like myself that he had run up against something too hot to handle, and for a moment I thought of advising him to send her a telegram saying it was all off and, this done, to pack a suitcase and catch the next boat to Australia. But feeling that this might give offense I merely asked him what the procedure was when you stood for Parliament— or ran for it, as they would say in America. Not that I particularly wanted to know, but it was something to talk about other than his frightful fiancée.

A cloud passed over his face, which, I ought to have mentioned earlier, was well worth looking at, the eyes clear, the cheeks tanned, the chin firm, the hair ginger and the nose shapely. It topped off, moreover, a body which also repaid inspection, being muscular and well knit. His general aspect, as a matter of fact, was rather like that presented by Esmond Haddock, the squire of Deverill Hall, where Jeeves's Uncle Charlie Silversmith drew his monthly envelope. He had the same poetic look, as if at any moment about to rhyme June with moon, yet gave the impression, as Esmond did, of being able, if he cared to, to fell an ox with a single blow. I don't know if he had ever actually done this, for one so seldom meets an ox, but in his undergraduate days he had felled people right and left, having represented the University in the ring as a heavyweight for a matter of three years. He may have included oxen among his victims.

"You go through hell," he said, the map still clouded as he recalled the past. "I had to sit in a room where you could hardly breathe because it was as crowded as the Black Hole of Calcutta and listen to addresses of welcome till midnight. After that I went about making speeches."

"Well, why aren't you down there making speeches now? Have they given you a day off?"

"I came up to get a secretary."

"Surely you didn't go there without one?"

"No, I had one all right, but my fiancée fired her. They had some sort of disagreement."

I had pursed the lips a goodish bit when he had told me about his fiancée and the cocktails, and I pursed them to an even greater extent now. The more I heard of this girl he had got engaged to, the less I liked the sound of her. I was thinking how well she would get on with Florence Craye if they happened to meet. Twin souls, I mean to say, each what a housemaid I used to know would have called an overbearing dishpot.

I didn't say so, of course. There is a time to call someone an overbearing dishpot, and a time not to. Criticism of the girl he loved might be taken in ill part, as the expression is, and you don't want an ex-Oxford boxing Blue taking things in ill part with you.

"Have you anyone in mind?" I asked. "Or are you just going to a secretary bin, accepting what they have in stock?"

"I'm hoping to get hold of an American girl I saw something of before I left London. I was sharing a flat with Boko Fittleworth when he was writing a novel, and she came every day and worked with him. Boko dictates his stuff, and he said she was tops as a secretary. I have her address, but I don't know if she's still there. I'm going round there after lunch. Her name's Magnolia Glendennon."

"It can't be."

"Why not?"

"Nobody could have a name like Magnolia."

"They could if they came from South Carolina, as she did. In the southern states of America you can't throw a brick without hitting a Magnolia. But I was telling you about this business of standing for Parliament. First, of course, you have to get the nomination."

"How did you manage that?"

"My fiancée fixed it. She knows one of the Cabinet Ministers, and he pulled strings. A man named Filmer."

"Not A. B. Filmer?"

"That's right. Is he a friend of yours?"

"I wouldn't say exactly a friend. I came to know him slightly owing to being chased with him on to the roof of a sort of summerhouse by an angry swan. This drew us rather close together for the moment, but we never became really chummy."

"Where was this?"

"On an island on the lake at my Aunt Agatha's place at Steeple Bumpleigh. Living at Steeple Bumpleigh, you've probably been there."

He looked at me with a wild surmise, much as those soldiers Jeeves has told me about looked on each other when on a peak in Darien, wherever that is.

"Is Lady Worpledon your aunt?"

"And how."

"She's never mentioned it."

"She wouldn't. Her impulse would be to hush it up."

"Then, good Lord, she must be your cousin."

"No, my aunt. You can't be both."

"I mean Florence. Florence Craye, my fiancée."

It was a shock, I don't mind telling you, and if I hadn't been seated I would probably have reeled. Though I ought not to have been so surprised. Florence was one of those

girls who are always getting engaged to someone, first team-
ing up with Stilton Cheesewright, then me, and finally
Percy Gorringe, who was dramatizing her novel *Spindrift*.
The play, by the way, had recently been presented to the
public at the Duke of York's theater, had laid an instanta-
neous egg, and had closed on the following Saturday. One
of the critics said he had perhaps seen it at a disadvantage
because when he saw it the curtain was up. I had wondered
a good deal what effect this had had on Florence's haughty
spirit.

"You're engaged to Florence?" I yipped, looking at him
with a wild surmise.

"Yes. Didn't you know?"

"Nobody tells me anything. Engaged to Florence, eh?
Well, well."

A less tactful man than Bertram Wooster might have
gone on to add "Oh, tough luck!" or something along those
lines, for there was no question but that the unhappy man
was properly up against it, but if there's one thing the
Woosters have in heaping measure, it is tact. I merely
gripped his hand, gave it a shake and wished him happiness. He thanked me for this.

"You're lucky," I said, wearing the mask.

"Don't I know it!"

"She's a charming girl," I said, still wearing as above.

"That just describes her."

"Intellectual, too."

"Distinctly. Writes novels."

"Always at it."

"Did you read *Spindrift*?"

"Couldn't put it down," I said, cunningly not revealing
that I hadn't been able to take it up. "Did you see the
play?"

"Twice. Too bad it didn't run. Gorringe's adaptation
was the work of an ass."

"I spotted him as an ass the first time I saw him."

"It's a pity Florence didn't."

"Yes. By the way, what became of Gorringe? When last heard of, she was engaged to him."

"She broke it off."

"Very wise of her. He had long side whiskers."

"She considered him responsible for the failure of the play and told him so."

"She would."

"What do you mean she would?"

"Her nature is so frank, honest and forthright."

"It is, isn't it?"

"She speaks her mind."

"Invariably."

"It's an admirable trait."

"Oh, most."

"You can't get away with much with a girl like Florence."

"No."

We fell into a silence. He was twiddling his fingers and a sort of what-d'you-call-it had come into his manner, as if he wanted to say something but was having trouble in getting it out. I remembered encountering a similar diffidence in the Rev. Stinker Pinker when he was trying to nerve himself to ask me to come to Totleigh Towers, and you find the same thing in dogs when they put a paw on your knee and look up into your face but don't utter, though making it clear that there is a subject on which they are anxious to touch.

"Bertie," he said at length.

"Hullo?"

"Bertie."

"Yes?"

"Bertie."

"Still here. Excuse me asking, but have you any cracked

423

gramophone-record blood in you? Perhaps your mother was frightened by one?"

And then it all came out in a rush as if a cork had been pulled.

"Bertie, there's something I must tell you about Florence, though you probably know it already, being a cousin of hers. She's a wonderful girl and practically perfect in every respect, but she has one characteristic which makes it awkward for those who love her and are engaged to her. Don't think I'm criticizing her."

"No, no."

"I'm just mentioning it."

"Exactly."

"Well, she has no use for a loser. To keep her esteem you have to be a winner. She's like one of those princesses in the fairy tales who used to set fellows some task to perform —it might be scaling a mountain of glass or bringing her a hair from the beard of the Great Cham of Tartary—and then gave them the brush-off when they couldn't make the grade."

I recalled the princesses of whom he spoke, and I had always thought them rather fatheads. I mean to say, what sort of foundation for a happy marriage is the bridegroom's ability to scale mountains of glass? A fellow probably wouldn't be called on to do it more than about once every ten years, if that.

"Gorringe," said Ginger, continuing, "was a loser, and that dished him. And long ago, someone told me, she was engaged to a gentleman jockey and she chucked him because he took a spill at the canal turn in the Grand National. She's a perfectionist. I admire her for it, of course."

"Of course."

"A girl like her is entitled to have high standards."

"Quite."

"But, as I say, it makes it awkward for me. She has set her

424

heart on my winning this Market Snodsbury election, heaven knows why, for I never thought she had any interest in politics, and if I lose it, I shall lose her, too. So—"

"Now is the time for all good men to come to the aid of the party?"

"Exactly. You are going to canvass for me. Well, canvass like a ton of bricks, and see that Jeeves does the same. I've simply got to win."

"You can rely on us."

"Thank you, Bertie, I knew I could. And now let's go in and have a bite of lunch."

4

HAVING RESTORED the tissues with the excellent nourishment which Barribault's hotel always provides and arranged that Ginger was to pick me up in his car later in the afternoon, my own sports model being at the vet's with some nervous ailment, we parted, he to go in search of Magnolia Glendennon, I to walk back to the Wooster GHQ.

It was, as you may suppose, in thoughtful mood that I made my way through London's thoroughfares. I was reading a novel of suspense the other day in which the heroine, having experienced a sock in the eye or two, was said to be lost in a maze of numbing thoughts, and that description would have fitted me like the paper on the wall.

My heart was heavy. When a man is an old friend and pretty bosom at that, it depresses you to hear that he's engaged to Florence Craye. I recalled my own emotions when I had found myself in that unpleasant position. I had felt like someone trapped in the underground den of the Secret Nine.

Though, mark you, there's nothing to beef about in her outer crust. At the time when she was engaged to Stilton Cheesewright I remember recording in the archives that she was tall and willowy with a terrific profile and luxuriant platinum-blond hair, the sort of girl who might, as far as looks were concerned, have been the star unit of the harem of one of the better-class sultans; and though I hadn't seen her for quite a while, I presumed that these conditions still prevailed. The fact that Ginger, when speaking of her, had gone so readily into his turtledove impersonation seemed to indicate as much.

Looks, however, aren't everything. Against this pin-up-ness of hers you had to put the bossiness which would lead her to expect the bloke she married to behave like a Hollywood yes-man. From childhood up she had been . . . I can't think of the word . . . begins with an i . . . no, it's gone . . . but I can give you the idea. When at my private school I once won a prize for Scripture Knowledge, which naturally involved a lot of researching into Holy Writ, and in the course of my researches I came upon the story of the military chap who used to say "Come" and they cometh and "Go" and they goeth. I have always thought that that was Florence in a nutshell. She would have given short shrift, as the expression is, to anyone who had gone when she said "Come" or the other way round. Imperious, that's the word I was groping for. She was as imperious as a traffic cop. Little wonder that the heart was heavy. I felt that Ginger, mistaking it for a peach, had plucked a lemon in the garden of love.

And then my meditations took a less somber turn. This often happens after a good lunch, even if you haven't had a cocktail. I reminded myself that many married men positively enjoy being kept on their toes by the little woman, and possibly Ginger might be one of them. He might take the view that when the little w made him sit up and beg and snap lumps of sugar off his nose, it was a compliment, really, because it showed that she was taking an interest.

Feeling a bit more cheerful, I reached for my cigarette case and was just going to open it, when like an ass I dropped it and it fell into the road. And as I stepped from the pavement to retrieve it there was a sudden tooting in my rear, and whirling on my axis I perceived that in about another two ticks I was going to be rammed amidships by a taxi.

The trouble about whirling on your axis, in case you didn't know, is that you're liable, if not an adagio dancer, to trip over your feet, and this was what I proceeded to do. My left shoe got all mixed up with my right ankle, I tottered, swayed, and after a brief pause came down like some noble tree beneath the woodman's ax, and I was sitting there lost in a maze of numbing thoughts, when an unseen hand attached itself to my arm and jerked me back to safety. The taxi went on and turned the corner.

Well, of course the first thing the man of sensibility does on these occasions is to thank his brave preserver. I turned to do this, and blow me tight if the b.p. wasn't Jeeves. Came as a complete surprise. I couldn't think what he was doing there, and for an instant the idea occurred to me that this might be his astral body.

"Jeeves!" I ejaculated. I'm pretty sure that's the word. Anyway, I'll risk it.

"Good afternoon, sir. I trust you are not too discommoded. That was a somewhat narrow squeak."

"It was indeed. I don't say my whole life passed before me, but a considerable chunk of it did. But for you——"

"Not at all, sir."

"Yes, you and you only saved me from appearing in tomorrow's obituary column."

"A pleasure, sir."

"It's amazing how you always turn up at the crucial moment, like the United States Marines. I remember how you did when A. B. Filmer and I were having our altercation with that swan, and there were other occasions too numerous to mention. Well, you will certainly get a rave notice in my prayers next time I make them. But how do you happen to be in these parts? Where are we, by the way?"

"This is Curzon Street, sir."

"Of course. I'd have known that if I hadn't been musing."

"You were musing, sir?"

"Deeply. I'll tell you about it later. This is where your club is, isn't it?"

"Yes, sir, just round the corner. In your absence and having completed the packing, I decided to lunch there."

"Thank heaven you did. If you hadn't, I'd have been— what's that gag of yours? Something about wheels."

"Less than the dust beneath thy chariot wheels, sir."

"Or, rather, the cabby's chariot wheels. Why are you looking at me with such a searching eye, Jeeves?"

"I was thinking that your misadventure had left you somewhat disheveled, sir. If I might suggest it, I think we should repair to the Junior Ganymede now."

"I see what you mean. You would give me a wash and brush-up?"

"Just so, sir."

"And perhaps a whiskey and soda?"

"Certainly, sir."

"I need one sorely. Ginger's practically on the wagon, so there were no cocktails before lunch. And do you know why he's practically on the wagon? Because the girl he's engaged to has made him take that foolish step. And do you know who the girl he's engaged to is? My cousin, Florence Craye."

"Indeed, sir?"

Well, I hadn't expected him to roll his eyes and leap about, because he never does no matter how sensational the news item, but I could see by the way one of his eyebrows twitched and rose perhaps an eighth of an inch that I had interested him. And there was what is called a wealth of meaning in that "Indeed, sir?" He was conveying his opinion that this was a bit of luck for Bertram, because a girl you have once been engaged to is always a lurking menace till she gets engaged to someone else and so cannot decide at any moment to play a return date. I got the message and thoroughly agreed with him, though naturally I didn't say so.

Jeeves, you see, is always getting me out of entanglements with the opposite sex, and he knows all about the various females who from time to time have come within an ace of hauling me to the altar rails, but of course we don't discuss them. To do so, we feel, would come under the head of bandying a woman's name, and the Woosters do not bandy women's names. Nor do the Jeeveses. I can't speak for his Uncle Charlie Silversmith, but I should imagine that he, too, has his code of ethics in this respect. These things generally run in families.

So I merely filled him in about her making Ginger stand for Parliament and the canvassing we were going to undertake, urging him to do his utmost to make the electors think along the right lines, and he said "Yes, sir" and "Very good, sir" and "I quite understand, sir," and we proceeded to the Junior Ganymede.

An extremely cozy club it proved to be. I didn't wonder that he liked to spend so much of his leisure there. It lacked the sprightliness of the Drones—I shouldn't think there was much bread and sugar thrown about at lunchtime, and you would hardly expect that there would be when you reflected that the membership consisted of elderly butlers and gentleman's gentlemen of fairly ripe years—but as regards comfort it couldn't be faulted. The purler I had taken left me rather tender in the fleshy parts, and it was a relief after I had been washed and brushed up and was on the spruce side once more to sink into a well-stuffed chair in the smoking room.

Sipping my whiskey and s, I brought the conversation round again to Ginger and his election, which was naturally the front-page stuff of the day. "Do you think he has a chance, Jeeves?"

He weighed the question for a moment, as if dubious as to where he would place his money.

"It is difficult to say, sir. Market Snodsbury, like so many English country towns, might be described as straitlaced. It sets a high value on respectability."

"Well, Ginger's respectable enough."

"True, sir, but, as you are aware, he has had a Past."

"Not much of one."

"Sufficient, however, to prejudice the voters, should they learn of it."

"Which they can't possibly do. I suppose he's in the club book—"

"Eleven pages, sir."

"—But you assure me that the contents of the club book will never be revealed."

"Never, sir. Mr. Winship has nothing to fear from that quarter."

His words made me breathe more freely.

"Jeeves," I said, "your words make me breathe more freely. As you know, I am always a bit uneasy about the club book. Kept under lock and key, is it?"

"Not actually under lock and key, sir, but it is safely bestowed in the secretary's office."

"Then there's nothing to worry about."

"I would not say that, sir. Mr. Winship must have had companions in his escapades, and they might inadvertently make some reference to them which would get into gossip columns in the press and thence into the Market Snodsbury journals. I believe there are two of these, one rigidly opposed to the Conservative interest, which Mr. Winship is representing. It is always a possibility, and the results would be disastrous. I have no means at the moment of knowing the identity of Mr. Winship's opponent, but he is sure to be a model of respectability whose past can bear the strictest investigation."

"You're pretty gloomy, Jeeves. Why aren't you gathering rosebuds? The poet Herrick would shake his head."

"I am sorry, sir. I did not know that you were taking Mr. Winship's fortunes so much to heart, or I would have been more guarded in my speech. Is victory in the election of such importance to him?"

"It's vital. Florence will hand him his hat if he doesn't win."

"Surely not, sir?"

"That's what he says, and I think he's right. His observations on the subject were most convincing. He says she's a perfectionist and has no use for a loser. It is well established that she handed Percy Gorringe the pink slip because the play he made of her novel only ran three nights."

"Indeed, sir?"

"Well-documented fact."

"Then let us hope that what I fear will not happen, sir."

We were sitting there hoping that what he feared would not happen, when a shadow fell on my whiskey and s and I saw that we had been joined by another member of the Junior Ganymede, a smallish, plumpish, Gawd-help-us-ish member wearing clothes more suitable for the country than the town, and a tie that suggested that he belonged to the Brigade of Guards, though I doubted if this was the case. As to his manner, I couldn't get a better word for it at the moment than "familiar," but I looked it up later in Jeeves's Dictionary of Synonyms and found that it had been unduly intimate, too free, forward, lacking in proper reserve, deficient in due respect, impudent, bold and intrusive. Well, when I tell you that the first thing he did was to prod Jeeves in the lower ribs with an uncouth forefinger, you will get the idea.

"Hullo, Reggie," he said, and I froze in my chair, stunned by the revelation that Jeeves's first name was Reginald. It had never occurred to me before that he had a first name. I couldn't help thinking what embarrassment would have been caused if it had been Bertie.

"Good afternoon," said Jeeves, and I could see that the chap was not one of his inner circle of friends. His voice was cold, and anyone less lacking in proper reserve and deficient in due respect would have spotted this and recoiled.

The Gawd-help-us fellow appeared to notice nothing amiss. His manner continued to be that of one who has met a pal of long standing.

"How's yourself, Reggie?"

"I am in in tolerably good health, thank you."

"Lost weight, haven't you? You ought to live in the country like me and get good country butter." He turned to me. "And you ought to be more careful, cocky, dancing about in the middle of the street like that. I was in that cab, and I thought you were a goner. You're Wooster, aren't you?"

"Yes," I said, amazed. I hadn't known I was such a public figure.

"Thought so. I don't often forget a face. Well, I can't stay chatting with you. I've got to see the secretary about something. Nice to have seen you, Reggie."

"Goodbye."

"Nice to have seen you, Wooster, old man."

I thanked him, and he withdrew. I turned to Jeeves, that wild surmise I was speaking about earlier functioning on all twelve cylinders.

"Who was that?"

He did not reply immediately, plainly too ruffled for speech. He had to take a sip of his liqueur brandy before he was master of himself. His manner, when he did speak, was that of one who would have preferred to let the whole thing drop.

"The person you mentioned at the breakfast table, sir. Bingley," he said, pronouncing the name as if it soiled his lips.

I was astounded. You could have knocked me down with a toothpick.

"Bingley? I'd never have recognized him. He's changed completely. He was quite thin when I knew him, and very gloomy, you might say, sinister. Always seemed to be brooding silently on the coming revolution, when he would be at liberty to chase me down Park Lane with a dripping knife."

The brandy seemed to have restored Jeeves. He spoke now with his customary calm.

"I believe his political views were very far to the left at the time when he was in your employment. They changed when he became a man of property."

"A man of property, is he?"

"An uncle of his in the grocery business died and left him a house and a comfortable sum of money."

"I suppose it often happens that the views of fellows like Bingley change when they come into money."

"Very frequently. They regard the coming revolution from a different standpoint."

"I see what you mean. They don't want to be chased down Park Lane with dripping knives themselves. Is he still a gentleman's gentleman?"

"He has retired. He lives a life of leisure in Market Snodsbury."

"Market Snodsbury? That's funny."

"Sir?"

"Odd, I mean, that he should live in Market Snodsbury."

"Many people do, sir."

"But when that's just where we're going. Sort of a coincidence. His uncle's house is there, I suppose."

"One presumes so."

"We may be seeing something of him."

"I hope not, sir. I disapprove of Bingley. He is dishonest. Not a man to be trusted."

"What makes you think so?"

"It is merely a feeling."

Well, it was no skin off my nose. A busy man like myself hasn't time to go about trusting Bingley. All I demanded of Bingley was that if our paths should cross he would remain sober and keep away from carving knifes. Live and let live is the Wooster motto. I finished my whiskey and soda and rose.

"Well," I said, "there's one thing. Holding the strong Conservative views he does, it ought to be a snip to get him to vote for Ginger. And now we'd better be getting along. Ginger is driving us down in his car, and I don't know when he'll be coming to fetch us. Thanks for your princely hospitality, Jeeves. You have brought new life to the exhausted frame."

"Not at all, sir."

5

GINGER TURNED UP in due course, and on going out to the car I saw that he had managed to get hold of Magnolia all right, for there was a girl sitting in the back and when he introduced us his "Mr. Wooster, Miss Glendennon" told the story.

Nice girl she seemed to me and quite nice-looking. I wouldn't say hers was the face that launched a thousand ships, to quote one of Jeeves's gags, and this was probably all to the good, for Florence, I imagine, would have had a word to say if Ginger had returned from his travels with something in tow calculated to bring a whistle to the lips of all beholders. A man in his position has to exercise considerable care in his choice of secretaries, ruling out anything that might have done well in the latest Miss America contest. But you could certainly describe her appearance as pleasant. She gave me the impression of being one of those quiet, sympathetic girls whom you could tell your troubles to in the certain confidence of having your hand held and your head patted. The sort of girl you could go to and say, "I say, I've just committed a murder and it's worrying me rather," and she would reply, "There, there, try not to think about it, it's the sort of thing that might happen to anybody." The little mother, in short, with the added attraction of being tops at shorthand and typing. I could have wished Ginger's affairs in no better hands.

Jeeves brought out the suitcases and stowed them away, and Ginger asked me to do the driving, as he had a lot of business to go into with his new secretary, giving her the lowdown on her duties, I suppose. We set out accordingly, with me and Jeeves in front, and about the journey down there is nothing of interest to report. I was in merry mood throughout, as always when about to get another whack at Anatole's cooking. Jeeves presumably felt the same, for he, like me, is one of that master skillet-wielder's warmest admirers, but whereas I sang a good deal as we buzzed along, he maintained, as is his custom, the silent reserve of a stuffed frog, never joining in the chorus, though cordially invited to.

Arriving at journey's end, we all separated. Jeeves attended to the luggage, Ginger took Magnolia Glendennon off to his office, and I made my way to the drawing room, which I found empty. There seemed to be nobody about, as so often happens when you fetch up at a country house latish in the afternoon. No sign of Aunt Dahlia, nor of Uncle Tom, her mate. I toyed with the idea of going to see if the latter was in the room where he keeps his collection of old silver, but thought better not. Uncle Tom is one of those enthusiastic collectors who, if in a position to grab you, detain you for hours, talking about sconces, foliation, ribbon wreaths in high relief and gadroon borders, and one wants as little of that sort of thing as can be managed.

I might have gone to pay my respects to Anatole, but there again I thought better not. He, too, is inclined to the long monologue when he gets you in his power, his pet subject being the state of his interior. He suffers from bouts of what he calls *mal au foie,* and his conversation would be of greater interest to a medical man than to a layman like myself. I don't know why it is, but when somebody starts talking to me about his liver I never can listen with real enjoyment.

On the whole, the thing to do seemed to be to go for a saunter in the extensive grounds and messuages.

It was one of those heavy, sultry afternoons when nature seems to be saying to itself, "Now shall I or shall I not scare the pants off these people with a hell of a thunderstorm?" but I decided to risk it. There's a small wooded bit not far from the house which I've always been fond of, and thither I pushed along. This wooded bit contains one or two rustic benches for the convenience of those who wish to sit and meditate, and as I hove alongside the first of these, I saw that there was an expensive-looking camera on it.

It surprised me somewhat, for I had no idea that Aunt Dahlia had taken to photography, but of course you never know what aunts will be up to next. The thought that occurred to me almost immediately was that if there was going to be a thunderstorm, it would be accompanied by rain, and rain falling on a camera doesn't do it any good. I picked the thing up, accordingly, and started off with it to take it back to the house, feeling that the old relative would thank me for my thoughtfulness, possibly with tears in her eyes, when there was a sudden bellow and an individual emerged from behind a clump of bushes. Startled me considerably, I don't mind telling you.

He was an extremely stout individual with a large pink face and a panama hat with a pink ribbon. A perfect stranger to me, and I wondered what he was doing here. He didn't look the sort of crony Aunt Dahlia would have invited to stay, and still less Uncle Tom, who is so allergic to guests that when warned of their approach he generally makes a bolt for it and disappears, leaving not a wrack behind, as I have heard Jeeves put it. However, as I was saying, you never know what aunts will be up to next, and no doubt the ancestor had had some good reason for asking the chap to come and mix, so I beamed civilly and opened the conversation with a genial "Hullo there."

"Nice day," I said, continuing to beam civilly. "Or,

rather, not so frightfully nice. Looks as if we were in for a thunderstorm."

Something seemed to have annoyed him. The pink of his face had deepened to about the color of his panama hat ribbon, and both his chins trembled slightly.

"Damn thunderstorms!" he responded—curtly, I suppose, would be the word, and I said I didn't like them myself. It was the lightning, I added, that I chiefly objected to.

"They say it never strikes twice in the same place, but then it hasn't got to."

"Damn the lightning! What are you doing with my camera?"

This naturally opened up a new line of thought.

"Oh, is this your camera?"

"Yes, it is."

"I was taking it to the house."

"You were, were you?"

"I didn't want it to get wet."

"Oh? And who are you?"

I was glad he had asked me that. His whole manner had made it plain to a keen mind like mine that he was under the impression that he had caught me in the act of absconding with his property, and I was glad to have the opportunity of presenting my credentials. I could see that if we were ever to have a good laugh together over this amusing misunderstanding, there would have to be a certain amount of preliminary spadework.

"Wooster is the name," I said. "I'm my aunt's nephew. I mean," I went on, for those last words seemed to me not to have rung quite right, "Mrs. Travers is my aunt."

"You are staying in the house?"

"Yes. Just arrived."

"Oh?" he said again, but this time in what you might call a less hostile tone of voice, though still not to be described as chummy. There followed a silence, presumably occupied

439

by him in turning things over in his mind in the light of my statement and examining them in depth, and then he said "Oh?" once more and stumped off.

I made no move to accompany him. What little I had had of his society had been ample. As we were staying in the same house, we would no doubt meet occasionally, but not, I resolved, if I saw him first. The whole episode reminded me of my first encounter with Sir Watkyn Bassett and the misunderstanding about his umbrella. That had left me shaken, and so had this. I was glad to have a rustic bench handy, so that I could sit and try to bring my nervous system back into shape. The sky had become more and more inky I suppose is the word I want, and the odds on a thunderstorm shorter than ever, but I still lingered. It was only when there came from above a noise like fifty-seven trucks going over a wooden bridge that I felt that an immediate move would be judicious. I rose and soon gathered speed, and I had reached the french window of the drawing room and was on the point of popping through, when from within there came the sound of a human voice. On second thoughts delete the word "human," for it was the voice of my recent acquaintance with whom I had chatted about cameras.

I halted. There was a song I used to sing in my bath at one time, the refrain or burthen of which began with the words "I stopped and I looked and I listened," and this was what I did now, except for the looking. It wasn't raining, nor was there any repetition of the truck-going-over-a-wooden-bridge noise. It was as though nature had said to itself, "Oh, to hell with it," and decided that it was too much trouble to have a thunderstorm after all. So I wasn't getting struck by lightning or even wet, which enabled me to remain in statu quo.

The camera bloke was speaking to some unseen companion, and what he said was: "Wooster, his name is. Says he's Mrs. Travers' nephew."

It was plain that I had arrived in the middle of a conversation. The words must have been preceded by a query, possibly "Oh, by the way, do you happen to know who that tall, slender, goodlooking—I might almost say fascinating —young man I was talking to outside there would be?" Though of course possibly not. That, at any rate, must have been the gist, and I suppose the party of the second part had replied, "No, sorry, I can't place him," or words to that effect. Whereupon the camera chap had spoken as above. And as he spoke as above a snort rang through the quiet room; a voice, speaking with every evidence of horror and disgust, exclaimed "Wooster!"; and I quivered from hairdo to shoe sole. I may even have gasped, but fortunately not loud enough to be audible beyond the french window.

For it was the voice of Lord Sidcup—or, as I shall always think of him, no matter how many titles he may have inherited, as Spode. Spode, mark you, whom I had thought and hoped I had seen the last of after dusting the dust of Totleigh Towers from the Wooster feet; Spode, who went about seeking whom he might devour and from early boyhood had been a hissing and a byword to all right-thinking men. Little wonder that for a moment everything seemed to go black and I had to clutch at a passing rosebush to keep from falling.

This Spode, I must explain for the benefit of the newcomers who have not read the earlier chapters of my memoirs, was a character whose path had crossed mine many a time and oft, as the expression is, and always with the most disturbing results. I have spoken of the improbability of a beautiful friendship ever getting under way between me and the camera chap, but the likelihood of any such fusion of souls, as I have heard Jeeves call it, between me and Spode was even more remote. Our views on each other were definite. His was that what England needed if it was to become a land fit for heroes to live in was fewer and

441

better Woosters, while I had always felt that there was nothing wrong with England that a ton of bricks falling from a height on Spode's head wouldn't cure.

"You know him?" said the camera chap.

"I'm sorry to say I do," said Spode, speaking like Sherlock Holmes asked if he knew Professor Moriarty. "How did you happen to meet him?"

"I found him making off with my camera."

"Ha!"

"Naturally, I thought he was stealing it. But if he's really Mrs. Travers' nephew, I suppose I was mistaken."

Spode would have none of this reasoning, though it seemed pretty sound to me. He snorted again with even more follow-through than the first time.

"Being Mrs. Travers' nephew means nothing. If he was the nephew of an archbishop he would behave in a precisely similar manner. Wooster would steal anything that was not nailed down, provided he could do it unobserved. He couldn't have known you were there?"

"No. I was behind a bush."

"And your camera looks like a good one."

"Cost me a lot of money."

"Then of course he was intending to steal it. He must have thought he had dropped into a bit of good luck. Let me tell you about Wooster. The first time I met him was in an antique shop. I had gone there with Sir Watkyn Bassett, my future father-in-law. He collects old silver. And Sir Watkyn had propped his umbrella up against a piece of furniture. Wooster was there, but lurking, so we didn't see him."

"In a dark corner, perhaps?"

"Or behind something. The first we saw of him, he was sneaking off with Sir Watkyn's umbrella."

"Pretty cool."

"Oh, he's cool all right. These fellows have to be."

"I suppose so. Must take a nerve of ice."

To say that I boiled with justifiable indignation would not be putting it too strongly. As I have recorded elsewhere, there was a ready explanation of my behavior. I had come out without my umbrella that morning, and completely forgetting that I had done so I had grasped old Bassett's, obeying the primeval instinct which makes a man without an umbrella reach out for the nearest one in sight, like a flower groping toward the sun. Unconsciously, as it were.

Spode resumed. They had taken a moment off, no doubt in order to brood on my delinquency. His voice now was that of one about to come to the high spot in his narrative.

"You'll hardly believe this, but soon after that he turned up at Totleigh Towers, Sir Watkyn's house in Gloucestershire."

"Incredible!"

"I thought you'd think so."

"Disguised, of course? A wig? A false beard? His cheeks stained with walnut juice?"

"No, he came quite openly, invited by my future wife. She has a sort of sentimental pity for him. I think she hopes to reform him."

"Girls will be girls."

"Yes, but I wish they wouldn't."

"Did you rebuke your future wife?"

"I wasn't in a position to then."

"Probably a wise thing, anyway. I once rebuked the girl I wanted to marry, and she went off and teamed up with a stockbroker. So what happened?"

"He stole a valuable piece of silver. A sort of silver cream jug. A cow-creamer they call it."

"My doctor forbids me cream. You had him arrested, of course?"

"We couldn't. No evidence."

443

"But you knew he had done it?"

"We were certain."

"Well, that's how it goes. See any more of him after that?"

"This you will *not* believe. He came to Totleigh Towers *again!*"

"Impossible!"

"Once more invited by my future wife."

"Would that be the Miss Bassett who arrived last night?"

"Yes, that was Madeline."

"Lovely girl. I met her in the garden before breakfast. My doctor recommends a breath of fresh air in the early morning. Did you know she thinks those bits of mist you see on the grass are the elves' bridal veils?"

"She has a very whimsical fancy."

"And nothing to be done about it, I suppose. But you were telling me about this second visit of Wooster's to Totleigh Towers. Did he steal anything this time?"

"An amber statuette worth a thousand pounds."

"He certainly gets around," said the camera chap with, I thought, a sort of grudging admiration. "I hope you had him arrested?"

"We did. He spent the night in the local jail. But next morning Sir Watkyn weakened and let him off."

"Mistaken kindness."

"So I thought."

The camera chap didn't comment further on this, though he was probably thinking that of all the soppy families introduced to his notice the Bassetts took the biscuit.

"Well, I'm very much obliged to you," he said, "for telling me about this man Wooster and putting me on my guard. I've brought a very valuable bit of old silver with me. I am hoping to sell it to Mr. Travers. If Wooster learns of this, he is bound to try to purloin it, and I can tell you that if he does, and I catch him, there will be none of this nonsense of a single night in jail. He will get the stiffest sentence the law can provide. And now how about a quick game of billiards before dinner? My doctor advises a little gentle exercise." ·

"I should enjoy it."

"Then let us be getting along."

Having given them time to remove themselves, I went in and sank down on a sofa. I was profoundly stirred, for if you think fellows enjoy listening to the sort of thing Spode had been saying about me, you're wrong. My pulse was rapid and my brow wet with honest sweat, like the village blacksmith's. I was badly in need of alcoholic refreshment, and just as my tongue was beginning to stick out and blacken at the roots, shiver my timbers if Jeeves didn't enter left center with a tray containing all the makings. St. Bernard dogs, you probably know, behave in a similar way in the Alps and are well thought of in consequence.

Mingled with the ecstasy which the sight of him aroused in my bosom was a certain surprise that he should be acting as cup-bearer. It was a job that should rightly have fallen into the province of Seppings, Aunt Dahlia's butler.

"Hullo, Jeeves!" I ejaculated.

"Good evening, sir. I have unpacked your effects. Can I pour you a whiskey and soda?"

"You can indeed. But what are you doing buttling? This mystifies me greatly. Where's Seppings?"

"He has retired to bed, sir, with an attack of indigestion consequent upon a too liberal indulgence in Monsieur Anatole's cooking at lunch. I am undertaking his duties for the time being."

"Very good of you, and very good of you to pop up at this particular moment. I have had a shock, Jeeves."

"I am sorry to hear that, sir."

"Did you know Spode was here?"

445

"Yes, sir."

"And Miss Bassett?"

"Yes, sir."

"We might as well be at Totleigh Towers."

"I can appreciate your dismay, sir, but fellow guests are easily avoided."

"Yes, and if you avoid them, what do they do? They go about telling men in panama hats you're a sort of cross between Raffles and one of those fellows who pinch bags at railway stations," I said, and in a few crisp words I gave him a resumé of Spode's remarks.

"Most disturbing, sir."

"Very. You know and I know how sound my motives were for everything I did at Totleigh, but what if Spode tells Aunt Agatha?"

"An unlikely contingency, sir."

"I suppose it is."

"But I know just how you feel, sir. Who steals my purse steals trash; 'tis something, nothing; 'twas mine, 'tis his, and has been slave to thousands. But he who filches from me my good name robs me of that which not enriches him and makes me poor indeed."

"Neat, that. Your own?"

"No, sir. Shakespeare's."

"Shakespeare said some rather good things."

"I understand that he has given uniform satisfaction, sir. Shall I mix you another?"

"Do just that thing, Jeeves, and with all convenient speed."

He had completed his St. Bernard act and withdrawn, and I was sipping my second rather more slowly than the first, when the door opened and Aunt Dahlia bounded in, all joviality and rosy complexion.

6

I NEVER SEE this relative without thinking how odd it is
that one sister—call her Sister A—can be so unlike another
sister, whom we will call Sister B. My Aunt Agatha, for
instance, is tall and thin and looks rather like a vulture in
the Gobi desert, while Aunt Dahlia is short and solid, like a
scrum half in the game of Rugby football. In disposition,
too, they differ widely. Aunt Agatha is cold and haughty,
though presumably she unbends a bit when conducting
human sacrifices at the time of the full moon, as she is
widely rumored to do, and her attitude toward me has always been that of an austere governess, causing me to feel
as if I were six years old and she had just caught me stealing
jam from the jam cupboard; whereas Aunt Dahlia is as
jovial and bonhomous as a pantomime dame in a Christmas pantomime. Curious.

I welcomed her with a huge Hello, in both syllables of
which a nephew's love and esteem could be easily detected,
and went so far as to imprint an affectionate kiss on her
brow. Later I would take her roundly to task for filling the
house with Spodes and Madeline Bassetts and bulging
bounders in panama hats, but that could wait.

She returned my greeting with one of her uncouth hunting cries—"Yoicks," if I remember correctly. Apparently,

447

when you've been with the Quorn and the Pytchley for some time, you drop into the habit of departing from basic English.

"So here you are, young Bertie."

"You never spoke a truer word. Up and doing, with a heart for any fate."

"As thirsty as ever, I observe. I thought I would find you tucking into the drinks."

"Purely medicinal. I've had a shock."

"What gave you that?"

"Suddenly becoming apprised of the fact that the blighter Spode was my fellow guest," I said, feeling that I couldn't have a better cue for getting down to my recriminations. "What on earth was the idea of inviting a fiend in human shape like that here?" I said, for I knew she shared my opinion of the seventh Earl of Sidcup. "You have told me many a time and oft that you consider him one of nature's gravest blunders. And yet you go out of your way to court his society, if court his society is the expression I want. You must have been off your onion, old ancestor."

It was a severe ticking off, and you would have expected the blush of shame to have mantled her cheeks, not that you would have noticed it much, her complexion being what it was after all those winters in the hunting field, but she was apparently imp-something, impervious, that's the word, to remorse. She remained what Anatole would have called as cool as some cucumbers.

"Ginger asked me to. He wanted Spode to speak for him at this election. He knows him slightly."

"Far the best way of knowing Spode."

"He needs all the help he can get, and Spode's one of those silver-tongued orators you read about. Extraordinary gift of the gab he has. He could get into Parliament without straining a sinew."

I dare say she was right, but I resented any praise of Spode. I made clear my displeasure by responding curtly, "Then why doesn't he?"

"He can't, you poor chump. He's a lord."

"Don't they allow lords in?"

"No, they don't."

"I see," I said, rather impressed by this proof that the House of Commons drew the line somewhere. "Well, I suppose you aren't so much to blame as I had thought. How do you get on with him?"

"I avoid him as much as possible."

"Very shrewd. I shall do the same. We now come to Madeline Bassett. She's here, too. Why?"

"Oh, Madeline came along for the ride. She wanted to be near Spode. An extraordinary thing to want, I agree. Morbid, you might call it. Florence Craye, of course, has come to help Ginger's campaign."

I started visibly. In fact, I jumped about six inches, as if a skewer or knitting needle had come through the seat of my chair.

"You don't mean Florence is here as well?"

"With bells on. You seem perturbed."

"I'm all of a twitter. It never occurred to me that when I came here I would be getting into a sort of population explosion."

"Whoever told you about population explosions?"

"Jeeves. They are rather a favorite subject of his. He says if something isn't done pretty soon—"

"I'll bet he said, If steps are not taken shortly through the proper channels."

"He did, as a matter of fact. He said, If steps are not taken shortly through the proper channels, half the world will soon be standing on the other half's shoulders."

"All right if you're one of the top layer."

"Yes, there's that, of course."

"Though even then it would be uncomfortable. Tricky sort of balancing act."

"True."

"And difficult to go for a stroll if you wanted to stretch the legs. And one wouldn't get much hunting."

"Not much."

We mused for awhile on what lay before us, and I remember thinking that present conditions, even with Spode and Madeline and Florence on the premises, suited one better. From this to thinking of Uncle Tom was but a step. It seemed to me that the poor old buster must be on the verge of a nervous breakdown. Even a single guest is sometimes too much for him.

"How," I asked, "is Uncle Tom bearing up under this invasion of his cabin?"

She stared incredibly, or rather, incredulously. "Did you expect to find him here playing his banjo? My poor half-witted child, he was off to the south of France the moment he learned that danger threatened. I had a picture postcard from him yesterday. He's having a wonderful time and wishes I was there."

"And don't you mind all these blighters overrunning the place?"

"I would prefer it if they went elsewhere, but I treat them with saintly forbearance because I feel it's all helping Ginger."

"How do things look in that direction?"

"An even bet, I would say. The slightest thing might turn the scale. He and his opponent are having a debate in a day or two, and a good deal, you might say everything, depends on that."

"Who's the opponent?"

"Local talent. A barrister."

"Jeeves says Market Snodsbury is very straitlaced, and if the electors found out about Ginger's past they would heave him out without even handing him his hat."

"Has he a past?"

"I wouldn't call it that. Pure routine, I'd describe it as. In the days before he fell under Florence's spell he was rather apt to get slung out of restaurants for throwing eggs at the electric fan, and he seldom escaped unjugged on Boat Race night for pinching policemen's helmets. Would that lose him votes?"

"Lose him votes? If it was brought to Market Snodsbury's attention, I doubt if he would get a single one. That sort of thing might be overlooked in the cities of the plain, but not in Market Snodsbury. So for heaven's sake don't go babbling about it to everyone you meet."

"My dear old ancestor, am I likely to?"

"Very likely, I should say. You know how fat your head is."

I would have what-d'you-call-it-ed this slur, and with vehemence, but the adjective she had used reminded me that we had been talking all this time and I hadn't inquired about the camera chap.

"By the way," I said, "who would a fat fellow be?"

"Someone fond of starchy foods who had omitted to watch his calories, I imagine. What on earth, if anything, are you talking about?"

I saw that my question had been too abrupt. I hastened to clarify it.

"Strolling in the grounds and messuages just now I encountered an obese bird in a panama hat with a pink ribbon, and I was wondering who he was and how he came to be staying here. He didn't look the sort of bloke for whom you would be putting out mats with 'Welcome' on them. He gave me the impression of being a thug of the first order."

My words seemed to have touched a chord. Rising nimbly, she went to the door and opened it, then to the french window and looked out, plainly in order to ascertain that nobody—except me, of course—was listening.

451

Spies in spy stories do the same kind of thing when about to make communications which are for your ears only.

"I suppose I'd better tell you about him," she said.

I intimated that I would be an attentive audience.

"That's L. P. Runkle, and I want you to exercise your charm on him, such as it is. He has to be conciliated and sucked up to."

"Why, is he someone special?"

"You bet he's someone special. He's a big financier, Runkle's Enterprises. Loaded with money."

It seemed to me that these words could have but one significance.

"You're hoping to touch him?"

"Such is indeed my aim. But not for myself. I want to get a round sum out of him for Tuppy Glossop."

Her allusion was to the nephew of Sir Roderick Glossop, the well-known nerve specialist and loony doctor, once a source of horror and concern to Bertram but now one of my leading pals. He calls me Bertie, I call him Roddy. Tuppy, too, is one of my immediate circle of buddies, in spite of the fact that he once betted me I couldn't swing myself from end to end on the rings above the swimming pool at the Drones, and when I came to the last one I found he had looped it back, giving me no option but to drop into the water in faultless evening dress. This had been like a dagger in the bosom for a considerable period, but eventually Time the great healer had ironed things out and I had forgiven him. He has been betrothed to Aunt Dahlia's daughter Angela for ages, and I had never been able to understand why they hadn't got around to letting the wedding bells get cracking. I had been expecting every day for ever so long to be called on to weigh in with the silver fish slice, but the summons never came.

Naturally I asked if Tuppy was hard up, and she said he wasn't begging his bread and nosing about in the gutters for cigarette ends, but he hadn't enough to marry on.

"Thanks to L. P. Runkle. I'll tell you the whole story."

"Do."

"Did you ever meet Tuppy's late father?"

"Once. I remember him as a dreamy old bird of the absentminded-professor type."

"He was a chemical researcher or whatever they call it, employed by Runkle's Enterprises, one of those fellows you see in the movies who go about in white coats peering into test tubes. And one day he invented what were afterwards known as Runkle's Magic Midgets, small pills for curing headaches. You've probably come across them."

"I know them well. Excellent for a hangover, though not, of course, to be compared with Jeeves's patent pick-me-up. They're very popular at the Drones. I know a dozen fellows who swear by them. There must be a fortune in them."

"There is. They sell like warm winter woollies in Iceland."

"Then why is Tuppy short of cash? Didn't he inherit them?"

"Not by a jugful."

"I don't get it. You speak in riddles, aged relative," I said, and there was a touch of annoyance in my voice, for if there is one thing that gives me the pip, it is an aunt speaking in riddles. "If these ruddy midget things belonged to Tuppy's father—"

"L. P. Runkle claimed they didn't. Tuppy's father was working for him on a salary, and the small print in the contract read that all inventions made on Runkle's Enterprises' time became the property of Runkle's Enterprises. So when old Glossop died, he hadn't much to leave his son, while L. P. Runkle went on flourishing like a green bay tree."

I had never seen a green bay tree, but I gathered what she meant.

"Couldn't Tuppy sue?"

"He would have been bound to lose. A contract is a contract."

I saw what she meant. It was not unlike that time when she was running that weekly paper of hers, *Milady's Boudoir*, and I contributed to it an article, or piece as it is sometimes called, on What the Well-dressed Man Is Wearing. She gave me a packet of cigarettes for it, and it then became her property. I didn't actually get offers for it from France, Germany, Italy, Canada and the United States, but if I had, I couldn't have accepted them. My pal Boko Littleworth, who makes a living by his pen, tells me I ought to have sold her only the first serial rights, but I didn't think of it at the time. One makes these mistakes. What one needs, of course, is an agent.

All the same, I considered that L. P. Runkle ought to have stretched a point and let Tuppy's father get something out of it. I put this to the ancestor, and she agreed with me.

"Of course he ought. Moral obligation."

"It confirms one's view that this Runkle is a stinker."

"The stinker supreme. And he tells me he has been tipped off that he's going to get a knighthood in the New Year's Honours."

"How can they knight a chap like that?"

"Just the sort of chap they do knight. Prominent business man. Big deals. Services to Britain's export trade."

"But a stinker."

"Unquestionably a stinker."

"Then what's he doing here? You usually don't go out of your way to entertain stinkers. Spode, yes. I can understand you letting him infest the premises much as I disapprove of it. He's making speeches on Ginger's behalf, and according to you doing it rather well. But why Runkle?"

She said "Ah!" and when I asked her reason for saying "Ah!" she replied that she was thinking of her subtle cunning, and when I asked what she meant by subtle cunning, she said "Ah!" again. It looked as if we might go on like this indefinitely, but a moment later, having toddled to the door and opened it and to the french window and peered out, she explained.

"Runkle came here hoping to sell Tom an old silver what-not for his collection, and as Tom had vanished and he had come a long way I had to put him up for the night, and at dinner I suddenly had an inspiration. I thought if I got him to stay on and plied him day and night with Anatole's cooking, he might get into mellowed mood."

She had ceased to speak in riddles. This time I followed her.

"So that you would be able to talk him into slipping Tuppy some of his ill-gotten gains?"

"Exactly. I'm biding my time. When the moment comes I shall act like lightning. I told him Tom would be back in a day or two, not that he will, because he won't come within fifty miles of the place till I blow the All Clear, so Runkle consented to stay on."

"And how's it working out?"

"The prospects look good. He mellows more with every meal. Anatole gave us his *Mignonette de Poulet Petit Duc* last night, and he tucked into it like a tapeworm that's been on a diet for weeks. There was no mistaking the gleam in his eyes as he downed the last mouthful. A few more dinners ought to do the trick."

She left me shortly after this to go and dress for dinner. I, strong in the knowledge that I could get into the soup and fish in ten minutes, lingered on, plunged in thought.

Extraordinary how I kept doing that as of even date. It just shows what life is like now. I don't suppose in the old days I would have been plunged in thought more than about once a month.

7

I need scarcely say that Tuppy's hard case, as outlined by the old blood relation, had got right in amongst me. You might suppose that a fellow capable of betting you you couldn't swing yourself across the Drones swimming pool by the rings and looping the last ring back deserved no consideration, but as I say, the agony of that episode had long since abated, and it pained me deeply to contemplate the spot he was in. For though I had affected to consider that the ancestor's scheme for melting L. P. Runkle was the goods, I didn't really believe it would work. You don't get anywhere by filling with rich foods a bloke who wears a panama hat like his; the only way of inducing the L.P. Runkle type of man to part with cash is to kidnap him, take him to the cellar beneath the lonely mill and stick lighted matches between his toes. And even then he would probably give you a dud check.

The revelation of Tuppy's hard-upness had come as quite a surprise. You know how it is with fellows you're seeing all the time; if you think about their finances at all, you sort of assume they must be all right. It had never occurred to me that Tuppy might be seriously short of doubloons, but I saw now why there had been all this delay in assembling the bishop and assistant clergy and getting the show on the road. I presumed Uncle Tom would brass up if given the green light, he having the stuff in heaping sackfuls, but Tuppy has his pride and would quite properly jib at the idea of being supported by a father-in-law. Of course he really oughtn't to have gone and signed Angela up with his bank balance in such a rocky condition, but love is love. Conquers all, as the fellow said.

Having mused on Tuppy for about five minutes, I changed gears and started musing on Angela, for whom I had always had a cousinly affection. A definitely nice young prune and just the sort to be a good wife, but of course the catch is that you can't be a good wife if the other half of the sketch hasn't enough money to marry you. Practically all you can do is hang around and twiddle your fingers and hope for the best. Weary waiting about sums it up, and the whole layout, I felt, must be g and wormwood for Angela, causing her to bedew her pillow with many a salty tear.

I always find when musing that the thing to do is to bury the face in the hands, because it seems to concentrate thought and keep the mind from wandering off elsewhere. I did this now, and was getting along fairly well, when I suddenly had that uncanny feeling that I was not alone. I sensed a presence, if you would prefer putting it that way, and I had not been mistaken. Removing the hands and looking up, I saw that Madeline Bassett was with me.

It was a nasty shock. I won't say she was the last person I wanted to see, Spode of course heading the list of starters, with L. P. Runkle in close attendance, but I would willingly have dispensed with her company. However, I rose courteously, and I don't think there was anything in my manner to suggest that I would have liked to hit her with a brick, for I am pretty inscrutable at all times. Nevertheless, behind my calm front there lurked the uneasiness which always grips me when we meet.

Holding the mistaken view that I am hopelessly in love with her and more or less pining away into a decline, this Bassett never fails to look at me, when our paths cross, with a sort of tender pity, and she was letting me have it now. So melting indeed was her gaze that it was only by reminding myself that she was safely engaged to Spode that I was able to preserve my equanimity and sangfroid. When she had been betrothed to Gussie Fink-Nottle, the peril of her making a switch had always been present, Gussie being the sort of spectacled newt-collecting freak a girl might at any moment get second thoughts about, but there was something so reassuring in her being engaged to Spode. Because, whatever you might think of him, you couldn't get away from it that he was the seventh Earl of Sidcup, and no girl who has managed to hook a seventh Earl with a castle in Shropshire and an income of twenty thousand pounds per annum is lightly going to change her mind about him.

Having given me the look, she spoke, and her voice was like treacle pouring out of a jug.

"Oh, Bertie, how nice to see you again. How are you?"

"I'm fine. How are *you*?"

"I'm fine."

"That's fine. How's your father?"

"He's fine."

I was sorry to hear this. My relations with Sir Watkyn Bassett were such that a more welcome piece of news would have been that he had contracted bubonic plague and wasn't expected to recover.

"I heard you were here," I said.

"Yes, I'm here."

"So I heard. You're looking well."

"Oh, I'm very very well, and oh so happy."

"That's good."

"I wake up each morning to the new day, and I know it's going to be the best day that ever was. Today I danced on the lawn before breakfast, and then I went round the garden saying good morning to the flowers. There was a sweet black cat asleep on one of the flower beds. I picked it up and danced with it."

I didn't tell her so, but she couldn't have made a worse

social gaffe. If there is one thing Augustus, the cat to whom she referred, hates, it's having his sleep disturbed. He must have cursed freely, though probably in a drowsy undertone. I suppose she thought he was purring.

She paused, seeming to expect some comment on her fatheaded behavior, so I said, "Euphoria."

"I what?"

"That's what it's called, Jeeves tells me, feeling like that."

"Oh, I see. I just call it being happy, happy, happy."

Having said which, she gave a start, quivered and put a hand up to her face as if she were having a screen test and had been told to register remorse.

"Oh, Bertie!"

"Hullo?"

"I'm so so sorry."

"Eh?"

"It was so tactless of me to go on about my happiness. I should have remembered how different it was for you. I saw your face twist with pain as I came in, and I can't tell you how sorry I am to think that it is I who have caused it. Life is not easy, is it?"

"Not very."

"Difficult."

"In spots."

"The only thing is to be brave."

"That's about it."

"You must not lose courage. Who knows? Consolation may be waiting for you somewhere. Some day you will meet someone who will make you forget you ever loved me. No, not quite that. I think I shall always be a fragrant memory, always something deep in your heart that will be with you like a gentle, tender ghost as you watch the sunset on summer evenings while the little birds sing their off-to-bed songs in the shrubbery."

"I wouldn't be surprised," I said, for one simply has to

say the civil thing. "You look a bit damp," I added, changing the subject. "Was it raining when you were out?"

"A little, but I didn't mind. I was saying good night to the flowers."

"Oh, you say good night to them, too?"

"Of course. Their poor little feelings would be so hurt if I didn't."

"Wise of you to come in. Might have got lumbago."

"That was not why I came in. I saw you through the window, and I had a question to ask you. A very, very serious question."

"Oh, yes?"

"But it's so difficult to know how to put it. I shall have to ask it as they do in books. You know what they say in books."

"What who say in books?"

"Detectives and people like that. Bertie, are you going straight now?"

"I beg your pardon?"

"You know what I mean. Have you given up stealing things?"

I laughed, one of those gay debonair ones. "Oh, absolutely."

"I'm so glad. You don't feel the urge any more? You've conquered the craving? I told Daddy it was just a kind of illness. I said you couldn't help yourself."

I remembered her submitting this theory to him—I was hiding behind a sofa at the time, a thing I have been compelled to do rather oftener than I could wish—and Sir Watkyn had replied in what I thought dubious taste that it was precisely my habit of helping myself to everything I could lay my hands on that he was criticizing.

Another girl might have left it at that, but not M. Bassett. She was all eager curiosity.

"Did you have psychiatric treatment? Or was it will-power?"

"Just willpower."

"How splendid. I'm so proud of you. It must have been a terrible struggle."

"Oh, so-so."

"I shall write to Daddy and tell him—"

Here she paused and put a hand to her left eye, and it was easy for a man of my discernment to see what had happened. The french window being open, gnats in fairly large numbers had been coming through and flitting to and fro. It's a thing one always has to budget for in the English countryside. In America they have screens, of course, which make flying objects feel pretty nonplused, but these have never caught on in England and the gnats have it more or less their own way. They horse around and now and then get into people's eyes. One of these, it was evident, had now got into Madeline's.

I would be the last to deny that Bertram Wooster has his limitations, but in one field of endeavor I am preeminent. In the matter of taking things out of eyes I yield to no one. I know what to say and what to do.

Counseling her not to rub it, I advanced, handkerchief in hand.

I remember going into the technique of operations of this kind with Gussie Fink-Nottle at Totleigh when he had removed a fly from the eye of Stephanie Byng, now the Reverend Mrs. Stinker Pinker, and we were in agreement that success could be achieved only by placing a hand under the patient's chin in order to steady the head. Omit this preliminary and your efforts are bootless. My first move, accordingly, was to do so, and it was characteristic of Spode that he should have chosen this moment to join us, just when we twain were in what you might call close juxtaposition.

I confess that there have been times when I have felt more at my ease. Spode, in addition to being constructed on the lines of a rather oversized gorilla, has a disposition like that of a short-tempered tiger of the jungle, and a nasty mind which leads him to fall a ready prey to what I have heard Jeeves call the green-eyed monster which doth mock the meat it feeds on—viz., jealousy. Such a man, finding you steadying the head of the girl he loves, is always extremely liable to start trying to ascertain the color of your insides, and to avert this I greeted him with what nonchalance I could muster.

"Oh, hullo, Spode old chap, I mean Lord Sidcup old chap. Here we all are, what? Jeeves told me you were here, and Aunt Dahlia says you've been knocking the voting public base over apex with your oratory in the Conservative interest. Must be wonderful to be able to do that. It's a gift, of course. Some have it, some haven't. I couldn't address a political meeting to please a dying grandmother. I should stand there opening and shutting my mouth like a goldfish. You, on the other hand, just clear your throat and the golden words come pouring out like syrup. I admire you enormously."

Conciliatory, I think you'll agree. I could hardly have given him the old salve with a more liberal hand, and one might have expected him to simper, shuffle his feet and mumble "Awfully nice of you to say so," or something along those lines. Instead of which, all he did was come back at me with a guttural sound like an opera basso choking on a fishbone, and I had to sustain the burden of the conversation by myself.

"I've just been taking a gnat out of Madeline's eye."

"Oh?"

"Dangerous devils, these gnats. Require skilled handling."

"Oh?"

"Everything's back to normal now, I think."

"Yes, thank you ever so much, Bertie."

It was Madeline who said this, not Spode. He continued

to gaze at me bleakly. She went on harping on the thing.

"Bertie's so clever."

"Oh?"

"I don't know what I would have done without him."

"Oh?"

"He showed wonderful presence of mind."

"Oh?"

"I feel so sorry, though, for the poor little gnat."

"It asked for it," I pointed out. "It was unquestionably the aggressor."

"Yes, I suppose that's true, but . . ." The clock on the mantelpiece caught her now de-gnatted eye, and she uttered an agitated squeak. "Oh, my goodness, is that the time? I must rush."

She buzzed off, and I was on the point of doing the same, when Spode detained me with a curt "One moment." There are all sorts of ways of saying "One moment." This was one of the nastier ones, spoken with an unpleasant rasping note in the voice.

"I want a word with you, Wooster."

I am never anxious to chat with Spode, but if I had been sure that he merely wanted to go on saying "Oh?" I would have been willing to listen. Something, however, seemed to tell me that he was about to give evidence of a wider vocabulary, and I edged toward the door.

"Some other time, don't you think?"

"Not some ruddy other time. Now."

"I shall be late for dinner."

"You can't be too late for me. And if you get your teeth knocked down your throat, as you will if you don't listen attentively to what I have to say, you won't be able to eat any dinner."

This seemed plausible. I decided to lend him an ear, as the expression is. "Say on," I said, and he said on, lowering his voice to a sort of rumbling growl which made him difficult to follow. However, I caught the word "read" and the word "book" and perked up a bit. If this was going to be a literary discussion, I didn't mind exchanging views.

"Book?" I said.

"Book."

"You want me to recommend you a good book? Well, of course, it depends on what you like. Jeeves, for instance, is never happier than when curled up with his Spinoza or his Shakespeare. I, on the other hand, go in mostly for whodunits and novels of suspense. For the whodunit, Agatha Christie is always a safe bet. For the novel of suspense . . ."

Here I paused, for he had called me an opprobrious name and had told me to stop babbling, and it is always my policy to stop babbling when a man eight foot six in height and broad in proportion tells me to. I went into the silence, and he continued to say on.

"I said that I could read you like a book, Wooster. I know what your game is."

"I don't understand you, Lord Sidcup."

"Then you must be as big an ass as you look, which is saying a good deal. I am referring to your behavior toward my fiancée. I come into this room and I find you fondling her face."

I had to correct him here. One likes to get these things straight. "Only her chin."

"Pah!" he said, or something that sounded like that.

"And I had to get a grip on it in order to extract the gnat from her eye. I was merely steadying it."

"You were steadying it gloatingly."

"I wasn't!"

"Pardon me. I have eyes and can see when a man is steadying a chin gloatingly and when he isn't. You were obviously delighted to have an excuse for soiling her chin with your foul fingers."

"You are wrong, Lord Spodecup."

"And, as I say, I know what your game is. You are trying to undermine me, to win her from me with your insidious guile, and what I want to impress upon you with all the emphasis at my disposal is that if anything of this sort is going to occur again, you would do well to take out an accident policy with some good insurance company at the earliest possible date. You probably think that being a guest in your aunt's house I would hesitate to butter you over the front lawn and dance on the fragments in hobnailed boots, but you are mistaken. It will be a genuine pleasure. By an odd coincidence I brought a pair of hobnailed boots with me."

So saying, and recognizing a good exit line when he saw one, he strode out, and after an interval of tense meditation I followed him. Repairing to my bedroom, I found Jeeves there, looking reproachful. He knows I can dress for dinner in ten minutes, but regards haste askance, for he thinks it results in a tie which, even if adequate, falls short of the perfect butterfly effect.

I ignored the silent rebuke in his eyes. After meeting Spode's eyes, I was dashed if I was going to be intimidated by Jeeves's.

"Jeeves," I said, "you're fairly well up in Hymns Ancient and Modern, I should imagine. Who were the fellows in the hymn who used to prowl and prowl around?"

"The troops of Midian, sir."

"That's right. Was Spode mentioned as one of them?"

"Sir?"

"I ask because he's prowling around as if Midian was his home town. Let me tell you all about it."

"I fear it will not be feasible, sir. The gong is sounding."

"So it is. Who's sounding it? You said Seppings was in bed."

"The parlormaid, sir, deputizing for Mr. Seppings."

"I like her wrist work. Well, I'll tell you later."

"Very good, sir. Pardon me, your tie."

"What's wrong with it?"

"Everything, sir. If you will allow me."

"All right, go ahead. But I can't help asking myself if ties really matter at a time like this."

"There is no time when ties do not matter, sir."

My mood was somber as I went down to dinner. Anatole, I was thinking, would no doubt give us of his best, possibly his *Timbale de Ris de Veau Toulousiane* or his *Sylphides à la Crème d'Écrivisses,* but Spode would be there and Madeline would be there and Florence would be there and L. P. Runkle would be there.

There was, I reflected, always something.

8

IT HAS BEEN well said of Bertram Wooster that when he sets
his hand to the plow he does not stop to pick daisies and let
the grass grow under his feet. Many men in my position,
having undertaken to canvass for a friend anxious to get
into Parliament, would have waited till after lunch next
day to get rolling, saying to themselves, Oh, what difference do a few hours make? and going off to the billiard
room for a game or two of snooker. I, in sharp contradistinction, as I have heard Jeeves call it, was on my way
shortly after breakfast. It couldn't have been much more
than a quarter to eleven when, fortified by a couple of kippers, toast, marmalade and three cups of coffee, I might
have been observed approaching a row of houses down by
the river to which someone with a flair for the *mot juste*
had given the name of River Row. From long acquaintance
with the town I knew that this was one of the posher parts
of Market Snodsbury, stiff with householders likely to favor
the Conservative cause, and it was for that reason that I was
making it my first port of call. No sense, I mean, in starting
off with the less highly priced localities where everybody
was bound to vote Labor and would not only turn a deaf
ear to one's reasoning but might even bung a brick at one.
Ginger no doubt had a special posse of tough supporters,
talking and spitting out of the side of their mouths, and

they would attend to the brick-bunging portion of the electorate.

Jeeves was at my side, but whereas I had selected Number One as my objective, his intention was to push on to Number Two. I would then give Number Three the treatment, while he did the same to Number Four. Talking it over, we had decided that if we made it a double act and blew into a house together, it might give the occupant the impression that he was receiving a visit from the plainclothes police and excite him unduly. Many of the men who live in places like River Row have a tendency to apoplectic fits as the result of high living, and a voter expiring on the floor from shock means a voter less on the voting list. One has to think of these things.

"What beats me, Jeeves," I said, for I was in thoughtful mood, "is why people don't object to somebody they don't know from Adam muscling into their homes without a—without a what? It's on the tip of my tongue."

"A With-your-leave or a By-your-leave, sir?"

"That's right. Without a With-your-leave or a By-your-leave, and telling them which way to vote. Taking a liberty, it strikes me as."

"It is the custom at election time, sir. Custom reconciles us to everything, a wise man once said."

"Shakespeare?"

"Burke, sir. You will find the apothegm in his *On the Sublime and Beautiful.* I think the electors, conditioned by many years of canvassing, would be disappointed if nobody called on them."

"So we shall be bringing a ray of sunshine into their drab lives?"

"Something on that order, sir."

"Well, you may be right. Have you ever done this sort of thing before?"

"Once or twice, sir, before I entered your employment."

"What were your methods?"

"I outlined as briefly as possible the main facets of my argument, bade my auditors goodbye, and withdrew."

"No preliminaries?"

"Sir?"

"You didn't make a speech of any sort before getting down to brass tacks? No mention of Burke or Shakespeare or the poet Burns?"

"No, sir. It might have caused exasperation."

I disagreed with him. I felt that he was on the wrong track altogether and couldn't expect anything in the nature of a triumph at Number Two. There is probably nothing a voter enjoys more than hearing the latest about Burke and his *On the Sublime and Beautiful,* and here he was, deliberately chucking away the advantages his learning gave him. I had half a mind to draw his attention to the Parable of the Talents, with which I had become familiar when doing research for that Scripture Knowledge prize I won at school. Time, however, was getting along, so I passed it up. But I told him I thought he was mistaken. Preliminaries, I maintained, were of the essence. Breaking the ice is what it's called. I mean, you can't just barge in on a perfect stranger and get off the mark with an abrupt "Hoy there. I hope you're going to vote for my candidate!" How much better to say "Good morning, sir. I can see at a glance that you are a man of culture, probably never happier than when reading your Burke. I wonder if you are familiar with his *On the Sublime and Beautiful?*" Then away you go, off to a nice start.

"You must have an approach," I said. "I myself am all for the jolly, genial. I propose, on meeting my householder, to begin with a jovial 'Hullo there, Mr. Whatever-it-is, hullo there,' thus ingratiating myself with him from the kickoff. I shall then tell him a funny story. Then, and only then, will I get to the nub,—waiting, of course, till he has stopped laughing. I can't fail."

"I am sure you will not, sir. The system would not suit me, but it is merely a matter of personal taste."

"The psychology of the individual, what?"

"Precisely, sir. By different methods different men excel."

"Burke?"

"Charles Churchill, sir, a poet who flourished in the early eighteenth century. The words occur in his 'Epistle to William Hogarth.' "

We halted. Cutting out a good pace, we had arrived at the door of Number One. I pressed the bell.

"Zero hour, Jeeves," I said gravely.

"Yes, sir."

"Carry on."

"Very good, sir."

"Heaven speed your canvassing."

"Thank you, sir."

"And mine."

"Yes, sir."

He pushed along and mounted the steps of Number Two, leaving me feeling rather as I had done in my younger days at a clergyman uncle's place in Kent when about to compete in the Choir Boys Bicycle Handicap open to all those whose voices had not broken by the first Sunday in Epiphany—nervous, but full of the will to win.

The door opened as I was running through the high spots of the laughable story I planned to unleash when I got inside. A maid was standing there, and conceive my emotion when I recognized her as one who had held office under Aunt Dahlia the last time I had enjoyed the latter's hospitality—the one with whom, the old sweats will recall, I had chewed the fat on the subject of the cat Augustus and his tendency to pass his days in sleep instead of bustling about and catching mice.

The sight of her friendly face was like a tonic. My morale, which had begun to sag a bit after Jeeves had left me, rose sharply, closing at nearly par. I felt that even if the fellow I was going to see kicked me downstairs, she would be there to show me out and tell me that these things are sent to try us, with the general idea of making us more spiritual.

"Why, hullo!" I said.

"Good morning, sir."

"We meet again."

"Yes, sir."

"You remember me?"

"Oh yes, sir."

"And you have not forgotten Augustus?"

"Oh no, sir."

"He's still as lethargic as ever. He joined me at breakfast this morning. Just managed to keep awake while getting outside his portion of kipper, then fell into a dreamless sleep at the end of the bed with his head hanging down. So you have resigned your portfolio at Aunt Dahlia's since we last met. Too bad. We shall all miss you. Do you like it here?"

"Oh yes, sir."

"That's the spirit. Well, getting down to business, I've come to see your boss on a matter of considerable importance. What sort of chap is he? Not too short-tempered? Not too apt to be cross with callers, I hope?"

"It isn't a gentleman, sir, it's a lady. Mrs. McCorkadale."

This chipped quite a bit off the euphoria I was feeling. I had been relying on the story I had prepared to put me over with a bang, carrying me safely through the first awkward moments when the fellow you've called on without an invitation is staring at you as if wondering to what he owes the honor of this visit, and now it would have to remain untold. It was one I had heard from Catsmeat Potter-Pirbright at the Drones, and it was essentially a *conte*

471

whose spiritual home was the smoking room or the men's washroom on an American train—in short, one by no means adapted to the ears of the gentler sex, especially a member of that sex who probably ran the local Watch Committee.

It was, consequently, a somewhat damped Bertram Wooster whom the maid ushered into the drawing room, and my pep was in no way augmented by the first sight I had of mine hostess. Mrs. McCorkadale was what I would call a grim woman. Not so grim as my Aunt Agatha, perhaps, for that could hardly be expected, but certainly well up in the class of Jael, the wife of Heber, and the Madame Whoever-it-was who used to sit and knit at the foot of the guillotine during the French Revolution. She had a beaky nose, tight, thin lips, and her eye could have been used for splitting logs in the teak forests of Borneo. Seeing her steadily and seeing her whole, as the expression is, one marveled at the intrepidity of Mr. McCorkadale in marrying her—obviously a man whom nothing could daunt.

However, I had come there to be jolly and genial, and jolly and genial I was resolved to be. Actors will tell you that on these occasions, when the soul is atwitter and the nervous system not like Mother makes it, the thing to do is to take a deep breath. I took three, and immediately felt much better.

"Good morning, good morning, good morning," I said. "Good morning," I added, rubbing it in, for it was my policy to let there be no stint.

"Good morning," she replied, and one might have totted things up as so far, so good. But if I said she said it cordially, I would be deceiving my public. The impression I got was that the sight of me hurt her in some sensitive spot. The woman, it was plain, shared Spode's view of what was needed to make England a land fit for heroes to live in.

472

Not being able to uncork the story and finding the way her eye was going through me like a dose of salts more than a little trying to my already dented sangfroid, I might have had some difficulty in getting the conversation going, but fortunately I was full of good material just waiting to be decanted. Over an after-dinner smoke on the previous night, Ginger had filled me in on what his crowd proposed to do when they got down to it. They were going, he said, to cut taxes to the bone, straighten out our foreign policy, double our export trade, have two cars in the garage and two chickens in the pot for everyone, and give the pound the shot in the arm it had been clamoring for for years. Than which, we both agreed, nothing could be sweeter, and I saw no reason to suppose that the McCorkadale gargoyle would not feel the same. I began, therefore, by asking her if she had a vote, and she said, Yes, of course, and I said, Well, that was fine, because if she hadn't had, the point of my argument would have been largely lost.

"An excellent thing, I've always thought, giving women the vote," I proceeded heartily, and she said—rather nastily, it seemed to me—that she was glad I approved. "When you cast yours, if cast is the word I want, I strongly advise you to cast it in favor of Ginger Winship."

"On what do you base that advice?"

She couldn't have given me a better cue. She had handed it to me on a plate with watercress round it. Like a flash I went into my sales talk, mentioning Ginger's attitude toward taxes, our foreign policy, our export trade, cars in the garage, chickens in the pot, and first aid for the poor old pound, and was shocked to observe an entire absence of enthusiasm on her part. Not a ripple appeared on the stern and rockbound coast of her map. She looked like Aunt Agatha listening to the boy Wooster trying to explain away a drawing-room window broken by a cricket ball.

I pressed her closely. Or do I mean keenly?

"You want taxes cut, don't you?"

"I do."

"And our foreign policy bumped up?"

"Certainly."

"And our exports doubled and a stick of dynamite put under the pound? I'll bet you do. Then vote for Ginger Winship, the man who with his hand on the helm of the ship of state will steer England to prosperity and happiness, bringing back once more the spacious days of Good Queen Bess." This was a line of talk that Jeeves had roughed out for my use. There was also some rather good stuff about this sceptered isle and this other Eden, demi-something, but I had forgotten it. "You can't say that wouldn't be nice," I said.

A moment before, I wouldn't have thought it possible that she could look more like Aunt Agatha than she had been doing, but she now achieved this breathtaking feat. She sniffed, if not snorted, and spoke as follows:

"Young man, don't be idiotic. Hand on the helm of the ship of state, indeed! If Mr. Winship performs the miracle of winning this election, which he won't, he will be an ordinary humble back-bencher, doing nothing more notable than saying 'Hear, hear' when his superiors are speaking and 'Oh' and 'Question' when the opposition has the floor. As," she went on, "I shall if I win this election, as I intend to."

I blinked. A sharp "Whatwasthatyousaid?" escaped my lips, and she proceeded to explain or, as Jeeves would say, elucidate.

"You are not very quick at noticing things, are you? I imagine not, or you would have seen that Market Snodsbury is liberally plastered with posters bearing the words 'Vote for McCorkadale.' An abrupt way of putting it, but one that is certainly successful in conveying its meaning."

It was a blow, I confess, and I swayed beneath it like an

aspen, if aspens are those things that sway. The Woosters can take a good deal, but only so much. My most coherent thought at the moment was that it was just like my luck, when I sallied forth as a canvasser, to collide first crack out of the box with the rival candidate. I also had the feeling that if Jeeves had taken on Number One instead of Number Two, he would probably have persuaded Ma McCorkadale to vote against herself.

I suppose if you had asked Napoleon how he had managed to get out of Moscow, he would have been a bit vague about it, and it was the same with me. I found myself on the front steps with only a sketchy notion of how I had got there, and I was in the poorest of shapes. To try to restore the shattered system I lit a cigarette and had begun to puff, when a cheery voice hailed me and I became aware that some foreign substance was sharing my doorstep. "Hullo, Wooster old chap," it was saying, and, the mists clearing from before my eyes, I saw that it was Bingley.

I gave the blighter a distant look. Knowing that this blot on the species resided in Market Snodsbury, I had foreseen that I mght run into him sooner or later, so I was not surprised to see him. But I certainly wasn't pleased. The last thing I wanted in the delicate state to which the McCorkadale had reduced me was conversation with a man who set cottages on fire and chased the hand that fed him hither and thither with a carving knife.

He was as unduly intimate, forward, bold, intrusive and deficient in due respect as he had been at the Junior Ganymede. He gave my back a cordial slap and would, I think, have prodded me in the ribs if it had occurred to him. You wouldn't have thought that carving knives had ever come between us.

"And what are *you* doing in these parts, cocky?" he asked.

I said I was visiting my aunt, Mrs. Travers, who had a

house in the vicinity, and he said he knew the place, though he had never met the old geezer to whom I referred. "I've seen her around. Red-faced old girl, isn't she?"

"Fairly vermilion."

"High blood pressure, probably."

"Or caused by going in a lot for hunting. It chaps the cheeks."

"Different from a barmaid. She cheeks the chaps."

If he had supposed that his crude humor would get so much as a simper out of me, he was disappointed. I preserved the cold aloofness of a Wednesday matinee audience, and he proceeded.

"Yes, that might be it. She looks a sport. Making a long stay?"

"I don't know," I said, for the length of my visits to the old ancestor is always uncertain. So much depends on whether she throws me out or not. "Actually I'm here to canvass for the Conservative candidate. He's a pal of mine."

He whistled sharply. He had been looking repulsive and cheerful; he now looked repulsive and grave. Seeming to realize that he had omitted a social gesture, he prodded me in the ribs.

"You're wasting your time, Wooster, old man," he said. "He hasn't an earthly."

"No?" I quavered. It was simply one man's opinion, of course, but the earnestness with which he had spoken was unquestionably impressive. "What makes you think that?"

"Never you mind what makes me think it. Take my word for it. If you're sensible, you'll phone your bookie and have a big bet on McCorkadale. You'll never regret it. You'll come to me later and thank me for the tip with tears in your—"

At some point in this informal interchange of thoughts by spoken word, as Jeeves's Dictionary of Synonyms puts it, he must have pressed the bell, for at this moment the door opened and my old buddy the maid appeared. Quickly adding the word "eyes," he turned to her.

"Mrs. McCorkadale in, dear?" he asked, and having been responded to in the affirmative he left me, and I headed for home. I ought, of course, to have carried on along River Row, taking the odd numbers while Jeeves attended to the even, but I didn't feel in the vein.

I was uneasy. You might say, if you happened to know the word, that the prognostications of a human wart like Bingley deserved little credence, but he had spoken with such conviction, so like someone who has heard something, that I couldn't just pass them off with a light laugh.

Brooding tensely, I reached the old homestead and found the ancestor lying on a chaise longue, doing the *Observer* crossword puzzle.

9

Thﾍere was a time when this worthy housewife, when tackling the *Observer* crossword puzzle, would snort and tear her hair and fill the air with strange oaths picked up from cronies on the hunting field, but consistent inability to solve more than about an eighth of the clues has brought a sort of dull resignation, and today she merely sits and stares at it, knowing that however much she licks the end of her pencil, little or no business will result.

As I came in, I heard her mutter, soliloquizing like someone in Shakespeare, "Measured tread of saint round St. Paul's, for God's sake," seeming to indicate that she had come up against a hot one, and I think it was a relief to her to become aware that her favorite nephew was at her side and that she could conscientiously abandon her distasteful task, for she looked up and greeted me cheerily. She wears tortoiseshell-rimmed spectacles for reading which make her look like a fish in an aquarium. She peered at me through these.

"Hullo, my bounding Bertie."

"Good morning, old ancestor."

"Up already?"

"I have been up some time."

"Then why aren't you out canvassing? And why are you looking like something the cat brought in?"

I winced. I had not intended to disclose the recent past,

but with an aunt's perception she had somehow spotted that in some manner I had passed through the furnace, and she would go on probing and questioning till I came clean. Any capable aunt can give Scotland Yard inspectors strokes and bisques in the matter of interrogating a suspect, and I knew that all attempts at concealment would be fruitless. Or is it bootless? I would have to check with Jeeves.

"I am looking like something the cat brought in because I am feeling like something the c b i," I said. "Aged relative, I have a strange story to relate. Do you know a local blister of the name of Mrs. McCorkadale?"

"Who lives in River Row?"

"That's the one."

"She's a barrister."

"She looks it."

"You've met her?"

"I've met her."

"She's Ginger's opponent in this election."

"I know. Is Mr. McCorkadale still alive?"

"Died years ago. He got run over by a municipal tram."

"I don't blame him. I'd have done the same myself in his place. It's the only course to pursue when you're married to a woman like that."

"How did you meet her?"

"I called on her to urge her to vote for Ginger," I said, and in a few broken words I related my strange story.

It went well. In fact, it went like a breeze. Myself, I was unable to see anything humorous in it, but there was no doubt about its entertaining the blood relation. She guffawed more liberally than I had ever heard woman guffaw. If there had been an aisle, she would have rolled in it. I couldn't help feeling how ironical it was that, having failed so often to be well received when telling a funny story, I should have aroused such gales of mirth with one that was so essentially tragic.

While she was still giving her impersonation of a hyena

which has just heard a good one from another hyena, Spode came in, choosing the wrong moment as usual. One never wants to see Spode, but least of all when someone is having a hearty laugh at your expense.

"I'm looking for the notes for my speech tomorrow," he said. "Hullo, what's the joke?"

Convulsed as she was, it was not easy for the ancestor to articulate, but she managed a couple of words.

"It's Bertie."

"Oh?" said Spode, looking at me as if he found it difficult to believe that any word or act of mine could excite mirth and not horror and disgust.

"He's just been calling on Mrs. McCorkadale."

"Oh?"

"And asking her to vote for Ginger Winship."

"Oh?" said Spode again. I have already indicated that he was a compulsive Oh-sayer. "Well, it is what I would have expected of him—" and with another look in which scorn and animosity were nicely blended and a word to the effect that he might have left those notes in the summerhouse by the lake, he removed his distasteful presence.

That he and I were not on Damon and Pythias terms seemed to have impressed itself on the aged relative. She switched off the hyena sound effects. "Not a bonhomous type, Spode."

"No."

"He doesn't like you."

"No."

"And I don't think he likes me."

"No," I said, and it occurred to me, for the Woosters are essentially fair-minded, that it was hardly for me to criticize Spode's Ohs when my Nos were equally frequent. Why beholdest thou the mote that is in thy brother's eye, but considerest not the beam that is in thine own eye, Wooster? I found myself asking myself, it having been one of the many good things I had picked up in my researches when I won that Scripture Knowledge prize at my private school.

"Does he like anyone?" said the relative. "Except, presumably, Madeline Bassett?"

"He seems fond of L. P. Runkle."

"What makes you think that?"

"I overheard them exchanging confidences."

"Oh?" said the relative, for these things are catching. "Well, I suppose one ought not to be surprised. Birds of a feather—"

"Flock together?"

"Exactly. And even the dregs of pond life fraternize with other dregs of pond life. By the way, remind me to tell you something about L. P. Runkle."

"Right ho."

"We will come to L. P. Runkle later. This animosity of Spode's, is it just the memory of old Totleigh days, or have you done anything lately to incur his displeasure?"

This time I had no hesitation in telling her all. I felt she would be sympathetic. I laid the facts before her with every confidence that an aunt's condolences would result.

"There was this gnat."

"I don't follow you."

"I had to rally round."

"You've still lost me."

"Spode didn't like it."

"So he doesn't like gnats either. Which gnat? What gnat? Will you get on with your story, curse you, starting at the beginning and carrying on to the end?"

"Certainly, if you wish. Here is the scenario."

I told her about the gnat in Madeline's eye, the part I had played in restoring her vision to mid-season form and the exception Spode had taken to my well-meant efforts. She whistled. Everyone seemed to be whistling at me today. Even the recent maid, on recognizing me, had puckered up her lips as if about to.

"I wouldn't do that sort of thing again," she said.

"If the necessity arose I would have no option."

"Then you'd better get one as soon as possible. Because if you keep on taking things out of Madeline's eye, you may have to marry the girl."

"But surely the peril has passed, now that she's engaged to Spode."

"I don't know. I think there's some trouble between Spode and Madeline."

I would be surprised to learn that in the whole W.1 postal section of London there is a man more capable than Bertram Wooster of bearing up with a stiff upper lip under what I have heard Jeeves call the slings and arrows of outrageous fortune; but at these frightful words I confess that I went into my old aspen routine even more wholeheartedly than I had done during my get-together with the relict of the late McCorkadale.

And not without reason. My whole foreign policy was based on the supposition that the solidarity of these two consenting adults was something that couldn't be broken or even cracked. He, on his own statement, had worshiped her since she was so high, while she, as I have already recorded, would not lightly throw a man of his eligibility into the discard. If ever there was a union which you could have betted with perfect confidence would culminate in a golden wedding with all the trimmings, this was the one.

"Trouble?" I whispered hoarsely. "You mean there's a what-d'you-call-it?"

"What would that be?"

"A rift within the lute which widens soon and makes the music mute. Not my own. Jeeves's."

"The evidence points in that direction. At dinner last night I noticed that he was refusing Anatole's best, while she looked wan and saintlike and crumbled bread. And talking of Anatole's best, what I wanted to tell you about L. P. Runkle was that zero hour is approaching. I am

482

crouching for my spring and have strong hopes that Tuppy will soon be in the money."

I clicked the tongue. Nobody could be keener than I on seeing Tuppy dip into L. P. Runkle's millions, but this was no time to change the subject.

"Never mind about Tuppy for the moment. Concentrate on the sticky affairs of Bertram Wilberforce Wooster."

"Wilberforce," she murmured, as far as a woman of her outstanding lung power could murmur. "Did I ever tell you how you got that label? It was your father's doing. The day before you were lugged to the font looking like a minor actor playing a bit part in a gangster film he won a packet on an outsider in the Grand National called that, and he insisted on you carrying on the name. Tough on you, but we all have our cross to bear. Your Uncle Tom's second name is Portarlington, and I came within an ace of being christened Phyllis."

I rapped her sharply on the topknot with a paper knife of Oriental design, the sort that people in novels of suspense are always getting stabbed in the back with.

"Don't wander from the *res*. The fact that you nearly got christened Phyllis will, no doubt, figure in your autobiography, but we need not discuss it now. What we are talking about is the ghastly peril that confronts me if the Madeline-Spode axis blows a fuse."

"You mean that if she breaks her engagement, you will have to fill the vacuum?"

"Exactly."

"She won't. Not a chance."

"But you said—"

"I only wanted to emphasize my warning to you not to keep on taking gnats out of Madeline's eyes. Perhaps I overdid it."

"You chilled me to the marrow."

"Sorry I was so dramatic. You needn't worry. They've only had a lovers' tiff such as occurs with the mushiest couples."

"What about?"

"How do I know? Perhaps he queried her statement that the stars were God's daisy chain."

I had to admit that there was something in this theory. Madeline's breach with Gussie Fink-Nottle had been caused by her drawing his attention to the sunset and saying sunsets always made her think of the Blessed Damozel leaning out from the gold bar of heaven, and he said "Who?" and she said "The Blessed Damozel," and he said "Never heard of her," adding that sunsets made him sick, and so did the Blessed Damozel. A girl with her outlook would be bound to be touchy about stars and daisy chains.

"It's probably over by now," said the ancestor. "All the same, you'd better keep away from the girl. Spode's an impulsive man. He might slosh you."

"He said he would."

"He used the word 'slosh'?"

"No, but he assured me he would butter me over the front lawn and dance on the remains with hobnailed boots."

"Much the same thing. So I would be careful if I were you. Treat her with distant civility. If you see any more gnats headed in her direction, hold their coats and wish them luck, but restrain the impulse to mix in."

"I will."

"I hope I have relieved your fears?"

"You have, old flesh and blood."

"Then why the furrows in your brow?"

"Oh, those? It's Ginger."

"What's Ginger?"

"He's why my brow is furrowed."

It shows how profoundly the thought of Madeline Bassett possibly coming into circulation again had moved me that it was only now that I had remembered Bingley and what he had said about the certainty of Ginger's finishing as an also-ran in the election. I burned with shame and remorse that I should have allowed my personal troubles to make me shove him down to the foot of the agenda paper in this scurvy manner. Long ere this I ought to have been inviting Aunt Dahlia's views on his prospects. Not doing so, amounted to letting a pal down, a thing I pride myself or , never being guilty of. Little wonder that I b'd with ᵒ and r.

I hastened to make amends, if those are what you make when you have done the dirty on a fellow you love like a brother.

"Did I ever mention a bloke called Bingley to you?"

"If you did, I've forgotten."

"He was my personal attendant for a brief space when Jeeves and I differed about me playing the banjolele. That time when I had a cottage down at Chuffnell Regis"

"Oh yes, he set it on fire, didn't he?"

"While tight as an owl. It was burned to a cinder' as was my banjolele."

"I've got him placed now. What about him?"

"He lives in Market Snodsbury. I met him this morning and happened to mention that I was canvassing for Ginger."

"If you can call it canvassing."

"And he told me I was wasting my time. He advised me to have a substantial bet on Ma McCorkadale. He said Ginger hadn't an earthly."

"He's a fool."

"I must say I've always thought so, but he spoke as if he had inside information."

"What on earth information could he have? An election isn't a horse race where you get tips from the stable cat. I don't say it may not be a close thing, but Ginger ought to win all right. He has a secret weapon."

"Repeat that, if you wouldn't mind. I don't think I got it."

"Ginger defies competition because he has a secret weapon."

"Which is?"

"Spode."

"Spode?"

"My lord Sidcup. Have you ever heard him speak?"

"I did just now."

"In public, fool."

"Oh, in public. No, I haven't."

"He's a terrific orator, as I told you, only you've probably forgotten."

This seemed likely enough to me. Spode at one time had been one of those dictators, going about at the head of a band of supporters in footer shorts shouting "Heil Spode," and to succeed in that line you have to be able to make speeches.

"You aren't fond of him, nor am I, but nobody can deny that he's eloquent. Audiences hang on his every word, and when he's finished cheer him to the echo."

I nodded. I had had the same experience myself when singing "The Yeoman's Wedding Song" at village concerts. Two or three encores sometimes, even when I blew up in the words and had to fill in with "Ding dong, ding dong, ding dong, I hurry along." I began to feel easier in my mind. I told her this, and she said "Your *what*?"

"You have put new heart into me, old blood relation," I said, ignoring the crack. "You see, it means everything to him to win this election."

"Is he so bent on representing Market Snodsbury in the Westminster menagerie?"

"It isn't that so much. Left to himself, I imagine he

486

could take Parliament or leave it alone. But he thinks Florence will give him the bum's rush if he loses."

"He's probably right. She can't stand a loser."

"So he told me. Remember what happened to Percy Gorringe."

"And others. England is strewn with ex-fiancés whom she bounced because they didn't come up to her specifications. Dozens of them. I believe they form clubs and societies."

"Perhaps calling themselves the Old Florentians."

"And having an annual dinner."

We mused on Florence for awhile; then she said she ought to be going to confer with Anatole about dinner tonight, urging him to dish up something special. It was vital, she said, that he should excel his always high standard.

"I was speaking just now, when you interrupted me and turned my thoughts to the name Wilberforce, of L. P. Runkle."

"You said you had an idea he might be going to cooperate."

"Exactly. Have you ever seen a python after a series of hearty meals?"

"Not to my knowledge."

"It gets all softened up. It becomes a kindlier, gentler, more lovable python. And if I am not greatly mistaken, the same thing is happening to L. P. Runkle as the result of Anatole's cooking. You saw him at dinner last night."

"Sorry, no, I wasn't looking. Every fiber of my being was concentrated on the foodstuffs. He would have repaid inspection, would he? Worth seeing, eh?"

"He was positively beaming. He was too busy to utter, but it was plain that he had become all amiability and benevolence. He had the air of a man who would start scattering largesse if given a word of encouragement. It is for

Anatole to see to it that this Christmas spirit does not evaporate but comes more and more to the boil. And I know that I can rely on him."

"Good old Anatole," I said, lighting a cigarette.

"Amen," said the ancestor reverently; then, touching on another subject, "Take that foul cigarette outside, you young hellhound. It smells like an escape of sewer gas."

Always glad to indulge her lightest whim, I passed through the french window in a far different mood from that in which I had entered the room. Optimism now reigned in the Wooster bosom. Ginger, I told myself, was going to be all right, Tuppy was going to be all right, and it would not be long before the laughing love god straightened things out between Madeline and Spode, even if he had talked out of turn about stars and daisy chains.

Having finished the gasper, I was about to return and resume conversation with the aged relative, when from within there came the voice of Seppings, now apparently restored to health, and what he was saying froze me in every limb. I couldn't have become stiffer if I had been Lot's wife, whose painful story I had had to read up on when I won that Scripture Knowledge prize.

What he was saying ran as follows:

"Mrs. McCorkadale, madam."

10

Leaning against the side of the house, I breathed rather in the manner copyrighted by the hart which pants for cooling streams when heated in the chase. The realization of how narrowly I had missed having to mingle again with this blockbusting female barrister kept me Lot's-wifed for what seemed an hour or so, though I suppose it can't have been more than a few seconds. Then gradually I ceased to be a pillar of salt and was able to concentrate on finding out what on earth Ma McCorkadale's motive was in paying us this visit. The last place, I mean to say, where you would have expected to find her. Considering how she stood in regard to Ginger, it was as if Napoleon had dropped in for a chat with Wellington on the eve of Waterloo or District Attorney Hamilton Burger on Perry Mason.

I have had occasion to mention earlier the advantages as a listening post afforded by the just-outside-the-french-window spot where I was standing. Invisible to those within, I could take in all they were saying, as I had done with Spode and L. P. Runkle. Both had come through loud and clear, and neither had had a notion that Bertram Wooster was on the outskirts, hearing all.

As I could hardly step in and ask her to repeat any of her remarks which I didn't quite catch, it was fortunate that the McCorkadale's voice was so robust, while Aunt

Dahlia's, of course, would be audible if you were at Hyde Park Corner and she in Piccadilly Circus. I have often thought that the deaf adder I read about when I won my Scripture Knowledge prize would have got the message right enough if the aged relative had been one of the charmers. I was able to continue leaning against the side of the house in full confidence that I shouldn't miss a syllable of either protagonist's words.

The proceedings started with a couple of Good mornings, Aunt Dahlia's the equivalent of "What the hell?" and then the McCorkadale, as if aware that it was up to her to offer a word of explanation, said she had called to see Mr. Winship on a matter of great importance. "Is he in?"

Here was a chance for the ancestor to get one up by retorting that he jolly well would be after the votes had been counted, but she let it go, merely saying, No, he had gone out, and the McCorkadale said she was sorry.

"I would have preferred to see him in person, but you, I take it, are his hostess, so I can tell you and you will tell him."

This seemed fair enough to me, and I remember thinking that these barristers put things well, but it appeared to annoy the aged relative.

"I am afraid I do not understand you," she said, and I knew she was getting steamed up, for if she had been her calm self, she would have said "Sorry, I don't get you."

"If you will allow me to explain. I can do so in a few simple words. I have just had a visit from a slimy slinking slug."

I drew myself up haughtily. Not much good, of course, in the circs, but the gesture seemed called for. One does not object to fair criticism, but this was mere abuse. I could think of nothing in our relations which justified such a description of me. My views on barristers and their way of putting things changed sharply.

Whether or not Aunt Dahlia bridled, as the expression is, I couldn't say, but I think she must have done, for her next words were straight from the Frigidaire.

"Are you referring to my nephew Bertie Wooster?"

The McCorkadale did much to remove the bad impression her previous words had made on me. She said her caller had not given his name, but she was sure he could not have been Mrs. Travers' nephew.

"He was a very common man," she said, and with the quickness which is so characteristic of me I suddenly got on to it that she must be alluding to Bingley, who had been ushered into her presence immediately after I had left. I could understand her applying those derogatory adjectives to Bingley. And the noun "slug," just right. Once again found myself thinking how well barristers put things.

The old ancestor, too, appeared what's the word beginning with m and meaning less hot under the collar. Mollified, that's it. The suggestion that she could not have a nephew capable of being described as a common man mollified her. I don't say that even now she would have asked Ma McCorkadale to come on a long walking tour with her, but her voice was definitely matier.

"Why do you call him a slug?" she asked, and the McCorkadale had her answer to that.

"For the same reason that I call a spade a spade—because it is the best way of conveying a verbal image of him. He made me a disgraceful proposition."

"*What?*" said Aunt Dahlia rather tactlessly.

I could understand her being surprised. It was difficult to envisage a man so eager to collect girlfriends as to make disgraceful propositions to Mrs. McCorkadale. It amazed me that Bingley could have done it. I never liked him, but I must confess to a certain admiration for his temerity. Our humble heroes, I felt.

"You're pulling my leg," said the aged relative.

The McCorkadale came back at her briskly.

"I am doing nothing of the kind. I am telling you precisely what occurred. I was in my drawing room going over the speech I have prepared for the debate tomorrow, when I was interrupted by the incursion of this man. Naturally annoyed, I asked him what his business was, and he said with a most offensive leer that he was Father Christmas bringing me manna in the wilderness and tidings of great joy. I was about to ring the bell to have him shown out, for of course I assumed that he was intoxicated, when he made me this extraordinary proposition. He had contrived to obtain information to the detriment of my opponent, and this he wished to sell to me. He said it would make my victory in the election certain. It would, as he phrased it, be a snip."

I stirred on my base. If I hadn't been afraid I might be overheard, I would have said "Aha!" Had circs been other than they were, I would have stepped into the room, tapped the ancestor on the shoulder and said, "Didn't I tell you Bingley had information? Perhaps another time you'll believe me." But as this would have involved renewing my acquaintance with a woman of whom I had already seen sufficient to last a lifetime, it was not within the sphere of practical politics. I remained, accordingly, where I was, merely hitching my ears up another couple of notches in order not to miss the rest of the dialogue.

After the ancestor had said "For heaven's sake!" or "Gorblimey!" or whatever it was, indicating that her visitor's story interested her strangely, the McCorkadale resumed. And what she resumed about unquestionably put the frosting on the cake. Words of doom is the only way I can think of to describe the words she spoke as.

"The man, it appeared, was a retired valet, and he belonged to a club for butlers and valets in London, one of the rules of which was that all members were obliged to record in the club book information about their employers. My visitor explained that he had been at one time in the employment of Mr. Winship and had duly recorded a number of the latter's escapades which, if made public, would be certain to make the worst impression on the voters of Market Snodsbury."

This surprised me. I hadn't had a notion that Bingley had ever worked for Ginger. It just shows the truth of the old saying that half the world doesn't know how the other three-quarters lives.

"He then told me without a blush of shame that on his latest visit to London he had purloined this book and now had it in his possession."

I gasped with horror. I don't know why, but the thought that Bingley must have been pinching the thing at the very moment when Jeeves and I were sipping our snootfuls in the next room seemed to make it particularly poignant. Not that it wouldn't have been pretty poignant anyway. For years I had been haunted by the fear that the Junior Ganymede club book, with all the dynamite it contained, would get into the wrong hands, and the hands it had got into couldn't have been more the sort of hands you would have wished it hadn't. I don't know if I make myself clear, but what I'm driving at is that if I had been picking a degraded character to get away with that book, Bingley was the degraded character I would have picked. I remember Jeeves speaking of someone who was fit for treasons, stratagems and spoils, and that was Bingley all over. The man was wholly without finer feelings, and when you come up against someone without finer feelings, you've had it.

The aged relative was not blind to the drama of the situation. She uttered an awed "Lord love a duck!" and the McCorkadale said she might well say "Lord love a duck," though it was not an expression she would have used herself.

"What did you do?" the ancestor asked, all agog, and the McCorkadale gave that sniffing snort of hers. It was partly like an escape of steam and partly like two or three cats unexpectedly encountering two or three dogs, with just a suggestion of a cobra waking up cross in the morning. I wondered how it had affected the late Mr. McCorkadale. Probably made him feel that there are worse things than being run over by a municipal tram.

"I sent him away with a flea in his ear. I pride myself on being a fair fighter, and his proposition revolted me. If you want to have him arrested, though I am afraid I cannot see how it can be done, he lives at Five Ormond Crescent. He appears to have asked my maid to look in and see his etchings on her afternoon off, and he gave her his address. But, as I say, there would seem not to be sufficient evidence for an arrest. Our conversation was without witnesses, and he would simply have to deny possession of the book. A pity. I would enjoy seeing a man like that hanged, drawn, and quartered."

She snorted again, and the ancestor, who always knows what the book of etiquette would advise, came across with the soothing syrup. She said Ma McCorkadale deserved a medal. "I'm sure we are most obliged to you."

"Not at all."

"It was splendid of you to turn the man down."

"As I said, I am a fair fighter."

"Apart from your revulsion at his proposition, it must have been very annoying for you to be interrupted when you were working on your speech."

"Especially as, a few moments before this person appeared, I had been interrupted by an extraordinary young man who gave me the impression of being half-witted."

"That would have been my nephew, Bertie Wooster."

"Oh, I beg your pardon."

"Quite all right."

"I may have formed a wrong estimate of his mentality. Our interview was very brief. I just thought it odd that he should be trying to persuade me to vote for my opponent."

"It's the sort of thing that would seem a bright idea to Bertie. He's like that. Whimsical. Moving in a mysterious way his wonders to perform. But he ought not to have butted in when you were busy with your speech. Is it coming out well?"

"I am satisfied with it."

"Good for you. I suppose you're looking forward to the debate?"

"Very keenly. I am greatly in favor of it. It simplifies things so much if the two opponents face one another on the same platform and give the voters a chance to compare their views. Provided, of course, that both observe the decencies of debate. But I really must be getting back to my work."

"Just a moment." No doubt it was the word "observe" that had rung a bell with the ancestor. "Do you do the *Observer* crossword puzzle by any chance?"

"I solve it at breakfast on Sunday mornings."

"Not the whole lot?"

"Oh yes."

"Every clue?"

"I have never failed yet. I find it ridiculously simple."

"Then what's all that song and dance about the measured tread of saints round St. Paul's?"

"Oh, I guessed that immediately. The answer, of course, is pedometer. You measure tread with a pedometer. Dome, meaning St. Paul's, comes in the middle and Peter, for St. Peter, round it. Very simple."

"Oh, very. Well, thank you. You have taken a great weight off my mind," said Aunt Dahlia, and they parted in complete amity, a thing I wouldn't have thought possible when Ma McCorkadale was one of the partners.

For perhaps a quarter of a minute after I had rejoined the human herd, as represented by my late father's sister Dahlia, I wasn't able to get a word in, the old ancestor being fully occupied with saying what she thought of the compiler of the *Observer* crossword puzzle, with particular reference to domes and pedometers. And when she had said her say on that subject, she embarked on a rueful tribute to the McCorkadale, giving it as her opinion that against a woman with a brain like that, Ginger hadn't the meager chance of a toupee in a high wind. Though, she added in more hopeful vein, now that the menace of the Ganymede Club book had been squashed, there was just a possibility that the eloquence of Spode might get his nose in front.

All this while I had been trying to cut in with my opening remark, which was to the effect that the current situation was a bit above the odds, but it was only when I had repeated this for the third time that I succeeded in obtaining her attention.

"This is a bit thick, what," I said, varying my approach slightly.

She seemed surprised as if the idea had not occured to her. "Thick?"

"Well, isn't it?"

"Why? If you were listening, you heard her say that, being a fair fighter, she had scorned the tempter and sent him away with a flea in his ear, which must be a most uncomfortable thing to have. Bingley was baffled."

"Only for the nonce."

"Nonsense."

"Not nonsense, nonce, which isn't at all the same thing. I feel that Bingley, though crushed to earth, will rise again. How about if he sells that book with all its ghastly contents to the *Market Snodsbury Argus-Intelligencer*?"

I was alluding to the powerful bi-weekly sheet that falls over itself in its efforts to do down the Conservative cause, omitting no word or act to make anyone with Conservative leanings feel like a piece of cheese. Coming out every Wednesday and Saturday with proofs of Ginger's past, I did not see how it could fail to give his candidature the left hook in the lower ribs.

I put this to the old blood relation in no uncertain terms. I might have added that that would wipe the silly smile off her face, but there was no necessity. She saw at once that I spoke sooth, and a crisp hunting-field expletive escaped her. She goggled at me with all the open dismay of an aunt who has inadvertently bitten into a bad oyster.

"I never thought of that!"

"Give it your attention now."

"Those *Argus-Intelligencer* hounds stick at nothing."

"The sky is notoriously their limit."

"Did you tell me Ginger had done time?"

"I said he was always in the hands of the police on Boat Race Night. And, of course, on Rugger Night."

"What's Rugger Night?"

"The night of the annual Rugby football encounter between the universities of Oxford and Cambridge. Many blithe spirits get even more effervescent then than when celebrating the boat race. Ginger was one of them."

"He really got jugged?"

"Invariably. His practice of pinching policemen's helmets insured this. Released next morning on payment of a fine, but definitely after spending the night in a dungeon cell."

There was no doubt that I had impressed on her the gravity of the situation. She gave a sharp cry like that of a stepped-on dachshund, and her face took on the purple tinge it always assumes in moments of strong emotion. "This does it!"

"Fairly serious, I agree."

"Fairly serious! The merest whisper of such goings-on

497

will be enough to alienate every voter in the town. Ginger's done for."

"You don't think they might excuse him because his blood was young at the time?"

"Not a hope. They won't be worrying about his ruddy blood. You don't know what these blighters here are like. Most of them are chapel folk with a moral code that would have struck Torquemada as too rigid."

"Torquemada?"

"The Spanish Inquisition man."

"Oh, *that* Torquemada?"

"How many Torquemadas did you think there were?"

I admitted that it was not a common name, and she carried on. "We must act!"

"But how?"

"Or, rather, you must act. You must go to this man and reason with him."

I h'med a bit at this. I doubted whether a fellow with Bingley's lust for gold would listen to reason.

"What shall I say?"

"You'll know what to say."

"Oh, shall I?"

"Appeal to his better instincts."

"He hasn't got any."

"Now don't make difficulties, Bertie. That's your besetting sin, always arguing. You want to help Ginger, don't you?"

"Of course I do."

"Very well, then."

When an aunt has set her mind on a thing, it's no use trying to put in a nolle prosequi. I turned to the door.

Halfway there a thought occurred to me. I said, "How about Jeeves?"

"What about him?"

"We ought to spare his feelings as far as possible. I repeatedly warned him that that club book was high-level explosive and ought not to be in existence. What if it fell into the wrong hands? I said, and he said it couldn't possibly fall into the wrong hands. And now it has fallen into about the wrongest hands it could have fallen into. I haven't the heart to say 'I told you so' and watch him writhe with shame and confusion. You see, up till now Jeeves has always been right. His agony on finding that he has at last made a floater will be frightful. I shouldn't wonder if he might not swoon. I can't face him. You'll have to tell him."

"Yes, I'll do it."

"Try to break it gently."

"I will. When you were listening outside, did you get this man Bingley's address?"

"I got it."

"Then off you go."

So off I went.

11

Considering how shaky was his moral outlook and how marked his tendency to weave low plots at the drop of a hat, you would have expected Bingley's headquarters to have been one of those sinister underground dens lit by stumps of candles stuck in the mouths of empty beer bottles such as abound, I believe, in places like Whitechapel and Limehouse. But no. Number Five Ormond Crescent turned out to be quite an expensive-looking joint with a nice little bit of garden in front of it well supplied with geraniums, bird baths and terra-cotta gnomes—the sort of establishment that might have belonged to a blameless retired Colonel or a saintly stockbroker. Evidently his late uncle hadn't been just an ordinary small-town grocer, weighing out potted meats and raisins to a public that had to watch the pennies, but something on a much more impressive scale. I learned later that he had owned a chain of shops, one of them as far afield as Birmingham, and why the ass had gone and left his money to a chap like Bingley is more than I can tell you, though the probability is that Bingley, before bumping him off with some little-known Asiatic poison, had taken the precaution of forging the will.

On the threshold I paused. I remember in my early days at the private school where I won my Scripture

Knowledge prize, Arnold Abney, M.A., the headmaster, would sometimes announce that he wished to see Wooster in his study after morning prayers, and I always halted at the study door a prey to uneasiness and apprehension, not liking the shape of things to come. It was much the same now. I shrank from the impending interview. But whereas in the case of A. Abney my disinclination to get things moving had been due to the fear that the proceedings were going to lead up to six of the best from a cane that stung like an adder, with Bingley it was a natural reluctance to ask a favor of a fellow I couldn't stand the sight of. I wouldn't say the Woosters were particularly proud, but we do rather jib at having to grovel to the scum of the earth.

However, it had to be done and, as I heard Jeeves say once, If it were done, then 'twere well 'twere done quickly. Stiffening the sinews and summoning up the blood, to quote another of his gags, I pressed the bell.

If I had had any doubts as to Bingley's now being in the chips, the sight of the butler who opened the door would have dispelled them. In assembling his domestic staff, Bingley had done himself proud, sparing no expenses. I don't say his butler was quite in the class of Jeeves's Uncle Charlie Silversmith, but he came so near it that the breath was taken. And like Uncle Charlie he believed in pomp and ceremony when buttling. I asked him if I could see Mr. Bingley, and he said coldly that the master was not receiving.

"I think he'll see me. I'm an old friend of his."

"I will inquire. Your name, sir?"

"Mr. Wooster."

He pushed off, to return some moments later to say that Mr. Bingley would be glad if I would join him in the library. Speaking in what seemed to me a disapproving voice, as though to suggest that, while he was compelled to carry out the master's orders, however eccentric, he would never have admitted a chap like me if it had been left to him.

"If you would step this way, sir," he said haughtily.

What with one thing and another I had rather got out of touch lately with that If-you-would-step-this-way-sir stuff, and it was in a somewhat rattled frame of mind that I entered the library and found Bingley in an armchair with his feet up on an occasional table. He greeted me cordially enough, but with that touch of the patronizing so noticeable at our two previous meetings.

"Ah, Wooster, my dear fellow, come in. I told Bastable to tell everyone I was not at home, but of course you're different. Always glad to see an old pal. And what can I do for you, Wooster?"

I had to say for him that he had made it easy for me to introduce the subject I was anxious to discuss. I was about to get going, when he asked me if I would like a drink. I said, No, thanks, and he said in an insufferably smug way that I was probably wise.

"I often thought, when I was staying with you at Chuffnell Regis, that you drank too much, Wooster. Remember how you burned that cottage down? A sober man wouldn't have done that. You must have been stewed to the eyebrows, cocky."

A hot denial trembled on my lips. I mean to say, it's a bit thick to be chided for burning cottages down by the very chap who put them to the flames. But I restrained myself. The man, I reminded myself, had to be kept in with. If that was how he remembered that night of terror at Chuffnell Regis, it was not for me to destroy his illusions. I refrained from comment, and he asked me if I would like a cigar. When I said I wouldn't, he nodded like a father pleased with a favorite son.

"I am glad to see this improvement in you, Wooster. I always thought you smoked too much. Moderation, moderation in all things, that's the only way. But you were going to tell me why you came here. Just for a chat about old times, was it?"

"It's with ref to that book you pinched from the Junior Ganymede."

He had been drinking a whiskey and soda as I spoke, and he drained his glass before replying.

"I wish you wouldn't use that word 'pinch,'" he said, looking puff-faced. It was plain that I had given offense. "I simply borrowed it because I needed it in my business. They'll get it back all right."

"Mrs. McCorkadale told my aunt you tried to sell it to her."

His annoyance increased. His air was that of a man compelled to listen to a tactless oaf who persisted in saying the wrong thing.

"Not sell. I would have had a clause in the agreement saying that she was to return it when she had done with it. The idea I had in mind was that she would have photostatic copies made of the pages dealing with young Winship without the book going out of my possession. But the deal didn't come off. She wouldn't cooperate. Fortunately I have other markets. It's the sort of property there'll be a lot of people bidding for. But why are you so interested, old man? Nothing to do with you, is it?"

"I'm a pal of Ginger Winship's."

"And I've no objection to him myself. Nice enough young fellow he always seemed to me, though the wrong size."

"Wrong size?" I said, not getting this.

"His shirts didn't fit me. Not that I hold that against him. These things are all a matter of luck. Don't run away with the idea that I'm a man with a grievance, trying to get back at him for something he did to me when I was staying at his place. Our relations were very pleasant. I quite liked

503

him, and if it didn't matter to me one way or the other who won this election, I'd just as soon he came out on top. But business is business. After studying form, I did some pretty heavy betting on McCorkadale, and I've got to protect my investments, old man. That's only common sense, isn't it?"

He paused, apparently expecting a round of applause for his prudence. When I remained sotto voce and the silent tomb, he proceeded.

"If you want to get along in this world, Wooster, old chap, you've got to grasp your opportunities. That's what I do. I examine each situation that crops up, and I ask myself, 'What is there in this for me? How,' I ask myself, 'can I handle this situation so as to do Rupert Bingley a bit of good?' and it's not often I don't find a way. This time I didn't even have to think. There was young Winship trying to get into Parliament, and here was I standing to win something like a couple of hundred quid if he lost the election and there was a club book with all the stuff in it which would make it certain he did lose. I recognized it at once as money for jam. The only problem was how to get the book, and I soon solved that. I don't know if you noticed, that day we met at the Junior Ganymede, that I had a large briefcase with me? And that I said I'd got to see the secretary about something? Well, what I wanted to see him about was borrowing the book. And I wouldn't have to find some clever way of getting him looking the other way while I did it, because I knew he'd be out to lunch. So I popped in, popped the book in the briefcase and popped off. Nobody saw me go in. Nobody saw me come out. The whole operation was like taking candy from a kid."

There are some stories which fill the man of sensibility with horror, repugnance, abhorrence and disgust. I don't mean anecdotes like the one Catsmeat Potter-Pirbright told me at the Drones, I am referring to loathsome revelations such as the bit of autobiography to which I had just been listening. To say that I felt as if the Wooster soul had been spattered with mud by a passing car would not be putting it at all too strongly. I also felt that nothing was to be gained by continuing this distasteful interview. I had had some idea of going into the possibility of Aunt Agatha's reading the contents of the club book and touching on the doom, desolation and despair which must inevitably be my portion if she did, but I saw that it would be fruitless or bootless. The man was without something and pity—ruth, would it be? I know it begins with r—and would simply have given me the horse's laugh. I was now quite certain that he had murdered his uncle and forged the will. Such a performance to such a man would have been mere routine.

I turned, accordingly, to the door, but before I got there he stopped me, wanting to know if when coming to stay with Aunt Dahlia I had brought Reggie Jeeves with me. I said I had, and he said he would like to see old Reggie again.

"What a cough drop!" he said mirthfully. The epithet was strange to me, but weighing it and deciding that it was intended to be a compliment and a tribute to his many gifts, I agreed that Jeeves was in the deepest and truest sense a cough drop.

"Tell Bastable as you go out that if Reggie calls to send him up. But nobody else."

"Right ho."

"Good man, Bastable. He places my bets for me. Which reminds me, have you done as I advised and put a bit on Ma McCorkadale for the Market Snodsbury stakes? No? Do it without fail, Wooster old man. You'll never regret it. It'll be like finding money in the street."

I wasn't feeling any too good as I drove away. I have described my heart-bowed-down-ness on approaching the Arnold Abney study door after morning prayers in the days when I was in statu pupillari, as the expression is, and I was equally apprehensive now as I faced the prospect of telling the old ancestor of my failure to deliver the goods in the matter of Bingley. I didn't suppose that she would give me six of the best, as A. Abney was so prone to do, but she would certainly not hesitate to let me know she was displeased. Aunts as a class are like Napoleon, if it was Napoleon; they expect their orders to be carried out without a hitch and don't listen to excuses.

Nor was I mistaken. After lunching at a pub in order to postpone the meeting as long as possible, I returned to the old homestead and made my report, and was unfortunate enough to make it while she was engaged in reading a Rex Stout—in the hard cover, not a paperback. When she threw this at me with the accurate aim which years of practice have given her, its sharp edge took me on the tip of the nose, making me blink not a little.

"I might have known you would mess the whole thing up," she boomed.

"Not my fault, aged relative," I said. "I did my best. Than which," I added, "no man can do more."

I thought I had her there, but I was wrong. It was the sort of line which can generally be counted on to soothe the savage breast, but this time it laid an egg. She snorted. Her snorts are not the sniffing snorts snorted by Ma McCorkadale, they resemble more an explosion in the larger type of ammunition dump and they send strong men rocking back on their heels as if struck by lightning.

"How do you mean you did your best? You don't seem to me to have done anything. Did you threaten to have him arrested?"

"No, I didn't do that."

"Did you grasp him by the throat and shake him like a rat?"

I admitted that that had not occurred to me.

"In other words, you did absolutely nothing," she said, and thinking it over I had to own that she was perfectly right. It's funny how one doesn't notice these things at the time. It was only now that I realized that I had let Bingley do all the talking, self offering practically nil in the way of a comeback. I could hardly have made less of a contribution to our conversation if I had been the deaf adder I mentioned earlier.

She heaved herself up from the chaise longue on which she was reclining. Her manner was peevish. In time, of course, she would get over her chagrin and start loving her Bertram again as of yore, but there was no getting away from it that an aunt's affection was, as of even date, at its lowest ebb.

She said gloomily, "I'll have to do it myself."

"Are you going to see Bingley?"

"I am going to see Bingley, and I am going to talk to Bingley, and I am going, if necessary, to take Bingley by the throat and shake him—"

"Like a rat?"

"Yes, like a rat," she said with the quiet confidence of a woman who had been shaking rats by the throat since she was a slip of a girl. "Five Ormond Crescent, here I come!"

It shows to what an extent happenings in and about Market Snodsbury had affected my mental processes that she had been gone at least ten minutes before the thought of Bastable floated into my mind, and I wished I had been able to give her a word of warning. That zealous employee of Rupert Bingley had been instructed to see to it that no callers were admitted to the presence, and I saw no reason to suppose that he would fail in his duty when the old ancestor showed up. He would not use physical violence—indeed, with a woman of her physique he would be unwise to attempt it—but it would be the work of an instant with him not to ask her to step this way, thus ensuring her departure with what Ma McCorkadale would call a flea in her ear. I could see her returning in, say, about a quarter of an hour a baffled and defeated woman.

I was right. It was some twenty minutes later, as I sat reading the Rex Stout which she had used as a guided missile, that heavy breathing became audible without and shortly afterward she became visible within, walking with the measured tread of a saint going round St. Paul's. A far less discerning eye than mine could have spotted that she had been having Bastable trouble.

It would have been kinder, perhaps, not to have spoken, but it was one of those occasions when you feel you have to say something.

"Any luck?" I inquired.

She sank onto the chaise longue, simmering gently. She punched a cushion, and I could see she was wishing it could have been Bastable. He was essentially the sort of man who asks, nay clamors, to be treated in this manner.

"No," she said. "I couldn't get in."

"Why was that?" I asked, wearing the mask.

"A beefy butler sort of bird slammed the door in my face."

"Too bad."

"And I was just too late to get my foot in."

"Always necessary to work quick on these occasions. The most precise timing is called for. Odd that he should have admitted me. I suppose my air of quiet distinction was what turned the scale. What did you do?"

"I came away. What else could I have done?"

"No, I can see how difficult it must have been."

"The maddening part of it is that I was all set to try to get that money out of L. P. Runkle this afternoon. I felt that today was the day. But if my luck's out, as it seems to be, perhaps I had better postpone it."

"Not strike while the iron is hot?"

"It may not be hot enough."

"Well, you're the judge. You know," I said, getting back to the main issue, "the ambassador to conduct the negotiations with Bingley is really Jeeves. It is he who should have been given the assignment. Where I am speechless in Bingley's presence, and you can't even get into the house, he would be inside and talking a blue streak before you could say What ho. And he has the added advantage that Bingley seems fond of him. He thinks he's a cough drop."

"What on earth's a cough drop?"

"I don't know, but it's something Bingley admires. When he spoke of him as one, it was with a genuine ring of enthusiasm in his voice. Did you tell Jeeves about Bingley having the book?"

"Yes, I told him."

"How did he take it?"

"You know how Jeeves takes things. One of his eyebrows rose a little and he said he was shocked and astounded."

"That's strong stuff for him. 'Most disturbing' is as far as he goes usually."

"It's a curious thing," said the aged relative thoughtfully. "As I was driving off in the car I thought I saw Jeeves coming away from Bingley's place. Though I couldn't be sure it was him."

"It must have been. His first move on getting the low-down from you about the book would be to go and see Bingley. I wonder if he's back yet."

"Not likely. I was driving, he was walking. There wouldn't be time."

"I'll ring for Seppings and ask. Oh, Seppings," I said, when he answered the bell. "Is Jeeves downstairs?"

"No, sir. He went out and has not yet returned."

"When he does, tell him to come and see me, will you?"

"Very good, sir."

I thought of asking if Jeeves, when he left, had had the

air of a man going to Number Five Ormond Crescent, but decided that this might be trying Seppings too high, so let it go. He withdrew, and we sat for some time talking about Jeeves. Then, feeling that this wasn't going to get us anywhere and that nothing constructive could be accomplished till he returned, we took up again the matter of L. P. Runkle. At least, the aged relative took it up, and I put the question I had been wanting to put at an earlier stage.

"You say," I said, "that you felt today was the day for approaching him. What gave you that idea?"

"The way he tucked into his lunch and the way he talked about it afterward. Lyrical was the only word for it, and I wasn't surprised. Anatole had surpassed himself."

"The *Suprême de Foie Gras au Champagne?*"

"*And* the *Neige aux Perles des Alpes.*"

I heaved a silent sigh, thinking of what might have been. The garbage I had had to insult the Wooster stomach with at the pub had been of a particularly lethal nature. Generally these rural pubs are all right in the matter of browsing, but I had been so unfortunate as to pick one run by a branch of the Borgia family. The thought had occurred to me as I ate that if Bingley had given his uncle lunch there one day, he wouldn't have had to go to all the bother and expense of buying little known Asiatic poisons.

I would have told the old relative this, hoping for sympathy, but at this moment the door opened, and in came Jeeves. Opening the conversation with that gentle cough of his that sounds like a very old sheep clearing its throat on a misty mountain top, he said, "You wished to see me, sir?"

He couldn't have had a warmer welcome if he had been the prodigal son whose life story I had had to bone up when I won that Scripture Knowledge prize. The welkin, what there was of it in the drawing room, rang with our excited yappings.

"Come in, Jeeves," bellowed the aged relative.

"Yes, come in, Jeeves, come in," I cried. "We were waiting for you with . . . with what?"

"Bated breath," said the ancestor.

"That's right. With bated breath and—"

"Tense, quivering nerves. Not to mention twitching muscles and bitten fingernails. Tell me, Jeeves, was that you I saw coming away from Five Ormond Crescent about an hour ago?"

"Yes, madam."

"You had been seeing Bingley?"

"Yes, madam."

"About the book?"

"Yes, madam."

"Did you tell him he had jolly well got to return it?"

"No, madam."

"Then why on earth did you go to see him?"

"To obtain the book, madam."

"But you said you didn't tell him—"

"There was no necessity to broach the subject, madam. He had not yet recovered consciousness. If I might explain. On my arrival at his residence he offered me a drink, which I accepted. He took one himself. We talked for a while of this and that. Then I succeeded in diverting his attention for a moment, and while his scrutiny was elsewhere I was able to insert a chemical substance in his beverage which had the effect of rendering him temporarily insensible. I thus had ample time to make a search of the room. I had assumed that he would be keeping the book there, and I had not been in error. It was in a lower drawer of the desk. I secured it and took my departure."

Stunned by this latest revelation of his efficiency and do-it-yourself-ness, I was unable to utter, but the old ancestor gave the sort of cry or yowl which must have rung over many a hunting field, causing members of the Quorn and the Pytchley to leap in their saddles like Mexican jumping beans.

"You mean you slipped him a Mickey Finn?"

"I believe that is what they are termed in the argot, madam."

"Do you always carry them about with you?"

"I am seldom without a small supply, madam."

"Never know when they won't come in handy, eh?"

"Precisely, madam. Opportunities for their use are constantly arising."

"Well, I can only say, Thank you. You have snatched victory from the jaws of defeat."

"It is kind of you to say so, madam."

"Much obliged, Jeeves."

"Not at all, madam."

I was expecting the aged relative to turn to me at this point and tick me off for not having had the sense to give Bingley a Mickey Finn myself, and I knew, for you cannot reason with aunts, that it would be no use pleading that I hadn't got any; but her jocund mood caused her to abstain. Returning to the subject of L. P. Runkle, she said this had made her realize that her luck was in, after all, and she was going to press it.

"I'll go and see him now," she yipped, "and I confidently expect to play on him as on a stringed instrument. Out of my way, young Bertie," she cried, heading for the door, "or I'll trample you to the dust. Yoicks!" she added, reverting to the patois of the old hunting days. "Tally ho! Gone away! Hard forrard!"

Or words to that effect.

12

HER DEPARTURE—at, I should estimate, some 60 mph—left behind it the sort of quivering stillness you get during hurricane time in America, when the howling gale, having shaken you to the back teeth, passes on to tickle up residents in spots further west. Kind of a dazed feeling it gives you. I turned to Jeeves, and found him, of course, as serene and unmoved as an oyster on the half shell. He might have been watching yowling aunts shoot out of rooms like bullets from early boyhood.

"What was that she said, Jeeves?"

"Yoicks, sir, if I am not mistaken. It seemed to me that madam also added Tally-ho, Gone away, and Hard forrard."

"I suppose members of the Quorn and the Pytchley are saying that sort of thing all the time."

"So I understand, sir. It encourages the hounds to renewed efforts. It must, of course, be trying for the fox."

"I'd hate to be a fox, wouldn't you, Jeeves?"

"Certainly I can imagine more agreeable existences, sir."

"Not only being chivvied for miles across difficult country but having to listen to men in top hats uttering those uncouth cries."

"Precisely, sir. A very wearing life."

I produced my cambric handkerchief and gave the brow a mop. Recent events had caused me to perspire in the manner popularized by the fountains at Versailles.

"Warm work, Jeeves."

"Yes, sir."

"Opens the pores a bit."

"Yes, sir."

"How quiet everything seems now."

"Yes, sir. Silence like a poultice comes to heal the blows of sound."

"Shakespeare?"

"No, sir. The American author Oliver Wendell Holmes. His poem, 'The Organ Grinders.' An aunt of mine used to read it to me as a child."

"I didn't know you had any aunts."

"Three, sir."

"Are they as jumpy as the one who has just left us?"

"No, sir. Their outlook on life is uniformly placid."

I had begun to feel a bit more placid myself. Calmer, if you know what I mean. And with the calm had come more charitable thoughts.

"Well, I don't blame the aged relative for being jumpy," I said. "She's all tied up with an enterprise of pith and something."

"Of great pith and moment, sir?"

"That's right."

"Let us hope that its currents will not turn awry and lose the name of action."

"Yes, let's. Turn what?"

"Awry, sir."

"Don't you mean agley?"

"No, sir."

"Then it isn't the poet Burns?"

"No, sir. The words occur in Shakespeare's drama *Hamlet*."

"Oh, I know *Hamlet*. Aunt Agatha once made me take her son Thos to it at the Old Vic. Not a bad show, I thought, though a bit highbrow. You're sure the poet Burns didn't write it?"

"Yes, sir. The fact, I understand, is well established."

"Then that settles that. But we have wandered from the point, which is that Aunt Dahlia is up to her neck in this enterprise of great pith and moment. It's about Tuppy Glossop."

"Indeed, sir?"

"It ought to interest you, because I know you've always liked Tuppy."

"A very pleasant young gentleman, sir."

"When he isn't looping back the last ring over the Drones swimming pool, yes. Well, it's too long a story to tell you at the moment, but the gist of it is this. L. P. Runkle, taking advantage of a legal quibble—is it quibble?"

"Yes, sir."

"Did down Tuppy's father over a business deal—no, not exactly a business deal. Tuppy's father was working for him, and he took advantage of the small print in their contract to rob him of the proceeds of something he had invented."

"It is often the way, sir. The financier is apt to prosper at the expense of the inventor."

"And Aunt Dahlia is hoping to get him to cough up a bit of cash and slip it to Tuppy."

"Actuated by remorse, sir?"

"Not just by remorse. She's relying more on the fact that for quite a time he has been under the spell of Anatole's cooking, and she feels that this will have made him a softer and kindlier financier, readier to oblige and do the square thing. You look dubious, Jeeves. Don't you think it will work? She's sure it will."

"I wish I could share madam's confidence, but—"

"But, like me, you look on her chance of playing on L. P. Runkle as on a stringed instrument as—what? A hundred-to-eight shot?"

"A somewhat longer price than that, sir. We have to take into consideration the fact that Mr. Runkle is . . ."

"Yes? You hesitate, Jeeves. Mr. Runkle is what?"

"The expression I am trying to find eludes me, sir. It is one I have sometimes heard you use to indicate a deficiency of sweetness and light in some gentleman of your acquaintance. You have employed it of Mr. Spode or, as I should say, Lord Sidcup, and, in the days before your association with him took on its present cordiality, of Mr. Glossop's uncle, Sir Roderick. It is on the tip of my tongue."

"A stinker?"

No, he said, it wasn't a stinker.

"A tough baby?"

"No."

"A twenty-minute egg?"

"That was it, sir. Mr. Runkle is a twenty-minute egg."

"But have you seen enough of him to judge? After all, you've only just met him."

"Yes, sir, that is true, but Bingley, on learning that he was a guest of madam's, told me a number of stories illustrative of his hardhearted and implacable character. Bingley was at one time in his employment."

"Good lord, he seems to have been employed by everyone."

"Yes, sir, he was inclined to flit. He never remained in one post for long."

"I don't wonder."

"But his relationship with Mr. Runkle was of more extended duration. He accompanied him to the United States of America some years ago and remained with him for several months."

"During which period he found him a twenty-minute egg?"

"Precisely, sir. So I very much fear that madam's efforts will produce no satisfactory results. Would it be a large sum of money that she is hoping to persuade Mr. Runkle to part with?"

"Pretty substantial, I gather. You see, what Tuppy's father invented were those Magic Midget things, and Runkle must have made a packet out of them. I suppose she aims at a fifty-fifty split."

"Then I am forced to the opinion that a hundred to one against is more the figure a levelheaded turf accountant would place upon the likelihood of her achieving her objective."

Not encouraging, you'll agree. In fact, you might describe it as definitely damping. I would have called him a pessimist, only I couldn't think of the word, and while I was trying to hit on something other than "Gloomy Gus," which would scarcely have been a fitting way to address one of his dignity, Florence came in through the french window, and he of course shimmered off. When our conversations are interrupted by the arrival of what you might call the quality, he always disappears like a family specter vanishing at dawn.

Except at meals I hadn't seen anything of Florence till now, she, so to speak, having taken the high road while I took the low road. What I mean to say is that she was always in Market Snodsbury, bustling about on behalf of the Conservative candidate to whom she was betrothed, while I, after that nerve-racking encounter with the widow of the late McCorkadale, had given up canvassing in favor of curling up with a good book. I had apologized to Ginger for this is pusillanimity the word? and he had taken it extraordinarily well, telling me it was perfectly all right and he wished he could do the same.

She was looking as beautiful as ever, if not more so, and at least 96 percent of the members of the Drones Club would have asked nothing better than to be closeted with

517

her like this. I, however, would willingly have avoided the tête-à-tête, for my trained senses told me that she was in one of her tempers, and when this happens the instinct of all but the hardiest is to climb a tree and pull it up after them. The overbearing dishpotness to which I alluded earlier and which is so marked a feature of her make-up was plainly to the fore.

She said, speaking abruptly, "What are you doing in here on a lovely day like this, Bertie?"

I explained that I had been in conference with Aunt Dahlia, and she riposted that the conference was presumably over by now, Aunt D being conspicuous by her absence, so why wasn't I out getting fresh air and sunshine?

"You're much too fond of frowsting indoors. That's why you have that sallow look."

"I didn't know I had a sallow look."

"Of course you have a sallow look. What else did you expect? You look like the underside of a dead fish."

My worst fears seemed to be confirmed. I had anticipated that she would work off her choler on the first innocent bystander she met, and it was just my luck that this happened to be me. With bowed head I prepared to face the storm, and then to my surprise she changed the subject.

"I'm looking for Harold," she said.

"Oh, yes?"

"Have you seen him?"

"I don't think I know him."

"Don't be a fool. Harold Winship."

"Oh, Ginger," I said, enlightened. "No, he hasn't swum into my ken. What do you want to see him about? Something important?"

"It is important to me, and it ought to be to him. Unless he takes himself in hand, he is going to lose this election."

"What makes you think that?"

"His behavior at lunch today."

"Oh, did he take you to lunch? Where did you go? I had

mine at a pub, and the garbage there had to be chewed to be believed. But perhaps you went to a decent hotel?"

"It was the Chamber of Commerce luncheon at the Town Hall. A vitally important occasion, and he made the feeblest speech I have ever heard. A child with water on the brain could have done better. Even you could have done better."

Well, I suppose placing me on a level of efficiency with a water-on-the-brained child was quite a stately compliment coming from Florence, so I didn't go further into the matter, and she carried on, puffs of flame emerging from both nostrils.

"Er, er, er!"

"I beg your pardon?"

"He kept saying Er. Er, er, er. I could have thrown a coffee spoon at him."

Here, of course, was my chance to work in the old gag about to err being human, but it didn't seem to me the moment. Instead, I said, "He was probably nervous."

"That was his excuse. I told him he had no right to be nervous."

"Then you've seen him?"

"I saw him."

"After the lunch?"

"Immediately after the lunch."

"But you want to see him again?"

"I do."

"I'll go and look for him, shall I?"

"Yes, and tell him to meet me in Mr. Travers' study. We shall not be interrupted there."

"He's probably sitting in the summerhouse by the lake."

"Well, tell him to stop sitting and come to the study," she said, for all the world as if she had been Arnold Abney, M.A., announcing that he would like to see Wooster after morning prayers. Quite took me back to the old days.

To get to the summerhouse you have to go across the

lawn, the one Spode was toying with the idea of buttering me over, and the first thing I saw as I did so, apart from the birds, bees, butterflies and what not which put in their leisure hours there, was L. P. Runkle lying in the hammock wrapped in slumber, with Aunt Dahlia in a chair at his side. When she sighted me, she rose, headed in my direction and drew me away a yard or two, at the same time putting a finger to her lips.

"He's asleep," she said.

A snore from the hammock bore out the truth of this, and I said I could see he was and what a revolting spectacle he presented, and she told me for heaven's sake not to bellow like that. Somewhat piqued at being accused of bellowing by a woman whose lightest whisper was like someone calling the cattle home across the sands of Dee, I said I wasn't bellowing, and she said, "Well, don't. He may be in a nasty mood if he's woken suddenly."

It was an astute piece of reasoning, speaking well for her grasp of strategy and tactics, but with my quick intelligence I spotted a flaw in it to which I proceeded to call her attention.

"On the other hand, if you don't wake him, how can you plead Tuppy's cause?"

"I said suddenly, ass. It'll be all right if I let nature take its course."

"Yes, you may have a point there. Will nature be long about it, do you think?"

"How do I know?"

"I was only wondering. You can't sit there the rest of the afternoon."

"I can if necessary."

"Then I'll leave you to it. I've got to go and look for Ginger. Have you seen him?"

"He came by just now with his secretary on his way to the summerhouse. He told me he had some dictation to do. Why do you want him?"

"I don't particularly, though always glad of his company. Florence told me to find him. She has been giving him hell and is anxious to give him some more. Apparently—"

Here she interrupted me with a sharp "Hist!" for L. P. Runkle had stirred in his sleep and it looked as if life was returning to the inert frame. But it proved to be a false alarm, and I resumed my remarks.

"Apparently he failed to wow the customers at the Chamber of Commerce lunch, where she had been counting on him being a regular—who was the Greek chap?"

"Bertie, if I wasn't afraid of waking Runkle, I'd strike you with a blunt instrument, if I had a blunt instrument. What Greek chap?"

"That's what I'm asking you. He chewed pebbles."

"Do you mean Demosthenes?"

"You may be right. I'll take it up later with Jeeves. Florence was expecting Ginger to be a regular Demosthenes, if that was the name, which seems unlikely, though I was at school with a fellow called Gianbattista, and he let her down, and this has annoyed her. You know how she speaks her mind when annoyed."

"She speaks her mind much too much," said the relative severely. "I wonder Ginger stands it."

It so happened that I was in a position to solve the problem that was perplexing her. The facts governing the relationship of guys and dolls had long been an open book to me. I had given deep thought to the matter, and when I give deep thought to a matter perplexities are speedily ironed out.

"He stands it, aged relative, because he loves her, and you wouldn't be far wrong in saying that love conquers all. I know what you mean, of course. It surprises you that a fellow of his thews and sinews should curl up in a ball when she looks squiggle-eyed at him and receive her strictures, if that's the word I want, with the meekness of a spaniel rebuked for bringing a decaying bone into the

521

drawing room. What you overlook is the fact that in the matter of finely chiseled profile, willowy figure and platinum-blond hair she is well up among the top ten, and these things weigh with a man like Ginger. You and I, regarding Florence coolly, pencil her in as too bossy for human consumption, but he gets a different slant. It's the old business of what Jeeves calls the psychology of the individual. Very possibly the seeds of rebellion start to seethe within him when she speaks her mind, but he catches sight of her sideways or gets a glimpse of her hair, assuming for purposes of argument that she isn't wearing a hat, or notices once again that she has as many curves as a scenic railway, and he feels that it's worth putting up with a spot of mind-speaking in order to make her his own. His love, you see, is not wholly spiritual. There's a bit of the carnal mixed up in it."

I would have spoken further, for the subject was one that always calls out the best in me, but at this point the old ancestor, who had been fidgeting for some time, asked me to go and drown myself in the lake. I buzzed off accordingly, and she returned to her chair beside the hammock, brooding over L. P. Runkle like a mother over her sleeping child.

I don't suppose she had observed it, for aunts seldom give much attention to the play of expression on the faces of their nephews, but all through these exchanges I had been looking grave, making it pretty obvious that there was something on my mind. I was thinking of what Jeeves had said about the hundred to one which a levelheaded bookie would wager against her chance of extracting money from a man so liberally equipped with one-way pockets as L. P. Runkle, and it pained me deeply to picture her dismay and disappointment when, waking from his slumbers, he refused to disgorge. It would be a blow calculated to take all the stuffing out of her, she having been so convinced that she was onto a sure thing.

I was also, of course, greatly concerned about Ginger. Having been engaged to Florence myself, I knew what she could do in the way of ticking off the errant male, and the symptoms seemed to point to the probability that on the present occasion she would eclipse all previous performances. I had not failed to interpret the significance of that dark frown, that bitten lip and those flashing eyes, nor the way the willowy figure had quivered, indicating, unless she had caught a chill, that she was as sore as a sunburned neck. I marveled at the depths to which my old friend must have sunk as an orator in order to get such stark emotions under way, and I intended—delicately, of course—to question him about this.

I had, however, no opportunity to do so, for on entering the summerhouse the first thing I saw was him and Magnolia Glendennon locked in an embrace so close that it seemed to me that only powerful machinery could unglue them.

13

IN TAKING THIS VIEW, however, I was in error, for scarcely had I uttered the first yip of astonishment when the Glendennon popsy, echoing it with a yip of her own such as might have proceeded from a nymph surprised while bathing, disentangled herself and came whizzing past me, disappearing into the great world outside at a speed which put her in the old ancestor's class as a sprinter on the flat. It was as though she had said, "Oh for the wings of a dove" and had got them.

I, meanwhile, stood rooted to the s, the mouth slightly ajar and the eyes bulging to their fullest extent. What's that word beginning with dis? Disembodied? No, not disembodied. Distemper? No, not distemper. Disconcerted, that's the one. I was disconcerted. I should imagine that if you happened to wander by accident into the steam room of a Turkish bath on Ladies Night, you would have emotions very similar to those I was experiencing now.

Ginger, too, seemed not altogether at his ease. Indeed, I would describe him as definitely taken aback. He breathed heavily, as if suffering from asthma; the eye with which he regarded me contained practically none of the chumminess you would expect to see in the eye of an old friend; and his voice, when he spoke, resembled that of an annoyed cinnamon bear. Throaty, if you know what I mean, and on the peevish side. His opening words consisted of a well-phrased critique of my tactlessness in selecting that particular moment for entering the summerhouse. He wished, he said, that I wouldn't creep about like a ruddy private eye. Had I, he asked, got my magnifying glass with me and did I propose to go around on all fours, picking up small objects and putting them away carefully in an envelope? What, he inquired, was I doing here, anyway?

To this I might have replied that I was perfectly entitled at all times to enter a summerhouse which was the property of my Aunt Dahlia and so related to me by ties of blood, but something told me that suavity would be the better policy. In rebuttal, therefore, I merely said that I wasn't creeping about like a ruddy private eye, but navigating with a firm and manly stride, and had simply been looking for him because Florence had ordered me to and I had learned from a usually well-informed source that this was where he was.

My reasoning had the soothing effect I had hoped for. His manner changed, losing its cinnamon-bear quality and taking on a welcome all-pals-togetherness. It bore out what I have always said, that there's nothing like suavity for pouring oil on the troubled w's. When he spoke again, it was plain that he regarded me as a friend and an ally.

"I suppose all this seems a bit odd to you, Bertie."

"Not at all, old man, not at all."

"But there is a simple explanation. I love Magnolia."

"I thought you loved Florence."

"So did I. But you know how apt one is to make mistakes."

"Of course."

"When you're looking for the ideal girl, I mean."

"Quite."

"I dare say you've had the same experience yourself."

"From time to time."

"Happens to everybody, I expect."

"I shouldn't wonder."

"Where one goes wrong when looking for the ideal girl is in making one's selection before walking the full length of the counter. You meet someone with a perfect profile, platinum-blond hair and a willowy figure, and you think your search is over. 'Bingo!' you say to yourself. 'This is the one. Accept no substitutes.' Little knowing that you are linking your lot with that of a female sergeant-major with strong views on the subject of discipline, and that if you'd only gone a bit further you would have found the sweetest, kindest, gentlest girl that ever took down outgoing mail in shorthand, who would love you and cherish you and would never dream of giving you hell, no matter what the circumstances. I allude to Magnolia Glendennon."

"I thought you did."

"I can't tell you how I feel about her, Bertie."

"Don't try."

"Ever since we came down here I've had a lurking suspicion that she was the mate for me and that in signing on the dotted line with Florence I had made the boner of a lifetime. Just now my last doubts were dispelled."

"What happened just now?"

"She rubbed the back of my neck. My interview with Florence, coming on top of that ghastly Chamber of Commerce lunch, had given me a splitting headache, and she rubbed the back of my neck. Then I knew. As those soft fingers touched my skin like dainty butterflies hovering over a flower—"

"Right ho."

"It was a revelation, Bertie. I knew that I had come to journey's end. I said to myself, 'This is a good thing. Push it along.' I turned. I grasped her hand. I gazed into her eyes. She gazed into mine. I told her I loved her. She said so she did me. She fell into my arms. I grabbed her. We stood murmuring endearments, and for a while everything was fine. Couldn't have been better. Then a thought struck me. There was a snag. You've probably spotted it."

"Florence?"

"Exactly. Bossy though she is, plain-spoken though she may be when anything displeases her, and I wish you could have heard her after that Chamber of Commerce lunch, I am still engaged to her. And while girls can break engagements till the cows come home, men can't."

I followed his train of thought. It was evident that he, like me, aimed at being a *preux chevalier,* and you simply can't be *preux* or anything like it if you go about the place getting betrothed and then telling the party of the second part it's all off. It seemed to me that the snag which had raised its ugly head was one of formidable—you might say king-size—dimensions, well calculated to make the current of whatever he proposed to do about it turn awry and lose the name of action. But when I put this to him with a sympathetic tremor in my voice, and I'm not sure I didn't clasp his hand, he surprised me by chuckling like a leaky radiator.

"That's all right," he said. "It would, I admit, appear to be a tricky situation, but I can handle it. I'm going to get Florence to break the engagement."

He spoke with such a gay, confident ring in his voice, so like the old ancestor predicting what she was going to do to L. P. Runkle in the playing-on-a-stringed-instrument line, that I was loath, if that's the word I want, to say anything to depress him, but the question had to be asked.

"How?" I said, asking it.

"Quite simple. We agreed, I think, that she has no use for a loser. I propose to lose this election."

Well, it was a thought, of course, and I was in complete agreement with his supposition that if the McCorkadale nosed ahead of him in the voting, Florence would in all

527

probability hand him the pink slip, but where it seemed to me that the current went awry was that he had no means of knowing that the electorate would put him in second place. Of course, voters are like aunts, you never know what they will be up to from one day to the next, but it was a thing you couldn't count on.

I mentioned this to him, and he repeated his impersonation of a leaky radiator.

"Don't you worry, Bertie. I have the situation well in hand. Something happened in a dark corner of the Town Hall after lunch that justifies my confidence."

"What happened in a dark corner of the Town Hall after lunch?"

"Well, the first thing that happened after lunch was that Florence got hold of me and became extremely personal. It was then that I realized that it would be the act of a fathead to marry her."

I nodded adhesion to this sentiment. That time when she broke her engagement with me my spirits had soared and I had gone about singing like a relieved nightingale.

One thing rather puzzled me and seemed to call for explanatory notes.

"Why did Florence draw you into a dark corner when planning to become personal?" I asked. "I wouldn't have credited her with so much tact and consideration. As a rule, when she's telling people what she thinks of them, an audience seems to stimulate her. I recall one occasion when she ticked me off in the presence of seventeen Girl Guides, all listening with their ears flapping, and she had never spoken more fluently."

He put me straight on the point I had raised. He said he had misled me. "It wasn't Florence who drew me into the dark corner, it was Bingley."

"Bingley?"

"A fellow who worked for me once."

"He worked for me once."

"Really? It's a small world, isn't it?"

"Pretty small. Did you know he'd come into money?"

"He'll soon be coming into some more."

"But you were saying he drew you into the dark corner. Why did he do that?"

"Because he had a proposition to make to me which demanded privacy. He—but before going on I must lay a proper foundation. You know in those Perry Mason stories how whenever Perry says anything while cross-examining a witness, the District Attorney jumps up and yells 'Objection, your honor. The S.O.B. has laid no proper foundation.' Well, then, you must know that this man Bingley belongs to a butlers' and valets' club in London called the Junior Ganymede, and one of the rules there is that members have to record the doings of their employers in the club book."

I would have told him I knew all too well about that, but he carried on before I could speak.

"Such a book, as you can imagine, contains a lot of damaging stuff, and he told me he had been obliged to contribute several pages about me which, if revealed, would lose me so many votes that the election would be a gift to my opponent. He added that some men in his place would have sold it to the opposition and made a lot of money, but he wouldn't do a thing like that because it would be low and in the short time we were together he had come to have a great affection for me. I had never realized before what an extraordinarily good chap he was. I had always thought him a bit of a squirt. Shows how wrong you can be about people."

Again I would have spoken, but he rolled over me like a tidal wave.

"I should have explained that the committee of the Junior Ganymede, recognizing the importance of this book, had entrusted it to him with instructions to guard it with his life, and his constant fear was that bad men would get wind of this and try to steal it. So what would remove a great burden from his mind, he said, would be if I took it into my possession. Then I could be sure that its contents wouldn't be used against me. I could return it to him after the election, and slip him a few quid, if I wished, as a token of my gratitude. You can picture me smiling my subtle smile as he said this. He little knew that my first act would be to send the thing by messenger to the offices of the *Market Snodsbury Argus-Intelligencer,* thereby handing the election on a plate to the McCorkadale and enabling me to free myself from my honorable obligations to Florence, who would, of course, on reading the stuff, recoil from me in horror. Do you know the *Argus-Intelligencer?* Very far to the left. Can't stand Conservatives. It had a cartoon of me last week showing me with my hands dripping with the blood of the martyred proletariat. I don't know where they get these ideas. I've never spilled a drop of anybody's blood except when boxing, and then the other chap was spilling mine—wholesome give and take. So it wasn't long before Bingley and I had everything all fixed up. He couldn't give me the book then, as he had left it at home, and he wouldn't come and have a drink with me because he had to hurry back because he thought Jeeves might be calling and he didn't want to miss him. Apparently Jeeves is a pal of his—old club crony, that sort of thing. We're meeting tomorrow. I shall reward him with a purse of gold, he will give me the book, and five minutes later, if I can find some brown paper and string, it will be on its way to the *Argus-Intelligencer.* The material should be in print the day after tomorrow. Allow an hour or so for Florence to get hold of a copy and say twenty minutes for a chat with her after she's read it, and I ought to be a free man well before lunch. About how much gold do you think I should reward Bingley with? Figures were not named, but I thought at least a hundred quid, because he certainly deserves something substantial for his scrupulous high-mindedness. As he said, some men in his place would have sold the book to the opposition and cleaned up big."

By what I have always thought an odd coincidence he paused at this point and asked me why I was looking like something the cat brought in, precisely as the aged relative had asked me after my interview with Ma McCorkadale. I don't know what cats bring into houses, but one assumes that it is something not very jaunty, and apparently, when in the grip of any strong emotion, I resemble their treasure trove. I could well understand that I was looking like that now. I find it distasteful to have to shatter a long-time buddy's hopes and dreams, and no doubt this shows on the surface.

There was no sense in beating about bushes. It was another of those cases of if it were done, then 'twere well 'twere done quickly.

"Ginger," I said, "I'm afraid I have a bit of bad news for you. That book is no longer among those present. Jeeves called on Bingley, gave him a Mickey Finn, and got it away from him. He now has it among his archives."

He didn't get it at first, and I had to explain.

"Bingley is not the man of integrity you think him. He is, on the contrary, a louse of the first water. You might describe him as a slimy slinking slug. He pinched that book from the Junior Ganymede and tried to sell it to the Mc-Corkadale. She sent him away with a flea in his ear because she is a fair fighter, and he tried to sell it to you. But meanwhile Jeeves nipped in and obtained it."

It took him perhaps a minute to absorb this, but to my surprise he wasn't a bit upset.

"Well, that's all right. Jeeves can take it to the *Argus-Intelligencer*."

I shook the loaf sadly, for I knew that this time those hopes and dreams of his were really due for a sock in the eye.

"He wouldn't do it, Ginger. To Jeeves that club book is sacred. I've gone after him a dozen times, urging him to destroy the pages concerning me, but he always remains as uncooperative as Balaam's ass, who, you may remember, dug his feet in and firmly refused to play ball. He'll never let it out of his hands."

He took it, as I had foreseen, big. He spluttered a good deal. He also kicked the table and would have splintered it if it hadn't been made of marble. It must have hurt like sin, but what disturbed him, I deduced, was not so much the pain of a bruised toe as spiritual anguish. His eyes glittered, his nose wiggled, and if he was not gnashing his teeth I don't know a gnashed tooth when I hear one.

"Oh, won't he?" he said, going back into the old cinnamon-bear routine. "He won't, won't he? We'll see about that. Pop off, Bertie. I want to think."

I popped off, glad to do so. These displays of naked emotion take it out of one.

14

THE SHORTEST WAY to the front of the house was across the lawn, but I didn't take it. Instead, I made for the back door. It was imperative, I felt, that I should see Jeeves without delay and tell him of the passions he had unchained and warn him to keep out of Ginger's way until the hot blood had had time to cool. I hadn't at all liked the sound of the latter's "We'll see about that," nor the clashing of those gnashed teeth. I didn't of course suppose that, however much on the boil, he would inflict personal violence on Jeeves—sock him, if you prefer the expression—but he would certainly say things to him which would wound his feelings and cause their relations, so pleasant up to now, to deteriorate. And naturally I didn't want that to happen.

Jeeves was in a deck chair outside the back door, reading Spinoza with the cat Augustus on his lap. I had given him the Spinoza at Christmas and he was constantly immersed in it. I hadn't dipped into it myself, but he tells me it is good ripe stuff, well worth perusal.

He would have risen at my approach, but I begged him to remain seated, for I knew that Augustus, like L. P. Runkle, resented being woken suddenly, and one always wants to consider a cat's feelings.

"Jeeves," I said, " a somewhat peculiar situation has popped up out of a trap, and I would be happy to have your comments on it. I am sorry to butt in when you are absorbed in your Spinoza and have probably just got to the part where the second corpse is discovered, but what I have to say is of great pith and moment, so listen attentively."

"Very good, sir."

"The facts are these," I said, and without further preamble or whatever they call it I embarked on my narrative. "Such," I concluded some minutes later, "is the position of affairs, and I think you will agree that the problem confronting us presents certain points of interest."

"Undeniably, sir."

"Somehow Ginger has got to lose the election."

"Precisely, sir."

"But how?"

"It is difficult to say on the spur of the moment, sir. The tide of popular opinion appears to be swaying in Mr. Winship's direction. Lord Sidcup's eloquence is having a marked effect on the electorate and may well prove the deciding factor. Mr. Seppings, who obliged as an extra waiter at the luncheon, reports that his lordship's address to the members of the Market Snodsbury Chamber of Commerce was sensational in its brilliance. He tells me that, owing entirely to his lordship, the odds to be obtained in the various public houses, which at one time favored Mrs. McCorkadale at ten to six, have now sunk to evens."

"I don't like that, Jeeves."

"No, sir, it is ominous."

"Of course, if you were to release the club book—"

"I fear I cannot do that, sir."

"No, I told Ginger you regarded it as a sacred trust. Then nothing can be done except to urge you to get the old brain working."

"I will certainly do my utmost, sir."

"No doubt something will eventually emerge. Keep eating lots of fish. And meanwhile stay away from Ginger as much as possible, for he is in ugly mood."

"I quite understand, sir. Stockish, hard and full of rage."

"Shakespeare?"

"Yes, sir. His *Merchant of Venice*."

I left him then, pleased at having got one right for a change, and headed for the drawing room, hoping for another quiet go at the Rex Stout which the swirling rush of events had forced me to abandon. I was, however, too late. The old ancestor was on the chaise longue with it in her grasp, and I knew that I had small chance of wresting it from her. No one who has got his or her hooks on a Rex Stout lightly lets it go.

Her presence there surprised me. I had supposed that she was still brooding over the hammock and its contents.

"Hullo," I said, "have you finished with Runkle?"

She looked up, and I noted a trace of annoyance in her demeanor. I assumed that Nero Wolfe had come down from the orchid room and told Archie Goodwin to phone Saul Panzer and Orrie what's-his-name, and things were starting to warm up. In which event she would naturally resent the intrusion of even a loved nephew whom she had often dandled on her knee—not recently, but when I was a bit younger.

"Oh, it's you," she said, which it was, of course. "No, I haven't finished with Runkle. I haven't even begun. He's still asleep."

She gave me the impression of being not much in the mood for chitchat, but one has to say something on these occasions. I brought up a subject which I felt presented certain points of interest.

"Have you ever noticed the remarkable resemblance between L. P. Runkle's daily habits and those of the cat Augustus? They seem to spend all their time sleeping. Do you think they've got traumatic symplegia?"

"What on earth's that?"

"I happened to come on it in a medical book I was reading. It's a disease that makes you sleep all the time. Has Runkle shown no signs of waking?"

535

"Yes, he did, and just as he was beginning to stir, Madeline Bassett came along. She said could she speak to me, so I had to let her. It wasn't easy to follow what she was saying, because she was sobbing all the time, but I got it at last. It was all about the rift with Spode. I told you they had had a tiff. It turns out to be more serious than that. You remember me telling you he couldn't be a member of Parliament because he was a peer. Well, he wants to give up his title so that he will be eligible."

"Can a fellow with a title give it up? I thought he was stuck with it."

"He couldn't at one time, at least only by being guilty of treason, but they've changed the rules and apparently it's quite the posh thing to do nowadays."

"Sounds silly."

"That's the view Madeline takes."

"Did she say what put the idea into Spode's fat head?"

"No, but I can see what did. He has made such a smash hit with his speeches down here that he's saying to himself, 'Why am I sweating like this on behalf of somebody else? Why not go into business for myself?' Who was it said someone was intoxicated with the exuberance of his own verbosity?"

"I don't know."

"Jeeves would. It was Bernard Shaw or Mark Twain or Jack Dempsey or somebody. Anyway, that's Spode. He's all puffed up and feels he needs a wider scope. He sees himself holding the House of Commons spellbound."

"Why can't he hold the House of Lords spellbound?"

"It wouldn't be the same thing. It would be like playing in the Market Snodsbury tennis tournament instead of electrifying one and all on the center court at Wimbledon. I can see his point."

"I can't."

"Nor can Madeline. She's all worked up about it, and I

can understand how she feels. No joke for a girl who thinks she's going to be Countess of Sidcup to have the fellow say 'April fool, my little chickadee. What you're going to be is Mrs. Spode.' If I had been told at Madeline's age that Tom had been made a peer and I then learned that he was going to back out of it and I wouldn't be able to call myself Lady Market Snodsbury after all, I'd have kicked like a mule. Titles to a girl are like catnip to a cat."

"Can nothing be done?"

"The best plan would be for you to go to him and tell him how much we all admire him for being Lord Sidcup and what a pity it would be for him to go back to a ghastly name like Spode."

"What's the next best plan?"

"Ah, that wants thinking out."

We fell into a thoughtful silence, on my part an uneasy one. I didn't at this juncture fully appreciate the peril that lurked, but anything in the nature of a rift within the lute between Spode and Madeline was always calculated to make me purse the lips to some extent. I was still trying to hit on some plan which would be more to my taste than telling Spode what a pity it would be for him to stop being the Earl of Sidcup and go back to a ghastly name like his, when my reverie was broken by the entry through the french window of the cat Augustus, for once awake and in full possession of his faculties, such as they were. No doubt in a misty dreamlike sort of way he had seen me when I was talking to Jeeves and had followed me on my departure, feeling, after those breakfasts of ours together, that association with me was pretty well bound to culminate in kippers. A vain hope, of course. The well-dressed man does not go around with kippered herrings in his pocket. But one of the lessons life teaches us is that cats will be cats.

As is my unvarying policy when closeted with one of these fauna, I made chirruping noises and bent down to tickle the back of the dumb chum's left ear, but my heart was not in the tickling. The more I mused on the recent conversation, the less I liked what the aged relative had revealed. Telling Augustus that I would be back with him in a moment, I straightened myself and was about to ask her for further details, when I discovered that she was no longer in my midst. She must suddenly have decided to have another pop at L. P. Runkle and was presumably even now putting Tuppy's case before him. Well, best of luck to her, of course, and nice to think she had a fine day for it, but I regretted her absence. When your mind is weighed down with matters of great pith and moment, it gives you a sort of sinking feeling to be alone. No doubt the boy who stood on the burning deck whence all but he had fled had this experience.

However, I wasn't alone for long. Scarcely had Augustus sprung onto my lap and started catching up with his sleep when the door opened and Spode came in.

I leaped to my feet, causing Augustus to fall to earth I knew not where, as the fellow said. I was a prey to the liveliest apprehensions. My relations with Spode had been for long so consistently strained that I never saw him nowadays without a lurking fear that he was going to sock me in the eye. Obviously I wasn't to be blamed if he and Madeline had been having trouble, but that wouldn't stop him blaming me. It was like the story of the chap who was in prison and a friend calls and asks him why and the chap tells him and the friend says, But they can't put you in prison for that, and the chap says, I know they can't, but they have. Spode didn't have to have logical reasons for setting about people he wasn't fond of, and it might be that he was like Florence and would work off his grouch on the first available innocent bystander. Putting it in a nutshell, my frame of mind was approximately that of the fellows in the hymn who got such a start when they looked over their shoulders and saw the troops of Midian prowling and prowling around.

It was with profound relief, therefore, that I suddenly got on to it that his demeanor was free from hostility. He was looking like somebody who has just seen the horse on which he had put all his savings, plus whatever he had been able to lift from his employer's till, beaten by a short head. His face, nothing to write home about at the best of times, was drawn and contorted, but with pain rather than the urge to commit mayhem. And while one would always prefer him not to be present, a drawn-and-contorted-with-pain Spode was certainly the next best thing. My greeting, in consequence, had the real ring of cordiality in it.

"Oh, hullo, Spode, hullo. There you are, what? Splendid."

"Can I have a word with you, Wooster?"

"Of course, of course. Have several."

He did not speak for a minute or so, filling in the time by subjecting me to a close scrutiny. Then he gave a sigh and shook his head.

"I can't understand it," he said.

"What can't you understand, Spode old man or rather Lord Sidcup old man?" I asked in a kind voice, for I was only too willing to help this new and improved Spode solve any little problem that was puzzling him.

"How Madeline can contemplate marrying a man like you. She has broken our engagement and says that's what she's going to do. She was quite definite about it. 'All is over,' she said. 'Here is your ring,' she said. 'I shall marry Bertie Wooster and make him happy,' she said. You can't want it plainer than that."

I stiffened from head to f. Even with conditions what they were in this disturbed postwar world, I hadn't been expecting to be turned into a pillar of salt again for some considerable time, but this had done it. I don't know how many of my public have ever been slapped between the eyes with a wet fish, but those who have will appreciate my emotions as the seventh Earl of Sidcup delivered this devastating bulletin. Everything started to go all wobbly, and through what is known as a murky mist I seemed to be watching a quivering-at-the-edges seventh Earl performing the sort of gyrations traveled friends have told me the Oulad Naïl dancers do in Cairo.

I was stunned. It seemed to me incredible that Madeline Bassett should have blown the whistle on their engagement. Then I remembered that at the time when she had plighted her troth Spode was dangling a countess's coronet before her eyes, and the thing became more understandable. I mean, take away the coronet and what had you got? Just Spode. Not good enough, a girl would naturally feel.

He, meanwhile, was going on to explain why he found it so bizarre that Madeline should be contemplating marrying me, and almost immediately I saw that I had been mistaken in supposing that he was not hostile. He spoke from between clenched teeth, and that always tells the story.

"As far as I can see, Wooster, you are without attraction of any kind. Intelligence? No. Looks? No. Efficiency? No. You can't even steal an umbrella without getting caught. All that can be said for you is that you don't wear a mustache. They tell me you did grow one once, but mercifully shaved it off. That is to your credit, but it is a small thing to weigh in the balance against all your other defects. When one considers how numerous these are, one can only suppose that it is your shady record of stealing anything you can lay your hands on that appeals to Madeline's romantic soul. She is marrying you in the hope of reforming you, and let me tell you, Wooster, that if you disappoint that hope, you will be sorry. She may have rejected me, but I shall always love her as I have done since she was so high, and I shall do my utmost to see that her gentle heart is not broken by any sneaking son of a what-not who looks like a chorus boy in a touring revue playing the small towns and cannot see anything of value without pocketing it. You will probably think you are safe from me when you are doing your stretch in Wormwood Scrubs for larceny, but I shall be waiting for you when you come out and I shall tear you limb from limb. And," he added, for his was a one-track mind, "dance on the fragments in hobnailed boots."

He paused, produced his cigarette case, asked me if I had a match, thanked me when I gave him one, and withdrew.

He left behind him a Bertram Wooster whom the dullest eye could have spotted as not being at the peak of his form. The prospect of being linked for life to a girl who would come down to breakfast and put her hands over my eyes and say "Guess who?" had given my morale a sickening wallop, reducing me to the level of one of those wee sleekit timorous cowering beasties Jeeves tells me the poet Burns used to write about. It is always my policy in times of crisis to try to look on the bright side, but I make one proviso—viz., that there has to be a bright side to look on, and in the present case there wasn't even the sniff of one.

As I sat there draining the bitter cup, there were noises off stage and my meditations were interrupted by the return of the old ancestor. Well, when I say return, she came whizzing in but didn't stop, just whizzed through, and I saw, for I am pretty quick at noticing things, that she was upset about something. Reasoning closely, I deduced that her interview with L. P. Runkle must have gone awry or, as I much prefer to put it, agley.

And so it proved when she bobbed up again some little time later. Her first observation was that L. P. Runkle was an illegitimate offspring to end all illigitimate offsprings, and I hastened to commiserate with her. I could have done with a bit of commiseration myself, but Women and Children First is always the Wooster slogan.

"No luck?" I said.

"None."

"Wouldn't part?"

"Not a penny."

"You mentioned that without his cooperation Tuppy and Angela's wedding bells would not ring out?"

"Of course I did. And he said it was a great mistake for young people to marry before they knew their own minds."

"You could have pointed out that Tuppy and Angela have been engaged for two years."

"I did."

"What did he say to that?"

"He said, 'Not nearly long enough.' "

"So what are you going to do?"

"I've done it," said the old ancestor. "I pinched his porringer."

15

I GOGGLED AT HER, 100 percent nonplused. She had spoken with the exuberance of an aunt busily engaged in patting herself between the shoulder blades for having done something particularly clever, but I could make nothing of her statement. This habit of speaking in riddles seemed to be growing on her.

"You what?" I said. "You pinched his what?"

"His porringer. I told you about it the day you got here. Don't you remember? That silver thing he came to try to sell to Tom."

She had refreshed my memory. I recalled the conversation to which she referred. I had asked her why she was entertaining in her home a waste product like L. P. Runkle, and she had said that he had come hoping to sell Uncle Tom a silver something for his collection and she had got him to stay on in order to soften him up with Anatole's cooking and put to him, when softened up, her request for cash for Tuppy.

"When he turned me down just now, it suddenly occurred to me that if I got hold of the thing and told him he wouldn't get it back unless he made a satisfactory settlement, I would have a valuable bargaining point and we could discuss the matter further at any time that suited him."

I was ap-what-is-it. Forget my own name next. Appalled,

that's the word, though shocked to the core would be about as good; nothing much in it, really. I hadn't read any of those etiquette books you see all over the place, but I was prepared to bet that the leaders of Society who wrote them would raise an eyebrow or two at carryings-on of this description. The chapter on Hints to Hostesses would be bound to have a couple of paragraphs warning them that it wasn't the done thing to invite people to the home and having got them settled in to pinch their porringers.

"But good Lord!" I ejaculated, appalled or, if you prefer it, shocked to the core.

"Now what?"

"The man is under your roof."

"Did you expect him to be on it?"

"He has eaten your salt."

"Very imprudent, with blood pressure like his. His doctor probably forbids it."

"You can't do this."

"I know I can't, but I have," she said, just like the chap in the story, and I saw it would be fruitless or bootless to go on arguing. It rarely is with aunts—if you're their nephew, I mean, because they were at your side all through your formative years and know what an ass you were then and can't believe that anything that you may say later is worth listening to. I shouldn't be at all surprised if Jeeves's three aunts don't shut him up when he starts talking, remembering that at the age of six the child Jeeves didn't know the difference between the poet Burns and a hole in the ground.

Ceasing to expostulate, therefore, if expostulate is the word I want, I went to the bell and pressed it, and when she asked for footnotes throwing a light on why I did this, I told her I proposed to place the matter in the hands of a higher power.

"I'm ringing for Jeeves."

"You'll only get Seppings."

"Seppings will provide Jeeves."

"And what do you think Jeeves can do?"

"Make you see reason."

"I doubt it."

"Well, it's worth a try."

Further chitchat was suspended till Jeeves arrived, and silence fell except for the ancestor snorting from time to time and self breathing more heavily than usual, for I was much stirred. It always stirs a nephew to discover that a loved aunt does not know the difference between right and wrong. There is a difference—at my school, Arnold Abney, M.A., used to rub it into the student body both Sundays and weekdays—but apparently nobody had told the aged relative about it, with the result that she could purloin people's porringers without a yip from her conscience. Shook me a bit, I confess.

When Jeeves blew in, it cheered me to see the way his head stuck out at the back, for that's where the brain is, and what was needed here was a man with plenty of the old gray matter who would put his points so that even a fermenting aunt would have to be guided by him.

"Well, here's Jeeves," said the ancestor. "Tell him the facts and I'll bet he says I've done the only possible thing and can carry on along the lines I sketched out."

I might have risked a fiver on this at say twelve to eight, but it didn't seem fitting. But telling Jeeves the facts was a good idea, and I did so without delay, being careful to lay a proper foundation.

"Jeeves," I said.

"Sir?" he responded.

"Sorry to interrupt you again. Were you reading Spinoza?"

"No, sir, I was writing a letter to my Uncle Charlie."

"Charlie Silversmith," I explained in an aside to the ancestor. "Butler at Deverill Hall. One of the best."

"Thank you, sir."

"I know few men whom I esteem more highly than your Uncle Charlie. Well, we won't keep you long. It's just that another problem presenting certain points of interest has come up. In a recent conversation I revealed to you the situation relating to Tuppy Glossop and L. P. Runkle. You recall?"

"Yes, sir. Madam was hoping to extract a certain sum of money from Mr. Runkle on Mr. Glossop's behalf."

"Exactly. Well, it didn't come off."

"I am sorry to hear that, sir."

"But not, I imagine, surprised. If I remember, you considered it a hundred-to-one shot."

"Approximately that, sir."

"Runkle being short of bowels of compassion."

"Precisely, sir. A twenty-minute egg."

Here the ancestor repeated her doubts with regard to L. P. Runkle's legitimacy, and would, I think, have developed the theme had I not shushed her down with a raised hand.

"She pleaded in vain," I said. "He sent her away with a flea in her ear. I wouldn't be surprised to learn that he laughed her to scorn."

"The superfatted old son of a bachelor," the ancestor interposed, and once more I shushed her down.

"Well, you know what happens when you do that sort of thing to a woman of spirit. Thoughts of reprisals fill her mind. And so, coming to the nub, she decided to purloin Runkle's porringer. But I mustn't mislead you. She did this not as an act of vengeance, if you know what I mean, but in order to have a bargaining point when she renewed her application. 'Brass up,' she would have said when once more urging him to scare the moths out of his pocketbook, 'or you won't get back your porringer.' Do I make myself clear?"

"Perfectly clear, sir. I find you very lucid."

"Now first it will have to be explained to you what a

porringer is, and here I am handicapped by not having the foggiest notion myself, except that it's silver and old and the sort of thing Uncle Tom has in his collection. Runkle was hoping to sell it to him. —Could you supply any details?" I asked the aged relative.

She knitted the brows a bit and said she couldn't do much in that direction. "All I know is that it was made in the time of Charles the Second by some Dutchman or other."

"Then I think I know the porringer to which you allude, sir," said Jeeves, his face lighting up as much as it ever lights up, he for reasons of his own preferring at all times to preserve the impassivity of a waxwork at Madame Tussaud's. "It was featured in a Sotheby's catalog at which I happened to be glancing not long ago. Would it," he asked the ancestor, "be a silver-gilt porringer on circular molded foot, the lower part chased with acanthus foliage, with beaded scroll handles, the cover surmounted by a foliage on a rosette of swirling acanthus leaves, the stand of tazza form on circular detachable feet with acanthus border joined to a multifoil plate, the palin top with upcurved rim?"

He paused for a reply, but the ancestor did not speak immediately, her aspect that of one who has been run over by a municipal tram. Odd, really, because she must have been listening to that sort of thing from Uncle Tom for years. Finally she mumbled that she wouldn't be surprised or she wouldn't wonder or something like that.

"Your guess is as good as mine," she said.

"I fancy it must be the same, madam. You mentioned a workman of Dutch origin. Would the name be Hans Conrael Brechtel of The Hague?"

"I couldn't tell you. I know it wasn't Smith or Jones or Robinson, and that's as far as I go. But what's all this in aid of? What does it matter if the stand is of tazza form or if the palin top has an upcurved rim?"

"Exactly," I said, thoroughly concurring. "Or if the credit for these tazza forms and palin tops has to be chalked up to Hans Conrael Brechtel of The Hague. The point, Jeeves, is not what particular porringer the ancestor has pinched, but how far she was justified in pinching any porringer at all when its owner was a guest of hers. I hold that it was a breach of hospitality and the thing must be returned. Am I right?"

"Well, sir . . ."

"Go on, Jeeves," said the ancestor. "Say I'm a crook who ought to be drummed out of the Market Snodsbury Ladies Social and Cultural Garden Club."

"Not at all, madam."

"Then what were you going to say when you hesitated?"

"Merely that in my opinion no useful end will be served by retaining the object."

"I don't follow you. How about that bargaining point?"

"It will, I fear, avail you little, madam. As I understand Mr. Wooster, the sum you are hoping to obtain from Mr. Runkle amounts to a good many thousand pounds."

"Fifty at least, if not a hundred."

"Then I cannot envisage him complying with your demands. Mr. Runkle is a shrewd financier—"

"Born out of wedlock."

"Very possibly you are right, madam; nevertheless he is a man well versed in weighing profit and loss. According to Sotheby's catalog the price at which the object was sold at the auction sale was nine thousand pounds. He will scarcely disburse a hundred or even fifty thousand in order to recover it."

"Of course he won't," I said, as enchanted with his lucidity as he had been with mine. It was the sort of thinking you have to pay topnotchers at the Bar a king's ransom for. "He'll simply say 'Easy come, easy go' and write it off as a business loss, possibly consulting his legal adviser as to whether he can deduct it from his income tax. Thank you, Jeeves. You've straightened everything out in your customary masterly manner. You're a—what were you saying the other day about Daniel somebody?"

"A Daniel come to judgment, sir?"

"That was it. You're a Daniel come to judgment."

"It is very kind of you to say so, sir."

"Not at all. Well-deserved tribute."

I shot a glance at the aged relative. It is notoriously difficult to change the trend of an aunt's mind when that mind is made up about this or that, but I could see at a g that Jeeves had done it. I hadn't expected her to look pleased, and she didn't, but it was evident that she had accepted what is sometimes called the inevitable. I would describe her as not having a word to say, had she not at this moment said one, suitable enough for the hunting field but on the strong side for mixed company. I registered it in my memory as something to say to Spode sometime, always provided it was on the telephone.

"I suppose you're right, Jeeves," she said, heavyhearted, though bearing up stoutly. "It seemed a good idea at the time, but I agree with you that it isn't as watertight as I thought it. It's so often that way with one's golden dreams. The—"

"—best-laid plans of mice and men gang aft agley," I said, helping her out. "See the poet Burns. I've often wondered why Scotsmen say 'gang.' I asked you once, Jeeves, if you recall, and you said they had not confided in you. You were saying, ancestor?"

"I was about to say—"

"Or, for that matter, 'agley.' "

"I was about to say—"

"Or 'aft' for 'often.' "

"I was about to say," said the relative, having thrown her Rex Stout at me, fortunately with a less accurate aim than the other time, "that there's nothing to be done but for me to put the thing back in Runkle's room where I took it from."

"Whence I took it" would have been better, but it was not to comment on her prose style that I interposed. I was thinking that if she was allowed to do the putting back, she might quite possibly change her mind on the way to Runkle's room and decide to stick to the loot after all. Jeeves's arguments had been convincing to the last drop, but you can never be sure that the effect of convincing arguments won't wear off, especially with aunts who don't know the difference between right and wrong, and it might be that she would take the view that if she pocketed the porringer and kept it among her souvenirs, she would at least be saving something from the wreck. "Always difficult to know what to give Tom for his birthday," she might say to herself. "This will be just the thing."

"I'll do it," I said. "Unless you'd rather, Jeeves."

"No, thank you, sir."

"Only take a minute of your time."

"No, thank you, sir."

"Then you may leave us, Jeeves. Much obliged for your Daniel come to judgmenting."

"A pleasure, sir."

"Give Uncle Charlie my love."

"I will indeed, sir."

As the door closed behind him, I started to make my plans and dispositions, as I believe the word is, and I found the blood relation docile and helpful. Runkle's room, she told me, was the one known as the Blue Room, and the porringer should be inserted in the left top drawer of the chest of drawers, whence she had removed it. I asked if she was sure he was still in the hammock, and she said he must be, because on her departure he was bound to have gone to sleep again. Taking a line through the cat Augustus, I found this plausible. With these traumatic symplegia cases waking is never more than a temporary thing. I have known Augustus to resume his slumbers within fifteen seconds of having had a shopping bag containing tins of cat food fall on him. A stifled oath, and he was off to dreamland once more.

As I climbed the stairs, I was impressed by the fact that L. P. Runkle had been given the Blue Room, for in this house it amounted to getting star billing. It was the biggest and most luxurious of the rooms allotted to bachelors. I once suggested to the aged relative that I be put there, but all she said was *"You?"* and the conversation turned to other topics. Runkle having got it in spite of the presence on the premises of a seventh Earl showed how determined the a.r. had been that no stone should be left unturned and no avenue unexplored in her efforts to soften him up; and it seemed ironical that all her carefully thought-out plans should have gone agley. Just shows Burns knew what he was talking about. You can generally rely on these poets to hit the mark and entitle themselves to a cigar or coconut according to choice.

The old sweats will remember, though later arrivals will have to be told, that this was not the first time I had gone on a secret mission to the Blue Room. That other visit, the old sweats will recall, had ended in disaster and not knowing which way to look, for Mrs. Homer Cream, the well-known writer of suspense novels, had found me on the floor with a chain round my neck, and it had not been easy to explain. This was no doubt why on the present occasion I approached the door with emotions somewhat similar to those I had had in the old days when approaching that of Arnold Abney, M.A., at the conclusion of morning prayers. A voice seemed to whisper in my ear that beyond that door there lurked something that wasn't going to do me a bit of good.

551

The voice was perfectly right. It had got its facts correct first shot. What met my eyes as I entered was L. P. Runkle asleep on the bed, and with my customary quickness I divined what must have happened. After being cornered there by the old ancestor he must have come to the conclusion that a hammock out in the middle of a lawn, with access to it from all directions, was no place for a man who wanted peace and seclusion, and that these were to be obtained only in his bedroom. Thither, accordingly, he had gone, and there he was. *Voilà tout*, as one might say if one had made a study of the French language.

The sight of this sleeping beauty had, of course, given me a nasty start, causing my heart to collide rather violently with my front teeth, but it was only for a moment that I was unequal to what I have heard Jeeves call the intellectual pressure of the situation. It is pretty generally recognized in the circles in which I move that Bertram Wooster, though he may be down, is never out, the betting being odds on that, given time to collect his thoughts and stop his head spinning, he will rise on stepping stones of his dead self to higher things, as the fellow said, and it was so now. I would have preferred, of course, to operate in a room wholly free from the presence of L. P. Runkle, but I realized that as long as he remained asleep there was nothing to keep me from carrying on. All that was required was that my activities should be conducted in absolute silence. And it was thus that I was conducting them, more like a specter or wraith than a chartered member of the Drones Club, when the air was rent, as the expression is, by a sharp yowl such as you hear when a cougar or a snow leopard stubs its toe on a rock, and I became aware that I had trodden on the cat Augustus, who had continued to follow me, still, I suppose, under the mistaken impression that I had kippered herrings on my person and might at any moment start loosening up.

In normal circumstances I would have hastened to make

my apologies and to endeavor by tickling him behind the ear to apply balm to his wounded feelings, but at this moment L. P. Runkle sat up, said "Wah-wah-wah," rubbed his eyes, gave me an unpleasant look with them and asked me what the devil I was doing in his room.

It was not an easy question to answer. There had been nothing in our relations since we first swam into each other's ken to make it seem likely that I had come to smooth his pillow or ask him if he would like a cooling drink, and I did not put forward these explanations. I was thinking how right the ancestor had been in predicting that, if aroused suddenly, he would wake up cross. His whole demeanor was that of a man who didn't much like the human race as a whole but was particularly allergic to Woosters. Not even Spode could have made his distaste for them plainer.

I decided to see what could be done with suavity. It had answered well in the case of Ginger, and there was no saying that it might not help to ease the current situation.

"I'm sorry," I said with an enchanting smile. "I'm afraid I woke you."

"Yes, you did. And stop grinning at me like a half-witted ape."

"Right ho," I said. I removed the enchanting smile. It came off quite easily. "I don't wonder you're annoyed. But I'm more to be pitied than censured. I inadvertently trod on the cat."

A look of alarm spread over his face. It had a long way to go, but it spread all right.

"Hat?" he quavered, and I could see that he feared for the well-being of his panama with the pink ribbon.

I lost no time in reassuring him.

"Not hat. Cat."

"What cat?"

"Oh, haven't you met? Augustus, his name is, though for purposes of conversation this is usually shortened to Gus.

He and I have been buddies since he was a kitten. He must have been following me when I came in here."

It was an unfortunate way of putting it, for it brought him back to his original theme.

"Why the devil did you come in here?"

A lesser man than Bertram Wooster would have been nonplused, and I don't mind admitting that I was, too, for about a couple of ticks. But as I stood shuffling the feet and twiddling the fingers I caught sight of that camera of his standing on an adjacent table, and I got one of those inspirations you get occasionally. Shakespeare and Burns and even Oliver Wendell Holmes probably used to have them all the time, but self not so often. In fact, this was the first that had come my way for some weeks.

"Aunt Dahlia sent me to ask you if you would come and take a few photographs of her and the house and all that sort of thing, so that she'll have them to look at in the long winter evenings. You know how long the winter evenings get nowadays."

The moment I had said it I found myself speculating as to whether the inspiration had been as hot as I had supposed. I mean, this man had just had a conference with the old ancestor which, unlike those between ministers of state, had not been conducted in an atmosphere of the utmost cordiality, and he might be thinking it odd that so soon after its conclusion she should be wanting him to take photographs of her. But all was well. No doubt he looked on her request as what is known as an olive branch. Anyway, he was all animation and eagerness to cooperate.

"I'll be right down," he said. "Tell her I'll be right down."

Having hidden the porringer in my room and locked the door, I went back to the aged relative and found her with Jeeves. She expressed relief at seeing me.

"Oh, there you are, my beautiful bounding Bertie. Thank goodness you didn't go to Runkle's room. Jeeves tells me Seppings met Runkle on the stairs and he asked him to bring him a cup of tea in half an hour. He said he was going to lie down. You might have run right into him."

I laughed one of those hollow, mirthless ones.

"Jeeves speaks too late, old ancestor. I did run into him."

"You mean he was *there?*"

"With his hair in a braid."

"What did you do?"

"I told him you had asked me to ask him to come and take some photographs."

"Quick thinking."

"I always think like lightning."

"And did he swallow it?"

"He appeared to. He said he would be right down."

"Well, I'm damned if I'm going to smile."

Whether I would have pleaded with her to modify this stern resolve and at least show a portion of her front teeth when Runkle pressed the button I cannot say, for as she spoke my thoughts were diverted. A sudden query presented itself. What, I asked myself, was keeping L. P. Runkle? He had said he would be right down, but quite a time had elapsed and no sign of him. I was toying with the idea that on a warm afternoon like this a man of his build might have had a fit of some kind, when there came from the stairs the sound of clumping feet, and he was with us.

But a very different L. P. Runkle from the man who had told me he would be right down. Then he had been all sunny and beaming, the amateur photographer who was not only going to make a pest of himself by taking photographs but had actually been asked to make a pest of himself in this manner, which seldom happens to amateur photographers. Now he was cold and hard like a picnic egg, and he couldn't have looked at me with more loathing if I really had trodden on his panama hat.

"Mrs. Travers!"

His voice had rung out with the clarion note of a coster-monger seeking to draw the attention of the purchasing public to his blood oranges and Brussels sprouts. I saw the ancestor stiffen, and I knew she was about to go into her grande dame act. This relative, though in ordinary circs so genial and matey, can on occasion turn in a flash into a carbon copy of a duchess of the old school reducing an underling to a spot of grease, and what is so remarkable is that she doesn't have to use a lorgnette, just does it all with the power of the human eye. I think girls in her day used to learn the trick at their finishing schools.

"Will you kindly not bellow at me, Mr. Runkle. I am not deaf. What is it?"

The aristocratic ice in her tone sent a cold shiver down my spine, but in L. P. Runkle she had picked a tough customer to try to freeze. He apologized for having bellowed, but briefly and with no real contrition. He then proceeded to deal with her query as to what it was, and with a powerful effort forced himself to speak quite quietly. Not exactly like a cooing pigeon, but quietly.

"I wonder if you remember, Mrs. Travers, a silver porringer I showed you on my arrival here."

"I do."

"Very valuable."

"So you told me."

"I kept it in the top left-hand drawer of the chest of drawers in my bedroom. It did not occur to me that there was any necessity to hide it. I took the honesty of everybody under your roof for granted."

"Naturally."

"Even when I found that Mr. Wooster was one of my fellow guests I took no precautions. It was a fatal blunder. He has just stolen it."

I suppose it's pretty much of a strain to keep up that grande dame stuff for any length of time, involving as it does rigidity of the facial muscles and the spinal column, for at these words the ancestor called it a day and reverted to the Quorn-and-Pytchleyness of her youth.

"Don't be a damned fool, Runkle. You're talking rot. Bertie would never dream of doing such a thing, would you, Bertie?"

"Not in a million years."

"The man's an ass."

"One might almost say a silly ass."

"Comes of sleeping all the time."

"I believe that's the trouble."

"Addles the brain."

"Must, I imagine. It's the same thing with Gus the cat. I love Gus like a brother, but after years of nonstop sleep he's got about as much genuine intelligence as a cabinet minister."

"I hope Runkle hasn't annoyed you with his preposterous allegations?"

"No, no, old ancestor, I'm not angry, just terribly terribly hurt."

You'd have thought all this would have rendered Runkle a spent force and a mere shell of his former self, but his eye was not dimmed nor his natural force abated. Turning to the door, he paused there to add a few words.

"I disagree with you, Mrs. Travers, in the view you take of your nephew's honesty. I prefer to be guided by Lord Sidcup, who assures me that Mr. Wooster invariably steals anything that is not firmly fastened to the floor. It was only by the merest chance, Lord Sidcup tells me, that at their first meeting he did not make off with an umbrella belonging to Sir Watkyn Bassett, and from there he has, as one might put it, gone from strength to strength. Umbrellas, cow creamers, amber statuettes, cameras, all are grist to his mill. I was unfortunately asleep when he crept into my room, and he had plenty of time before I woke to do what he had come for. It was only some minutes after he had slunk out that it occurred to me to look in the top left-hand drawer of my chest of drawers. My suspicions were confirmed. The drawer was empty. He had got away with the swag. But I am a man of action. I have sent your butler to the police station to bring a constable to search Wooster's room. I, until he arrives, propose to stand outside it, making sure that he does not go in and tamper with the evidence."

Having said which in the most unpleasant of vocal deliveries, L. P. Runkle became conspic by his a, and the ancestor spoke with considerable eloquence on the subject of fat slobs of dubious parentage who had the immortal crust to send her butler on errands. I, too, was exercised by the concluding portion of his remarks.

"I don't like that," I said, addressing Jeeves, who during the recent proceedings had been standing in the background giving a lifelike impersonation of somebody who wasn't there.

"Sir?"

"If the fuzz search my room, I'm sunk."

"Have no anxiety, sir. A police officer is not permitted to enter private property without authority, nor do the regulations allow him to ask the owner of such property for permission to enter."

"You're sure of that?"

"Yes, sir."

Well, that was a crumb of comfort, but it would be deceiving my public if I said that Bertram Wooster was his usual nonchalant self. Too many things had been happening one on top of the other for him to be the carefree boulevardier one likes to see. If I hoped to clarify the various situations which were giving me the pip and erase the dark circles already beginning to form beneath the eyes, it would, I saw, be necessary for me to marshal my thoughts.

"Jeeves," I said, leading him from the room, "I must marshal my thoughts."

"Certainly, sir, if you wish."

"And I can't possibly do it here with crises turning handsprings on every side. Can you think of a good excuse for me to pop up to London for the night? A few hours alone in the peaceful surroundings of the apartment are what I need. I must concentrate, concentrate."

"But do you require an excuse, sir?"

"It's better to have one. Aunt Dahlia is on a sticky wicket and would be hurt if I deserted her now unless I had some good reason. I can't let her down."

"The sentiment does you credit, sir."

"Thank you, Jeeves. Can you think of anything?"

"You have been summoned for jury duty, sir."

"Don't they let you have a longish notice for that?"

"Yes, sir, but when the post arrived containing the letter from the authorities, I forgot to give it to you, and only delivered it a moment ago. Fortunately it was not too late. Would you be intending to leave immediately?"

"If not sooner. I'll borrow Ginger's car."

"You will miss the debate, sir."

"The what?"

"The debate between Mr. Winship and his opponent. It takes place tomorrow night."

"What time?"

"It is scheduled for a quarter to seven."

"Taking how long?"

"Perhaps an hour."

"Then expect me back at about seven-thirty. The great thing in life, Jeeves, if we wish to be happy and prosperous, is to miss as many political debates as possible. You wouldn't care to come with me, would you?"

"No, thank you, sir. I am particularly anxious to hear Mr. Winship's speech."

"He'll probably only say 'Er,' " I riposted rather cleverly.

16

IT WAS WITH HEART definitely bowed down and the circles beneath my eyes darker than ever that I drove back next day in what is known as the quiet evenfall. I remember Jeeves saying something to me once about the heavy and the weary weight of this unintelligible world—not his own, I gathered, but from the works of somebody called Wordsworth, if I caught the name correctly—and it seemed to me rather a good way of describing the depressing feeling you get when the soup is about to close over you and no life belt in sight. I was conscious of this heavy and weary weight some years ago, that time when my cousins Eustace and Claude without notifying me inserted twenty-three cats in my bedroom, and I had it again, in spades, at the present juncture.

Consider the facts. I had gone up to London to wrestle in solitude with the following problems:

(a) How am I to get out of marrying Madeline Bassett?

(b) How am I to restore the porringer to L. P. Runkle before the constabulary come piling on the back of my neck?

(c) How is the ancestor to extract that money from Runkle?

(d) How is Ginger to marry Magnolia Glendennon while betrothed to Florence?

and I was returning with all four still in statu quo. For a night and day I had been giving them the cream of the Wooster brain, and for all I had accomplished I might have been the aged relative trying to solve the *Observer* crossword puzzle.

Arriving at journey's end, I steered the car into the drive. About halfway along it there was a tricky right-hand turn, and I had slowed down to negotiate this, when a dim figure appeared before me, a voice said "Hoy!" and I saw that it was Ginger.

He seemed annoyed about something. His "Hoy!" had had a note of reproach in it, as far as it is possible to get the note of reproach into a "Hoy!" and as he drew near and shoved his torso through the window I received the distinct impression that he was displeased.

His opening words confirmed this.

"Bertie, you abysmal louse, what's kept you all this time? When I lent you my car, I didn't expect you'd come back at two o'clock in the morning."

"It's only half-past seven."

He seemed amazed.

"Is that all? I thought it was later. So much has been happening."

"What has been happening?"

"No time to tell you now. I'm in a hurry."

It was at this point that I noticed something in his appearance which I had overlooked. A trifle, but I'm rather observant.

"You've got egg in your hair," I said.

"Of course I've got egg in my hair," he said, his manner betraying impatience. "What did you expect me to have in my hair, Chanel Number Five?"

"Did somebody throw an egg at you?"

"Everybody threw eggs at everybody. Correction. Some of them threw turnips and potatoes."

561

"You mean the meeting broke up in disorder, as the expression is?"

"I don't suppose any meeting in the history of English politics has ever broken up in more disorder. Eggs flew hither and thither. The air was dark with vegetables of every description. Sidcup got a black eye. Somebody plugged him with a potato."

I found myself of two minds. On the one hand I felt a pang of regret for having missed what had all the earmarks of having been a political meeting of the most rewarding kind; on the other, it was like rare and refreshing fruit to hear that Spode had got hit in the eye with a potato. I was conscious of an awed respect for the marksman who had accomplished this feat. A potato, being so nobbly in shape, can be aimed accurately only by a master hand.

"Tell me more," I said, well pleased.

"Tell you more be blowed. I've got to get up to London. We want to be there bright and early tomorrow in order to inspect registrars and choose the best one."

This didn't sound like Florence, who, if she ever gets through an engagement without breaking it, is sure to insist on a wedding with bishops, bridesmaids, full choral effects, and a reception afterwards. A sudden thought struck me, and I think I may have gasped. Somebody made a noise like a dying soda-water syphon, and it was presumably me.

"When you say 'we,' do you mean you and M. Glendennon?"

"Who else?"

"But how?"

"Never mind how."

"But I do mind how. You were Problem (d) on my list, and I want to know how you have been solved. I gather that Florence has remitted your sentence——"

"She has, in words of unmistakable clarity. Get out of that car."

"But why?"

"Because if you aren't out of it in two seconds, I'm going to pull you out."

"I mean why did she r your s?"

"Ask Jeeves," he said, and attaching himself to the collar of my coat he removed me from the automobile like a stevedore hoisting a sack of grain. He took my place at the wheel, and disappeared down the drive to keep his tryst with the little woman, who presumably awaited him at some prearranged spot with the bags and baggage.

He left me in a condition which can best be described as befogged, bewildered, mystified, confused and perplexed. All I had got out of him was (a) that the debate had not been conducted in an atmosphere of the utmost cordiality; (b) that at its conclusion Florence had forbidden the banns; and (c) that if I wanted further information Jeeves would supply it. A little more than the charmers got out of the deaf adder, but not much. I felt like a barrister, as it might be Ma McCorkadale, who has been baffled by an unsatisfactory witness.

However, he had spoken of Jeeves as a fount of information, so my first move on reaching the drawing room and finding no one there was to put forefinger to bell button and push.

Seppings answered the summons. He and I have been buddies from boyhood—mine, of course, not his—and as a rule when we meet conversation flows like water, mainly on the subject of the weather and the state of his lumbago, but this was no time for idle chatter.

"Seppings," I said, "I want Jeeves. Where is he?"

"In the servants' hall, sir, comforting the parlormaid."

I took him to allude to the employee whose gong work I had admired on my first evening, and, pressing though my business was, it seemed only humane to offer a word of sympathy for whatever her misfortunes might be.

"Had bad news, has she?"

"No, sir, she was struck by a turnip."

"Where?"

"In the lower ribs, sir."

"I mean where did this happen?"

"At the Town Hall, sir, in the later stages of the debate."

I drew in the breath sharply. More and more I was beginning to realize that the meeting I had missed had been marked by passions that recalled the worst excesses of the French Revolution.

"I myself, sir, narrowly escaped being hit by a tomato. It whizzed past my ear."

"You shock me profoundly, Seppings. I don't wonder you're pale and trembling." And indeed he was, like a badly set blancmange. "What caused all this turmoil?"

"Mr. Winship's speech, sir."

This surprised me. I could readily believe that any speech of Ginger's would be well below the mark set by Demosthenes, if that really was the fellow's name, but surely not so supremely lousy as to start his audience throwing eggs and vegetables; and I was about to institute further inquiries when Seppings sidled to the door, saying that he would inform Mr. Jeeves of my desire to confer with him. And in due season the hour produced the man, as the expression is.

"You wished to see me, sir?" he said.

"You can put it even stronger, Jeeves. I yearned to see you."

"Indeed, sir?"

"Just now I met Ginger in the drive."

"Yes, sir, he informed me that he was going there to await your return."

"He tells me he is no longer betrothed to Miss Craye, being now affianced to Miss Glendennon. And when I asked him how this switch had come about, he said that you would explain."

"I shall be glad to do so, sir. You wish a complete report?"

"That's right. Omit no detail, however slight."

He was silent for a space. Marshaling his thoughts, no doubt. Then he got down to it.

"The importance attached by the electorate to the debate," he began, "was very evident. An audience of considerable size had assembled in the Town Hall. The Mayor and corporation were there, together with the flower of Market Snodsbury's aristocracy and a rougher element in cloth caps and turtleneck sweaters who should never have been admitted."

I had to rebuke him at this point. "Bit snobbish, that, Jeeves, what? You are a little too inclined to judge people by their clothes. Turtleneck sweaters are royal raiment when they're worn for virtue's sake, and a cloth cap may hide an honest heart. Probably frightfully good chaps, if one got to know them."

"I would prefer not to know them, sir. It was they who subsequently threw eggs, potatoes, tomatoes and turnips."

I had to concede that he had a point there.

"True," I said. "I was forgetting that. All right, Jeeves. Carry on."

"The proceedings opened with a rendering of the national anthem by the boys and girls of Market Snodsbury elementary school."

"Pretty ghastly, I imagine?"

"Somewhat revolting, sir."

"And then?"

"The Mayor made a short address, introducing the contestants, and Mrs. McCorkadale rose to speak. She was wearing a smart coat in fine quality repp over a long-sleeved frock of figured marocain pleated at the sides and finished at the neck with—"

"Skip all that, Jeeves."

"I am sorry, sir. I thought you wished every detail, however slight."

"Only when they're—what's the word?"

"Pertinent, sir?"

"That's right. Take the McCorkadale's outer crust as read. How was her speech?"

"Extremely telling, in spite of a good deal of heckling."

"That wouldn't put her off her stroke."

"No, sir. She impressed me as being of a singularly forceful character."

"Me, too."

"You have met the lady, sir?"

"For a few minutes—which, however, were plenty. She spoke at some length?"

"Yes, sir. If you would care to read her remarks? I took down both speeches in shorthand."

"Later on, perhaps."

"At any time that suits you, sir."

"And how was the applause? Hearty? Or sporadic?"

"On one side of the hall extremely hearty. The rougher element appeared to be composed in almost equal parts of her supporters and those of Mr. Winship. They had been seated at opposite sides of the auditorium, no doubt by design. Her supporters cheered, Mr. Winship's booed."

"And when Ginger got up, I suppose her lot booed him?"

"No doubt they would have done so, had it not been for the tone of his address. His appearance was greeted with a certain modicum of hostility, but he had scarcely begun to speak when he was rapturously received."

"By the opposition?"

"Yes, sir."

"Strange."

"Yes, sir."

"Can you elucidate?"

"Yes, sir. If I might consult my notes for a moment. Ah, yes. Mr. Winship's opening words were, 'Ladies and gentlemen, I come before you a changed man.' A voice: 'That's good news.' A second voice: 'Shut up, you bleeder.' A third voice . . .'"

"I think we might pass lightly over the voices, Jeeves."

"Very good, sir. Mr. Winship then said, 'I should like to begin with a word to the gentleman in the turtleneck sweater in that seat over there who kept calling my opponent a silly old geezer. If he will kindly step onto this platform, I shall be happy to knock his ugly block off. Mrs. McCorkadale is *not* a silly old geezer.' A voice—Excuse me, sir, I was forgetting. 'Mrs. McCorkadale is *not* a silly old geezer,' Mr. Winship said, 'but a lady of the greatest intelligence and grasp of affairs. I admire her intensely. Listening to her this evening has changed my political views completely. She has converted me to hers, and I propose, when the polls are opened, to cast my vote for her. I advise all of you to do the same. Thank you.' He then resumed his seat."

"Good Lord, Jeeves!"

"Yes, sir."

"He really said that?"

"Yes, sir."

"No wonder his engagement's off."

"I must confess it occasioned me no surprise, sir."

I continued amazed. It seemed incredible that Ginger, whose long suit was muscle rather than brain, should have had the ingenuity and know-how to think up such a scheme for freeing himself from Florence's clutches without forfeiting his standing as a fairly *preux chevalier*. It seemed to reveal him as possessed of snakiness of a high order, and I was just thinking that you never can tell about a fellow's hidden depths, when one of those sudden thoughts of mine came popping to the surface.

"Was this you, Jeeves?"

"Sir?"

"Did you put Ginger up to doing it?"

"It is conceivable that Mr. Winship may have been influenced by something I said, sir. He was very much exercised with regard to his matrimonial entanglements and he did me the honor of consulting me. It is quite possible that I may have let fall some careless remark that turned his thoughts in the direction they took."

"In other words, you told him to go to it?"

"Yes, sir."

I was silent for a space. I was thinking how jolly it would be if he could dish up something equally effective with regard to me and M. Bassett. The thought also occurred to me that what had happened, while excellent for Ginger, wasn't so good for his backers and supporters and the Conservative cause in general.

I mentioned this.

"Tough on the fellows who betted on him."

"Into each life some rain must fall, sir."

"Though possibly a good thing. A warning to them in future to keep their money in the old oak chest and not risk it on wagers. May prove a turning point in their lives. What really saddens one is the thought that Bingley will now clean up. He'll make a packet."

"He told me this afternoon that he was expecting to do so."

"You mean you've seen him?"

"He came here at about five o'clock, sir."

"Stockish, hard and full of rage, I suppose?"

"On the contrary, sir, extremely friendly. He made no allusion to the past. I gave him a cup of tea, and we chatted for perhaps half an hour."

"Strange."

"Yes, sir. I wondered if he might not have had an ulterior motive in approaching me."

568

"Such as?"

"I must confess I cannot think of one. Unless he entertained some hope of inducing me to part with the club book, but that is hardly likely. Would there be anything further, sir?"

"You want to get back to the stricken parlormaid?"

"Yes, sir. When you rang, I was about to see what a little weak brandy and water would do."

I sped him on his errand of mercy and sat down to brood. You might have supposed that the singular behavior of Bingley would have occupied my thoughts. I mean, when you hear that a chap of his well-established crookedness has been acting oddly, your natural impulse is to say "Aha!" and wonder what his game is. And perhaps for a minute or two I did ponder on this. But I had so many other things to ponder on that Bingley soon got shoved into the discard. If I remember rightly, it was as I mused on Problem (b), the one about restoring the porringer to L. P. Runkle, and again drew a blank, that my reverie was interrupted by the entrance of the old ancestor.

She was wearing the unmistakable look of an aunt who has just been having the time of her life, and this did not surprise me. Hers since she sold the weekly paper she used to run, the one I did that piece on What the Well-Dressed Man Will Wear for, has been a quiet sort of existence, pleasant enough but lacking in incident and excitement. A really sensational event such as the egg-and-vegetable-throwing get-together she had just been present at must have bucked her up like a week at the seaside.

Her greeting could not have been more cordial. An aunt's love oozed out from every syllable.

"Hullo, you revolting object," she said. "So you're back."

"Just arrived."

"Too bad you had that jury job. You missed a gripping experience."

"So Jeeves was telling me."

"Ginger finally went off his rocker."

With the inside information which had been placed at my disposal I was able to correct this view. "It was no rocker that he went off, aged relative. His actions were motivated by the soundest good sense. He wanted to get Florence out of his hair without actually telling her to look elsewhere for a mate."

"Don't be an ass. He loves her."

"No longer. He's switched to Magnolia Glendennon."

"You mean that secretary of his?"

"That identical secretary."

"How do you know?"

"He told me so himself."

"Well, I'll be blowed. He finally got fed up with Florence's bossiness, did he?"

"Yes, I think it must have been coming on for some time without him knowing it, subconsciously, as Jeeves would say. Meeting Magnolia brought it to the surface."

"She seems a nice girl."

"Very nice, according to Ginger."

"I must congratulate him."

"You'll have to wait a bit. They've gone up to London."

"So have Spode and Madeline. And Runkle ought to be leaving soon. It's like one of those great race movements of the Middle Ages I used to read about at school. Well, this is wonderful. Pretty soon it'll be safe for Tom to return to the nest. There's still Florence, of course, but I doubt if she will be staying on. My cup runneth over, young Bertie. I've missed Tom sorely. Home's not home without him messing about the place. Why are you staring at me like a halibut on a fishmonger's slab?"

I had not been aware that I was conveying this resemblance to the fish she mentioned, but my gaze must certainly have been on the intent side, for her opening words had stirred me to my depths.

"Did you say," I yes I suppose vociferated would be the word, "that Spode and Madeline Bassett had gone to London?"

"Left half an hour ago."

"Together?"

"Yes, in his car."

"But Spode told me she had given him the push."

"She did, but everything's all right again. He's not going to give up his title and stand for Parliament. Getting hit in the eye with that potato changed his plans completely. It made him feel that if that was the sort of thing you have to go through to get elected to the House of Commons, he preferred to play it safe and stick to the House of Lords. And she, of course, assured that there was going to be no funny business and that she would become the Countess of Sidcup all right, withdrew her objections to marrying him. Now you're puffing like Tom when he goes upstairs too fast. Why is this?"

Actually, I had breathed deeply, not puffed, and certainly not like Uncle Tom when he goes upstairs too fast, but I suppose to an aunt there isn't much difference between a deep-breathing nephew and a puffing nephew, and anyway I was in no mood to discuss the point.

"You don't know who it was who threw that potato, do you?" I asked.

"The one that hit Spode? I don't. It sort of came out of the void. Why?"

"Because if I knew who it was, I would send camels bearing apes, ivory and peacocks to his address. He saved me from the fate that is worse than death. I allude to marriage with the Bassett disaster."

"Was she going to marry you?"

"According to Spode."

A look almost of awe came into the ancestor's face.

"How right you were," she said, "when you told me once

571

that you had faith in your star. I've lost count of the number of times you've been definitely headed for the altar with apparently no hope of evading the firing squad, and every time something has happened which enabled you to wriggle out of it. It's uncanny."

She would, I think, have gone deeper into the matter, for already she had begun to pay a marked tribute to my guardian angel, who, she said, plainly knew his job from soup to nuts, but at this moment Seppings appeared and asked her if she would have a word with Jeeves, and she went out to have it.

And I had just put my feet up on the chaise longue and was starting to muse ecstatically on the astounding bit of luck which had removed the Bassett menace from my life, when my mood of what the French call *bien être* was given the sleeve across the windpipe by the entrance of L. P. Runkle, the mere sight of whom, circs being what they were, was enough to freeze the blood and make each particular hair stand on end like quills upon the fretful porpentine, as I have heard Jeeves put it.

I wasn't glad to see him, but he seemed glad to see me.

"Oh, there you are," he said. "They told me you had skipped. Very sensible of you to come back. It's never any good going on the run, because the police are sure to get you sooner or later, and it makes it all the worse for you if you've done a bolt."

With cold dignity I said I had had to go up to London on business. He paid no attention to this. He was scrutinizing me rather in the manner of the halibut on the fishmonger's slab to which the ancestor has referred in our recent conversation.

"The odd thing is," he said, continuing to scan me closely, "that you haven't a criminal face. It's a silly fatuous face, but not criminal. You remind me of one of those fellows who do dances with the soubrette in musical comedy."

Come, come, I said to myself, this is better. Spode had compared me to a member of the ensemble. In the view of L. P. Runkle I was at any rate one of the principals. Moving up in the world.

"Must be a great help to you in your business. Lulls people into a false security. They think there can't be any danger from someone who looks like you, they're off their guard, and *wham!* you've got away with their umbrellas and cameras. No doubt you owe all your successes to this. But you know the old saying about the pitcher going too often to the well. This time you're for it. This time—"

He broke off, not because he had come to an end of his very offensive remarks but because Florence had joined us, and her appearance immediately claimed his attention. She was far from being dapper. It was plain that she had been in the forefront of the late battle, for whereas Ginger had merely had egg in his hair, she was, as it were, festooned in egg. She had evidently been right in the center of the barrage. In all political meetings of the stormier kind these things are largely a matter of luck. A escapes unscathed, B becomes a human omelet.

A more tactful man than L. P. Runkle would have affected not to notice this, but I don't suppose it ever occurred to him to affect not to notice things.

"Hullo!" he said. "You've got egg all over you."

Florence replied rather acidly that she was aware of this.

"Better change your dress."

"I intend to. Would you mind, Mr. Runkle, if I had a word with Mr. Wooster alone?"

I think Runkle was on the point of saying "What about?" but on catching her eye he had prudent second thoughts. He lumbered off, and she proceeded to have the word she had mentioned.

She kept it crisp. None of the "Er" stuff which was such a feature of Ginger's oratory. Even Demosthenes would have been slower in coming to the nub, though he, of course, would have been handicapped by having to speak in Greek.

"I'm glad I found you, Bertie."

A civil "Oh, ah" was all the reply I could think of.

"I have been thinking things over, and I have made up my mind. Harold Winship is a mere lout, and I am having nothing more to do with him. I see now that I made a great mistake when I broke off my engagement to you. You have your faults, but they are easily corrected. I have decided to marry you, and I think we shall be very happy."

"But not immediately," said L. P. Runkle, rejoining us. I described him a moment ago as lumbering off, but a man like that never lumbers far if there is a chance of hearing what somebody has to say to somebody else in private. "He'll first have to do a longish stretch in prison."

His reappearance had caused Florence to stiffen. She now stiffened further, her aspect similar to that of the old ancestor when about to go into her grande dame act.

"Mr. Runkle!"

"I'm here."

"I thought you had gone."

"I hadn't."

"How dare you listen to a private conversation!"

"They're the only things worth listening to. I owe much of my large fortune to listening to private conversations."

"What is this nonsense about prison?"

"Wooster won't find it nonsense. He has sneaked a valuable silver porringer of mine, a thing I paid nine thousand pounds for, and I am expecting a man any minute now who will produce the evidence necessary to convict. It's an open-and-shut case."

"Is this true, Bertie?" said Florence with that touch of the prosecuting district attorney I remembered so vividly, and all I could say was "Well . . . I . . . er . . . well."

With a guardian angel like mine working overtime, it was enough. She delivered judgment instantaneously.

"I shall not marry you," she said, and went off haughtily to de-egg herself.

"Very sensible of her," said L. P. Runkle. "The right course to take. A man like you, bound to be always in and out of prison, couldn't possibly be a good husband. How is a wife to make her plans—dinner parties, holidays, Christmas treats for the children, the hundred and one things a woman has to think of, when she doesn't know from one day to another whether the head of the house won't be telephoning to say he's been arrested again and no bail allowed? Yes?" said Runkle, and I saw that Seppings had appeared in the offing.

"A Mr. Bingley has called to see you, sir."

"Ah, yes, I was expecting him."

He popped off, and scarcely had he ceased to pollute the atmosphere when the old ancestor blew in.

She was plainly agitated, the resemblance to a cat on hot bricks being very marked. She panted a good deal, and her face had taken on the rather pretty mauve color it always does when the soul is not at rest.

"Bertie," she boomed, "when you went away yesterday, did you leave the door of your bedroom unlocked?"

"Of course I didn't."

"Well, Jeeves says it's open now."

"It can't be."

"It is. He thinks Runkle or some minion of his has skeleton-keyed the lock. Don't yell like that, curse you."

I might have retorted by asking her what she expected me to do when I suddenly saw all, but I was too busy seeing all to be diverted into arguments about my voice production. The awful truth had hit me as squarely between the eyes as if it had been an egg or a turnip hurled by one of the Market Snodsbury electorate.

"Bingley!" I ejaculated.

"And don't sing."

"I was not singing, I was ejaculating 'Bingley!' or vociferating 'Bingley!' if you prefer it. You remember Bingley, the fellow who stole the club book, the chap you were going to take by the throat and shake like a rat. Aged relative, we are up against it in no uncertain manner. Bingley is the Runkle minion you alluded to. Jeeves says he dropped in to tea this afternoon. What simpler for him, having had his cuppa, than to nip upstairs and search my room? He used to be Runkle's personal attendant, so Runkle would naturally turn to him when he needed an accomplice. Yes, I don't wonder you're perturbed," I added, for she had set the welkin ringing with one of those pungent monosyllables so often on her lips in the old Quorn-and-Pytchley days. "And I'll tell you something else which will remove your last doubts, if you had any. He's just turned up again, and Runkle has gone out to confer with him. What do you suppose they're conferring about? Give you three guesses."

The Quorn trains its daughters well. So does the Pytchley. She did not swoon, as many an aunt would have done in her place, merely repeated the monosyllable in a slightly lower tone—meditatively as it were, like some aristocrat of the French Revolution on being informed that the tumbril waited.

"This tears it," she said, the very words such an aristocrat would have used, though speaking, of course, in French. "I'll have to confess that I took his foul porringer."

"No, no, you mustn't do that."

"What else is there for me to do? I can't let you go to chokey."

"I don't mind."

"I do. I may have my faults—"

"No, no."

"Yes, yes. I am quite aware that there are blemishes in my spiritual makeup which ought to have been corrected at my finishing school, but I draw the line at letting my nephew do a stretch for pinching porringers which I pinched myself. That's final."

576

I saw what she meant, of course. Noblesse oblige and all that. And very creditable, too. But I had a powerful argument to put forward, and I lost no time in putting it.

"But wait, old ancestor. There's another aspect of the matter. If it's—what's the expression?—if it's bruited abroad that I'm merely an as-pure-as-the-driven-snow innocent bystander, my engagement to Florence will be on again."

"You're what to who?" It should have been "whom" but I let it go. "Are you telling me that you and Florence—?"

"She proposed to me ten minutes ago and I had to accept her because one's either *preux* or one isn't, and then Runkle butted in and pointed out to her the disadvantages of marrying someone who would shortly be sewing mailbags in Wormwood Scrubbs, and she broke it off."

The relative seemed stunned, as if she had come on something abstruse in the *Observer* crossword puzzle.

"What is it about you that fascinates the girls? First Madeline Bassett, now Florence, and dozens of others in the past. You must have a magnetic personality."

"That would seem to be the explanation," I agreed. "Anyway, there it is. One whisper that there isn't a stain on my character, and I haven't a hope. The Bishop will be notified, the assistant clergy and bridesmaids rounded up, the organist will start practicing 'The Voice That Breathed O'er Eden,' and the limp figure you see drooping at the altar rails will be Bertram Wilberforce Wooster. I implore you, old blood relation, to be silent and let the law take its course. If it's a choice between serving a life sentence under Florence and sewing a mailbag or two, give me the mailbags every time."

She nodded understandingly, and said she saw what I meant.

"I thought you would."

"There is much in what you say." She mused awhile. "As a matter of fact, though, I doubt if it will get as far as mail-

577

bags. I'm pretty sure what's going to happen. Runkle will offer to drop the whole thing if I let him have Anatole."

"Good God!"

"You may well say 'Good God!' You know what Anatole means to Tom."

She did not need to labor the point. Uncle Tom combines a passionate love of food with a singular difficulty in digesting it, and Anatole is the only chef yet discovered who can fill him up to the Plimsoll mark without causing the worst sort of upheaval in his gastric juices.

"But would Anatole go to Runkle?"

"He'd go to anyone if the price was right."

"None of that faithful old retainer stuff?"

"None. His outlook is entirely practical. That's the French in him."

"I wonder you've been able to keep him so long. He must have had other offers."

"I've always topped them. If it was simply another case of outbidding the opposition, I wouldn't be worrying."

"But when Uncle Tom comes back and finds Anatole conspicuous by his absence, won't the home be a bit in the melting pot?"

"I don't like to think of it."

But she did think of it. So did I. And we were both thinking of it when our musings were interrupted by the return of L. P. Runkle, who waddled in and fixed us with a bulging eye.

I suppose if he had been slenderer, one might have described him as a figure of doom, but even though so badly in need of a reducing diet, he was near enough to being one to make my interior organs do a quick shuffle-off-to-Buffalo as if some muscular hand had stirred them up with an egg whisk. And when he began to speak, he was certainly impressive. These fellows who have built up large commercial empires are always what I have heard Jeeves call orotund. They get that way from dominating meetings of shareholders. Having started off with "Oh, there you are, Mrs. Travers," he went into his speech, and it was about as orotund as anything that has ever come my way. It ran, as nearly as I can remember, as follows:

"I was hoping to see you, Mrs. Travers. In a previous conversation, you will recall that I stated uncompromisingly that your nephew, Mr. Wooster, had purloined the silver porringer which I brought here to sell to your husband, whose absence I greatly deplore. That this was no mere suspicion has now been fully substantiated. I have a witness who is prepared to testify on oath in court that he found it in the top drawer of the chest of drawers in Mr. Wooster's bedroom, unskillfully concealed behind socks and handkerchiefs."

Here, if it had been a shareholders' meeting, he would probably have been reminded of an amusing story which may be new to some of you present this afternoon, but I suppose in a private conversation he saw no need for it. He continued, still orotund.

"The moment I report this to the police and acquaint them with the evidence at my disposal, Wooster's arrest will follow automatically, and a sharp sentence will be the inevitable result."

It was an unpleasant way of putting it, but I was compelled to admit that it covered the facts like a bedspread. Dust off that cell, Wormwood Scrubbs, I was saying to myself, I shall soon be with you.

"Such is the position. But I am not a vindictive man. I have no wish, if it can be avoided, to give pain to a hostess who has been to such trouble to make my visit enjoyable."

He paused for a moment to lick his lips, and I knew he was tasting again those master dishes of Anatole's. And it was on Anatole that he now touched.

"While staying here as your guest, I have been greatly

impressed by the skill and artistry of your chef. I will agree
not to press charges against Mr. Wooster provided you consent to let this gifted man leave your employment and enter mine."

A snort rang through the room, one of the ancestor's
finest. You might almost have called it orotund. Following
it with the word "Ha!" she turned to me with a spacious
wave of the hand.

"Didn't I tell you, Bertie? Wasn't I right? Didn't I say
the child of unmarried parents would blackmail me?"

A fellow with the excess weight of L. P. Runkle finds it
difficult to stiffen all over when offended, but he stiffened
as far as he could. It was as if some shareholder at the meeting had said the wrong thing.

"Blackmail?"

"That's what I said."

"It is not blackmail. It is nothing of the sort."

"He is quite right, madam," said Jeeves, appearing from
nowhere. I'll swear he hadn't been there half a second before. "Blackmail implies the extortion of money. Mr. Runkle is merely extorting a cook."

"Exactly. A purely business transaction," said Runkle,
obviously considering him a Daniel come to judgment.

"It would be very different," said Jeeves, "were somebody to try to obtain money from him by threatening to
reveal that while in America he served a prison sentence
for bribing a juror in a case in which he was involved."

A cry broke from L. P. Runkle's lips, somewhat similar
to the one the cat Gus had uttered when the bag of cat food
fell on him. He tottered and his face would, I think, have
turned ashy white if his blood pressure hadn't been the sort
that makes it pretty tough going for a face to turn ashy
white. The best it could manage was something Florence
would have called sallow.

The ancestor, on the other hand, had revived like a floweret beneath the watering can. Not that she looks like a floweret, but you know what I mean.

"What?" she ejaculated.

"Yes, madam, the details are all in the club book. Bingley recorded them very fully. His views were very far to the left at the time, and I think he derived considerable satisfaction from penning an exposé of a gentleman of Mr. Runkle's wealth. It is also with manifest gusto that he relates how Mr. Runkle, in grave danger of a further prison sentence in connection with a real-estate fraud, forfeited the money he had deposited as security for his appearance in court and disappeared."

"Jumped his bail, you mean?"

"Precisely, madam. He escaped to Canada in a false beard."

The ancestor drew a deep breath. Her eyes were glowing more like twin stars than anything. Had not her dancing days been long past, I think she might have gone into a brisk buck-and-wing. The lower limbs twitched just as if she were planning to.

"Well," she said, "a nice bit of news that'll be for the fellows who dole out knighthoods. 'Runkle?' they'll say. 'That old lag? If we made a man like that a knight, we'd never hear the last of it. The boys on the Opposition benches would kid the pants off us.' We were discussing yesterday, Runkle, that little matter of the money you ought to have given Tuppy Glossop years ago. If you will step into my boudoir, we will go into it again at our leisure."

17

THE FOLLOWING DAY dawned bright and clear, at least I suppose it did, but I wasn't awake at the time. When eventually I came to life, the sun was shining, all nature appeared to be smiling, and Jeeves was bringing in the breakfast tray. Gus the cat, who had been getting his eight hours on an adjacent armchair, stirred, opened an eye and did a sitting high jump on to the bed, eager not to miss anything that was going.

"Good morning, Jeeves."

"Good morning, sir."

"Weather looks all right."

"Extremely clement, sir."

"The snail's on the wing and the lark's on the thorn, or rather the other way round, as I've sometimes heard you say. Are those kippers I smell?"

"Yes, sir."

"Detach a portion for Gus, will you? He will probably like to take it from the soap dish, reserving the saucer for milk."

"Very good, sir."

I sat up and eased the spine into the pillows. I was conscious of a profound peace.

"Jeeves," I said, "I am conscious of a profound peace. I wonder if you remember me telling you a few days ago that I was having a sharp attack of euphoria?"

"Yes, sir. I recall your words clearly. You said you were sitting on top of the world with a rainbow round your shoulder."

"Similar conditions prevail this morning. I thought everything went off very well last night, didn't you?"

"Yes, sir."

"Thanks to you."

"It is very kind of you to say so, sir."

"I take it the ancestor came to a satisfactory arrangement with Runkle?"

"Most satisfactory, sir. Madam has just informed me that Mr. Runkle was entirely cooperative."

"So Tuppy and Angela will be joined in holy wedlock, as the expression is?"

"Almost immediately, I understood from madam."

"And even now Ginger and M. Glendennon are probably in conference with the registrar of their choice."

"Yes, sir."

"And Spode has a black eye, which one hopes is painful. In short, on every side one sees happy endings popping up out of traps. A pity that Bingley is flourishing like a green what-is-it, but one can't have everything."

"No, sir. *Medio de fonte leporum surgit amari aliquid in ipsis floribus angat.*"

"I don't think I quite followed you there, Jeeves."

"I was quoting from the Roman poet Lucretius, sir. A rough translation would be 'From the heart of this fountain of delights wells up some bitter taste to choke them even among the flowers.'"

"Who did you say wrote that?"

"Lucretius, sir, 99–55 B.C."

"Gloomy sort of bird."

"His outlook was perhaps somewhat somber, sir."

"Still, apart from Bingley, one might describe joy as reigning supreme."

"A very colorful phrase, sir."

"Not my own. I read it somewhere. Yes, I think we may say everything's more or less oojah-cum-spiff. With one exception, Jeeves," I said, a graver note coming into my voice as I gave Gus his second helping of kipper. "There remains a fly in the ointment, a familiar saying meaning—well, I don't quite know what it does mean. It seems to imply a state of affairs at which one is supposed to look askance, but why, I ask myself, shouldn't flies be in ointment? What harm do they do? And who wants ointment, anyway? But you get what I'm driving at. The Junior Ganymede club book is still in existence. That is what tempers my ecstasy with anxiety. We have seen how packed with trinitrotoluol it is, and we know how easily it can fall into the hands of the powers of darkness. Who can say that another Bingley may not come along and snitch it from the secretary's room? I know it is too much to ask you to burn the beastly thing, but couldn't you at least destroy the eighteen pages in which I figure?"

"I have already done so, sir."

"What?"

"Yes, sir."

You wouldn't be far wrong in saying that I was visibly moved—so visibly, indeed, that Gus the cat, who had gone to sleep on my solar plexus, shot some inches in the air and showed considerable annoyance.

"Jeeves," I started to vociferate, but he cut in first.

"In taking this step, sir, I do not feel that I have inflicted any disservice on the Junior Ganymede club. The club book was never intended to be light and titillating reading for the members. Its function is solely to acquaint those who are contemplating taking new posts with the foibles of prospective employers. This being so, there is no need for the record contained in the eighteen pages in which you figure. For I may hope, may I not, sir, that you will allow me to remain permanently in your service?"

"You may indeed, Jeeves. It often beats me, though, why with your superlative gifts you should want to."

"There is a tie that binds, sir."

"A what that whats?"

"A tie that binds, sir."

"Then heaven bless it, and may it continue to bind indefinitely. Fate's happenstance may oft win more than toil, as the fellow said."

"What fellow would that be, sir? Thoreau?"

"No, me."

"Sir?"

"A little thing of my own. I don't know what it means, but you can take it as coming straight from the heart."

"Very good, sir."

"Yes, I didn't think it was bad myself," I said, and after a bit more kidding back and forth he shimmered out, leaving me to grapple with the problem—call it Problem (e)—of how to get up and have my bath without waking Gus, who had now transferred himself to my Adam's apple.